THE
SNOWFANG
BRIDE

MERRY RAVENELL

The SnowFang Bride

copyright © 2016 Merry Ravenell

All rights reserved.

The SnowFang Bride is a work of fiction. Names, characters, places, and incidents are either the products of the author's imagination or are used fictitiously. Any resemblance to actual persons, living or dead, events, or locales is entirely coincidental.

For Dad.

You would have approved.

PRESSURE

The werewolves lacked females. A male with a mate had the goddess Gaia's favor.

A female without a mate was considered unlucky at best, and exiled at worst.

Being twenty, I was well past the age when most she-wolves found the soul Gaia had chosen for them. If I had been anyone else's daughter it would have been dismissed as simple misfortune. How unlucky that we couldn't find my mate, or what a shame he had died too soon. All just very bad luck, tsk tsk, what a shame.

But my father was Elder Alpha Rodero, Chronicler of the Werewolves, and his daughter being unpaired was easy gossip fodder for his rivals. Rumor maintained I was Unwanted: a female with a soul so flawed Gaia had no use for her, and She had not paired me with another. I had no place in the future She wanted for us.

Unwanted meant total exile. It heaped shame on the she-wolf's family and pack. It didn't matter that there was no way to conclusively prove Unwanted versus simple bad luck. It didn't matter if an Unwanted had been born that way, or acted so badly that Gaia stripped her of her worth. Packs shared in the glory, and packs shared in the shame. It wasn't a word thrown around lightly. It wasn't something anyone said.

Except now someone had gone and said it.

Two days later and my veins still vibrated under my skin.

I perched on one of the uncomfortable barstools at my father's main drafting table and tried not to fidget. Evidence of his work surrounded us: ancient tombs of our history, huge sheets of paper tacked onto the walls and covered in tiny, neat print, stacks of mail sorted into piles. Many days I was down there helping him sort through the mail, but that day it was going to be more pictures, more men, more aggravating a political sore.

The cause of all this (as I saw it) was my father openly used his position as Chronicler to track down my mate, and it wasn't just limited to exploiting the troves of knowledge in his care. He also invited himself to other packs under the banner of official business, took me with him, and claimed I was his *assistant*. I enjoyed the privilege but not the guilt. Only *apprentices* traveled with Chroniclers, or received such an education on the details of our Law and history, or acquired such familiarity with the private matters of other lives.

My father would never go to such lengths for anyone else. Of all the she-wolves in the world, I literally had every opportunity and no excuses. The inevitable conclusion drawn by aggravated wolves? Unwanted.

It was good logic.

It hadn't been a family member who had finally had enough and taken my father aside to speak with him. It had been the Alpha of a rural, barely-there pack called SaltPaw. A few days earlier we had gone to SaltPaw to impose on their hospitality. The whole pack had greeted us at the end of their drive and their had Alpha looked my father in the eye, spoken my name, and then the word.

Unwanteds had to be exiled or risk Gaia's wrath, so if the SaltPaw Alpha truly believed I was Unwanted, he had only been defending his pack. More than likely, he had just taken the chance to growl at an Elder Alpha and snitch some prestige. I was a big, squishy target with no defense against the claim, except for my father's swift, violent, anger.

It wouldn't be long before the other Elders couldn't ignore the situation anymore, and even my own SilverPaw joined in.

My father reached across the table and pushed

photographs my way.

"Photographs?" Normally it was email attachments, webpages, printouts, not glossy photographs.

He gestured with his pen. "Photographs capture someone's impression better than images on a screen. They have a little more substance."

SaltPaw's rancor must have left more of an impression than he cared to admit. Dutifully, I shuffled through the dozen headshots. The men ranged from about my age to much older, perhaps upwards of fifty, all shirtless males shot from the shoulders up, posed against plain backdrops in muted colors. I squinted at the pictures, searching for clues as to who they were, or what packs they might be from. My father never revealed the details of the faces.

Damn. Nothing. There was just nothing about them.

He shifted forward on his stool and craned his neck to see what picture I had at front. "Something that interests you?"

"No." Meeting in person was best, but we could feel a connection from photographs or videos. These photos were like flipping through a yearbook found at a yard sale. "What happens now?"

"You've never asked me that before."

"You've never had anyone call me Unwanted. To your face, I mean." The first time for *me* had been about a year ago. Some nasty little teenage she-wolves had whispered the word, then run away giggling while I stood like a stunned buffalo. From there it had continued, like every wolf my age had gotten some kind of memo.

He brushed it off. There were a few faded, slightly crusted scratches on his cheek. The SaltPaw Alpha hadn't been all words. "It's nastiness that has nothing to do with you."

"I'm just the soft exposed underbelly of your prestige." That was the whole point. It had *everything* to do with me.

He snorted. "You aren't Unwanted. My daughter is not

Unwanted. You have a mate. I just have to find him."

"Are you in denial or do you honestly still believe that?" I dared to ask.

He stared at me. "Do *you* believe you're Unwanted?"

I shrugged.

"Have you done something to make Gaia despise you? Is there something you need to confess?" His shoulders stiffened.

I was no darling little ball of purity and fluff, but depravity wasn't in my skill set. "Of course not. If I'm Unwanted, I was born this way."

He frowned, looked at the wad of pictures again, and tossed them into the trash. "You weren't born Unwanted."

There was something in his voice that plucked a string, like a catch of breath. So Dad was thinking about it. I gnawed on the inside of my cheek, then forged ahead with the conversation. "It's possible that we won't find him. Dad, the way things are going... maybe you should let it go."

This wasn't only about a mate we couldn't find. This was about me being the patient zero, the moment everything for our species went straight to hell.

We were on the brink of a true population crisis. Sometime around five hundred years ago, Alphas had started using mate pairs to play political chess with lives, bloodlines and wealth, just like humans. If a female's mate hadn't been found among suitably advantageous males, Alphas called off the search and declared the female without a mate. There had been no stigma, nor any question. Perhaps he had been too far away, perhaps he had died before they could meet. The world had been huge and dangerous, after all. The packs grew wealthy off bride-prices instead of having to pay dowries, and pack rivals could be eradicated in a generation.

It was a violation of Gaia's will, and our Law, but since there was no way to prove if a pair was legitimate or not, the Law was easy to ignore. The justification had always been "for the good of the pack", and that too was Law. In fact, guarding the living whole of the pack was our First Law. The Law about accepting mates was lower down the list, so in true lawyer fashion (species not withstanding) there were many arguments about which Law took precedence.

With pups produced outside of a mated pair considered pariahs and born under unlucky stars, these sorts of politics made population decline inevitable. Sister by sister, mother by daughter, aunt by niece, one female family after another disappeared as they died without producing offspring. Many of the remaining female lines were closely related, and Gaia never paired close relatives.

In retrospect it seemed obvious, but it had taken the better part of four hundred years for the Elder Council to recognize the coming crisis, and another generation before my grandfather figured out the cause. Not a blight or disease or divine wrath. Just stupidity, with an easy but very unpopular solution: stop playing power games.

But even SilverPaw resisted. Many honestly believed quietly rejecting a pairing needed to remain an option. Many more didn't want to give up the power and deal with the political headaches that were sure to come. The Elder Council had been fighting over it my entire life, and my father had picked up where his father had left off: Gaia's will must be obeyed without question, or we would go extinct.

Me being declared Unwanted would have destroyed him in front of his peers.

Right now it was all murmurs and rumors. If I quietly disappeared, it might settle down. I believed, with the vague awareness that humans called women's intuition but werewolves called the Moon's Gift, that the SaltPaw were the last warning we were going to get.

His annoyed voice jarred me out of my thoughts. "Let me worry about my work, and this pack. We will keep looking."

We weren't humans; we didn't have population in the billions. I had probably been presented with at least a thousand, perhaps two thousand, males. "Where is there left to look?"

He scratched behind his ear. "I wanted you to mate into some prestige," he sounded more like he was talking to himself, "but that doesn't seem to be Gaia's will."

I had been his tag-along long enough to know what that meant. Now it was time to look at the males no father would otherwise consider: criminals, abusers, idiots, the disgraced. Feel along the mucky bottom, no stone unturned, no name not considered. "Perhaps it's better if we stop now."

"And let the old ways that are killing us win? There are still males left. We have to show the other wolves that Gaia's will must be obeyed, even when it's cruel."

"My mate could have died, but now everyone wants blood and will say I'm Unwanted and destroy your work! A tactical retreat isn't surrender."

"No, this is about faith in Gaia. You are not Unwanted. There are still some names. They all have... ah... serious problems. But never mind. You have other things to do."

"What kind of serious problems?"

"That's not your business. It's mine."

"Not my business! Criminals? Are they in prison? Rogues who haven't been caught yet? Blank pedigrees? Maybe some humans?"

He snapped, "Be quiet. Humans. You are not that stupid, Winter. Stop behaving like a little girl!"

"There have been human mates before."

"Which is worse than no mate at all!"

"Gaia's will." I parroted back at him, knowing it was childish and petty, but how could he tell me this wasn't my business! "How is finding my mate down in the marshes or with humans any better for SilverPaw than me being Unwanted? Dammit, Dad, can't you see how deep this—"

He growled and flicked his hand toward the stairs. "What I see is a little she-wolf who has forgotten her place. Go. Now."

I clutched the edge of the drafting table and held my ground under his stare. Defying an Alpha was stupid, and the punishment would be severe, but my anger and despair gave me a wild kind of courage. I had to defend the SilverPaw, and if the Alpha was going to keep chasing some mythical white stag, it was time to disobey.

He stood. "*Go.*"

The wild courage hummed, but a cool thread of logic slipped from the back of my mind. My father was my only ally, fighting with him would be supremely stupid. Perhaps I was just tired and ready for everything to stop, even if it meant the worst of outcomes for me. That wasn't true courage or sacrifice; it was just selfish weakness.

Obediently, I bowed my head and averted my gaze to show the appropriate submission, slid off the stool and retreated up the stairs. I'd be patient.

For a little while longer.

EXPECTATIONS

Meatloaf grease had a way of burrowing through all anti-stick barriers and burning itself onto pans. No matter how much spray stuff I used, or how many nights the pans soaked, I always ended up scrubbing hard enough to work up a sweat. It wasn't the upper body workout that I objected to, scrubbing pans just wasn't how I liked to get one.

I glared at the pan. Stubborn bits of charred grease clung to the corners and mocked me, daring me to ruin my fingernails scraping at it.

Fingernails it was then. They'd grow back.

Glass rattled as Jerron yanked open the fridge door. He guzzled huge mouthfuls of apple juice, the excess dripping down his throat onto his bare chest and onward to the hem of his sweatpants. If one more woman told me how hot he was, I'd bite her. My brother's good looks and charming smile got him out of everything, including his most recent selfish screw-up.

He should have been up hours earlier to deposit his paycheck. Instead, he had cashed it after work and headed off to the local bar. Round after round with some cousins and local boys, then a case for the road, and driven (unwisely) out to our back pasture and shot bottles off the fence until they had run out of bullets. Now there was $2.12 to run the house until his next payday.

And once again, Dad had just shrugged it off. The misguided antics of a young male, my father had explained, and assured me, again, that Jerron would mature like a fine wine. Jerron could go drink the grocery money, but I wasn't allowed to know the names of potential suitors.

My temper stretched tight. "What the hell are we supposed to do until your next payday, Jerron?"

It wasn't like he and our father wouldn't expect three hot meals a day.

He shrugged and returned the apple juice to the shelf. "Figure it out."

"Figure it out! There isn't any legal accounting that's going to turn two bucks into two weeks of groceries!"

Jerron slammed the fridge door shut. "Lay off, Winter. Some of us were out late."

"You knew you needed to deposit that check, not drink it!"

"Yeah, and maybe you'd find your mate and get some friends if you didn't have that stick in your butt. Stop being a nag."

"That's a cheap shot." He knew I was trapped on our remote spread for weeks on end, the only times I left were to go to our tiny town for errands, or to travel with our father to be paraded about like a prize cow at a county fair. Once my high school friends and cousins had moved away, I had been alone. Belly-crawling jerk to rub my snout in it.

"It's my paycheck, Winter, and if I want to drink it, I will." Jerron's glare was an imitation of our father's, and a damn convincing one at that. He might have mastered the mannerisms of an Alpha, but he still lacked the presence.

Jerron seemed to think he'd be the SilverPaw Alpha one day. Pedigree counted for something, but it was as much about merit as lineage. The rest of the SilverPaw leadership wouldn't suffer Jerron's self-entitled attitude for long. At four years older than me, Jerron wasn't exactly setting a blazing pace up that maturity curve. He better get around to becoming a fine wine sometime soon.

I bristled. "You know that's not how it works! You want to *eat,* don't you?"

There was some food in our deep freeze, but enough for a few days, not weeks. Even when he turned over his paycheck like he should, there was barely enough to get by,

not replenish stores. I might be able to get some rabbits, maybe a tiny deer, but the snow was already here, and the lean season started. Anything bigger would mean a call to our relatives an hour away to come hunt with me, and as soon as my father found out,
he'd tell me to stop being lazy and bring in dinner on my own.

Jerron couldn't keep doing this! It wasn't how an Alpha acted. An Alpha put the good of the pack before his own. An Alpha went hungry before anyone else did.

"So go tattle. Oh wait, you already have." He waved his fingers at me over his shoulder and disappeared down the hallway.

It wasn't about tattling! It was about pack, family, and responsibilities. Jerron's bread didn't get buttered on both sides. If he wanted to keep his paycheck to himself, then he needed to move out and pay his pack tribute like every other wolf.

I turned my attention back to my pans and growled at the greasy water.

If they had let me get a job, I would have, and Jerron could have done the cooking and cleaning. I would have gone to college, studied, had a career. Maybe trade school. Welding was a family tradition.

In a few things our father was progressive, but in most others, he was entrenched in tradition and the old ways. That meant females didn't need college or careers. He had barely cared if I had graduated high school. I could have just barely graduated and he'd have been content. He had thought nothing of taking me from school for days at a time to pursue my mate. Missing days of class, labs, exams, and my grades getting docked for it all? Unimportant.

My mother had always been honest: for Rodero of SilverPaw's daughter there would be no college, no career. Better to hope my mate would be more modern in his

water.

That evening, I contemplated my reflection and tried to figure out how to present myself. Make up? How much? Do my hair or just put it in a ponytail? If Sterling was the soul Gaia had chosen for me seduction wasn't required, but I still wanted to leave a decent impression.

If he was the wolf my *father* had chosen for me, first impressions mattered even more.

One of the concerns I had never had was my mate being unattractive. When things could end so badly, good looks become a meaningless criteria. Concern shifts to things like "doesn't drink himself into a stupor every night," "has a job," "won't beat me into a pulp," and, most importantly, "is smarter than a pet rock." If Gaia had allowed me to name just one thing I wanted in my mate, it would have been intelligence. A sweet-natured idiot sounded worse than a brilliant monster.

Being goddess-ordained pairs didn't assure happiness. Gaia paired souls in infancy, but each wolf had a life they led before finding their other half. Life's events could change wolves, but almost never changed the bond between souls. More than a few pairs were miserable, and burdened with things like addiction, abuse, trauma, and illness.

Since Sterling was flying out on short notice, his mortal flaw wasn't grinding poverty.

"Making yourself pretty?"

I glared at my brother. "Don't you knock?"

Jerron leaned against the frame of my door, arms crossed, and a smirk on his lips. He had inherited our father's amber-brown eyes and dark hair. I favored our mother: red hair and green eyes. He was tall and lanky, I was more petite.

"Your door was *mostly* open," he pointed out.

"You're a pest, Jerron." Pest wasn't the word I wanted to use. Selfish, self-absorbed asshat was more like it.

It was a bad thing when two wolf-sibs didn't like each

other. Another ill-luck omen. Deep down, my dislike for my brother was shamefully genuine. Maybe that was proof of a fatal flaw within me.

"So. Sterling Mortcombe of SnowFang."

"He's just coming for a visit," I retorted.

"Dad's really scraping the bottom of the barrel if he's letting Sterling sniff you." Jerron growled, his anger genuine under his quip.

"Don't you have something better to do? Like eat some rat poison? Get into some antifreeze?"

Jerron glared at me, like this was somehow all my fault.

"You know I don't get a say in any of this. Go away, Jerron."

He didn't move. "Only thing he has going for him is he's stupid rich."

So what? Wealth and power were Jerron's ambitions, not mine. "I said get lost, Jerron!"

"Think he'll have to dunk you in some flea-dip and teach you to shake?" Jerron sneered.

My temper burst into a boiling heat, and my vision washed silver and red. The mist rose in my blood, and the exquisite shiver of a coming shift flitted over my skin. He was my brother, and he should be here to commiserate with me instead of torment me. This wasn't like when I had been five and he had ruined my favorite toys with black markers. This was my life, possibly my soul, and if Jerron was smart, he'd realize that our father bringing questionable wolves to the house eroded the prestige of the pack Jerron wanted to lead one day. Stupid, stupid wolf. He should be downstairs convincing our father this was a bad idea all around, not up here dancing back and forth singing *nyah nyah nyah!*

I could drop into wolf form, snake my jaw forward, bite that perfect calf of his, clamp down, hold on, listen to him squeal and squirm until he was forced to twist around and bite at me to free himself, and then we'd see how big a wolf he really was.

"She-wolves," he huffed, but he stepped out of range.

I slammed the door in his face for his safety as much as mine.

AN UNCOMMON LINE

Wolves considered it very lucky when a daughter favored her mother. I had inherited more from my mother than just my outward appearance.

All she-wolves had a little gift from Gaia's daughter, the Moon. Humans called it a sixth sense. It was almost always a passive gift, and confined to feelings or the occasional dream. Just a little bit beyond what a male would call "good instincts."

My mother, however, had had enough of the Moon's Gift that she had been able to scry in bowls and water. I had inherited enough that she had started to teach me to use it. She had never mentioned it to my father, and while my Gift had come early, I had never been haunted by dreams or visions. Just an early bloom, a little more than most, but not worth mentioning. I had rarely thought about it.

That night I woke from a dream knowing, with absolute certainty, a storm was on its way, riding Sterling's shoulders.

My heart thumped under my ribs, a heavy but slow rhythm, as the dream retreated from my memory, but transmuted into a firm, steel awareness.

Sterling would be the soul Gaia had chosen, or he would be the end of this. My father would force us together, or the SilverPaw would force me out.

One way or the other, it would be over.

I was grateful, and held a tiny sliver of hope that I didn't need to doubt my father, or his work, or his mission, or that Gaia had abandoned all of us.

At breakfast Jerron mentioned something about the meeting. He wanted to be there when I met Sterling.

He just wanted to watch me like I was a slug squirming under a dusting of salt. I didn't think so. "No, I don't want you there."

My father nodded agreement.

"What?" my brother squawked. "But I'm her brother!"

He only cared about that when it got him something he wanted. Vermin.

"It's the female's right to decide who's there." Our father took a bite of his eggs. "You can wait outside. I'm sure Sterling won't be any trouble and we won't need extra hands."

Jerron bristled at the statement about the "female's right." He wasn't allowed to carry on with human females (although I knew he did, I just never ratted him out), and he resented that werewolf females were such creatures of importance. Perhaps I would have felt the same way if I had been a male, but I wasn't, and right then, I didn't feel very gracious.

Jerron got to have a job, a life, an education, his freedom. Only once I was paired off (or written off), our father would turn his attention to finding Jerron's mate. If there was no soul waiting for him, he wouldn't suffer. It'd be a disappointment, but with so many males not having a mate, it couldn't be a mark against him. The only real consequence for him would be never having children.

The coming storm pressed between my shoulder blades. This was no time to be squabbling with Jerron, I wanted to get a bit more information about Sterling before this meeting. "Is there anything to know about Sterling? His pedigree? His pack? How old is he?"

My father shrugged. "If he's your mate, it changes nothing. If he isn't, the details matter even less."

So Jerron got to know all about Sterling, but I wasn't even allowed to know how old he was.

Dammit. Should not have lost my temper the previous evening. Playing along and letting Jerron feel like he was Big Bad Alpha would have caused his mouth to run in a useful direction.

Sterling was due to arrive at eleven, so a whole day of pins and needles wouldn't happen. It'd be over quickly.

I chose to have my hair down, and wore a white sweater and green skirt. Clean and neat seemed the best course of action.

"You look nice." My father smiled at me when I came into the living room.

"Thank you." I blushed. He wasn't frequent with his compliments.

He didn't seem nervous or concerned with the outcome. There was an air of curious anticipation around him, almost an eagerness. Dad was not the jittery-for-Christmas-morning type, and being male, could not possibly have heard any whispers from the Moon. His anticipation made no sense.

I dug my fingernails into my thighs. No matter what, it *would* end and I'd get all my answers very soon.

I still jumped when the doorbell rang at exactly 11:01.

Fear seized my blood. It was here, the final moment, the axe hanging just a hair off my neck.

Jerron answered the door and greeted the man on the other side with a surly tone, still angry about not being included. Then, another voice, deep-toned, masculine. I *felt* him, I swear to Gaia, rolling towards me like the front of a storm.

For some reason my mind had expected Sterling Mortcombe to be a rugged woodsman type with dark hair and a beard and earth-colored eyes, and broad, thick hands. The man who walked into the sitting room was marble transmuted to living flesh, tall and handsome in the way a steel blade was beautiful. Lean, strong, his posture one of austere, grave pride that was completely out of place with his apparent youth.

He couldn't have been much older than Jerron, but his hair had grayed to a swept silvery-white hue, and his eyes were a pale shade of hazel.

My father greeted him, but Sterling ignored him.

His eyes filled my whole field of vision. The world narrowed to just him. My entire being liquefied and rolled down toward him, as if I had suddenly become matter rushing toward a black hole. Silver mist felt like it rose from every pore in my body. I smelled the moon, wolf, man, and him.

The storm rolled over my head, clouds crashing and tumbling in a thunder that drowned out everything else.

"Winter," Sterling's voice reached me through the thunder, strumming me with little electrical charges. Every hair and pore prickled. "I am Sterling Mortcombe, Alpha of SnowFang."

I should have greeted him formally, and Gaia knew I normally did such things by rote, but speech abandoned me. His scent was masculine, pine and woods and snow and rain and musk and raw desire. It pulled me toward him, beckoned me, blocked out everything except for him.

He took a step, then another. I should not have worn heels. I rocked on the little spike-like tops. That single random thought kept me tethered to the corporeal world by only the thinnest of thread. The rest of my world spun around this silver werewolf, spiraling, and I saw the moon shifting from new to crescent to full, and seasons passing. His eyes were scrying mirrors and the visions of years and seasons and the turning dome of the sky burned into my very bones.

Another step, and the sensations snapped the last ties to my logical, human mind, as if a vortex surrounded his entire body and ensnared me within it. I drowned and spun in its clutches.

His hands closed over my arms, steadying me before I tumbled away with the clouds. Shocks of lightning snapped through me. It was too intense. There was barely enough of me to encompass it all. It was too much! I threatened to crack under the weight of the storm. Words were impossible. Breathing was impossible. Everything was impossible except existing long enough for the clouds to roll past.

His lips pressed to mine. It was a relief akin to a humid day shattered by a cloudburst. Our lips met, his tongue slid against mine and seared my entire body with an exquisite, agonizing sensation that burned our souls, melting us as candles placed too close, the wax mingling and merging and reforming.

The spell released us once the wax had cooled.

His strong hands still held my arms, and prevented me from falling, or escaping.

The room came back into focus: my father, the carpet, the faint scent of coffee, the smell of my shampoo, my brother's lingering scent. Over top of it all was Sterling.

My breathing came fast and shallow, my heart raced.

He was here.

It had happened. I wasn't Unwanted. My father wasn't a hypocrite. The future I had abandoned unfurled before me as a dark, endless hallway of hidden possibilities and secrets. My fingers curled into the fabric of his jacket, unwilling to believe he was real. Steel forearms did not yield under my fingertips.

Sterling.

Sterling's stunned shock came to my nose too, as my instincts and senses attuned themselves to him. Now he was in my awareness, like the beating of my heart, or if I were to concentrate on a particular patch of skin. Just under the surface, as if he had always been there. Shock and astonishment were in the twitch of the pulse under his shaven jaw, the rigid tension of his shoulders under his impeccable suit. A dark charcoal gray suit, brilliant lime green shirt. Unbuttoned collar and no tie.

Shaking seized me.

His gaze of powerful certainty never faltered, and his

fingers tightened another notch, steadying me on my feet.

He was my storm. My storm summoned from some dark, distant horizon.

I was his moon come down from the sky. For him I was a revelation, a promise that had been kept.

His hands fell with slow grace to his sides. He and I both knew they would be upon me again very soon.

My father's tense, cable-taunt voice cut through our silence. "Wait outside, Sterling."

It was now just 11:10. The whole encounter had taken less than ten minutes.

AN UNCARING MOON

Sterling's head snapped to the side. He didn't appreciate the dismissal from the room.

My father twitched his chin. Sterling nodded, then another look passed between us before he left.

My lips burned, still tasted of him, still felt the imprint of his fingertips on my skin, the way he had seemed like a frost-covered piece of stone under my hands. But I still managed to ask, "Why did you send him out?"

He had been summoned, he had showed up, he was the one, and now my father told him to wait outside?

"Because I want to talk to him alone."

My brain was wrapped in dream-fog and haze, and I couldn't argue. I looked in the direction of Sterling's scent, and my thoughts drifted after him. A poking pain formed in my right temple.

My father's face was schooled to flat ice. "So. We've found him."

The cold tone yanked me back to the present. Who was Sterling? Where the hell did he live? How old? His pedigree? How large was the SnowFang? What was the fatal flaw—why had I not met him sooner?

"Let it sink in," my father said. "It's overwhelming."

He wasn't happy. That much reached my brain through its spin-cycle whirling. He wasn't happy, or even a little relieved? I wasn't Unwanted. The rumors could be laid to rest. Couldn't they? I rubbed my head. I couldn't think straight. I could barely *see* straight. Everything in the room seemed to blur and be haloed with a pale silvery-blue light.

Lucky for me, I didn't have to think straight just then. There was time. Nobody expected newly-found mates to scamper right off together. The rush to find partners was about preventing other relationships from forming and breeding heartache. Not because anyone wanted to see a couple of teenagers play house.

My mind slowed a little, absolved of its responsibility to process everything right away.

My father added, in that cold tone that seemed to mask disgust more than relief, "It's a strong bond, but I don't need to tell you that."

The poking pain now started up in my left temple. "I thought you'd be happy, Dad. It's over."

"It's a good match," he acknowledged, albeit unwillingly.

My brain teetered but pulled itself up along some mental wall. "What are you talking about? If that's true, I should have met him long ago. You told me all that was left were wolves with problems. He's one of the ones with problems, isn't he?"

His eyes shifted away from me for just an instant. Alphas never broke eye contact. His eyes returned to mine so quickly I wondered if I had seen it at all. "I only mean that he's the last descendant of his female line. He has a rare pedigree. I was speaking as a Chronicler."

No, he had looked away from me. I was sure of it. "And the top side of his pedigree?"

He shook his head. "You can ask him these questions. It'll give you two something to talk about."

The brush-off meant as much as what he refused to say. Pedigrees *mattered*. My female family was one of the more common. Good, ancient, noble breeding, which was why it still existed, and also had closed off the potential mate pool considerably. My father would have known about Sterling's existence the moment he was recorded, and I should have met Sterling years ago based *purely* on his pedigree. There had to be some major blemish on Sterling for him to have been excluded this long.

Anxiety and suspicion needled me. "At least tell me about his female family. Is it a good family?"

"In recent generations, obscure. Jumping from one pack to the next. But a long time ago it was a noble line. Hard times come, Winter. It doesn't necessarily speak badly of a bloodline."

Even more suspect. I made another bid for information. "And his father?"

"An uncommon line." He didn't elaborate on if that meant uncommon-good or uncommon-bad. Given how forthcoming he was *not* being, and his tone, it must have been uncommon-bad. Or uncommon-and-let's-not-talk-about-it. Perhaps Sterling was the product of an unmated pair, or maybe even the top side of his pedigree was blank because his dam refused to disclose who had fathered him. That usually meant the sire was too shameful to reveal. The stigma associated with either was severe.

My brain balked at any further thinking.

"It's overwhelming," my father repeated. "Just sit. Let it all soak in. Your being needs to adjust. It is very intense for some pairs as your souls complete themselves. I need to go deal with Sterling now."

Deal with Sterling?

He headed out of the room with a grumble. That would have been Jerron's cue to come in and gloat, but he didn't show up. Instead, the sound of male voices drifted up the hallway, growing louder in volume and anger. One of them was Sterling's, one was my father's. I couldn't make out the words, just the angry tones.

There wasn't anything to argue about. Sterling was my mate, we had accepted each other, my father had accepted the pairing. It was done. I kicked my brain into working another ten minutes. My mate and my family were arguing, and like hell I wasn't going to know what it was about.

I crept to the doorway and tip-toed down the hall.

I wasn't going to go barging in there, just eavesdrop. Getting between fighting males was never a good idea, and that day it was uncertain which side I should pick. Technically, Sterling should have my first loyalty. But if I sided with Sterling, I had no idea what he was about. If I sided with my father, it would humiliate Sterling. Best to use my little-sister-honed eavesdropping skills, and avoid immediate involvement.

"...you can't be serious," Sterling's voice said, smoldering with anger and authority. "This is outrageous, Rodero!"

"I'll say you've rejected her." The venom in my father's voice curdled my blood.

The word hit me hard enough I gagged. Rejection was even being *discussed?* Someone had said *that* word?

"You know damn well that's not what I'm intending to do, I'm just not going to let you browbeat me!" Sterling's voice seemed to hit the walls.

Not many Alphas had the fortitude to argue with my father. By my estimation, Sterling had lasted a solid ten minutes, with no sign of backing down.

"This isn't for negotiation. I will expect you back here tomorrow morning at ten. If you don't show up, start running. There will be a Hunt on you by five after."

A Hunt! What in Gaia's name is he talking about!

A hot, angry pause. I plastered myself against the wall, heart thumping and barely able to breathe.

Not another word. Footsteps, the storm door's usual screech, whine, and metallic rattle as it slammed back into its frame.

Oh Gaia.

"You think he'll be here?" Jerron asked.

"He'll be here. He's not stupid." My father's voice was ugly, rancid, and graceless.

Jerron's footsteps came closer, and he strode out of the kitchen across the hallway to the next room. He didn't see me lurking. It had all sounded like a foreign language: *rejection, Hunt, don't leave town.*

Time for some Gaia-damned answers, and this time I wasn't going to be put off. What the hell was my father going to do to me anyway? Throw me out? Call a Hunt on *me?*

My father brewed tea. Under the scent of the tea the kitchen reeked of anger. My father's anger, Jerron's anger, and Sterling's anger, which was more like incensed and disgusted than simply angry.

I peered through the mud room's door and feigned innocent inquiry, "Where are Jerron and Sterling?"

"Jerron is about. Sterling left." My father didn't *appear* to be angry or rattled now, but the fight had not been my imagination, and the anger in the air wasn't either.

"Why did he leave? Did he reject me?" I asked plainly.

"Of course not. He just has things to attend to. He was going to leave tonight, but now he needs to make arrangements for tomorrow." He stared at the bubbling water on the stove. He didn't even try to explain the smell of male anger.

"Arrangements for what?" The emotions of the past year pulled tight, like a muscle expecting a blow.

"For you to go with him, of course."

My skin leapt off my bones, my blood bubbled and a bark bloomed in the base of my throat. I clapped my hands over my mouth and dug my fingers into my cheeks, reeling in the feral urge to drop into wolf-form and start barking.

It had been years since I had force-shifted.

He didn't notice. "There's no reason for you to delay."

"Nobody forces mates together like that!"

Not even a hundred years ago, or two hundred, or five hundred. Females were never treated like something put into a box and shipped to parts unknown!

He poured himself tea and did not offer me any.

What in Gaia's name was this? "Why?"

"There's no reason for you to wait," he repeated, calmly sipping his tea.

"Aside from it's *never* done?!"

He faced the backsplash over the stove and only glanced at me once from the corner of his eye, like I was a wolf not even worth his full attention.

"You won't even tell me how old he is or his pedigree or where the hell I'm even going! Do you even know where he's taking me?"

"New York City," he supplied in a dismissive tone.

Realization bloomed like sunrise. "By Gaia, you don't care. You don't even fucking *care*. Are you going to have me wait out by the front gate? Set me on the front step like a naughty dog?"

"If that's where you want to wait, that's your business. You will leave with him tomorrow."

His authority drowned under the years of anguish bubbling up within me. Years of walking on hot coals but not daring to flinch because every mistake was seen through the magnifying glass of a male who wasn't there, and a father abusing his powers to find him. And somehow, it all ends like this, as if it was all *my* fault. The daughter who took too long, the daughter who dared to be born bound to a wolf too shameful to speak of publicly.

My fingernails dug gouges in my palms. "Tell me why you're doing this. Why was he here like this? No escort, in secret, now you're sending me away before anyone knows. You owe me that much! Tell me! Answer a damn question for once!"

The man who looked at me wasn't my father, but the Alpha of SilverPaw, giving me the same look he would give any other mouthy rival. "I owe you nothing. You are a mated female now. Put your fangs away before I rip them out, and instead put whatever you can into a suitcase. Your mate will provide the rest. His pack is small, and you'll easily adjust to each other. I'll record the pairing myself. There's no reason for you to file it."

Anger washed away and tears eroded my voice to a wheeze. "You're my father. Tomorrow I will be SnowFang but tonight I am still SilverPaw and you are still my Alpha. You will *always* be my father. You've set me out like I betrayed you. This is Gaia's will. Isn't it what all of us wanted? What we all needed? What *you* shed blood for a week ago?"

He stared at the wall in front of him, lost in thoughts that I was no longer a part of.

THE MATTER OF PRICE

Breakfast the next morning was silent. I kept glancing at the old clock over the door every few seconds.

An emotional crater sat in my middle, like a comet had smashed into the Earth with no warning. The shockwave alone flattened and incinerated trees, the earth compressed downward, and debris sprayed up into the sky.

Jerron reeked of smugness, my father of vague disgust, anger, resentment, betrayal.

My father's disgust was one thing, but what the hell did Jerron have to be so damn smug about? Not like he had been nagging for his turn on the Find-A-Mate-Merry-Go-Round. He had never complained once about it. Given how allergic he seemed to adult responsibilities, settling down wasn't high on his list of priorities. Maybe Jerron was just gloating over how I had been flung out, and there wouldn't be anyone to remind him about his less fun responsibilities, like *not* guzzling down his paycheck. He probably wouldn't be gloating when there was nobody to cook his dinner.

Not one single relative or packmate had been called to tell the good news. My father hadn't gleefully spread the word, pleased at his vindication and triumph. Instead, he sat glaring over the lip of his coffee mug, angry like a wet cat having to lick its paws.

Sterling was on time. To the minute.

His presence caught me off guard for a moment, but I was too wrung out to be knocked completely off my feet by a handsome man. The intense attraction that bit through my emotions was unexpected, but the effect diminished.

I looked up at him, feeling much like a puppy who had been tied into a sack and tossed into the river. It would have been easy to do what instinct told me I could do: he was my mate, I could fling myself at him and seek comfort in his fur. But I also barely knew him, and the tiny bit I did know meant I shouldn't let down my guard yet.

"Winter," he greeted me a little too politely. "Good morning. Are you ready to go?"

His tone said there wasn't anything good about the morning. He didn't greet my father or brother, and they didn't acknowledge him.

It was cold, but the sky was pure blue with wispy strands of white, and the trees were just a week past their autumn glory. The air was clear and fresh, and if I tried hard enough, I could smell the metallic scent of the little spring-fed pond in the woods. "Yes, I am."

Five paces behind Sterling, another man waited by the black SUV. He wore a nondescript dark blue suit and red tie. He stepped forward for my suitcases. That was my cue to say goodbye, but it wasn't even clear what, or why, I was leaving.

I only remember my father's cold, stiff embrace. He pushed me away within a heartbeat. I might have said goodbye to Jerron, perhaps I didn't. The next memory was being in the backseat, my eyes swimming with tears I fought to hold back, and Sterling next to me. The car passed the rusted livestock gate at the end of the driveway, then onto gravel road.

Soon we'd cross the SilverPaw boundary line.

Sterling looked up the drive, and something passed over his face, like he had smelled something unpleasant.

"You don't have to say anything." I pressed my forehead to the window and watched the forests of my home pass by. Rural Montana was a long way from New York. Under other circumstances, I may have noticed or even been impressed by the cloud-gray leather interior and the soft music that seemed like a cocoon. Just then it was all lost on me. My father had finished his work and sent me down the lane, while brow-beating Sterling into it. Nobody in that car had any reason to be chipper.

"For what it's worth," he spoke with an air of caution, "I wasn't prepared for this either."

"I overheard the fight."

His attention focused on me, a little too sharp and intense. "So this is a shock to you as well?"

"Of course. Nobody does things this way." My voice got a little raw, ragged on the edges of his obvious distrust.

Sterling stared out his window, frigid and unmoving, and under layers of ice, seething.

He had every damn right to be mad, and to be wondering what the hell had just happened to his life. I was wondering what the hell had just happened to *my* life, and once I was done feeling like my father had punched me in the throat, it'd be anger and not sadness inside me.

Unless a reasonable explanation came along. Logic could usually appease me, but hell if I could spot any logic in this.

I tried to appraise Sterling without obviously staring at him. City wolf. It was the polished shoes that told me that more than his clothes, and the slight silk sheen on his dress socks. More than that I didn't risk trying to take in. He was bristling and wary. His seething didn't seem violent, but that didn't mean he couldn't be provoked. Poking at angry Alpha males was never a good idea.

Still, the silence became too much. "What time is our plane?"

"Two."

"Two? We won't make it." It was just before eleven-thirty now. It was a solid two hours to the airport.

Sterling shook his head. "It will be fine."

If he said so.

I knew exactly where the SilverPaw boundary line was, and when the vehicle crossed it, I shivered. There was nothing mystical to it. Just something final that flicked in my mind. I tucked my hands under my arms and gripped my sweater.

I was a SnowFang now.

"Winter?" his voice saying my name pulled on my tired soul.

"That was the SilverPaw boundary." I managed to say. Hopefully he was not so much of a city wolf he didn't understand what it meant.

He didn't say anything, and there wasn't anything I wanted to hear.

The rest of the trip was in silence. At some point his phone picked up a signal, and he focused on some task that kept him busy until the signs for the airport appeared. Twenty miles, ten miles, five miles, now the exit. I straightened in my seat as the driver headed down a long road that bypassed all the regular terminals. Great Falls Airport is not a very large airport at all, and it was easy to see we weren't going to the regular passenger terminals.

He said, "I half expected to be followed."

I looked sideways at him.

"To make sure I left the SilverPaw territory without any unexpected detours," he elaborated, watching for my reaction.

"An escort in and out is normally how it's done," I admitted.

"I doubt it's because they trust you to keep me on my good behavior," he said dryly.

"I'm not sure if I should be insulted or not, or who I should feel insulted by."

The road opened up onto hangers and a plain of asphalt. The driver slowed, turned right and I found myself confronted with the broad side of a small white jet.

Now I say "small" because compared to commercial jets it was tiny. It was also no little crop duster. The door of the plane was open and the stairs folded down, and as the car pulled up a man wearing dark pants and a white shirt appeared on the top stair. In the pointy nose of the plane were two men silhouetted by the sun.

Sterling Mortcombe was wealthy, but how wealthy was wealthy? He hadn't expected me to come back with him. This wasn't a ploy to look big to me. This was how the man traveled. I wondered where he had slept the previous night. Not too many options out our way, the nearest "inn" from my home was forty minutes north, and that was just a couple who rented out a room.

He gestured for me to go toward the jet. "After you."

The inside of the plane was something I had only seen in movies and TV shows. The smell of leather, wood and recycled air hit me first. Polished wood veneers, wide leather seats in a buttery cream color, a table, a television. I did not want to stand gawking and cataloging everything so I quickly sat down at what probably was my seat. Before me was a crescent-shaped table set with a bowl of fruit and two cups of water.

Sterling flung himself down into the opposite seat and fished around in his pocket for his phone. The attendant, Patrick, came and gathered up our coats and asked if we'd like anything to drink. I asked for hot tea. My throat was so dry. Sterling wanted coffee.

If I had had any coffee I probably would have jumped out of my skin.

Perhaps some people would have been seduced or mollified by a private jet, but it made me dizzy.

One of the pilots came out of the cockpit. He tipped his hat at me, "Ma'am. Sterling," he addressed him by first name, "wheels up in twenty minutes. Should have you to New York about eleven local time."

Just a quick jaunt across the country. Like it was nothing. To them, I'm sure it was nothing. That crater got a little bigger, and a little deeper.

"Have you flown before?" Sterling inquired.

I grabbed for the bits of dignity his ugly tone sent rattling down the edges of the crater. "Yes."

Once. I had been on a passenger plane once before. Little illegal crop dusters owned by my crazy neighbor were a different matter, and as to the question of if I had ever flown said crop dusters... no comment.

He acknowledged my reply with the slightest huff of breath, as if he were relieved he wouldn't have to deal with some backwoods idiot plastering her nose up against the window and exclaiming about how gosh darn high up we were.

Patrick brought us our drinks, and handed Sterling several newspapers. I took one of them and tried to remind myself Sterling's day wasn't going any better than mine.

The teacup was actual china, and instead of a teabag there was a pretty silver tea ball. It certainly beat a little foam cup in cattle class.

I read the first couple of stories in the paper, but my surroundings distracted me. The beautiful hibiscus tea bothered me. Patrick sitting near at hand, but unobtrusive, ready to jump up and cater to my any whim. Thirty-some-odd thousand feet in the sky, and way over my head.

After his second cup of coffee Sterling folded his paper and tossed it down on the table. "Why did your father do this?"

So he was a male who wouldn't pussyfoot and would come right at his prey. This I could handle. Unfortunately, I didn't have the answers either of us were after. "I don't know."

Sterling scoffed, "Don't play me for an idiot, Winter. I'm not the son of an Elder, but if I'm halfway versed on my traditions, your first loyalty is now to me. Not him."

That was, of course, true. Now I was a SnowFang, and like a compass needle swinging north, so did my loyalty change. That was just our nature. "Obviously. And I'm telling you, I don't know. The rest of the family hasn't been told yet, unless my father was whispering into the phone all night. You tell me why he did this. He stonewalled me."

Sterling didn't move, except for a twitch in his fingers as if he wanted to grab something living and squeeze until it popped. "He wouldn't tell me, but I can guess why, considering he wouldn't name your bride-price."

I almost spilled my tea. "What?"

Bride prices were *always* named and paid before the female left. There were never exceptions. There was always *some* payment, even if it had been buttons or an egg.

If anything, an Alpha historically used bride-prices to stymie pairings, either by naming an outrageous price, or refusing payment because he disapproved of how it had been earned or the form it took. Arguments over wanting gold instead of cows, or not accepting stolen pearls. Now the Law was very specific about how prices could be paid, and attitudes towards what was an appropriate amount had changed, but the price was *always* paid.

Given the nature of the family bank account, and the only slightly less dire state of the SilverPaw coffers, this was impossible to comprehend. I had thought Jerron's smugness might have been over the windfall that my mate was wealthy, but if the price hadn't been named, Jerron had nothing to gloat over. It couldn't have been prestige, as Sterling had no prestige for Jerron to take.

Prestige was a complex game between males (and slightly less so among females), and Jerron guarded what he had jealously. The mechanics of prestige discouraged powerful males from being menaces to lesser males, since a loss of any sort transferred commensurate amounts of prestige from the loser to the victor. Jerron wouldn't have risked a shred of it on Sterling.

Prestige was what had made Sterling coming to the SilverPaw heart so extremely bizarre: the invitation to the home of a far, far more powerful wolf conferred prestige on its own. It meant Sterling was worth dealing with, he mattered, and he could be trusted.

Perhaps that had been my father's ploy: a way to very quietly grant Sterling some prestige as a final fatherly gesture. If he had done that, it would mean Sterling's fatal flaw wasn't something truly awful, no worse perhaps than a blank pedigree. My being with Sterling and honoring Gaia's will would only empower my father's work before the other Elders. Prestige was the one thing my father could afford to spend.

My heart fluttered and lifted just a breath. But only a breath. A prestige transfer perhaps explained the secrecy and abruptness, but refusing to name my price crushed that theory. The price was *always* paid.

Sterling watched my reactions, even as I tried to keep them from his sight. It was impossible. Males were driven to observe every small detail of their partner and pups, tend to their worries and anxieties and fears. Even if Sterling didn't realize it, even if he didn't want to, he still would learn my every small reaction and nuance. Eons of evolution wouldn't let him do otherwise.

There weren't many secrets between pairs.

He resettled himself and folded his hands in his lap. His knuckles were chapped and marred by abrasions. The hands of a man who knew how to impose his will. On second, closer inspection, his jaw was not soft, he probably could have grown a full beard if he had wanted to. His build was lean, the suit was tailored to a strong, muscular frame, not a lanky specimen. Even though he was a city wolf, perhaps he was as comfortable in a wolf's fur as a bespoke suit.

His hazel gaze was direct and imposing.

Many Alphas were Alphas only in name. Others had it in their muscle and bone and blood.

"He would not name your bride-price," he repeated, as if

I had not heard him the first time. "Why not?"

I stumbled over the answer. "I—I don't know."

"Do you know why?" he pressed, every syllable an accusation.

"No. Did he say if he'd name it, or am I a free sample?"

My bitterness backed him off a notch, but he still had that rough edge, "No, you aren't. I suppose whatever price he eventually sees fit to demand will have to be paid."

"So that's what the fight was about. You had to take me with you right away, and without paying the price. Or else."

"Threatening me with a Hunt got my attention. Does your father normally go to such outrageous extremes?"

It was easy to see where his train of thought was headed, so I cut off his next statement, "Sterling, the SilverPaw don't know about you or this. When they find out I've left, which won't be too long from now, they'll ask about the bride-price. My father shares control of the coffers with five other SilverPaw. Given the financial situation, they won't be happy. There will be questions."

"What is this financial situation?"

"Desperate."

He frowned, visibly reshuffling his mental cards as he considered the hand he held. "Hmm. I thought Rodero had full control of the purse strings."

"No, never in a pack that large."

"And the whole pack is impoverished."

"It is a carefully kept secret." I didn't care about keeping it anymore. My father should have thought about that before tossing me out without explanation.

"Because you see what I suspect, of course."

"Even if he was going to name an outrageous price, he could have done it right then, and if you refused, crucify you for refusing to pay. If he doesn't want SilverPaw to know about this, it's not the way to go about it. He could have just demanded you pay *him* and deposit the money into the family's account, then split off whatever price seemed reasonable. I guess that might be what he's trying to do but..."

"Is your father capable of this kind of duplicity?" he asked.

"If you had asked me before yesterday, I would have slapped you for suggesting it," I admitted.

"You think he might not ask for anything at all."

My fingernail traced the rim of my empty teacup. Perhaps the source of Sterling's money was too disgusting for my father to stomach. Disgusting or not, he still had to face the practical challenge of no money, no food in the freezer, and a pack who couldn't dine on principles. He'd have to name my price. "No, he can't afford that. He might want to, but he can't."

Sterling watched me for a few heartbeats. His eyes were such pale, sharp hazel. His direct gaze was not aggressive, but penetrating and unavoidable. A man who didn't want a fight, but was willing if that's what it came to. He did not move, not even his fingers, just sat very still, very controlled. He picked over the things he wanted to say, and selected one. "I will pay what is asked. I *want* him to ask. He *should* ask."

"So... this," I gestured to the cabin around us and made another delicate attempt at learning something before Sterling's carefully offered kindness conjured forth tears. At least someone thought I was worth something. "You own a jet, Sterling?"

"No. It's a rental. Makes more sense."

Of course it did. Because renting a private jet was so much more practical than flying commercial. It wasn't like planes didn't fly to Great Falls. Wasn't like big planes with first class didn't fly to Great Falls. Wasn't like statistics didn't bear out that commercial aviation was much safer than private. I sipped my fresh tea and did my best to keep my distress from turning into mean-spirited comments.

Chewing on him would not be becoming of a Luna.

All werewolf packs had one leader. If it was a female, she was the Luna and her mate became the Alpha. Most packs had Alphas, because most packs were predominantly male, and the Luna came later. Complications arose when a leader ended up with a mate not suitable to fulfill their role. Yet another reason many pairs had been quietly (and depending on who you talked to, logically) rejected over the years.

In a pack as tiny as SnowFang, two leaders was superfluous, but it didn't change how things were done. It also meant that I also had formal responsibilities and obligations to this tiny little pack. I knew what they were on paper, but no firm idea how to carry them out. My parents hadn't groomed me for the job. This was going to be a lot more than just me joining a new pack as a mated female.

"How many members of SnowFang are there?" I asked.

"Five, counting you. Males."

Four males. So very tiny. Tiny was probably good for a neonate Luna.

Sterling asked, "My turn. Have you ever lived in anything resembling civilization before?"

It wasn't an insulting question to a werewolf. "Not really. I've lived in a few different places, but all rural."

"So you're a feral."

"That would be a fair statement." I took it as a compliment. For centuries, if not millennia, a feral wolf meant one of our kind who was wild and dangerous, the sort who had inspired human folklore and panic. Now we called those brutes, and a feral wolf just meant one from a rural area. Wolves who knew how to track and hunt, alone and in a pack, scout, patrol and defend territory, and lived more like the wolves of old, before humanity had encroached on our territories, built cities around us and compelled us to constantly be wary of cameras and social media.

Impressive that Sterling, who reeked of city wolf, knew

the difference. I had met wolves who didn't even know the term "feral," they just derided us as their country bumpkin cousins.

That was the end of the questions until the lights of the coast appeared. Sterling pulled out his phone. "I don't have your number."

"Don't have one."

"What?"

"Don't get a signal out where I li—out there. The number you have is the house landline."

He put his phone back in his pocket. "And here I thought your father was just playing keep-away with you."

What an odd thing to say in light of our current situation.

"We'll fix that tomorrow," he said.

"There's no point paying for something when you can't use it." I found his comment insulting.

"I agree, but you can use it in New York."

The lights of the city beckoned below. So bright, an astonishing sea of lights. I managed not to plaster my face against the window, but the pure ocean of light! It outshone the stars. "Where are we landing?"

"Teterboro."

"Is that a little airport?"

"It's in New Jersey. This jet can't fly into the major airports. Not important enough. It's only about half an hour drive this time of night."

It was very late, but my body was two hours behind and I was amped on nerves, trying to outrun the anguish. "Where do you live?"

He told me the address, which meant nothing to me but I committed it to memory.

Once landed, the plane taxied off the tarmac, and a black town car waited outside for us.

"Ready?" Sterling asked me as Patrick went to open the

door and lower the stairs.

"Yes," I lied. He offered me his hand. After a bit of hesitation, I took it, the jolt of his skin against mine not unexpected but painful and exciting all the same. I bit the inside of my lip, torn between excitement and the misery of how all this had happened.

It wasn't supposed to be like this.

The cold wind snapped across my bare calves, cutting through my clothes. I hurried across the tarmac to the open car door and slid inside without a thought. Sterling's leg brushed mine, and my skin rushed with the instinctual thrill of his presence.

"Is Sterling your birth name?" I asked him just so I could blurt out something before my skin warmed from something other than the air.

"Yes," he said.

"I'm sorry, that was rude of me." Of course it was his birth name. It was an odd name for a werewolf, considering silver would kill us faster than a dinner of rat poison with an antifreeze chaser, but that was no excuse for me to be so damn rude.

He gave me a little, wry smile, a warmth creeping into his eyes. "No offense taken. You're not the first to ask. My mother jokes I was born with my first gray hairs."

"I am sorry." My rudeness shocked me. How dare I question someone's name like that! My nerves were ahead of me.

His smile intensified just a degree. My blunder bothered me more than him. I swallowed around all his attention on me, warm under his gaze, and aware of his presence under my own skin. His hand unconsciously slipped over my hip. The caress of his hand, even through layers of clothing, ripped another shiver off my skin.

Change the subject. A good, chilling conversation about my new pack seemed a good idea. "Do you live with your pack?"

"They live with me," he corrected. "Or, now, us."

Us.

SLEEPING ARRANGEMENTS

Over a bridge and into Manhattan itself, lit up bright as day. It was huge, there was no other way for me to describe the sheer scope of it, the cluster of smells, the noise and motion. At midnight on a Thursday it was still a buzzing hive.

The car pulled up to a tall steel-and-glass building with multiple flags hanging out front. The building's top disappeared into the night sky. I had stood on hillsides and even small mountains, but I had never seen a building that climbed into cloud cover.

The city assaulted with its myriad of scents and noises, including the vague scent of other wolves. The concrete was cold and unforgiving. Was Gaia even present, or was She buried under a dozen feet of poured concrete, and speared through with rebar?

Sterling ushered me into the massive lobby and to the elevators. I tried not to gawk at the size, polish, the glass and marble, and quiet elegance that silently stated how far from anything familiar I was.

The elevator went up and up. And up. Then it stopped. Sterling took out a little keycard from his coat pocket and pressed it against a glass panel on the elevator board. Something went ding and the elevator continued onward. "I'll get you one of these tomorrow."

"What is it?"

"The very top floors are single units," he explained.

"So you have to have a key to get the elevator to go to those levels."

"You mean the whole floor of the building?" I hoped I didn't sound as astonished as I felt. For all the television and internet videos and what-not covering the lives of the wealthy, when you're actually confronted with anything resembling it, it hits hard.

I had never longed to be a princess in a castle with silks and delicate trays of tasty morsels and jewels in my hair, servants catering to my every whim. My daydreams had always been me as a great hunter, moonlight shining through my fur, and packs from all over in awe of my sharp senses and cunning prowess.

"Yes." Sterling fell back into his maddening neutral tone. One day he wouldn't be able to use that dead-center voice to hide what he really felt.

The elevator stopped and opened onto an extravagant marble foyer. There were two doors in recessed alcoves, a single round table, and a double set of doors at the end of the small space. It was to these doors—also requiring a keycard—that I followed Sterling.

I stepped into an open space of marble, high ceilings and floor-to-ceiling windows overlooking the top of the Manhattan skyline. To my far left was a recessed spot in the floor with three couches arranged around a massive flat screen pressed into the wall. Two heads relaxed against the back of the couches.

My new pack. The SnowFang. Most of it, anyway.

Sterling tossed down his keys onto a little side table. The clatter shook the two men off their couches and over to us. One was Chinese and also one of the biggest men I had ever seen. His far-too-small tee shirt didn't cover his abs and barely accommodated his massive biceps. The other was a lanky, dusky-skinned man with jet-black hair, possibly of some Slavic extraction. He had on just some ripped jeans and a beaten up flannel shirt that had two buttons done. They were both about twenty or so, give or take a few years.

"Gaia's tits." The dark man told the huge guy. "She actually came with him."

"Medieval," the huge guy replied.

They shook their heads.

Only a great deal of experience pretending to be at ease with being discussed kept my tears at bay. This part was familiar, at least, watching strange wolves discuss the merit of my being present at all.

"Winter," Sterling kept his eyes were on his packmates. "That is Jun," he indicated the huge guy, then the other one, "and that's Burian."

"Hey," Burian told me.

"Hi." Jun had an American accent. Burian had a slight accent I couldn't quite place.

"Where's Cye?" He had expected his whole pack present to meet the new addition.

"Kitchen." Jun jerked his thumb in that direction. To me, he asked, "Why did you come with him?"

"The SilverPaw Alpha saw no reason to delay." My throat almost betrayed me again, but my voice only had a slight, strangled rasp around each word.

Burian dusted his hands together and told Jun, "Cold. Just pack her off and buh-bye."

"I thought you got to get to know your mate first," Jun said.

"So did I." I answered without thinking. I instantly regretted it. Speaking badly of SilverPaw or my father hadn't been my intention.

Jun shrugged his huge shoulders. "Welcome to SnowFang."

His greeting was genuine and surprisingly sympathetic. I hadn't expected sympathy. Burian was more callous candor, but I appreciated that too. "Thank you."

Sterling retrieved Cye, who was also tall, very thin, and with gorgeous sea-green eyes. He had on an apron that read *DTF: Down To Fondant.*

"I made something to celebrate," he informed us in a shy tone.

"Celebrate? Well, I guess that's what we can call it," Burian said.

Sterling gave Burian a warning look.

"Thank you," I told Cye. I knew nothing about these men, except that two of them had been founding members and had possibly questionable backgrounds. It still was hard not to like them outright. We were all thrown in together, no point snarling at each other, and everyone seemed game to make the best of it.

"Did you take care of the room?" Sterling asked Cye.

"Of course," Cye said indignantly. He went back towards the kitchen. "Show her around and I'll finish up the food."

"I'm starving," Jun whined after Cye.

Sterling showed me around the palatial apartment. Polished marble, burnished woods, smooth paint, steel fixtures, glass panels. Huge open spaces and rooms and everything was very quiet. Padding under the hardwood and heavily insulated walls, he told me. Beyond playing potential landlord showing off a property, he didn't say a thing, and his voice was a brittle cold that rattled me with each word.

"Your room is this way," he told me.

"My room?" I balked. Up until that moment I hadn't considered sleeping arrangements. Thinking about being in Sterling's bed, or that Sterling might want pups sooner rather than later had been too much. Now it came front of my mind, because Sterling sleeping by himself wasn't how it was supposed to be.

All of this wasn't how it was supposed to be, but this was within my control. Sort of.

"Your room," he repeated.

I frowned at him, not understanding.

"I was not going to presume I could join you," he told my expression. Gaia, I hated that tone! Just some forced veneer to cover up his anger and frustration.

"Mates do not sleep apart." Any mate would presume

they had the right to share sleeping space with their other half. Everyone in the flat would notice he wasn't with me, which would be weird for everyone (if they knew it was weird, and perhaps that was a big assumption on my part) and then when he did join me, everyone would notice that too.

I wanted one thing to be like it was supposed to be. Dark hilarity that the thing on offer was sleeping arrangements! Gaia had a sense of humor.

Sterling needed to sleep with me or explain why he didn't want to.

And he didn't want to, but it was hard to pin down exactly why. The twitch of his jaw said he was nervous or doubtful, the set of his shoulders said angry.

Sterling had been prepared to be resentful and distrustful of me, certain I was playing along with some ploy to part him from a large chunk of his wealth, or ruin him in some way. Knowing that wasn't the case had to have been the final insult. Him believing he had been bullied and played, just to find out he wasn't even worth toying with.

Sadly, for both of us, it wasn't as simple as me being my father's pawn.

This would have been a hell of a lot more straightforward if I was just bait, and Sterling the nice woolly sheep being led in for fleecing. That arrangement would be very clear.

Him sleeping apart from me wouldn't make things any better between us, or easier on the pack. It'd make things worse.

Sterling's lips compressed a little tighter.

"I won't make off with your virtue," I told him.

A glint in his hazel eyes, like a knife twitching in and out of direct light. I bit my lower lip and tried not to squirm as he leaned forward, his voice like a hand through my fur, "Whatever virtue I had was made off with long ago."

Good going, Winter. Way to just fling yourself at him.

A little color crept to my cheeks, my insides squirmed, but not from fear. What would those hands feel like on my skin? Rough like the scrapes and callouses on them, or gentler? Angry, perhaps. His fingers pulling through my hair, perhaps just a little too rough.

One thing at a time. Maybe I should find out how his hands got that scraped up before I let him touch me with them.

Sterling kept watching me, observing, learning my every nuance and tick, as mates—especially Alphas—will do. He came to the conclusion my body wasn't actually on offer just yet. "You trust me to not lay a paw upon you."

"Should I not?" I asked.

He leaned closer, his breath on my cheek, his lips very close to mine. "When I shake off the shock, Winter, *I* would not trust me."

His words were like a rough caress, sending fire over my skin and a single shock through me. Desire overrode the haze of rattled anger and insult. I think I might have whispered something monosyllabic, and certainly imbecilic. It didn't matter. He closed the final breath of distance between us, his strong body pressed mine against the wall, and kissed me.

I had never been kissed like that. Hard. Rough. Hungry.

I couldn't trust me either. My fingers found his shirt and jawline, one set twisting into the fabric, the other raking fingernails along his flesh, enjoying the painful bristle of his unshaven skin.

He grabbed a handful of my thigh, lifted me against him, his touch rough and everything I had never known I needed. No, not rough enough, not nearly enough. He felt *so* strong, so solid, so *rough* under those tailored human clothes.

The heat clouded out everything else, there was nothing at all between us except the warmth of where souls joined and melted together.

I gathered myself and pried him back a few degrees. "Not

tonight," I breathed. "Gaia may have chosen you for me, but I want to see why."

"This is not proof enough?" he asked, in almost a low growl, angry at having been caught off-guard by his instincts, and still well within their clutches. He pushed me against the wall, every inch and dip and line of his body fitted against mine, "I could take you behind those doors right now, Winter. You want me to. Your lips might tell me differently, but your scent says something else."

He kissed the hollow of my throat, inhaling the scent of desire that bloomed across my chest. I did. Gaia, I did. His body pressed against mine, all of him, the thought of his naked skin against mine sent a violent shudder down my spine, almost more than I could stand.

All it would have taken was one uttered, single-word invitation. My lips moved to do just that. His hands held me tight, and he would have used them to take me into that bedroom, kick the door shut, and do exactly what feral, base instinct wanted.

No. Not when it was all mixed up with pain and anger and I didn't even have the faintest idea who he was. I needed to have a *little* common sense. "I don't think it's a good idea."

Of course I had the gall to say that when I was tangled up with him and had my fingers in his skin and my thighs wrapped around him. I had the *right* to say it, but it was a sure way to irritate him.

He clicked his teeth, as if hunting, his eyes a storm of anger and desire , but he released me. "Probably. And I don't want you to think I have no patience, or think that this is five hundred years ago."

Patience? If there was one thing Sterling didn't strike me as, it was *patient*. "I doubt you are a patient man."

"Only when I'm hunting. That anticipation is always worth savoring."

Sterling, how in Gaia's name did you end up on that

list... and what does it say that you are the other part of me?

ERRANDS & ARMOR

Sterling and I negotiated a minor compromise: he'd move in to the master bedroom the next day. Given the late hour that was the most reasonable course of action. I had one night in the massive bed by myself, and it was too empty. Things moving too fast with Sterling still would have meant someone would have been nearby. What was "too fast" with your divine-chosen partner anyway? I kept telling myself I did *not* know him, the circumstances were so strange, I could *not* get tangled up in the easy lust and lies of the bond.

He was my mate. Instinct urged me to trust him completely, rely on him, that I was safe with him. But that could be a lie. I knew mated pairs who were miserable and in all practical terms, hated each other. That might be us when the shiny lust wore off.

Running two hours behind New York time had been to my benefit the night before, but it was not the next morning.

I oozed out of bed. My jaw threatened to split my face from yawns. When I saw myself in the bathroom mirror I had to wonder what Sterling would think. An old, too-large tee shirt and pair of faded shorts that hung off my body. My hair was a red tousled mess. Somehow I did not think he would have approved.

"Good morning!" Cye practically chirped.

There was no dining room, just a large table in the area next to the equally large kitchen. Everyone else already sat reading newspapers or hunkered over phones, except for Cye, who buzzed around the kitchen wielding a spatula.

If Cye cooked breakfast most mornings that was the best news I had gotten in a month.

Sterling glanced at me from his seat, already dressed in fashionably abused jeans and a deceptively casual three-button top of heathered green. His lips twisted a few degrees. My happiness switched into a cold jolt that then transmuted into a deep, oozing shame.

See. Told you to be careful.

Jun shoveled food onto his plate.

"What do you want to drink, Winter?" Cye asked me from the kitchen.

"Coffee. I'll get it." He didn't need to wait on me.

Sterling gathered up his own mug. "Sit. How do you take it?"

"Cream," I murmured, averting my gaze from his face. Seeing that skeptical, faintly displeased look on the faces of strangers had been bad enough.

Jun handed me a plate from the stack near him. Cye certainly put out a spread. I concerned myself with my coffee and food. Didn't seem anyone else was much for conversation in the morning. Burian acknowledged me only with a glance and only after Sterling growled at him, but not that Sterling so much as said a word to me over his paper, and Jun was too busy shoveling food into his face at a rate that would have won any eating contest.

Outside the city waited. It was just about dawn, the city suspended between evening lights and morning's red glow.

"We need to go downstairs," Sterling told me, "get dressed and we can head out when you're ready."

Get dressed to go downstairs? This would end badly.

As I contemplated my suitcases I realized I had nothing approaching Sterling's level of polish. The best I could do was a sweater in pale cream wool and jeans. The height of fashion back home was a fresh plaid shirt and jeans with the seams still pressed crisp.

When I reappeared Sterling didn't give me that same mildly offended look, instead he just whisked me out the doors to the marble alcove.

Through the lobby again to the other side of the

building, down a hallway to a single door, where an overly-attentive concierge greeted us. She handed over the various keys I'd need to come and go as I wished, while giving me a questioning look, her pen hovering over her desk. I shriveled, small and grubby. I was as out of place in this glossy building as muddy boots.

She stretched a smile across her face, made a few notes on her blotter and murmured something conciliatory to Sterling about how nice it was to see him.

Sterling gave her the same polite frost that he gave me while my whole being tried to melt off my bones, slide off the chair and slip down into the cracks where the sewers waited to receive me.

Even though it only took twenty minutes, it felt like three hours, and the vast building was too small, and there was no where to run. Outside the windows was just concrete and steel and endless dismal gray, and mobs of people and chains of cars.

When we returned upstairs, a small box had arrived with Sterling's name on it. Inside was a sleek silver phone, which he handed to me. "It should have all my contacts on it. And," he took it back a moment and tapped on the screen, "my number."

"Thank you." I put it in my pocket, and caught myself before nerves caused me to stupidly quip about old girlfriends. It wasn't my business who or what he had done before me, all I cared about was there weren't any ghosts to haunt us.

Jun watched this from his place in the kitchen, but he said nothing. Instead, he shoved a celery stick into a pale flesh-colored shake, the veins of his massive biceps visibly throbbing. "Got ya' keys, Winter?"

"Yes. What is that?" Whatever the slop in the huge cup was, it smelled revolting, like cold chicken, peanut butter and chocolate.

"Post-lift chicken shake. Want a sip?"

"No, thanks."

He took a huge swig. "You don't know what you're missing!"

Nope. No, I didn't, and I would die at peace with my decision.

Sterling checked his watch. "I have to run. Someone will be by in forty minutes to pick you up."

I didn't recall having any conversation about this. "Who and why and where are they taking me?"

"I'm not quite sure who and I don't know where," Sterling informed me. "But to take you shopping. Salon. That sort of thing."

"Excuse me?"

"Your father didn't really give you a chance to pack much." For an instant Sterling looked like a deer in headlights. He visibly scrambled for a moment, but regained his frigid composure. "I don't know anything about it, so I asked someone who does to give you a hand."

"Who is this someone?" I growled. I hadn't imagined his disapproving look. I was sort of grateful for the rescue, but at the same time, mortified at not being given a chance to fix it on my own.

"A friend of mine is a music agent," Sterling said. "Some of his staff specialize in this sort of thing."

Think he'll have to teach you how to shake?

I slapped the shame aside and picked up the pieces of my pride. I was done being road kill. "You mean clean up people so they're presentable to polite society. That sort of thing."

"I didn't say that."

"Did you need to?" I snapped.

"Winter, I'm not trying to start a fight—"

"What did you think was going to happen? You tell me you're going to pawn me off to someone so I can be made to look presentable? Were you embarrassed this morning? The way I looked standing next to you?"

"No."

"That's not the look you gave me at breakfast." He wasn't lying, but he also wasn't telling the truth. I bit down hard on the urge to throw the previous night in his face. Had he been so disgusted touching me? Good enough to fuck, not good enough to introduce to his friends? Had he run off to wash his hands and rinse out his mouth, maybe scrape his tongue and wonder what the hell he had been thinking?

He said nothing.

Years of being called bad luck, a disappointment, whispers that the only reason I had come to anything at all was my father's misplaced indulgence. Now this: Sterling's marionette, dancing on strings to the jerking motion of unsympathetic hands.

"Call your friend," my throat felt torn and I fought to get the words out, "I'm not going."

"You're going."

"Like hell I am! I am not a piece of livestock being prepared for the county fair!"

He moved close to me. His hot intensity bore into my flesh. The scent of impatient anger rose off his skin. There was nothing pleasant about it, and a flash of fear drained the heat from my cheeks and replaced it with an icy chill. I held my ground and dug deeper. If this was going to provoke a violent rage, well then, guess I'd just learn sooner than later what he was capable of.

Go ahead. Hit me. Do it. Do it!

"In case you haven't noticed, this is a city, not a county fair," he hissed, so scathing it could have peeled enamel off teeth. "I am not going to argue with you. We have a gala in three days, and there are expectations. You not liking those expectations won't change them!"

"I am not some trophy wolf being hunted for her hide!"

He did not relent. "Humans outnumber us. We live in

their world. It's armor. It's not plate and chain and leather. It's jewels and clothing and shoes. If you don't come prepared, they will eat you, me, and this pack. So you are going to go and you are going to play your part and that means looking the part. Do less and you *will* end up as a very pretty throw rug!"

Then why not just say so! Instead he dragged me around by the ruff like I was some naughty dog beyond logical thought. Dragging me off to the flea dip because woe was him, Gaia had given him a mate who knew how to hunt bear, not walk in six inch heels.

Good enough to grope, dirty enough someone needed to take me out back and clean me up.

"I'm sorry if this art gala party is not the outdoor under-the-moon paper plate and red plastic cup affair you are used to," he added before I could say anything.

"Oh, I don't know. I enjoy getting my paws dirty and snarling at a real enemy, not cowering to some soft pink human's disapproval because I don't know the proper fork to use!"

"It's easier to play by human rules and costs me nothing I value. But good you know that not all forks are equal."

"So you're a very good human but have never been much of a wolf?" I spat.

He looked to the side, ignoring the bait and disengaging from the fight without yielding a backward step. "Whoever is coming will be here soon. I have things to do. I'll be back this evening."

Just like that, the fight was over, like my father had so often just *stopped* a conversation. Sterling didn't even slam the door on his way out.

My anger evaporated into cold sadness. He had just decided the fight was over, I wasn't worth arguing with, and left. Me. His Luna, his mate, just not worth arguing with. He was right, I was wrong. Whoever was coming, and whatever they did to me, it didn't matter to Sterling so long as I returned home in time to decorate his arm for the party.

Jun hadn't moved and had seen everything. "You okay?"

"Yes." I wadded up my feelings and squished them deep down within myself.

"You sure?" Jun pressed. "'Cause I didn't like him leaning in on you like that, and I don't like what he said. You seem pretty upset."

Speaking against the Alpha was risky, his concern was touching. "It was just a spat."

Jun sounded doubtful, "Looked like more than that. Sterling can be a jerk but he—"

"I can handle it. Now I just have to go play dress up doll." I pulled at a strand of my hair. It was one thing to be told you aren't good enough. It's another to be told that... and know it's true. I wasn't prepared for whatever this gala was. I didn't have enough time to figure it out on my own... but Sterling had made it so... degrading.

"You're gorgeous like you are," Jun said. "Don't let anyone else tell you different. You're classy and beautiful and fuck anyone who says different."

"Well, right now I'm not the right kind of classy or beautiful," I gestured to our surroundings. "Maybe I'll feel better after I get polished. Like putting a rock in a tumbler."

"Don't say that kind of stuff. Sterling's not usually the rich-brat privileged asshole, if it makes you feel better. I'd have punched his teeth down his throat a while back if he was." Jun's face stilled with more seriousness than I had initially credited him with.

I twisted the hair around my finger. My scalp protested, and I mumbled to myself, "He should have just asked."

"I don't know what goons Sterling's passed you to for this outing," Jun said. "They're probably straight up, but you want me to come along?"

Bringing protection would be insulting, and I didn't

want to antagonize Sterling further. I had to share a bed with him. "I'm sure it will be fine."

"You got my number in your new phone?"

"Yes."

"You text me if you need me."

I managed a smile.

THE GAMES HUMANS PLAY

About thirty minutes after Sterling left, the door chimed. Jun went to get it. He gave the tall, lanky man on the other side of the door a mean mug, and followed him into the kitchen area where I waited.

"I'm Mint," the man introduced himself to me.

There was nothing green about him. Not even his eyes or a tattoo or a dyed eyebrow. He was tall, dark haired, tanned to perfection and impeccably dressed in a fitted smoke-colored suit, complete with bright purple waistcoat under the jacket.

"Winter." I hoped he wouldn't make a joke about candy flavors.

Jun stood very close to Mint. Mint ignored him and instead looked me up and down. He put a hand on his chin as he thought and made a little frown-like noise.

Jun growled at him, "Tell her she's pretty."

"Oh, she's gorgeous," Mint said as if he had huge guys growling at him all the time. "Natural redhead. Those are pretty rare, and such a dark red too."

"Jun, I'm sure it's fine." I wasn't sure how to deal with this.

"I can stand here and breathe on him all day. Allll day." He breathed out very loudly to prove his point. Mint ignored him.

"I'm sure it's fine," I repeated.

Mint gestured for me to turn around.

I was not going to twirl around on command like some little dancing dog. "What exactly did Sterling tell you?"

"I didn't talk to Mr. Mortcombe."

"So what were you told about this assignment?"

"That you're from Montana and need a New York look."

That was the nicest possible way of translating "take her out back and wash her off."

Mint had been honest with me, I should be honest with him. If he thought he was going to be dealing with a woman delirious with excitement and grateful for a makeover, he should be disabused of that notion. I was tired of being treated like everyone else's property, or up for everyone else's perusal... or heavy petting. "I'm not thrilled about this."

This was news to Mint. "No?"

"No."

Mint frowned in a serious way, as if he was a doctor and I had revealed some grave symptoms. "You're not the first person I've dealt with who isn't enthused about this process."

That wasn't what I expected him to say. "What process would that be?"

"Realizing you don't meet the expectations of your audience."

I had always envisioned wealthy society hen-pecking as only as harmful as one let it be. Sort of like a bunch of overgrown teenagers who had never really left high school. Sterling, under the rancor, acted like it was much more serious than that and I was an idiot for thinking otherwise. But he had grown up in that world, so to him it might have acquired more importance than it deserved.

Mint telling me the same thing didn't erase my bruised feelings, but I was willing to consider Sterling hadn't been exaggerating. "Is this audience very blood-thirsty and predatory? Looking to add my hide as a throw rug in front of their fire?"

"You haven't seen how one bad choice of earrings can make the news?"

"That's starlets and movies," I shook my head.

"No difference. Nothing is sacred or too petty. Anything to pull you down even half a rung so their head can be that much higher. Hair, makeup, shoes, clothes. All those are avoidable mistakes. That's my job. Avoidable mistakes."

I picked up on his unspoken meaning. "But there are people in your agency who do personality coaching."

"Yes. I'm not one of them."

Forced to choose between needing a washing or needing training, I'd take the shampoo. It would be stupid for my first social faux pas to be something avoidable like shoes. At some point I would probably say something too blunt, and then if I had the wrong dress on, that would just give them ammo about not only was I poorly bred, I looked it too.

It was all prestige, a game of rank and microaggressions, same as any wolf pack.

Sterling hadn't had to be so cruel about it.

I sighed.

Mint guided me out the door.

Our first stop was a posh salon. I could not remember the last time my hair had had more than a trim. Another man, who had introduced himself by the name Tony, clutched handfuls of my red hair and arranged it this way and that while Mint supervised. In hushed, grave tones they discussed the possibilities: my hair was so long, so full, natural waves, my neck slender, my skin pale, my shoulders, but perhaps my face was too round, or perhaps this or that color tint would draw out my eyes, or my hair was too long, how much to trim.

Someone appeared during all this to soak my fingers in little dishes of soapy water and followed me as I moved through all the hair-care steps. An assortment of people rubbed lotion into my hands, and little oils, and jabbed at my cuticles with a pointy stick. While my hair was rinsed and my face prone another person came to trim and pluck my eyebrows.

It was a production line.

Mint remained watchful just behind my right shoulder.

He would not let anything outlandish happen, like blue hair or shaved eyebrows, even though the amount of hair Tony started to cut made me nervous. I finally had to protest, and was assured that it would be fine. Mint's reflection nodded at me. I fidgeted while my hair was clipped and twisted and combed and brushed. The shape began to take form and I wondered at the transformation. Subtle, yet clearly there.

It was still long and full, and still red, but it looked different. It felt different on my head too, and my eyes looked even more green-blue than usual. I had expected to hate it. Or not notice a difference. I didn't know how to feel about any of this.

Mint asked, "Unhappy?"

"I thought it would not be me."

"Of course it's you. I'm not turning you into someone."

"But you do that. Turn people into a totally different look. You can do it."

"All the time. With your pale skin and bone structure, I could transform you into a gothic beauty. You wouldn't recognize yourself. But that's not what you wanted." He gave me a wry smile, as if he understood. He ran his hands along the outline of my red hair. "This is just the New York you, Winter. When in Rome, and all."

"I wouldn't have minded having this hair in Montana," I confessed.

"Good luck finding someone who can do highlights like this on natural red hair in Montana."

He smiled, but he hadn't been joking, and he probably wasn't wrong. My lips trembled a little as they smiled for him.

There were worse things than being polished to a shine. I was still just bruised with what had happened up until this point, and this was the unfortunate spot where Sterling had bitten down.

He took me up to the third floor for my nails. I chose a

burnished copper shade like the setting sun. Insistence on acrylics made me balk. Sometimes fake nails retracted into the claw sheath when in wolf form, but usually they just popped off instead. Mint didn't know this, and Mint clearly didn't care about my resistance. "You have no nails, Winter. You have to have acrylics. Period."

I wouldn't be casually shifting in New York, and if I had to shift, a lost acrylic would be the least of my problems.

It was already five in the evening, but Mint took me to a third-story loft next. It was quiet and exquisite, and waiting for us was some food and two other people, both men in suits. There were also several steel racks of clothes, and more clothes laid out on tables.

The building sounded empty. Everyone on the other floors had already gone home. I was alone with men I barely knew. Anyone could storm in through that hundred-year old door with its frosted glass panel.

I undressed behind a beautiful screen and spotted a window that had a fire escape, and decided if something happened, I would drop to wolf and dart out that window. In the chaos and semi-dark perhaps a white wolf would not be noticed right away.

But everyone in New York would notice a white wolf running down the street. Perhaps a crazy naked woman might attract less attention.

Before I was even undressed Mint's disembodied hand shoved an outfit at me from beyond the screen.

From there he tasked me with trying on innumerable sets of clothing. I dared not ask what strange, surreal world I was in. My own private clothing shop, it seemed. Mint directed what I was to put on, came over, would arrange a scarf or tug at some buttons. Some of the things I liked, many I did not, a few I loved, some I liked but Mint did not.

There was also an entire table devoted to the matter of delicate apparel. I had never had anything so fancy or beautiful as some of those dainties. Chemises, bras, panties of all types, garters, stockings with beautiful lace tops. I admired all of them, and as I ran the silk of a chemise through my fingers, I remembered Sterling was supposed to share a bed with me that night.

Would he think I was wearing them for him? And would it be wrong of him to think I was, because maybe one day I would?

The thought of Sterling looking at me like he had that morning made me hurt.

"Do you prefer more conservative lingerie?" Mint asked.

"I was thinking about something else."

If I wanted to wear fancy panties, that's what I'd wear. I'd deal with Sterling when it was necessary to deal with him. When that time came I'd probably want to be in something pretty rather than one of my faded old bras.

Maybe one day I'd wear things like this for Sterling, but right then, I'd wear them for me.

In the end, it was dark, nearly nine, I was exhausted and stood in the loft wrapped in a bathrobe while my chosen items were packed. Mint handed me an outfit. "Here. Wear this. Your old things will disappear."

Not a surprise. "Will they at least go to good use?"

Mint caught his breath as if he had been about to say something else. "I'll take care of it. So was it as bad as you expected?"

"No," I confessed, even if this now meant confronting a victorious Sterling. "Maybe a lot of people don't tell you this, Mint, but I've never had makeover fantasies."

"Not everyone does. Some of my charges agreed to be dolls, or were told they had to be dolls. You just got an updated look."

"You mean you took me out back and hosed me off." I slid the second heel onto my foot with a sigh.

Mint chuckled. "I didn't say that. I'm sure I'd look like an idiot if I showed up in your hometown dressed like this."

"You'd get a lot of looks."

"And now you won't get those looks here. You'll get all the right kind of looks. Your choice."

We'd see each other again the next afternoon to find a dress to wear to the gala.

The closer we got to my new home, the more reality gnawed its way back into my bones. I crossed the threshold, the marble lobby, the shiny elevator. Bellboys in tow with my parcels. My heels clicking on the marble...

If I showed up in Montana wearing these shoes, I'd get laughed at. *Culture shock. That's all it is.*

Deep breath before going through the double doors.

I dropped my keys on the low table and walked into the front area. The skyline struck me with its awesome, but unnatural, beauty. I would have liked to see the trees or mountains from this height, the light-punctuated blocks of steel and stone seemed so strange.

"Down the hall," I told the bellboys, gesturing in the direction they were to go. It allowed me to turn away from Sterling.

The bellboys disappeared into the closet to hang the bags, and placed parcels on the low table, as if they knew exactly how to do this. They probably knew more about it than I did.

The men disappeared as swiftly as they had come, leaving me with my silent Alpha.

"You're looming, Sterling."

"It's late." He came around to face me.

"You could have texted if you were concerned."

A small frown bent his features, but he didn't share his thoughts as he looked me up and down.

I tried not to glare at him. My soul was no different for my body having been cut and faceted and polished. Were we going to have another fight over this?

He noted each small changed detail, then, "Are you sure about me being in here with you?"

"Yes." Mates shared a bed, they shared a den. My parents had clashed often enough, but they had never slept apart.

He shifted his weight, and studied me again, as if I were the solution to whatever rattled him. Not that I had any clue what could have him off center, aside from the obvious, but it seemed more than that. Perhaps he wanted to feel out if I held a grudge about earlier and planned on strangling him in his sleep.

Lucky for him I preferred my prey to be conscious.

Then, "I'm sorry about earlier. I didn't mean to make you feel ashamed. That's not what I meant. I want you to know that."

It was hard to believe it *hadn't* been what he meant, and instead he just regretted I had seen it. "Then what did you mean? I saw that look. Don't deny it, Sterling."

He rubbed the space between his eyes. "It was worry. Not shame or disapproval."

"Worry about what? That you might need to teach me to shake paws, or how many dips in a flea bath it would take to wash the woods off me?"

"That *this* would happen when I told a feral she needs her hair done."

I drew in a deep breath through my nose, held it for three beats, let it out slowly. "It's not *what* you said. It's *how* you said it."

"Which is what I'm apologizing for. How I spoke to you. I was angry about... something else. This thing coming up is important, and let's not kid ourselves by saying you were prepared. It's a lot of hoops to jump through, but I didn't want there to be any misunderstanding you've *got to* jump through them. I should have been more gracious."

It took a very, very large wolf to come right out and offer an apology, and I liked him even better that he didn't back away from his expectations, or what he needed. Hell, it was better than my father's infinite silence and stonewalling. Finally, someone who would *talk* to me!

He waited, not expecting me to accept his apology.

"I'll be out in a bit," I told him, "and apology accepted."

Sterling nodded and left. I put away my purchases, then soaked myself in the shower. Our sleeping arrangements didn't enter my mind. Only where to find an actual dinner, and then proceed onward to sleep.

Humans seemed to love talking about when they first met a partner, how delirious it all had been. They might have felt differently if they had known their partner was *their* partner, the final word on it, the one they were destined for, that was it, for better or worse, no matter what. Werewolves never seemed to talk about that sort of thing, how anyone had met anyone else, or what it had been like.

This must be why. The first few weeks were awful and nobody wanted to think about it ever again, and didn't want to scare the youngsters.

But Sterling had apologized, and it wasn't hard to understand why his temper was short, and his stress levels high. I had swallowed my pride and accomplished the mission. The day wasn't a complete failure.

I shrugged a green silk robe over my shoulders. The thin, plush lining felt wonderful on my skin. No point in getting fully dressed just to get undressed for bed in an hour.

The men had not moved from their places on the couch. Sterling and Burian bent over laptops, but Jun watched the television with a bowl of popcorn on his lap.

The fridge was well stocked, flawlessly organized and sparkling clean. If there was anything that could be removed and eaten without causing the whole arrangement to tumble, it eluded me.

"I saved you some dinner!" Cye practically chirped at me. He bustled into the kitchen as a sort of terrifying force, nudging me away from the fridge with a smile stretched across his face.

"Do you have bodies buried in that fridge?" I asked the territorial glint in his eyes. I didn't move and his shoulder burrowed between my breasts. His gentle and passing nudge was not going to be taken as such.

"No, of course not." He looked down at his arm, realized his very grave mistake trying to physically push me around, and edged back. "I just, um, I just have it organized a certain way. Besides, I set a plate for you!"

He broke eye contact and slunk over to the microwave. "See?" he brought me back a plate wrapped neatly with foil.

Burian and Jun teased Cye about *his* kitchen now being *my* kitchen.

Nope, Cye could *have* the kitchen.

There were three nice couches arranged around the much-abused table. Burian sat on one, Sterling on another, and Jun and Cye on the third. I nudged my way past Jun's legs and sat down next to Sterling with plate and fork in hand.

Out of the corner of my eye I spotted scrolling charts and graphs and columns of numbers.

He had to do something to afford this place. At least I hoped so. Him being a trustfund baby would have been disappointing.

His hands were even more scraped up than the previous day, with skin gouged out of his knuckles and blue stains under two fingernails to match the half-healed scrapes from earlier. Did he punch concrete for recreation? The corded muscles of his wrists moved as he typed, shifting like the cables of a suspension bridge in strong wind.

Jun took his television very seriously and that night was a costume drama from China that he devoured with rapt attention. There were no subtitles so I had no idea what was going on, but it was beautiful to look at, and Jun gave us the summary during commercials. Cye made off with my plate once I had finished. I tried to protest I'd bus my own plate, but he ignored me.

"Cye, if your belly was any lower you'd be a snake," Burian said.

"I like the kitchen organized a certain way. I don't ask you guys to do anything!" Cye protested.

"Just shove your tail between your legs. And shove your balls up into your belly while you're at it."

"Shut up. My show is back on!" Jun demanded.

Sterling glanced up from his work. He made note of where everyone was, then he looked back down.

The day hit me once Jun's show was over. Normally I wasn't a lightweight, and they seemed like they were going to stay up for another few hours, but I was done.

Sterling came to bed shortly after me. He moved quietly, but it was his presence that woke me. He reminded me of a forest in winter: still, quiet, yet vast, and filling my whole awareness. I couldn't help but find it pleasant, and he caused an unbidden shiver of pleasure when he entered the room. Instinct rewarded me for him being near.

And then a sudden intense rush of anxiety as everything was not familiar, and there was a nearly naked (or maybe naked) man I barely knew getting into bed next to me because I had asked him to, and he had warned me not to trust him, and how stupid it was, because I had *invited* him.

His presence brushed mine like invisible fur.

"I know you're awake, Winter," he said in the darkness.

What did I say? What did him saying anything mean? I had not stood on ceremony and had chosen one of my new silk chemises to wear to bed. Rarely had I slept in more than a nightshirt (and more often nude) so I wasn't going to start and then shed layers as I grew more comfortable. My chemise now felt flimsy and flirty and like a very bad idea.

The bed was large enough that we weren't touching, and

he'd have had to make a clear effort to cross the distance between us. He seemed to press against every inch of my skin.

"Did you want to talk about something?" My throat was dry.

His tone lightened very slightly. "I just wanted to tell you 'good night,' since you are awake to hear it."

"Good night, Sterling." He had apologized. It had all been an ugly misunderstanding between us, but what if it happened again? What if I made some glorious gaffe at the gala and screwed everything up?

I didn't want to be the woman he amused himself with in private, but dreaded every time he had to take out in public.

I closed my eyes in the darkness and waited.

He shifted in the bed, twisting the blankets as he sat up. The cool air touched my back. "You're afraid."

Invoked by his words, the inexplicable fear bloomed across my back and between my breasts.

"I'm here because you wanted me to be, Winter." He moved closer, the warmth of his skin against mine, the strength of him. My skin pleaded for the touch of his hands, even through the din of hot anxiety. The unexpected gentleness of his tone magnified everything, good and bad. "I will leave if you've changed your mind. Gaia put us together, but you *can* change your mind on what that means."

"It's not about that." I had no idea what any of this was about, but it wasn't me wanting to sleep alone.

His hand, chapped and calloused, lightly caressed my hip, bunching layers of silk as it moved. His fingertips found the hollows of my hip and pulled at the string of my panties.

I froze in place, barely able to sip air, unsure if the touch of his hand was terrifying or an exquisite torment that should never stop. The previous night it had made sense, but now it didn't, or maybe that had just been the thrill of the hunt, and this wasn't.

His hand retreated away. "You put on a good show, Winter. You almost convinced me."

If I could have found my vocal cords, I might have asked him *convinced you of what?*

He returned to his side of the bed.

I did not sleep for a very long time.

THE BODEGA ENCOUNTER

Sterling woke me up as he got out of bed the next morning, and I watched him from behind slitted eyes as he shook silver hair out of his face and rubbed his jaw. I expected to see a naked man as he cast off the sheets, but he was clad in boxers. Blue plaid boxers.

How lovely and normal of us. He came to bed in his boxers, and I came to bed in a little silk chemise nighty, and should a cat burglar have broken into the room they would have said what a lovely young couple. Nothing out of the ordinary here. Nothing at all.

I rolled onto my back and contemplated the ceiling. Decided I needed some coffee. The clock said six-twenty, but my body still said four-twenty.

Cye had half-finished breakfast. Burian wasn't there yet, but Jun was, in yet another far too small tee shirt and a faded pair of boxers that had a most unfortunate and inadequate fit. I almost said something, then decided I simply didn't care enough. Sterling was the only one who flustered me.

I couldn't look at the skyline without feeling queasy and jittery. Too big and unforgiving and hostile, and this box of glass and steel too confining.

Sitting around was nothing I ever did. Too much emotion, too little sweating. Sterling noted that I mangled my breakfast more than ate it, but didn't say anything.

He left with Burian around seven-fifteen without explanation. No idea where he was headed, when he'd be back or what he was doing. Since nobody else commented, it must have been routine. Cye set out to sanitize the kitchen, and Jun headed for the gym.

Their days proceeded on their usual tracks. It wasn't their job to babysit me or play host to me. This was my home now.

It was like the worst first day of school ever, and after the chaos of figuring out where your classes were and all the introductions, you're faced with the horrible ritual of the lunch room, holding your tray and looking out over the vast and crowded sea of people, all of whom pretend they don't see you.

I peered down at the sidewalk below. So many people, like ants marching to and from their hill. In between the ants wove other, faster-moving ants, and then even faster moving ants. Runners.

Well, why not?

With my new phone, there was no chance of me getting lost, and the whole city was mostly laid out on a grid anyway. I could just run in one direction for however many blocks, then turn around and run back. Sweat out all these feelings, get some endorphins going through my system. Do something familiar.

I changed, grabbed my keys and phone, and headed out.

Running had once meant running in the woods, or along dirt trails and country roads. Now it meant jogging around the city. Instead of dodging branches and stones, I wove through pedestrians and obeyed crosswalks.

The blistering cold city fascinated me with its momentum, its smells, the press of people, the constant noise, how everything seemed covered in soot or dirt or grime or a poster. Even if I hated the way the asphalt sucked the energy from my legs and gave nothing back, it was a new challenge that lifted my tired spirit.

I normally ran longer distances, but since I didn't know the area very well, decided to play it safe with just a small circuit. Halfway back I stopped at a little corner bodega for a bottle of water. From the outside it looked derelict and filthy, but it was mobbed with people. Curiosity lured me more than thirst, but thirst was a convenient excuse.

Inside, every spare inch of real estate was taken with some

item, and the assortment of things I could have purchased ranged from the afore-mentioned water bottles to tourist bait to snacks to notebooks to USB cables to little pills promising to solve any sexual dysfunction I might have. It smelled of people, incense, fried foods and tobacco. I pulled a bottle from the freezer and lined up in the six-deep line, trying not to play the gawking tourist.

Under the innumerable smells I caught the scent of something familiar. Another wolf.

Urban areas were neutral ground, with a pack's "territory" limited to their apartment or building. Ambitious packs might push that envelope and try to claim a whole city block. Even so, if this shop had been on such a claimed territory, it still wasn't off-limits. The Elder Council had declared that packs could lay absolutely no claim to streets or sidewalks, nor obstruct a wolf's passage from one point to another, and nonresidential places like shops or office buildings could not be claimed.

Cities were too small and densely populated with humans for wolves to draw territory lines. It's why I hadn't asked Sterling about it. Perhaps I should have. The Law was one thing, but local custom was another.

The wolf was male, and if I could smell him, he could smell me. I felt his keen gaze and intense focus. It was strange, we were two wolves passing on neutral ground and even if I was stepping on toes, the level of intensity was too high, even for an interested male. I resisted the urge to look back around, paid for my water and left the bodega.

He dumped whatever he was going to buy. With a huge step of one skinny leg he swung wide around me and planted both feet. I yanked up to avoid bumping into him, and was met with the grin on his narrow, thin face.

Tall, skinny, and dressed in worn jeans and camel-colored boots he leaned close, eyes boring into me. No wolf would just *loom* over a female like that unless he meant to be very aggressive.

Well, duh, you stupid little bumpkin. That's exactly what's happening.

Nobody passing by noticed any of this, much less cared.

"You're new." He pushed to within inches of my face, and inhaled the scent of my hair. His scent reminded me of dirty fryer vats and cigarette butts.

Every other time in my life I had had family or pack members near me, or *someone,* who would have grabbed this vermin by his collar.

Human women get told "use your voice," and "make a fuss," but werewolf females are taught only to bark at meaningful threats, otherwise to ignore them as below notice. Slimeball males trying to bait females into a confrontation *wanted* her to make a fuss. That meant the offending male was a worthy threat, and by extension, worthy of male pack members dealing with them.

Preventing this guy from becoming an actual threat anywhere but his own mind was a top priority.

I side-stepped. He jumped to block my way, his grin spreading across his cheeks.

How much of a threat *was* he? Under his bravado was the scent of anticipation and uncertainty. The same sort of nerves pups had on their first hunt. It didn't really change my situation, because yelling, shouting, or punching him in the face would have justified his existence. He'd have crawled back to whatever low-life friends he had and snicker about it all, and Gaia so help me if they found out who I was. They would have a *spectacular* laugh at SnowFang's expense.

I snapped to the other side, he jumped, but I was ready and ducked about him, and struck off at my regular pace. Sprinting would be fleeing and that was a no-no. I needed an alternative.

Or for him to have really bad cardio and fade back.

He fell into step next to me, laboring around his heavy

boots. "Don't run, gorgeous. Let's talk about you coming back to my place, eh? Put my tongue between those sweet little thighs of yours."

Only if you're into cold, dead corpses.

Each huffed pant contained some obscenity, all the while reeking of fryer vats and a revolting desire that sent my skin crawling. Nobody on the sidewalk noticed the vermin dangling off me. They just cursed at both of us for taking up too much room and being in the way.

Two blocks, he was still hanging on and I needed a plan. At the second crosswalk he leaned so close his breath almost gagged me, "You smell fancy. Which pack gets a pretty thing like you giving them head? Too good to even look at me, princess? You're a fancy pedigreed bitch, aren't you?"

Maybe it would be worth it to punch him in the nose. The more he talked the more he worked himself up, and the more creative he got. Didn't have the true criminal edge of a rogue, nor would I insult lone wolves by calling him one. He was just disgusting, the sort who lacked the balls to actually go full criminal. Big city, crowded street, he seemed to be alone, who would ever know if I punched him?

The way my luck had been lately, this wolf would prove to be a shill sent by another pack to bait me into a mistake. For all I knew Sterling had a ton of enemies in New York, and this was some kind of city wolf warfare I knew nothing about. Best to play it by the strict rules of noble etiquette and prestige as long as I could.

The wolf pushed closer, the sloppy grin from before narrowing into something more serious. He had seen me flinch, or caught the scent of my fear amid everything else. Blood in the water now.

My phone buzzed. And buzzed. And buzzed again.

I risked a glance at it as the light changed. Five texts from Sterling demanding to know where the hell I was, and it was also late. I needed to meet Mint in an hour and I was at least a two miles from the flat, with this dingleberry clinging to me.

The light changed and we marched across the crosswalk.

He snaked forward in the press of people. I dodged but slammed into two guys. They shoved back and pushed me right into him. He laughed and seized my tricep. I yelped. His fingers clamped down. "Hey there, gorgeous."

He pulled me forward with the current.

No way! I shoved myself into him and twisted. He hadn't been prepared for me to get closer and lost his grip. This time I wretched myself backward, knocking into a man behind me, bounced forward, and pressed myself through the crowd. The crowd, however, pressed back, pissed that anyone was trying to race through. There was an art to cutting through these crowds, and I didn't know it.

He was right back on me. "Well, well, you are a feisty thing, aren't you? Where did you get imported from? I'm gonna enjoy you on my lap."

I gagged. His stench told me exactly what he was going to do to me, and how excited the thought made him, as if his thick, rancid tone wasn't bad enough. My lungs begged for fresh air.

I looked around for what was immediately at hand. Various shops, but half a block down, a gym. Three levels, glass panels giving the people on treadmills a look of the street. Good option. Possible back entrance, and had a good vantage point if I ended up treed and had to tell Sterling to retrieve me.

Like a goddamn cat up a tree.

I crossed the street again, continuing to ignore his filth as he worked his way closer and closer, his lips so close I heard them smacking together, and ducked into the gym.

He did not follow, but waited right outside the glass doors, grinning.

My phone buzzed again. Now I was up to eight texts

from Sterling. Safe for a moment, I read the most recent one.

Sterling >> I am coming to find you if you do not text me in the next 2 minutes

Winter >> I'll be back in 10 minutes

Sterling kept at bay for a few minutes, now I had to extract myself from this lurking wolf as discreetly as was still possible. I went up to the desk, and asked the man organizing folders, "Is there a back door to this place?"

He looked up at me. "Excuse me?"

"The creepy guy lurking outside. Do you have a back door I can use?"

He briefly glanced at my stalker. His face registered that the creep was indeed full creep. "You want me to call the cops?"

"No," I shook my head. No, the *last* thing I wanted. "Just some weirdo bum with a thing for redheads. Another way out of here?"

He nodded towards the back. "Hallway on the right, all the way at the end."

"Thanks."

A quick consult of my phone told me I was more than ten minutes from the flat. Crap. I'd have to sprint the whole way.

At the end of the long hallway was a large door marked EXIT. It opened up onto an alley. An alley was still better than the wolf. I bolted to the left, where the streets waited.

THE APPROACHING STORM, ERR, PARTY

That stench of cigarettes, dried urine, and day-old fryer vats would linger with me for a long time.

My legs trembled from the sprint and massive adrenaline and endorphin dump that at least had the cosmic courtesy to wait until I staggered through the front doors of the building. Fifteen minutes, and Sterling had texted three times past the ten-minute mark. I hadn't had time to check my phone between sprints across streets but nobody else would have texted me, so Sterling was a safe deduction and—

Sterling strode across the lobby. I blinked sweat from my eyes. He had on a long coat, still in the suit from that morning. I pulled up, panting, and let the storm come to me.

"Where have you *been?*" He gave me a quick up and down look, then circled around me once.

"Running." I pushed past him, crunched up the water bottle and tossed it into a nearby recycling bin. Normally I kept water bottles to put into the freezer, but that particular bottle needed to be out of my life. "What are *you* doing?"

"Coming to find you. Did you think I wasn't serious?"

I pulled out my phone and saw that the last text, dated four minutes earlier, had promised he would in fact come find me if I wasn't home within sixty seconds.

In the elevator he leaned close, catching the scents I carried with me. Male werewolves had a keener sense of smell than females, especially in human form. I tolerated it for a moment, then pushed him away. I needed some space. I was still panting from the run, and I could still smell that wolf, and it was nauseating, the little closed confines of the elevator made it worse.

In the flat I headed straight for the kitchen sink. Flushed, sweating, and panting, and Sterling still looming. I pulled down a glass and filled it. The water tasted of chemicals.

"Are you okay?" Cye was in the kitchen.

"Fine." I braced my hands on either side of the sink, willing myself to not gag on the water, or the air that was clogged with unfamiliar smells, or the way my arm thundered as if the wanderer had branded me. I was not his! I was not for him!

"You aren't fine," Sterling growled.

"Just a rotten smell up my nose." I shuddered and rubbed my tricep, cringing. He had touched me. Just like that, grabbed me, *hauled me around* (if even for a few steps), reeked of disgusting sexual desire, in broad daylight, on the street, while all of New York just walked by like it wasn't their business.

"The city takes a while to get used to," Cye sympathized.

I needed a shower.

The water ran over my head and skin. I held the bar of soap to my nose to try and purge the stench from my system. In the privacy of the shower I let myself shake, feel sick, feel dirty, feel ashamed. Feel all the things a pack didn't expect or want a female to feel. The shower hid my tears.

Soon Mint would be by and we'd go get a dress for the human survival games. No more abandoned buildings with Mint.

Sterling was sitting on the bed when I emerged from the shower.

I clutched my towel in front of my breasts. "Don't you have work to do?"

"I always have work to do. You disappeared for two hours, and now you are distressed."

"I didn't disappear. I went for a run. Nobody told me I was a princess locked up in a castle," my voice cracked.

"What happened? Don't hide it, Winter. I can still smell it. Soap doesn't wash distress away."

My stomach curled and shifted, queasy and greasy, like the scent had settled there to mingle with acid. I only had about twenty minutes before Mint arrived, and I should eat something to sop up the stress. "Mint is going to be here in twenty minutes, Sterling. I don't want to get upset talking about it."

He didn't relent. "You've been crying."

"And I don't want to start again! I've got to go play doll with Mint and get a gown for this party. Just let me go eat my lunch in peace. I'll tell you about it later."

Of course I would tell him. He had to know, and I needed to know what had attacked me on the street. I just couldn't right *then*.

I only managed two bites of my sandwich before my throat refused to take anymore.

"It's not bad," Cye said mildly. "Perhaps the honey wasabi is a little weird but—"

"I'm just not hungry yet, Cye."

"Of course you're hungry. You ran like how many miles?"

It wasn't the running that had killed my appetite.

"Working out hard releases a chemical in your brain that suppresses appetite," Jun said around a mouthful of food. He reached for my plate and pulled it closer to his own.

"Riiight. And you're just fighting it and force-feeding yourself."

Burian, more interested in his tablet than his own meal, paused to ask me, "What do you study, Winter? Or did you stop at high school?"

His tone was a little ugly, and his question was random. That made for two ambushes in one day.

"Dude, what the hell," Jun said. "Don't be a jerk."

"I stopped at high school." It was the truth, no covering it up. Not something I had chosen or was proud of. My father hadn't even left it open for conversation. The answer had been, and always remained, an absolute, total, not-for-discussion *no.*

Sterling shifted his attention back to me. "Choice or circumstance?"

"My father forbid it." It was such a sore spot in a week of sore spots I couldn't keep the bitterness out of my voice. "I wanted to study mathematics. Statistics."

"What made you interested in that?" Burian asked.

"What? You think I should have gotten a masters in Housekeeping for the Modern Woman?"

"I—"

"Enough, Burian." Sterling growled.

Of course, males always seemed so shocked, but why couldn't I like math? It had been the complex formula that calculated how much an Alpha could demand in tribute from his wolves that sparked my fascination with math and statistics. Reducing Gaia's creation to math? That had been when I was in grade school, and my interest had never waned.

Mint would be here any moment. Now I could duck out of this conversation before it became about why the SilverPaw Alpha had not permitted me to continue my education. "Mint will be here soon."

Sterling got to his feet as well. "I will come with you."

"I don't need supervision." I had been out the previous evening until ten with Gaia-knew-who. And good job on warning me about wolves that stank of fryer vats, especially since he had made such a point to address other aspects of my ignorance.

He apologized for all that. Be more gracious, and it's probably best if he comes along.

"My plans for this afternoon changed." His hazel eyes narrowed very slightly even though his tone remained mild.

"Glad to know I'm your first priority. When it suits you, of course." My voice cracked again. The urge to just start barking balled in my throat. Or crying. Maybe both.

Cye and Jun tucked their heads down into their food like ostriches plunging for the nearest bit of sand.

I left to go find some shoes or boots or something to have on my feet.

It could be worse, that little voice told me. It could be so much worse than it was.

Sterling waited with Mint, my coat folded over his right forearm. He seemed to tower over Mint, although Mint was actually taller. Sterling's eyes touched mine, and I felt something within me. It hurt. It was a sort of wretched, raw pain, like a trapped sob, and I wanted to fling myself at him and sob into his chest and weep at everything that had gone so fucking wrong that week.

"You look lovely today, Winter," Mint said.

I managed a smile that Mint saw right through. "Thank you, Mint."

Downstairs, Sterling took the seat opposite me in the car. "Is it later yet?"

"Mint is right there, Sterling." Gaia, did he have no manners or sense? We could not have this conversation around Mint!

"And you're still upset," Sterling retorted, bristling with frustration.

"Keep stewing," I snapped.

"I do not stew, Winter."

Mint shifted in his seat, leaning toward us as if he was going to intervene. Then Sterling held up both hands, his hostility evaporating, and conceded. "Fine. I will wait."

The dress shop was nothing like the third story loft from the day before, although it was formal and very quiet. A salon, Mint called it. I went into the back with Mint, and Sterling remained outside in a sitting area intended for entertaining tagalongs. An array of dresses had already been set out. I stared and could not really process them. They just blurred into a lump of colors and fabrics.

"Which one would you like to try first?" Mint peered into my face. My eyes were still red-rimmed from crying, and the tears that kept trying to escape.

"I don't care." I took the silk robe an attendant offered me and hugged myself. I rubbed my tricep again. "Whichever one."

"No preference?" Mint tried again.

"Mint, I'm not in the mood to do this today. Will you pick out something for me? Something I'll like tomorrow. Because right now I won't like anything." My arm hurt where the wolf had touched it, even though it was just my imagination, a bruise on my pride, not my body. Mint seemed to be my only ally in any of this, and that was absurd. Sometimes it was just easier to confide in a stranger. Everyone else in my pack would care too much, feel obliged to care or worse, not care at all. Mint cared, and didn't need to ask questions to justify his giving a damn.

He nodded.

I obediently tried on an assortment of dresses. Mint enjoyed draping me in whatever struck his fancy. In the end he chose a sea-green silk dress that hung off the shoulders, was littered with sequins and had a slit up one thigh that was too daring. He gathered up my hair in an impromptu bun and said to my reflection, "This one."

"If you say so." I tried not to look because I knew my reflection would be colored by the day, and I didn't want to hold it against the dress. All of this could just stay in today, and tomorrow could be new.

"And I know just the jewelry to go with it. Just the necklace and earrings. Are your ears pierced?" he pulled at one lobe. "Yes, they are. Perfect."

I kept my head turned to the side.

Mint put his hands on my bare shoulders "Do you need help, Winter?"

I may have been from Montana, but I understood what his question was right away. I twisted my head around to look at him.

"Do you need help?" he said in that low, low tone.

"No, Mint, I don't. It's not like that." To his doubtful questioning look I said, "Mint, it's an... ah... arranged pairing. I didn't even know him before three days ago."

I didn't expect him to understand what I said, much less accept it. Mint's face, however, sort of softened over. He squeezed my shoulders and didn't say anything else.

"Mint," my voice cracked. "I'll like this dress in two days, won't I? Because I want to like it."

"You'll love it. Promise."

While I changed and composed myself, Mint went to go talk to Sterling. I don't know what they discussed. Sterling didn't seem the least bit rattled. It had probably just been paying for the dress.

Sterling rose from the sofa as I entered the sitting room. He straightened his jacket. Mint gave me a reassuring smile and told me he'd have the minor adjustments done to the dress by the next day. Mint and Sterling shook hands.

Sterling asked, "Would you like to get some coffee and sit before going home?"

I didn't, but I agreed anyway.

On the sidewalk he offered me his arm. I hesitated, looking around, expecting to see a thin, grinning face peering at me from behind the walls of people.

"Winter?"

"Nothing." I slid my arm through the crook. The sensation of peace and safety and wholeness caught me off guard, and assaulted the raw spots. Why did kindness make tears so much closer to the surface? Instinctively, I turned my head into his arm, the wool of his coat a little rough on my forehead, and inhaled his scent. The city mingled with it, and the smell of fabric, and starch, but under that there was him.

Tears burned and I held my breath, fighting them off.

I think this was why so many unhappy pairs stay together. Because even under all the bad parts there were those glimmers of something better.

He took me to a little coffee shop two blocks away. The place was quiet before the evening rush, with just half a dozen people sitting at the white-varnished tables crouched over tablets and laptops.

"What happened?" Sterling said once we had our drinks and shared a cozy little table in a corner by the street-facing window.

"Nothing we can really talk about here," I mumbled.

"I'm clever and can fill in blanks, and I have been roasting long enough. Time to let me out of the broiler."

My coffee was something laced with cranberries, the tart flavor nipped my tongue. I looked out the window, still searching the crowds for that face before Sterling recaptured my attention with my name. With as much dignity as I could muster, I told him what had happened, and steeled myself for his burst of anger at my stupidity. I knew better than to wander off on unfamiliar ground.

Sterling clenched his teeth, then hissed, "A wanderer."

"I don't know what that is."

"No, I guess you wouldn't. The Elders don't acknowledge their existence. They're a city blight. Every major city has them."

He explained how wanderers were wolves that came to big cities and never left. They came for all the same reasons that humans went to a big city: looking for opportunities, to disappear, to start over, to escape. Werewolf Law still classified them as "lone wolves," but in the cities a second term had emerged to separate Law-abiding wolves from disreputable ones. Wanderers could vary from garden-variety vagrants to a rogue that just hadn't been caught yet. Most wanderers were common low-lifes and petty criminals.

"They cluster together in groups of like-minded vermin." Sterling gestured with one hand. "Called hives, or nests. They're like cockroaches. Where there's one, there are more, and they all seem to know each other. If they go rogue, they get hunted, but as long as they don't stray too far, nobody deals with them. Most of the problems can be handled by the city's justice system."

Most of them.

He continued, "If you ask me, everyone is afraid of them. The problem just builds on itself. It's not going away, and it's not getting better. The Law won't recognize them, the unspoken agreement is avoidance. Attempts to clean things up have always resulted in trouble. Get mixed up with them, get out on your own. But I still think if you were to deal with enough of them, they'd learn."

His cold tone shocked me. I had once taken a swipe at a fire ant mound. They were just ants, after all.

Bad idea. Really, really bad idea.

And if enough bodies started showing up in morgues the humans would catch on. Still, if it was like he said, what was the solution to the problem? Trusting the eyes of humanity and the arm of their justice to contain a werewolf problem? Sterling wasn't lying, I had seen a wanderer with my own eyes, but I had never heard of this problem. Surely the Elders had to be aware of them. I had been to Great Meetings and overheard many of the Council arguments, listened to the gossip and chatter from wolves all over the world. I had never heard of wanderers, by that name or any other.

I frowned. "And I just had the bad luck to bump into one?"

Sterling grimaced. "There's a hive that's become a bit of an uptown problem. It's not a conversation for here."

"Your hands," I said softly.

Sterling glanced at his right knuckles and shrugged. "It's different for a male. Unless you object to me having to get my hands dirty on ambitious street scum."

I shook my head.

"I should have warned you. I was going to. I just didn't expect you to get out from under my eye so fast, and after the throw rug fight..."

I managed a tired smile.

He was not placated. "I was careless. I know how restless that hive is, I should have been much more careful with you. These hives are all male. The rumor is women are of intense interest."

My hand trembled as I nervously sipped from my coffee cup.

"Did something else happen?"

"He made it very clear what he was going to do to me, and how much he'd enjoy it." I rubbed my tricep again.

He stood up, buttoned his coat and offered me his hand. As he drew me up, he said, "I promise, Winter, this won't happen again. I won't *let* it happen."

"I shouldn't have gone out in strange territory," I muttered.

"No," he corrected. "You did nothing wrong. Those dogs don't own this city."

What was this wolf's mortal flaw that had put him so far to the bottom of the list? His words helped, and I ran my thumb over the healing scratches on his knuckles, searching for clues. He had a temper, and a vicious streak, but I also believed his promise.

* * * * *

Mint delivered my dress the next morning, then whisked me off to the spa and salon. But not before Jun presented himself in a pair of jeans and a sweatshirt, and informed everyone he was going with me. Mint just shrugged and said to stay out of the way.

Jun sat and read newspapers while I got slathered with pastes and layered with cucumbers and swaddled in wraps.

Mint chose my nail polish, handed Tony several crystal-encrusted hair combs and directed him how to arrange my hair. I tried to get in a few words edgewise, to which Mint said, "Avoidable mistakes, Winter. Trust me."

It wasn't until I stared at my reflection while Tony carefully pinned and twisted coils of my hair in an intricate arrangement designed by a city planning commission that I asked, "Mint?"

"Yes, ma'am." He stepped forward.

"Where am I going tonight? I just got told 'be there.'"

"Art gallery. Several new artists on display."

"I don't know anything about art."

Mint leaned down by my ear. "Most people at those things don't. Read a couple of articles on the internet and you'll be fine."

Gaia flicked Her finger at me again. *How now, little wolf? How now.*

"Please tell me this is a bad, bad dream, Mint," I pled with him.

"Nope." Mint winked at me. "You lucky, lucky woman."

The party started at seven, but Mint returned me to the flat at five. "If anything happens, makeup smudge, hair falls down, anything, just call me. I'll rush right over with a trauma team."

"What if I punch someone and break a nail?" That could happen. There was a distinct possibility of that happening.

"I don't handle behavior issues or incident containment, but I know who does. Text me and I'll pass you along." Mint handed me a little bag containing my shoes and a bag of makeup for touching up, then showed himself out the door.

"Gaia's tits," Jun told me after Mint left. "You look amazing but that production was ridiculous."

I rolled my heavily made-up eyes. I had flat-out refused fake lashes (which had been my only successful fight of the day), and the mascara was piled on thick and dark. "I have so much makeup on I feel like my face might crack. I'm going to go find Sterling."

Sterling was in the gym.

"Must be nice," I said upon walking in. I spent hours getting my body scrubbed and painted, and he got to be at the gym. Although I did enjoy his stunned expression. "Suitable?"

"You look beautiful." His sincerity made my spine tingle.

The way he looked at me encouraged the tingle to expand. Half of me quivered with anticipation of whatever fun and games might come along. Half of me didn't believe in fun and games anymore, and that everything was going to end up complicated and difficult. Either way, I'd need to figure out how to play my hand.

I traded my spine tingles for dredged-up annoyance. "All a man has to do is shower. I spend five hours being painted and decorated."

Sterling placed a hand over his heart. "You are a work of art. I am only a blunt object."

I had the craziest urge to walk over to him and slide my manicured hands over his shoulders and rake my glittery nails gently along the nape of his neck. He would like the measured rake against his flesh, peeling up a few layers of skin and threatening so much worse.

I swallowed, and grasped for something else to say. "Tell me where we're going. I need to do reading so I can fake small talk."

"A gallery event. It's a debut showing for three new artists that society is hot on this fall. I am certain the art is completely forgettable and will, in fact, be forgotten by next fall."

"Then why bother going?"

"To go. To be seen. To talk to people."

"Then I'm going to go read so I can play these human games."

"Winter," his voice caught me like a hand on my shoulder. "This is very important."

"I know the difference between a private joke and a public front, Sterling."

"Just making sure."

I paused at the door. "But tell me something."

"Hmm?"

"How old are you? What do you do? I should know these things." It would be very awkward if I suddenly needed this information. My father had been right about one thing: Sterling was the soul Gaia had chosen for me, and in the chaos and feeling him so close against me, details like age and profession had fallen to the back of my mind.

Disconcerting. I needed to pay closer attention to those things. Details. Mistakes always got made in details.

"You—don't know?" Sterling paused unwrapping his hands.

"Is your work illegal?" I sighed. That was the fatal flaw. Maybe he was a seedy criminal defense attorney. Sketchy stockbroker. Lobbyist. Human politician. Maybe money that wasn't *dirty,* but wasn't exactly noble either. Well, if that's what my father had objected to (and he would have), then that wasn't *so* bad.

"No, of course not. I was just thinking your father was playing coy with me about you."

"So he didn't tell you anything about me?"

"Not a thing. Just your name."

"How the—what—he made it sound like you had been asking after me. For months. And that he had been putting you off."

Sterling finished rolling up his wraps. "Really. Isn't that interesting. Because he didn't even tell me you were his daughter."

"*What?*" I spun around and marched back into the gym.

"Out of the blue I got an email from him. Just your

picture. Nothing else. I took one look at the picture and realized what he was about. I replied that whoever you were, *you* were the one and I had to meet you. He told me to be at an address in Montana within twenty-four hours, and that your name was Winter. Didn't give it a second thought until it dawned on me somewhere over North Dakota that you were probably his daughter."

The information clouded my brain like steel wool. "He said he had finally decided to humor your curiosity."

We frowned at each other.

Sterling tossed the wraps into a corner. He came over to me, took my hand and swept low in a courtly bow that made me laugh. "My name is Sterling. That is my birth name, the one my mother gave me. I am twenty-four years old, my birthday is in May, and I am a speculative investor in renewable resources and green tech. Mostly. Some medical research thrown in there. I was born in nowhere, Pennsylvania, and speak Pennsylvania German passably well. And you?"

"Winter. Twenty, born in Alaska, I know how to hunt small and large game, maintain wild territory and I've spent the past three years as a Chronicler's assistant."

"So you are an expert on Law, custom, and history. A wolf lawyer, hmm?"

"And historian. Why, do you have need of either?" What a flattering thing to say! Such things didn't exist, but if they did, I would be one! Until he said it, I hadn't realized that I probably was one of the most well-educated wolves outside the Chroniclers and Elders.

"You would be the judge of that."

I withdrew my fingers from his grasp before something happened that would smudge my makeup. "Now I have reading to do. Since nobody in that art gallery should know my area of legal expertise."

The gallery's website was easy enough to find, and

pretentious blurbs about the three artists being showcased in ample supply. So superficial! I wanted to sink my claws into each canvas and rip it to pieces. The art was ugly to my eyes. Just a lot of lines and circles and splatters, while the descriptions of the works discussed "use of color" and "bold meaning" and "daring construction."

There wasn't anything daring or bold about the works except someone being brave enough to put them forth as "art."

Burian took the opposite couch and flipped on the television. "You look pissed. Pretty. But pissed."

"Just not understanding why this stuff is art."

"Art is baseball cards for rich people."

That made sense. I suppressed a laugh, but only because Sterling had made it clear this entire matter deserved some degree of respect.

Sterling was already in our room, shaving off his silvery stubble.

I stepped into my dress and wriggled it over my hips and shoulders, but I had to appeal to Sterling to zip me the rest of the way. The touch of his fingertips along the small of my back was absolute, beautiful, agony.

He leaned close by my ear, his breath on my neck. "You do look beautiful."

"Thank you," my whisper sounded torn even to my ears.

He bent low and brushed the small hairs at the nape of my neck, then kissed my spine. He held me against him, his lips trailed to the next vertebrae, then to my exposed shoulder. His fingertips curled into the soft hollow of my hip.

"Beautiful," he whispered to himself.

My dress felt so tight I couldn't breathe, I was just going to have to rip it off.

Maybe later.

"I keep telling myself," he murmured, "I need to be

patient."

"Why?" I asked simply.

"I have something for you," he ignored my question, but his fingers dug into my hip, tugging me against him, his breath hot on my neck.

"Oh?" His other hand caressed the length of my dress' zipper, as if he planned on pulling that zipper right down again. "Is this the something?"

My skin pled with him as if it were parched plains needing rain.

Such reckless attraction, attraction so needful it went beyond infatuation or crush, to where our souls touched and warmed together and I was aware of him, knowing that I would never be whole without him.

Sterling released me with a low growl, frustration lacing his scent. "No, wait here. Temptress."

A GREAT & MEANINGFUL LACK OF GLUE

Sterling retrieved a large, flat, velvet box. My smile fled, and my mouth dried up.

He didn't say anything as he opened the box and presented me with its contents. The emerald and diamond necklace, complete with matching earrings, was quite possibly the most beautiful thing I had ever seen.

I had no idea what to say.

He lifted the necklace. I tensed as the metal slid over my neck, expecting the raw acid-like burn of silver on my skin. I had a little resistance to silver. Many wolves had none at all, or were especially sensitive. But even for me, having it against my skin for hours would cause burns, bruises and once the first few layers of skin peeled back and blood vessels were exposed, the silver would enter my bloodstream and the cytotoxin-like effects would begin.

The burn, however, didn't come. The necklace was platinum.

His fingertips caressed my skin as he secured the clasp.

I knew what those lips felt like on me, and I wanted to feel them again, his chapped hands moving over my skin, the touch that didn't apologize or hesitate.

Sterling's hand slid down my spine to the small of my back. "Come, Winter. We have human games to play."

My dress was not warm, nor was the sheer silk wrap draped over my shoulders. As we left the building the cold autumn breeze ripped right through the fabric and burned my skin numb. One of the doormen held my door, and I paused just as Sterling stopped at the driver's side. He raised his chin, a frown on his face, and looked at me.

The smell of fryer vats and cigarettes.

"Ma'am?" the doorman prompted me. I kept my eyes on Sterling, too unsure to look around. I feared if I turned the wolf would be right there on my left, looming over me.

Sterling scanned the illuminated streets, then he slid into the driver's seat.

"They're lurking." My voice shook. "Are they hunting?"

"If they are smart, they aren't."

At each stoplight I expected to see a sallow, dirty face burst out from the streetlights and fling itself in front of the car. There were many faces, the streets were clogged with people, but not the one I was looking for. *So* many people. In Montana you could drive miles without seeing a soul.

"Tell me you get used to it," I said without thinking.

Sterling looked at the pillars obscuring the sky. "Mostly."

I was expecting the gallery to be something modern and polished and drenched in light to go with the tuxedo-wearing, besparkled party-goers. While the gallery itself was drenched in light, the building was older, with a wood floor that reminded me of my family's house. Not exactly rustic, it was just—

"Urban." One older man in a tuxedo said to the two people with him, like it was just so quaint.

I had met people like that in Montana. People with too much money and no sense, who had shown up in our town to "get away from it all," and thought the locals were there for their entertainment. On occasion I had been asked things like did I know how to grow corn, and could I shoot a squirrel from a hundred feet. Upon finding out I could do neither, they had seemed quite disappointed.

The three artists were also there, and they looked like stereotypes brought to life. Two men, one woman, all dressed in black. One of the men even wore a little beret to go with his glasses. The woman was painfully rail-thin, ashen white like a corpse, and her hair hung in ungroomed curls like she had just gotten up from bed.

The guests had spent hours getting ready to come to their little party, and the hosts couldn't have bothered to at least brush their hair?

Everyone who wasn't an artist was either in a tuxedo or a formal gown. There were in fact several women who had opted to wear tuxedos. They looked fabulous and way more comfortable than I was teetering on the heels Mint had picked for me. Caterers silently moved among us carrying uplifted trays of dainty hors d'oeuvres and flute-necked champagne glasses and tumblers of juices and waters and sodas.

Sterling covered my hand with his and guided me to a cluster of older men in cookie-cutter tuxedos. His was actually a very intense dark gray-blue, not black, and the difference became obvious against the more traditional backdrop. The shortest member of the group sized Sterling up, even though he grinned and shoved his hand out towards us. "Sterling!"

Sterling shook his hand, but spoke to me. "Winter, this is Jack. Jack. Winter."

"A pleasure." Jack shook my hand. His eyes made a quick dart for my cleavage. No surprise, Mint's choice did offer up my breasts for perusal. Sterling certainly had wandering eyes. What shocked me was how skilled the old guy was at it. Damn. He was deft. Must have had practice. Lots and lots of practice.

Sterling knew the other men in passing and made introductions all the way around. Nobody asked what my association with Sterling was, and that was a good thing, because in human terms, there wasn't one. It was not polite in this layer of society to make public assumptions about anyone's relationship to anyone else. Many assumptions were made in private.

"Haven't seen your father," Jack told Sterling.

His father! My father had made it sound like Sterling's

pedigree was blank, but his father was in the picture after all!

"He's in Europe with my mother." Sterling lifted two champagne flutes off a passing tray, and handed me one.

Not that I was old enough to drink.

"So he sent you, eh?" Juan, one of the men asked, not realizing how patronizing he sounded, and probably not caring.

"He just asked me to make sure you were still breathing, since I was going to be here." Sterling didn't waste much effort being diplomatic. He disliked all three of these men, and wanted nothing to do with them.

Jack chortled, and the third one ribbed Juan, and they all guffawed. Juan grinned and saluted Sterling with his flute. There was some respect in the gesture, but just as much contempt and it practically screamed *run along, pup.* The tuxedo-trio drew together to rag on each other about better stop dodging phone calls.

Aggravated, Sterling drew me away to a different group, and we repeated the introduction, suffered a bit more tame, bland, slightly patronizing pleasantries that required me to say nothing at all and just keep my face stretched in a smile. The cycle repeated itself over and over again until Sterling and I got separated by my needing to use the bathroom (I really needed a break so I wouldn't burst out laughing and start saying what I was thinking) and as I made my way back, I stopped to look at some of the artwork, trying to figure out how a blank canvas splattered with the blue imprint of a hand was art.

Unless it's from the hands of a five-year-old child. Specifically, *your* five-year-old child.

What everyone cooed over eluded me. The art deserved an honest chance before I dismissed this entire thing as the modern version of the *Emperor's New Clothes.*

"Aren't they something?" a female voice asked me.

Oh, they were something all right. I looked at the tall,

older woman who wore a lovely gown in a surprising shade of yellow, and being cornered, I chose an agreeable answer. "Yes."

She seemed to marvel at the canvases.

"I think the second one is my favorite," I ventured. Maybe she could enlighten me to what was so appealing about them. The second one featured a grid of ragged blue lines with alternating green and red handprints, sort of like a bad game of tic-tac-toe.

She indicated the one with the handprint and splatters. "I like this one best. So strong, so bold, and challenging."

This wasn't happening. I was not standing in an art gallery in Manhattan wearing emeralds and platinum and a gown talking about paint splatters. My cheeks twitched with what might have been laughter, or tears. She waited for my reply, so I grasped for something to say. "I think it's quite frightening."

Oh, it was frightening. Verrrrry frightening.

She gave me all of her attention. "Really!"

I needed to say something. Anything. "Ah... yes. I just think of a hand pressed against a window. You know, trying to get out."

"But you find *that* frightening, not like it's pushing through a glass ceiling?"

"Doesn't look like they've succeeded." I said with a bit more sarcasm than I should have.

"I think it's about the struggle."

Was I having this conversation? I was having this conversation.

Gaia's tits.

Crime statistics said that during the entire pointless conversation at least two women had been raped and five people assaulted, and I was there discussing something that looked like a toddler's finger-painting efforts. And might have just managed to gravely insult someone who probably was important and it might even get back to my future in-laws what a feral I was.

Instead of getting angry, the woman grabbed my elbow. "Come! Let me introduce you to the artists!"

"Oh, I'd like that." I had the presence of mind to lie.

The artist, Royce, reeked. Not of earth and musk, as so many breathless people murmured, but of underarms. The woman fawned over Royce's work, and told him about our brief conversation but made it sound like we had had this intense discussion about world peace. Royce bobbed his head at disinterested and appropriate intervals, too cool to care. He must have had rich people telling him how amazing he was all the time.

I excused myself but was accosted by another woman who dragged me off for introductions to the other two artists.

The other two artists happened to be in the same place, so I only had to go through the introductions and fawning once. Of the three artists, Royce proved the least ridiculous. Bernie—the woman—was absolutely insufferable, and Eddard, the guy in the beanie, peppered everything he said with either the name of someone famous or a burning profanity.

A man in the little audience asked Bernie to explain one of her paintings. I nudged my way to the front of the little group and listened with rapt attention while Bernie gestured to a large canvas painted entirely in black. Large swathes of rose and flesh paint, so thick it looked like smears and formed ridges, all twirled about. An assortment of craft buttons had been set into the canvas using dollops of pink paint.

She gestured dismissively to the work and in a flat, bored voice, explained to us that it was about the creative struggle and the void of inner angst and the true suffering every legitimate artist experiences while creating, and that the ribbons symbolized the agony of the birthing process and the little squished buttons were unfertilized artistic eggs.

I had to ask. I just couldn't stop myself from asking. I had passed eighth grade sex ed and knew how the human period worked. "If the buttons are free-floating unfertilized artistic eggs, why did you choose to use an artist's paint to attach them instead of clear glue?"

Clearly, it was the champagne talking.

Murmurs from the small group of people around me as they pondered and nodded like I had said something intriguing. All eyes craned towards the artist.

Bernie's thin fingers twitched and jerked, her rail-thin chest bone heaved against her skin. It took her a minute, but she answered that the use of paint had been to symbolize that artists are never really free of their ideas and are always birthing new ones.

All that sounded logically flawed to me but everyone else seemed satisfied.

You ask me? Bernie had suffered from a great and meaningful lack of glue.

COLD SHOWER

And that was how I unwittingly became the center stage attraction, with everyone wanting to introduce me to someone else and talk art. I switched to soda water because a third champagne flute would have had me running my mouth, and I wouldn't have kept my tone so saccharine sweet. I managed to group-hop enough that I finally was within grabbing distance of Sterling.

"Winter," he greeted me as I pressed against his arm. I resisted clinging to him and begging him to get me out of there before I did something really stupid. I was at my limit, and having detailed fantasies of ripping a canvas off the wall, putting it on my head and twirling around while demanding everyone admire my fancy new hat.

Sterling moved his fingers against mine. I gulped at his touch. He put his other hand very, very lightly on my jaw, leaned close and whispered, "We're almost done."

I flushed all over, distracted from the pressure of the gallery. He drew away, but not too far, his fingertips still on my jaw and his eyes in my field of vision, pulling at me like the tide. For a second it was only him and I, and in my mind I saw shades. Then it slipped from my grasp as if it had never been present at all.

"Almost done," he assured me again.

I whispered, "Buy me one of these paintings so I can set it on fire in the street?"

Now he smiled mischievously, a devilish glint in his eye. "If you want one."

"Don't tempt me. I might get a reputation for performance art." My insides fluttered at the unexpected shared mischief.

"Perhaps it's a hidden talent."

"I hope not." I glanced around again, afraid to leave his side. We were getting some dirty glances for whispering like lovers, but the alternative seemed to be me faking my way as an art aficionado, and eventually someone was going to see my expertise was as fake as my nails.

Sterling placed his drink on a passing tray. "We can leave."

"You just said—" I protested. I could handle it, even if it made me twitchy.

"And if we stay, I'm going to buy every painting here and you're going to have a bonfire. I've done my good deed."

The frigid air outside the gallery smelled of city, people, garbage, soot and fuel fumes. The sky was a narrow sliver squished between towering buildings and the stars faint marks, compared to the massive, brilliance-speckled dome of Montana's sky.

Sterling yanked his bowtie loose as we waited for the valet to bring his car. A disapproving glance from another, older couple said this was improper. Sterling ignored them and let the ends of the tie hang loose, then he tugged the button at his neck.

"Wait," I murmured. The little buttons on his tuxedo shirt defied his fingers. My nails more easily slipped under the edge and plucked it through the tiny slit. Gaia, that collar was snug. How did he even stand it, and with the tie too! He heaved a breath once free.

I waited until we were in the car before I asked, "If it bothers *you* so much, why go?"

"Necessary evil," he told me like the words tasted extremely bad. "The parties at museums or the opera aren't so insufferable. The private gallery parties are the worst. For reasons you have just become acquainted with. Your performance art idea was brilliant."

"*Why* is it necessary?" Sterling hadn't seemed to be talking business, and me fluttering about trying to fake knowing something about modern art couldn't be important, nor a good idea.

"The world of wealth at our level is small. Everyone knows everyone else. It's never a good idea to be a lone wolf. It's a pack. A very strange pack. And just like a pack, once you're out it's hard to work your way back in."

That made sense. Wolves were the same way. Willingly leaving a pack made it very difficult to find another pack. There were always questions about what you had run away from, or why you had left. Wolves had to be loyal to their pack. The pack had to be loyal to the wolf.

Packs let wolves live with them for a while before asking for final vows. When those final promises were made, they were promises on death and life. If a wolf was clearly unhappy in a pack, or the pack was unhappy with the wolf, the Alpha would usually try to transfer that wolf to another pack instead of throw them out.

The only exception was a young male wolf (but never a female) who struck out on their own from their birth pack. Packs were often so overburdened with males that a young bachelor got a one-time pass to seek his own fortunes.

"And what does this pack offer us?" Aside from the obvious that it was better to be in a pack than not in a pack.

"They're sometimes valuable allies, and always dangerous enemies to have."

"Hmm." I digested this. My estimation from earlier hadn't been wrong. "So the rules for prestigious wolves and prestigious humans aren't so different after all."

"I wouldn't know about the former," Sterling said with a hint of dryness.

"And I know nothing about the latter," I retorted. My comment hadn't been personal; he didn't need to get his panties in a wad. Mine were in a wad. Or, as much of a wad as a thong could be in. Mint had insisted I had to wear a thong with my dress, and after a few hours the little seams were chafing in all the wrong places. I added, "I think you'd learn quickly. It's not that much different. Just fewer forks."

Sterling laughed, "Actually, Winter, confession time. That back there is more my father's pack than mine. He and I both got invites. He's the one they wanted there, but he's on vacation. I was going to duck out, but he needed me to go and lean on Jack and his cronies. We don't normally tag-team, but he's my father and I can spare him a big favor."

"Oh, so *that's* what that was about." It also explained why Sterling had been a little forceful about me being prepared for tonight. It wasn't *his* affairs I might have screwed up. Being entrusted with another pack's affairs was no small thing.

Sterling shrugged. "Well, I leaned, and I even had to drag you into it. Dad owes me."

I wanted to ask about his father. Sterling spoke like there was nothing amiss there, but my father had played keep-away with the information. It'd have to wait a little longer, now wasn't the right time.

It was midnight by the time we got back to the flat. Everyone had gone to bed. Light slid out from under the door to Burian's room, and there was Cye's snoring from the other.

In our room, Sterling tossed his tie down on the bed, and shrugged off his tuxedo jacket. I set down my little purse and pulled my earrings off, and replaced them in their box. The seams of my dress pulled in protest as I stretched, and I savored it for just a second. It'd make being free that much better. "Sterling."

He paused in mid-unbutton of his shirt.

"Help with my necklace and dress."

He stepped behind me and deftly unclasped my necklace. He placed the glittering form in its box, then his fingers brushed my skin before he slowly drew the zipper down.

My skin raced as the zipper revealed the curve of my

spine to the air, and to his gaze. He could have stopped at the midpoint of my shoulders, but he drew the zipper to its inevitable conclusion just above the cleft of my rump. His hand lingered an instant too long, then his fingertips moved upwards along my spine.

He could have raked me with his claws for the way my skin surged.

"Shall I step out?" I knew from his tone he had no intention of leaving, even if I asked.

He moved away and resumed unbuttoning his shirt. His expression dared me to do or say something. Like turn around or avert my gaze or demand he do the same.

He undid the last button and shrugged off his shirt.

Every movement seemed like he was made of chiseled, living marble that had sprung from a master artist's hand. Part of my brain urged me to look away and have a little good sense. The other part told me to keep right on looking. I liked what I saw and Sterling dared me to look away. That meant I needed to keep right on watching his little show.

For a man who had told me he needed to be patient, the hook was baited. What was he up to? Was I supposed to flinch?

He crumpled his shirt in one palm and threw it onto the bed with his tie and jacket. Then his hands went to his belt. His lips curled a little bit. I was sorely tempted to just watch him strip for my amusement, but that was too easy. Sterling had far more experience playing flesh games than I did, and whatever upper hand he seemed to have he'd maintain by virtue of experience.

He expected me to flinch. He taunted me. He expected me to quickly cast my eyes elsewhere, blush and make some whimpering noises.

Really, Sterling?

He had said he needed to be patient, whatever that meant. So his little show was just to press my buttons? Press his buttons? Fine, I'd play along with that game and press *all* the buttons.

Slow and deliberate, I turned my head. My cheeks burned with what I was about to do. I swallowed the sudden lump of nervous giggles and daring. I shrugged my shoulders once. My dress slid over my arms, my breasts, until it caught on my hips. I gave the fabric a little push over my curves, and it fell into a pool of silk and sequins at my feet.

I stepped over the fabric, and gave Sterling an eyeful of my delicate panties and rump. This moment made it worth every bit of chafing suffered on account of the thong's sequins and beads. I paused so Sterling could get a second helping, then sauntered into the bathroom for my shower.

I had to suppress giggles. Naughty giggles, nervous giggles, giggles that half expected him to storm in after me and put his hands all over the flesh that I had just paraded before him. I removed my bra and panties, tossed them outside the shower and waited to see what happened.

Buttons pushed. With *both* hands.

Sterling appeared about two minutes after I had taken up residence under the delightfully hot water. The giggles had passed, and the burst of maidenly nerves as well. Now I was just smug. So smug. So the brave Alpha hadn't known what to do, hmm? He thought he got to call all the shots, hmm?

He started it, now it was his move.

The steam carried his scent. He smelled of desire, frustration, the musk of competitive spirit and rankled anger. I closed my eyes, inhaled deeply and took fierce pleasure in having provoked him so completely. The consequences were going to be hard to complain about.

"I can smell your smugness," his tone was rough.

I laughed. "Oh, can you now, dear Alpha?"

His shadow moved outside the steamy glass. I turned my head just as he yanked open the shower door. He was not naked, but in his robe. His eyes remained rooted above my neckline, and his neck muscles ticked as they struggled to keep his gaze above my shoulders.

I smirked and taunted him, "You can look."

He made a noise somewhere between laughter, frustration, and a curse. Then he slammed the door. It throbbed on its hinges.

"Am I too intimidating, Alpha?" I called over the water, then collapsed into snickers.

"You are taking too long," he informed me with raw dignity. "I will shower in the guest room."

"How cold a shower will it be, dear Alpha?!"

He slammed the bathroom door behind him.

LEMON CREAM COOKIES

"How was the party?" Burian asked over breakfast.

I scowled. "Intolerable."

"Winter contemplated some performance art," Sterling said.

"Because," Burian's face morphed into an unconvincing grin, "guess who made the society page!"

He passed me his tablet. Staring right back at me was... me.

Sterling peered over my shoulder.

"What the hell is this?!" The newspaper article had some headline about the gallery showing and right there, center stage in a triptych of pictures, were Sterling and I. There had been some photographers wandering around snapping shots but we hadn't posed for anything.

"Gaia's ass," Sterling muttered.

"Clearly you two were the best looking couple there." Burian handed the tablet to the eager Cye and Jun. "Ergo, you made the paper."

"Sterling Mortcombe and his date, Winter," Cye read the caption out loud. He and Jun giggled like adoring schoolgirls.

Burian snickered. "It says you have quite the appreciation for modern art."

"Dart me with silver and skin me alive," I snatched my coffee cup towards my lips.

"You two look so great!" Cye said. Jun nodded excitedly.

It was six-thirty in the morning and I had never been much of a drinker, but I wanted to upend an entire bottle of whiskey into my mouth.

Sterling was not the least bit amused. "I hate art gallery parties."

"What were these brilliant observations? Because I know they're bullshit." Burian grinned at me.

In Burian's weird way that was a compliment: I had infiltrated the gallery party and passed as one of their own. I told him about the horrible uterus painting. Burian guffawed and Cye descended into giggles. Jun was confused, so Burian gave him a brief lesson in how female reproduction worked in mammals, and called up some diagrams on his tablet while I laid my head down on the table and Sterling suffered in regal silence.

Other Lunas perhaps were negotiating alliances with other packs, overseeing the care of pups, mediating disputes, planning pack events. I fulfilled my mandate to see to the education of my pack by making sure they knew how babies were made.

Come to think of it, if they didn't already know how babies got made... well, that was very important.

"Is it so bad?" Cye asked in a timid tone. "I mean, it's just nice, isn't it? Someone thought you were worth putting in the paper."

Worth putting in the paper? My worth had nothing to do with a damned paper, and I wasn't a human who felt the need to parade my glitz everywhere.

Memories of Greater Meetings trampled in, and I suppressed a sigh. If werewolves could have their own paparazzi, they probably would. Greater Meetings were full of long looks and estimations of fur, fangs (especially the fangs on males), the beauty and strength of human form, and even the ferocity of war-form. Earrings were quite fashionable and could be very extravagant, because they would stay in position through shifts. Females would sport necklaces, and more than a few males had carefully done tattoos or scarification, and many warriors would display their hard-won scars with pride.

Guilty. We'd parade our version of glitz if we could.

Damn. Indignant rage defused.

Sterling snorted, "Cye, somewhere at some country club are a few cranky people sniffing about how Winter's dress was too high on her thigh, or I didn't have gold cuff links."

"I thought that slit was a bit too high." I had kept expecting someone to tell me my panties were showing. But cufflinks? Sterling's cufflinks had been platinum inset with some green stone, perhaps a polished malachite. Gold wouldn't have suited him, no one should ever have expected him to wear it, fashion or no.

"Doesn't matter. You looked amazing," Sterling corrected.

I blushed.

Sterling once again left with Burian, but this time at least told me where he was going: meetings. He had an office about eight blocks over, although he only kept it to have a place to send mail and host meetings. The primary residents were his two assistants.

Cye had class, and Jun had a personal training client. I didn't want to risk bumping into wanderers again, so despite having a huge city to explore, I resigned myself to a day alone in the flat.

I spent a little time trying to figure out how Cye had the fridge organized, decided I couldn't safely remove anything, then discovered some lemon-creme cookies hidden way back in the pantry. The kind that came in cheap crinkly plastic, cost a few dollars and were probably made in a chemical factory. I munched lemon cookies and got sucked into playing games on my phone.

I debated the merits of learning how to make simple games. I seemed to have nothing but time (between formal parties), so why not?

Sterling returned a few hours later, rankled. It was just him and I, so I slid towards the kitchen, trying to figure out which direction his bad temper would fly off to.

"They were waiting for me," Sterling growled.

"Who was?" I could guess, I just wanted to confirm my fears.

Sterling glared at the wall. "Wanderers. Waiting when I left, followed me, waiting for me when I got back."

My insides twisted and slid over each other in an oily mass. So much for hoping my encounter with them had been isolated.

"You didn't go out, did you?"

"No. What do they want?" Every wolf wanted something, even if it was another wolf's goat.

He paced back and forth across the kitchen tiles, seeming to vibrate just under his skin with angry energy. "I don't have any contacts here, so I don't know much. Wolf contacts, I mean."

Normally Alphas had sources within their own pack of lower rank and prestige, where relationships between wolves were less guarded. They maintained the threads and flow of information. At least that's how it worked in SilverPaw. He glanced at me sideways, expecting judgment for his lack of influence and prestige, but there was nothing for me to judge.

Allegiances weren't easy to form, and even friendships were difficult. Every wolf's first priority was service to their own pack, at the expense of nearly everything else. The living whole of the pack meant more than any single wolf within it. As prestige of individuals changed, the distance created strained friendships. Those connections could diminish or imperil the living whole of a pack, and when that happened, they were unacceptable. Every wolf had to be aware of what they gave, and what they received, in any relationship.

Prestige was what mattered the most. Technically Sterling and I were an Alpha and Luna, but there was no prestige to prop up those ranks. They were tin crowns. Outside SnowFang they meant almost nothing, and were more risk than reward. The only thing of value we had was Sterling's wealth, and only to wolves willing to trade prestige and alliances for association with that wealth. But any wolf willing to sell their prestige was probably in a sort of trouble so serious we couldn't afford to be involved.

However, Sterling did have a single source, and after a moment of strained quiet, told me, "From what Burian managed to glean, they're trying to lay claim to the area. Not as territory. Extort money from the wolves here. Pay up, we'll leave you alone. Don't, we'll be like ticks and cause a scene. You'll be forced to acknowledge us one way or the other."

So they would try to stay largely on the human side of the law, getting picked up for petty crimes at worst, like minor trespassing, but offending the etiquette of wolves. Pay up, keep your dignity. Refuse, get mange.

Sterling went on, "They've been lurking around this building, pop up every once in a while, but haven't made a move yet. Imagine if they had a huge hive here in uptown, Winter, drawn by the amassed wealth, and they were able to control movement through here. I can up and move, slip in and out, but what about the wolves who can't? Wolves here would become a herd of milkers."

"And violate the law of neutral ground?"

"The Elder Council doesn't even acknowledge they exist, but I can't see how they don't know. Besides, do you really think any wolf is going to go crying to the Elder Council that they're getting milked? I wouldn't."

Wolves paying off other wolves to just make them go away... that wasn't just hard currency. That was the darkest kind of prestige. The sort that no wolf ever wanted to acknowledge existed, much less mattered. No, Sterling was right. The Elder Council *had* to know wanderers existed. While most Elder packs kept their hearts out of urban areas, there were a few who kept a strong presence in large cities like Tokyo.

Sterling growled, "I wonder if they harass the GranitePaw."

The GranitePaw were not an Elder pack, but they were large, wealthy and had a strong hold over New York, insomuch as any pack could legally claim a city as territory. I fiddled with one of my fake nails. "I doubt it. No reason if they can get what they want from easier prey."

SnowFang had just the five of us, no allies, no contacts, no friends, no resources except Sterling's wealth. If we stirred up the hornet's nest we'd be on our own, and if SnowFang died, we'd be just an entry in the Chronicler's records. A pack that lived, died and nobody remembered even existed.

Four years doubting I'd have any future, now these wanderers threatened to take it away. I intended to keep it!

My vision shimmered like the surface of a pond. I saw something over Sterling's shoulder. His head was turned, he didn't notice. On the marble floor beyond him, were three little puppies. Little pups, still in their first fuzzy fur, in a playful, wriggling heap. Two silver, one dark russet.

I blinked, and the vision was gone.

Cold prickles raised each hair on my skin one at a time.

Sterling shifted, my attention yanked to him now. I realized he had been talking, "... I'm not sure I could make you more appealing if I tied several million dollars in non-sequential bills around your neck and sent you outside in a lace teddy!"

I looked over his shoulder again. No puppies.

"You look like you've seen a ghost. I'm not going to put you in a lace teddy—"

"No, no. Sorry. Just a thought." I shook my head quickly. Checked over his shoulder again. No puppies. He gave me a skeptical look. "I'm fine. I'm fine. You go get cleaned up. I'm sure Cye will kick you out of the kitchen to start dinner soon."

"It's my kitchen," he reminded me.

"Our kitchen. And unless you want to cook, let Cye have it."

Sterling muttered something about still having some phone calls to make and retreated back into his office. I leaned on the counter and put my head in my hands.

Right in the thick of this mess. The Elder Council had to know about them, and had to be suppressing the matter. The idea didn't sit well with me, but it did make sense. If they recognized them, there would be expectations to deal with them. Sterling made it sound like they were historically more of a nuisance, but this new hive had gotten clever. Dealing with one rogue, or two, or half a dozen. That was one thing. But dozens, hundreds, maybe thousands of petty criminals with nothing to lose? They were like fleas, sucking blood and leaping away. You'd scratch yourself raw before they'd die off.

The puppies. That had been too much. Some kind of warning of the future from the Moon, or perhaps just my brain flopping around like an exhausted fish. Probably fish-brain.

Cye came in the front door, a brown bag of groceries crinkling in his arms. "You all right?"

I lifted my head. "Yes, yes. Where's the booze in this place?"

He opened the cabinets under the sink.

"Of course. With the cleaning products and household chemicals. Makes perfect sense."

"It's a long story," he sounded sheepish. "What would you like?"

"Whiskey. The first bottle you find if there's more than one."

Time for my brain to get a bath, and my liver to do the heavy lifting.

Cye put the bottle in front of me, then brought a crystal tumbler with a single large round ice cube. He poured the first drink, then left me to it. This wasn't drinking for pleasure.

It took two tumblers and half a third before my feelings gave up and slid beneath the surface of their liquor bath.

Now if I saw puppies again I could blame it on the booze.

Before dinner Sterling summoned us to the living room. He took up a place on one couch's arm. I was nursing my third drink, and all but licked my lips looking at him. Sterling was nothing if not a perfect physical specimen to my eyes, and that night wearing an Alpha's purpose, dressed in iron gray slacks and a green polo and his dress-socked feet on the cushions he looked like a casually glorious Adonis come down from his pedestal for a nightcap.

The irony sinews under his forearms moved as his fingers laced together. The hard glint in his eye, the tension in his jaw, the worry and anger that possessed his whole form. Mostly it was those muscled forearms as he twisted his fingers together. I sipped my drink, pondering what his fangs might look like, and if I could convince him to shift and show them to me...

Winter. Pack meeting. Do not reveal your blood alcohol level by ogling the Alpha at a pack meeting.

A tiny little meeting of a tiny little pack was still a pack meeting, and that meant a certain level of decorum. Me being even slightly intoxicated was disgraceful. I'd have to fake it.

Sterling glanced at me before he started talking. "Those wanderers are back, and this time they're here to stay."

Grunts.

"They've spotted Winter, they know she's here, pedigreed and presumably, mine. They tracked us to the gala last night, they trailed me today. They're serious this time."

My pleasant numbness started to wear off very fast.

Jun leaned forward on his knees and glared at Sterling. "Dude, seriously? She's been here like four days and they're on her like fleas?"

"I think it's worse than fleas. They've got her scent. Not sure for what."

Burian rolled his eyes. "Gaia's sweet ass, you idiots. Ransom. Daughter of an Elder Alpha, Luna of a rich wolf. Nothing but sport and a money-day. You guys are shocked?"

Nobody argued with him.

Burian grimaced as if we were all hopeless morons. "I told you this was a stupid idea, Sterling."

"Shut up with that shit," Jun growled. "We all know how you feel about it, and it doesn't matter. Sterling was never gonna get another chance with her."

"Oh please. If she's the one, then he'd get another chance. He's got zero competition! He'd put it in his pocket and say I'm not sure, delay or some shit. Instead he raced off after the pussy, or like a little lapdog called to its master. It was a stupid idea to bring a female here. Period. We can't handle it."

"You clearly have never dealt with an Elder Alpha," Sterling told Burian in a dry tone.

"I wouldn't even have gone. What the hell was he going to do to you anyway, Sterling? You had plenty of chances to walk away but you kept right on into that lovely blazing fire."

It was laughably obvious Burian had absolutely no idea what an Elder Alpha was capable of, much less Elder Chronicler Rodero of SilverPaw.

Burian also had no idea what had happened in Montana, and I sure as hell didn't want his opinion on any of it. I stared at Sterling, hoping he understood not to talk about it.

Sterling's voice was edged with ice, "I'm not justifying this to you, Burian. I saw her picture, I knew, it's that simple. One chance was all I was ever going to get from the SilverPaw. You might *think* otherwise, but I *know*, and I don't need to explain further."

Burian rolled his eyes a third time. "Way to play that Alpha card."

"You want the job?" Sterling growled at the disrespect, sending excited prickles along my skin.

"Fuck, no, I don't want the job. Fine, Alpha Sterling. You brought this mess here against the advice of the pack, you figure it out."

"You mean your advice," Jun snapped. "Cye and I told him to go get her! We're a goddamn pack, we're in it together, even if you don't like it. Get with the fucking program!"

"So if Sterling told us to jump off the Whitestone we all would? Fine, go chase your damn mate, but don't bring her back here! Tell Rodero to warehouse her for a few months. Like everyone else does? Duh?"

A throbbing ache started as the crater re-opened. Once again I was the inconvenient burden to my pack. Jun's defense didn't change the legitimacy of what Burian argued: I was a burden, they hadn't been prepared, my father hadn't let anyone prepare.

Sterling swung his attention to Jun. "You'll help keep an eye on her. I don't want her trapped here all day. We'll share that duty."

"Hell, yeah. No problem." Jun slapped his thick thigh and nodded. He gave Burian a scalding look, shoulders pushed forward, a posture that said *act proper, chump*.

Burian flipped him the finger before going back to his room.

Sterling holed up in his office, dinner got scrapped, Jun ordered a pizza and I decided the only reasonable thing to do was celebrate it all with another drink.

NEVER SO HAPPY FOR HOMEWORK

I parked myself between Jun and Cye on the couch.

"Eat it." Jun shoved a piece of pizza at me.

"No."

"You gotta eat something. Soak up all that booze."

The pizza was greasy and probably delicious, but I only tasted cardboard.

Sterling walked past us without a word about ten, I held out until midnight, hoping he'd be asleep when I came to bed.

Instead, he was propped up on pillows and tapping away at his phone. Something else had his full attention now, and he didn't even seem to realize I was there until I had changed.

Then he glanced up. His intense appreciation was balanced against a more intense distraction.

I slid under the covers, the wall of booze between me and the gleam of his gaze. "You have something on your mind."

Whatever it was, no point letting it fester till morning.

"Hmm," was his answer.

Fine. He didn't want to talk about it. I was too tired and a little too drunk to trust myself, lest I say something stupid that won Sterling to Burian's side of thinking: that I hadn't been worth it.

His hazel eyes slid to toward me. Again, that tick in his neck as he caught himself from glancing down below my neckline. Not like a dainty silk nightie did anything but beg his eyes to travel downward. His forced restraint aggravated me. Gaia, dammit! "Sterling, not looking is a hell of a lot less subtle than just looking!"

"You make it sound like you don't want either," his tone was angry and frustrated. This wasn't what he had had on his mind, but now it was front and center.

"If you don't want to look I'm not going to shove your head between my breasts! It's obvious you do, so just look!"

His expression tightened. "You don't get it, do you?"

So I tell the man he can look, and he gets angry at me? "I'd have thought you'd be relieved to know you don't have to deal in strained modesty around me."

"Telling me I can look because you find me not looking more irritating than me looking makes me feel like I'll do the wrong thing no matter what."

"I'll tell you what feels wrong to me. You obviously not looking. If you want to look, look. If you don't want to look, don't. Don't get a crick in your neck over it."

His pulse throbbed in one vein of his neck. Beat. Beat. Beat. The scent of a hundred different things rose off him, but they changed so quickly and were mixed with so many other things it was only churning and turmoil.

This made no sense. Jerron had always complained females should just say what they wanted. Male acquaintances in high school had echoed the sentiment. If Sterling wanted to look, I wanted him to look. There! I had said what I wanted! Wasn't that what I was supposed to do?

Sterling should look. Looking would be normal, and normal was at a premium just then.

Perhaps I wasn't being properly demure to suit his human sensibilities, because there were a lot of humans that believed in that kind of thing. He was so confusing! I studied him, trying to figure out what he wanted from me. Being strong and showing skin in public was fine, but perhaps he wanted to lead the dance in bed. Maybe even a double standard: he could taunt me with his nudity, but I wasn't allowed to taunt him with mine.

Dammit, that wouldn't be any fun.

There was that expression on him again. The one where he sorted through little mental note cards of all the things on his mind until he selected a topic to broach. "This isn't what

I wanted to talk about."

I let him change the subject, although I debated if I should just grab his head and shove it between my breasts. The mental image of Sterling mumbling protests while being smothered and flailing about almost made me giggle. Only problem with that plan was my breasts were not nearly large enough to smother him.

He grumbled deep in his throat. Sometimes even being around him exhausted me. He turned and roiled like a fussy storm that couldn't decide if it wanted to crack open or dissipate.

He set his phone aside. He started to say something, then stopped, then started again. "Winter, there are more things we need to do."

I waited for the downpour.

"I just don't want to keep throwing thing after thing at you."

"I'm fine." I wasn't, but the great cosmic fist would get tired eventually. "So what's on your mind, Sterling?"

"There are many things we need to do, but there is one that should come before all others. Especially with this wanderer business spreading to you. We can't take any chances."

"I'm listening."

He said with an air of wary anticipation, "We need to get married."

In the eyes of werewolf society we were married. More than married.

However, formalizing a pairing for human society was a logical and common thing. Many pairs even had fancy human-style weddings with cakes and gowns and the works, especially if either member of a pair had many human friends.

Sterling was so wealthy that I had figured a quickie wedding wasn't on the calendar, and it was something we'd eventually get around to. Give him some time to make sure I wasn't some crazy she-wolf that would run amuck (or run off) with his considerable fortune.

I was indifferent to his proposal. "Okay."

All the arguments he had been prepared to make visibly evaporated. "Okay?" he echoed, completely nonplussed. "Just like that?"

"How should I act?"

"I expected some kind of indignant refusal or anger or..." his voice trailed off. He tilted his head to the side and gave me a very curious look.

The canine mannerism made me smile.

He plowed on right ahead with his stored-up justifications. "It's just that I want you to be taken care of. In case something happens to me. You need to be able to take care of the pack."

The society page jumped back into my head. In Montana the big local weddings had made our small town paper, along with engagement announcements. Sterling had a lot of human acquaintances. I'd marry him without hesitation but like hell was I going to have a big society wedding. "You didn't want a big fancy wedding, right?"

"No. Unless you want to—"

"No," I interrupted him. "Just making sure."

He cocked his the other way. "I was prepared for a tussle."

His confusion was almost adorable. I smiled and shook my head.

He stared at me for a bit, very intensely. His fingers rubbed a fold of the soft sheets. "I feel like there should be a fight over this."

"No, no fight."

He kept up with the fidgeting. I didn't understand what had him so knotted. My own knots had nothing to do with this marriage business. Getting married wasn't serious. Gaia had paired us, and getting a little piece of paper to ward off human complications was a smart, practical move.

Perhaps to the far more human Sterling this was a big deal. To me, as long as he wasn't going to expect me to climb into a fancy white gown, throw around flowers, and smile for a thousand pictures, I was content.

"I'm sorry about what Burian said. You shouldn't have heard that."

Ugh. That tightened all the knots within me. I shrugged as if it had been nothing so we didn't have to talk about it.

This time the silence was uncomfortable. I reconsidered my plan to smother him with my breasts.

Sterling fished around. "So math. You wanted to study math."

If Sterling had hoped to bring my stress level down, talking about my thwarted academic aspirations wasn't the way to do it. "I did."

Why the sudden change of subject? Did it have to do with marrying me? Was he circling toward something?

Sterling was an educated man. I didn't know what his degrees were in, or where he had gone to school, but I couldn't imagine he didn't have a fancy education to go along with his sharp mind. A tiny little glimmer of hope entered my chest, flitting like a tiny bird. Would he want me, no, *need* me, to go to college so I'd conform to expectations? That was an expectation I'd embrace!

"Math," he mused.

He wasn't getting to his point, and I couldn't stand it anymore! "Why are we talking about this?"

"I was going to suggest you study math."

"What?"

He didn't seem to notice my reaction. "There are colleges here in the city. Pick one."

New York schools. The hummingbird in my chest collapsed to the ground. Pick one! Even little bumpkin me knew it wasn't that easy. Those colleges were fancy schools. Schools for students with academic pedigrees. "There's no point. I'm from a crappy little school in Montana, and I graduated middle of my class."

"You're not stupid. I don't believe you weren't near the top, Winter."

The compliment warmed me a bit. "My father didn't care about where I graduated as long as I did. I missed a lot of my senior year. Grades just got docked. No makeup on labs and the like."

"If you want to go, go," he repeated with raised, expectant brows. "If you don't, don't. Just a suggestion. You could get in somewhere. Work your way up."

"Why are you suggesting this now?"

"I figured you might want to end the day with a win."

I didn't believe him, so I prodded with something crazy. "So I could get my PhD if I wanted."

"I don't see why not."

I almost couldn't breathe around the lump in my throat. I searched his face for clues he was not being honest with me. "Don't toy with me, Sterling. Not about this."

One half of his mouth smiled in a sort of wry, lopsided grin.

He meant it!

I flung my arms around his neck. He froze as stiff as a board and made a sound. I yanked back, looked him full in the face (he seemed somewhat terrified), squealed something incoherent and dissolved into wolf-form. I yipped, tore off the bed, and sprinted circles around the floor, all while barking gleefully.

I could go to school! I could go to school! Really go!

I leapt up onto the bed, ran all over the covers, ran under the covers, shot out the end of the bed, and ran in circles until I fell on my side. I laid panting on the floor.

I could go. I could go. I could go.

I rolled onto my belly. Sterling watched me from the bed, reeking of astonishment and under that, amusement. In fact, all the smells of the room hit my nose.

Crap.

So much excitement and I had just shifted. I got to my paws, chagrined. Losing control of forms was a nasty habit all wolves fought to avoid. Females, because we could shift almost instantly, tended to be more prone. I hadn't accidentally shifted for years. It had been a problem when I was younger.

It also felt good to be in wolf form. I shook myself from head to tail and faced Sterling. I wagged my tail slowly from left to right and my tongue hung out.

He picked up my discarded chemise from the sheets and held it up in one fist. "I believe this belongs to you."

I took the hint. Granted, wolf-hair in the sheets was itchy on human skin. I did as he wanted, then straightened the sheets I had made a mess of.

"Do you force-shift often?"

"First time in years." In the morning, I would be disturbed at how easily it had happened, and how dangerous it was in the city, and how concerned he had seemed, but that night, I didn't give it a thought.

"I didn't know your schooling meant so much to you."

"It does." I drew my knees up and hugged myself, determined to enjoy my dopey moment of glee and triumph. I wasn't Unwanted, and I could go to college. Everything was strange and foreign, but those two facts were most welcome. I closed my eyes and held onto them.

"I see where you got your name," he commented.

Eyes still closed, I replied, "Oh, yes, that. I'm one of those who the hair doesn't match the fur."

He smirked.

"Oh! You know what I meant, Sterling!"

"Indeed I do. Now."

I giggled.

A smile dwelled on the corner of Sterling's lips.

He leaned across to me. His hand steadied my cheek, but he kissed my neck. I inhaled, and remembered his declaration he could not be trusted. His lips lingered as my skin shivered. He whispered, "Goodnight, Winter."

HUNTING THE MOON

A few mornings later, while I brushed my teeth, Sterling —who was already dressed and had been awake since about four a.m.—appeared behind me in the mirror. Here I was brushing my teeth, foaming at the mouth. The door was cracked. *Cracked.* But to Sterling a cracked door was an open door.

College research had been easier than expected, and having stumbled upon an opportunity, I needed to talk to him. Even though it made me a little nauseated to think about it. Jerron had never been ashamed about mooching money from anyone, but had always made me feel like such a slimeball telling him I needed money to pay a bill or buy groceries... the groceries he ate. For him it was *his* money and groveling was required.

Jerron was one feature of my past life I did not miss in the least.

If I didn't ask Sterling this morning, he'd disappear for the rest of the day, and the registration deadline loomed. But first I needed to finish brushing my teeth.

"Mmmph," I told him.

"What?" he asked my reflection.

"Mmmph!" I pointed with my free hand to the door.

He looked out the door. I twitched my finger. He took the hint. He stepped back outside, but just outside, still watching me. It was like when Jerron would hover his finger just over my nose and I'd screech and he'd gleefully declare he wasn't actually touching me.

Gaia spare Sterling, because I was going to strangle him. Were all males such pests?

I finished brushing my teeth and nudged past him. "Morning," I told him by way of greeting. "You were up early."

"Not so early." He followed me and took up a position outside this door too.

I looked through my racks of still unfamiliar clothes. Mint had sent up another batch of things to wear, based off my previous selections, and I still had no idea what most of it was. Or how some of the pieces were to be worn. Fashion was a sort of weird alchemy and I feared making mud, not gold.

"You seem nervous, Sterling."

"Do I? *You* seem nervous. That's why I'm here."

Hell. I had heard that some males became overly aware of their partner's moods and state of mind. I had always dismissed it as, of course, people who cared for each other grew sensitive to their partner, but that morning, I realized there was more to it. He seemed a little bewildered by his instinctual need to be there too. The need to provide, protect, fix, resolve.

Perhaps the wanderers had Sterling's instincts a little over-caffeinated.

I had hoped to work my way around to my request, now I was cornered and would just have to blurt it out. Before my first cup of coffee. Not fair.

"One of the better schools offers non-credit online courses," I tried to sound casual and expectant. "I want to take some, the deadline to sign up for this semester is in a few days."

"So you take the course and do the work but don't get credit? I thought you wanted a degree."

"I do, but it's too late to get everything done to apply for spring semester. I'll apply for next fall."

Sterling shifted his shoulders. "Whatever you want to do, Winter."

"I need tuition money, Sterling." Ugh, not the way to start the morning.

Sterling said, with understanding, "Oh, yes, I guess you

would."

I stared at him, not sure what I was supposed to do next. So he'd buy me expensive diamond necklaces and gowns, but I couldn't have money for online classes? I suppose there was a good argument the classes served no practical purpose, but I wanted to take them.

He disappeared for a moment. I heard a drawer squeak open, then he returned holding a manila envelope. Without explanation he offered it to me.

I slid a fingernail under the frog clasp, peeled it open, and upended the contents into my palm. A number of credit and debit cards fell out. They were in various shades of jet-black, gray and azure blue.

Oh. I set the envelope aside and corralled the half-dozen pieces of plastic in one hand. The imprint of the top card had my name on it. My married name. *Winter Mortcombe.*

Words escaped me. My mouth dried up. *Winter Mortcombe.* I hadn't had time to really think about my name changing.

So far away from where I had started only a few days ago. Now art galas, wanderers, credit cards, and even Sterling himself.

Money. Such a delicate subject that ripped mates apart, destroyed families, and devastated packs. I plucked one of the cards from the pile and held it between two of my nails. Money. Destroyer of worlds. Was having an endless supply of it more or less complicated than having very little?

I had a number of questions, but settled on the one that I'd ask about anything dangerous. "What should I know about these?"

"There's not much to know."

It was money, of course there was a great deal to know. Efforts at delicacy gave way to tacky bluntness, "Sterling, it's money. There's always something to know. Be straight with me."

He cast a glance at the closet around us and then back to me. "That's complicated. Do you want the summary or the balance sheets?"

It was pre-coffee. "I'll take the summary for now. But you still owe me that explanation of all the pies you have your fingers in."

He told me a rough amount.

I prodded my addled brain to conjure a mental picture of how many zeros and commas that was. Jerron would have swooned with delight. I swooned for a different reason.

"I think it is very disrespectful to put your partner on an allowance. Unless you are going to make a habit of buying exotic cars, yachts, small islands, or entire skyscrapers, you aren't going to harm anything. Take as many classes as you want. Oh, and buy as many pairs of fancy panties as you want."

I gasped indignantly. Well, of course he had seen one pair on a previous evening. Thank goodness I had decided to get fancy panties or else I would have had granny drawers under there.

I patted myself on the back for that one.

He snorted a little half-laugh. "I wasn't going through your dainties. I just got the bill."

His ill-feigned blassé made me even more embarrassed. My face must have matched my hair from his expression. With bruised dignity I said, "I think I will, thank you very much."

"My favorite color is blue."

His comment seemed completely random until I realized what he meant.

"No teasing before coffee!" I flung the nearest object at him. Which happened to be the pair of panties on top of the dresser that I had pulled out to wear. He hooked them around his index finger and took stock of the yellow silk and lace. I didn't think those panties were especially risqué, but when he held them like that they sure looked skimpy.

"Let me get dressed in peace," I fumed.

His smirk stretched a little wider. He extended his hand to me.

I snatched the panties off his finger. "Out!"

He swept low in a grand bow before leaving.

* * * * * *

I signed up for all my classes without difficulty. It left me giddy and I squealed like a puppy when my welcome email came through. I relished the extensive list of work and lectures I'd need to catch up on. The work was way over my head, since I was coming in late and these online offerings were already left-over seats from unfilled classes that had already started. Mid-level logic, linear algebra and a trig course. But that made it an even better hunt, now that I had to outrun my disadvantage.

Nobody else was home just then, and that was a good thing. Squeals and giggles are best left for little kids.

No matter what, this was mine. *This* was mine. It wasn't a degree, or a degree program, but it was what I wanted, and now it was mine. I didn't let myself think about the what-ifs of if I never got accepted to college, or the wanderers never lost interest.

This was mine. This little, small thing was mine. And I was smart enough to do the work, and I would catch up, and I would manage a passing grade, even if it didn't count toward anything.

I would know I had done it, and as Sterling had said, I was a wolf lawyer and historian, and adding some more education on top of that wasn't a bad thing. It caused a tingling blush to race up and down my spine when I thought of myself that way. I wasn't just some little flake who had tagged along after her powerful daddy on outings.

Between dinner and the nightly ritual of television and desert, I took my drink and went to stand by the massive windows. The lack of total darkness, with the light-dot windows of other buildings and the endless motion of the trees, just didn't sit well. A forest made of concrete and steel. Supposedly Central Park was green and vast, but also dangerous and surely off-limits, at least for now. If I thought too much on it, the urge to smell something besides car exhaust, people, and the briny scent of the harbor's polluted water gnawed on my spine.

I sensed Sterling before my eyes focused on his reflection in the window.

He came very close behind my shoulder, so close I felt the warmth and weight and strength of his body. He bent over my shoulder to speak to me in a low tone that played along my senses like rough velvet against my skin.

"Marriage," he reminded me.

"You have *such* a way with words."

"Next Tuesday."

He had already set the date. I looked at him through a few falls of my red hair. "What's involved?"

He shifted in a slight, dismissive gesture. "Some paperwork, a few signatures, a few words exchanged in front of a judge. All very anticlimactic. Oh, a set of rings."

He was not looking for a response, and continued, "I thought you may like to pick out your own rings. Everyone else has been dictating your wants and needs of late."

For many wolves rings had become a symbol of a mate-bond. I had not really thought about it beyond the assumption that one day I too would wear rings. I had also thought my rings would be chosen for me, because after all, wasn't that how it worked?

Sterling hadn't known me long enough to know what I might want to wear the rest of my life. In high school the girls had all looked online and in magazines comparing their fantasy rings, dresses, and hairstyles. I hadn't given it a thought.

Sterling's reason sank deeper and touched a raw part of me I had become too accustomed to. Wearing a ring wasn't an obligation. Picking it out wasn't required. I didn't even have to care about it. Like everything else in this city, it could just be purchased and brought to the door within a few hours, even pre-selected to be suitable for parties and polite company.

I did care. I cared great deal, and being able to choose what I liked—what we liked, since one of the rings would be his—and have something that was ours, and not what had been chosen, ordained or handed to us like Cye handed us our dinner plate... suddenly, I wanted that.

"As long as we go together," I told him.

Sterling had always intended for us to go together. He had also, rightly, guessed I would say yes, because he had already set up an appointment at a shop.

"Just one shop?" I mustered light teasing through my swimming emotions. "Sterling."

His smile widened and the sensation of his amusement and pleasure at my little jab hit me right in the belly, and warmth crept through my awareness like ice cracking. "There are many such shops between here and the ends of the world," his tone was laced with a growl, "I would not see you less than pleased."

Sterling wasn't talking about rings just then.

Cye brought in desert, with Jun and Burian behind him.

"Knock it off, lovebirds," Burian said. "Different kind of sugar waiting for everyone."

SPEAK OF THE WOLF

Jun came along when Sterling and I went to the jewelers.

"Hell," Jun grumbled, spotting the three faces loitering across the street. One of them even waved to Jun.

Sterling ignored the wanderers, and nudged me into the backseat of the car. He slid in after me, while Jun flipped the wanderers off with both hands.

Jun climbed in next to me. "Gaia's ass."

"We must have worked our way to the top of their list," Sterling said.

Jun opened and closed his immense right hand. "Who needs a job when you're just hassling folks for money? Ass clowns."

They ghosted after us, easily keeping pace in the Manhattan traffic. Sterling pretended to ignore them, but he noted every move and step.

"Don't worry about it," Jun told me. "I'll twist their weedy little arms off."

That wasn't going to solve the ultimate problem, and might just step up hostilities. The only protection we had was Sterling's wealth; that enabled us to pull humanity around us like a soft, protective cloak. So far it seemed only Sterling or I were the targets, which was expected. Jun, Cye and Burian had no real value as wolf targets. They didn't have much prestige to steal, and no rank to honor, no mates or pups to menace. The most they could do to them was beat them up. Anything more would have attracted human attention. As long as they didn't go looking for a fight, the wanderers would (hopefully) leave them alone.

The wanderers didn't dare follow us all the way to the diamond district. It was a place of extreme vigilance, cameras, gates and door buzzers. For a little while, we were free. Jun, not completely convinced, waited outside.

In an exquisitely posh glass-and-light store that shone like the business surface of a disco ball, I wondered if my children would need to be fostered out so they wouldn't *only* know this world. Perhaps sent to live with another pack of lesser means. My children always needed to know how to shop for their own groceries, and understand the merit of simple underthings.

Two older gentlemen in impeccable dark suits and elegant cravats presented Sterling and I with velvet trays of ring. When I did not care for any of the rings presented, trays of gems and settings were brought out. The scattered diamonds strewn across black velvet were like spilled sugar. It seemed impossible to choose anything because it was all so very beautiful.

Sterling watched it all in a warm and content silence. We had chosen our wedding bands with relative ease: simple platinum bands with scrollwork on the side. Sterling chose to have small blue diamonds set in his. My engagement ring was more complicated. I knew I wanted blue diamonds as well, but choosing the center stone proved difficult.

The jeweler, somewhat indulgently, told me that the right gem would speak to me.

I, believing in Gaia, thought it might be true. Diamonds, like all gemstones, were a gift of Her affection for Her children.

As I considered the blazing diamonds in brilliant white and sea-blue, Sterling picked up the delicate jeweler's tongs and nudged the one he liked best.

"Unless you want something larger after all?" he asked me in a light, jesting tone.

"No." Some of the trays had contained huge gems that were the very definition of "boulder." The jewelers had used phrases like "extravagant" and "make a statement" but all I could think was "tacky" and "excessive." The gem Sterling had chosen was of a marked size, and shone with a fierce beauty. It threw off any light that dared hit in a brilliant rage. It was wholly extravagant in a completely different way.

Perhaps the right stone spoke to him *and* I. If it had been just me, I preferred a different gem. But when I thought about us as a pair, the gem he had pointed out matched that feeling.

The jewelers promised our rings in three days.

"Any problems?" Sterling asked Jun. His eyes scanned the street for trouble, as his gloved hand slid into mine.

Jun shook his shaggy head.

But they were there: waiting two blocks down where they had left us. They trailed us back to our building and when we arrived, at least three more had taken up posts across the street, and a fourth half a block down lounging beside a newspaper bin.

Sterling bristled with anger on the elevator ride up, and Jun bluntly asked, "What are you gonna do about it?"

"Two or three I can handle. They're scrappy, but no training." Sterling said.

"I counted more than three, Alpha."

At the foyer, Sterling nudged me out of the elevator. "I'm going back downstairs. I'm outnumbered, but I have a few more resources than most. I'll be back in twenty minutes."

After he was gone, Jun told me, "This is balls."

Jun hadn't seemed like one to needle an Alpha, especially not in front of his mate. I asked, "How long have you been with SnowFang?"

"Since the beginning. Me and Burian. Burian and Sterling go way back."

"When did Cye come along?"

"About six months ago."

Why was I playing twenty questions? He had to know I was looking for a history lesson. "How did you meet Sterling?"

"Through Burian." He frowned at me as I pulled a bag of chips from the pantry. "You shouldn't eat junk food. Have a carrot."

Burian and Sterling being long-time acquaintances wasn't exactly a surprise, I had figured as much, but Burian's gracelessness made me wary of him. Jun shoved a carrot at me. I pushed his hand away. "How did you meet Burian? Do I need a flow chart for this?"

Jun looked uncomfortable. He tried shoving some carrots in his mouth to hide it, but I had hit a nerve. He squirmed, but confessed, "I'm the youngest of seven. All boys. My folks, you know, they wanted a girl. So they kept trying. Unlucky number seven. Too many boys. Not enough to go around. I came here as sorta a lone wolf."

Interesting, but it didn't explain how he had met Burian. And what was a *sorta* lone wolf? Did he mean he technically hadn't been a lone wolf because he was still a member of his birthpack? Had his birthpack thrown him out? Had he taken the one-time pass bachelor males got? The stain of being expelled from a pack would linger forever. There would always be questions about how he had become a solitary male. His lack of clarity concerned me, it mattered, but at the same time, I was probably too used to hearing wolves speak in careful specifics.

"So how did you meet Burian?" That was what I was really after, as it sounded like Jun had just been a spare pup. Family wanted girls, got boys, and pushed Jun out the door to seek his own fortunes. Spare parts. Not worth the trouble.

My mind prodded me with the vision of three pups: two silver, one brown, squirming on marble tiles.

My temples pounded and my throat refused to swallow my chips.

Jun didn't notice, and kept on talking. "I was bouncing and he was in a bathroom fight. Broke it up, dragged him out. He was drunk and bloody as shit. I got him to give me his phone, went through it and called the New York number he swapped the most texts with. Sterling showed up."

Sterling returned at that exact moment and headed toward our bedroom. I excused myself from Jun, expecting more bad news, but only Sterling's frazzled irritation was on the other side of the door. "What did you do?"

"Spoke with building security. I can't involve humans directly, but they can be useful obstacles and eyeballs. I'm working on something more permanent."

More permanent sounded good, but options seemed limited. "What would—"

He pulled his watch off. "For what it's worth, Winter, I'm sorry about this."

It wasn't his fault. It wasn't anyone's fault. Unless it wasn't, in which case it was absolutely *not* our fault. "That's not—"

His phone buzzed. He looked at the screen and his face went glacial. "A Montana area code."

A DIFFERENT SORT OF BETRAYAL

Cold sweat broke out over my shoulders and under my breasts.

Sterling answered the call. "Daniel. No, you and I have never spoken before."

Daniel was the SilverPaw Beta. There were three Betas due to the large size of the pack, and Daniel was first among them. At pack meetings Daniel hadn't been afraid to argue with my father, and he had often heavily criticized my father's politics and leadership. He thought my father put too much emphasis on what was best for werewolves, and that that had often left SilverPaw shouldering an unfair share of burdens.

His arguments had had merit, and had certainly been seductive, although I had never been wholly convinced that the well-being of a pack took precedence over the well-being of the species. The *species* was the logical, long-term extension of the pack. Human encroachment was real. The gender imbalance was real. The population crisis was coming. Thinking about what benefited individual wolves and packs wasn't going to help the species. We *had* been doing that, and look what it had gotten us: spare pups like Jun, females treated like broodstock, and wanderers filling cities, with an Elder Council seemingly unwilling to even admit the problem existed.

In more immediate concerns, Daniel calling, for any reason, was *not* a good sign. He had no reason to call. My pairing with Sterling didn't involve the pack. It was a private family matter.

Very, very private.

Sterling's tone took on that steel edge that peeled fine wafers of skin from bone. "Oh, is that so. Why am I speaking to you? This is not between you and I."

My bride-price! It had to be about the bride-price! Dazed, I moved to stand. I didn't want to hear this. No more of this! Sterling could tell me later, the thought of a one-sided conversation that didn't even involve my father... bride prices were negotiated by the father, or the Alpha! It was never given to anyone else. It *couldn't* be. I didn't know why Daniel was involved, and with sudden, terrified instinct, I didn't want to.

Sterling clamped his hand over my thigh.

"I don't want to hear this," I pleaded in a whisper.

Stay, his lips said. His grip remained tight.

Sterling listened to the voice on the other end. Then he chilled over, eyes a storm, shoulders tight. My pulse jumped to a painful thump. The thundering hit my windpipe, each beat threatening to make me gag.

"Rodero insisted that I leave with her immediately, and without even naming her price. Now he thinks so little of both of us he will not call me to discuss his own daughter? You have the job?"

The thumping in my throat stopped.

My heart waited to learn how much this would hurt before it felt anything at all.

"I wanted to deal with this prior to my leaving. Alpha Rodeo refused. Now he gets you to voice his unreasonable demands? Is this how the SilverPaw honor their daughters? How an Alpha honors a female? Like *this*?! That price honors nothing but your pockets, this method is an insult! The mighty SilverPaw can't even afford to honor their own politics or their daughter?!"

I clapped my hands over my mouth to hold in my gasp. Oh Gaia! Daniel may have been a Beta, but he was still the first Beta of an Elder pack! I shook my head emphatically, then grabbed at Sterling's arm. This entire thing was a mess, no doubt about it, but Sterling might not know what a greedy price was. He shook my hand off.

"Sterling, don't say things like that!" I grabbed at his bicep again. "What do they want? It might not be unreasonable!"

Sterling yanked the phone from his ear and pressed the mute button. "Winter, aside from the fact that your father sent his Beta to negotiate your bride-price with me, which is —"

Tears pooled on the edge of my eyelids.

Sterling didn't finish his sentence. He jumped ahead, "What your father wants is obscene. This is *exactly* what I was expecting him to do, but he insults *you* by using this mouthpiece called a Beta?! It's too damn far, Winter! You are his *daughter,* and even if I am shit on a boot, *you* deserve better than this!"

There were no sobs. The emotions just had to come out somehow, so they transmuted themselves to tears and escaped through my eyes. "What does he want, Sterling?"

"The traditional ten percent."

It hit like a fist.

The traditional bride-price was ten percent of a male's worth. Centuries ago that had been simple. A few cows, a horse, some chickens, furs, pelts, perhaps gold and silver. Now it was more complicated. A man could not give ten percent of his condo or car, and just because he had those things didn't mean he could produce ten percent of that worth in cash. The ten percent rule had fallen out of favor as archaic and impractical, and now was seen as a way to profit off a female, or stonewall a pairing.

My father had not paid ten percent for my mother, and he (like the majority of Elders) actively discouraged anyone else from demanding it. Don't make a new pair's life more difficult through greed. Don't use it as leverage. Don't make the mistakes of the past. Ask for a token to prove esteem and nothing more. It was one of the few things most Elders agreed on. I had *heard* my father chastise other Alphas during mediations on the very subject!

Yes, SilverPaw needed money badly, but to demand *so* much! For that price they were selling prestige and honor, and needlessly! Even one percent would have been a nice sum. Why go for ten?

Like an idiot, I had dismissed that this had been their plan all along. Sterling had been right. He had been set up.

"I will not be fleeced like a lamb!" Sterling barked at Daniel.

Sterling's whole body stilled as he listened to Daniel's reply. His rage intensified, vibrating just beneath the surface of his skin.

"I will consider it," he spat. He flung his phone down onto the bed.

Tears dripped down my neck. I didn't try to stop them. It would have been futile.

Sterling raked at his hair. "I figured this is what would happen. Cut a little extra flesh, fine, I don't care, but this traditional-to-honor-the-old-ways is bullshit!"

"I'm sorry. I'm so sorry, I didn't think that—"

"Your arguments against it made sense, except you were wrong. There *are* other wolves in on it. I guess they need more than a lone wolf to bring me down. The *hypocrisy*. Even I know the Elders don't approve of that price. Daniel was playing that damn formal card so hard he didn't even call your father by name. Oh no, not to a wolf like me. I'm too filthy to even *hear* that name. I have to be reminded at every sentence just how lowly I am, lest I forget!"

My lungs shuddered. The smell of fryer vats, cigarette butts and boiled peanuts wafted up from my memory to torment me. The walls pressed in. The concrete many stories below seemed to rise up and grab my feet. I grasped for some other explanation. "My father and Daniel are often at odds."

Sterling considered that idea, then discarded it. "Daniel knew too much about what happened, Winter. He got it from your brother or your father, but he knew too much. He isn't working alone."

It started to sink in, slowly, like rain soaking through layers of clothing. If this was true, if it was all true, I had been used as a pawn. A worthless pawn, easily played, easily sacrificed. Not even worth my father calling himself to finish the deal.

The tears didn't stop. The sobs didn't come. Just tears. Just hot, hot tears as my body worked to shed grief as fast as possible.

Sterling traced a tear along one of my cheeks. "I'm not angry about the money. I figured your father was going to screw me, but to throw *you* into it this way? I—I have no idea why any father would do that. Treat me like no-prestige garbage, fine, I know what I am to wolves like him, but your own *daughter?*"

"Ten percent. Nobody asks for ten percent," I whispered. "Not him. Not my father."

"Apparently, he does. Daniel told me if I do not pay it, it will be known I refused to pay what you are worth when fully capable of doing so. You know what that means, in all its hypocritical glory."

Sterling would be declared a rogue, and I'd be honorbound to dispose of him for dishonoring me and breaking the Law. There was no defense before the Elder Council. My father had broken no actual laws save that of decency, which wasn't a law. He could easily spin it that he had honored Sterling with a shred of prestige and faith by letting me leave as I did. He'd say what was ten percent to a man like Sterling? Not when it would benefit the werewolves to see it spread around.

For SilverPaw, all it would come to would be a minor embarrassment, shaken heads, clucked tongues. My father could withstand the impact, and SilverPaw was too hungry to care about a minor bruise.

For Sterling, it would be death. And how could I, in good conscience, kill him for a crime he didn't commit?

He said, "I'm not inclined to pay. It's not about the money. I can make more money. It's about... you know what it's about, don't you? Will your father make good on the threat? He forced you to leave with me, but would he *really* force you to kill me, or die with me? You dying as a rogue would cost him dearly."

"Maybe not as dearly as you think," I managed to whisper. "There were already rumors I was Unwanted. Maybe... he'd spin it as... *she was my daughter, I loved her, not seeing her flaws.* He's already sacrificed me. I'm already gone."

"You, Unwanted?" Sterling didn't believe me.

"It was said," I mumbled.

Sterling didn't know what to make of this. My father had denied it until the last, but now he could use it to serve his interests. My father had always been inscrutable, but I had always trusted in his honor, and that he had raised me to be honorable as well. Pragmatic, of course, but honorable in a world that no longer valued honor as it once had. Honor always came with a cost, not a price, which was the whole point. It wasn't for sale. It had to be earned, then defended and protected.

My dying as a rogue at Sterling's side would smear SilverPaw. But, how much? Enough for them to care? The sobs had worked their way up my throat and wanted to escape.

No. I refused to cry until I knew why, what, and who I was grieving.

We sat for a long time.

I struggled with what seemed to be an obvious truth. "Maybe there is something we're not understanding."

He put his arm around me and pulled me against his side. "It's not the damned money, Winter. Fuck the money. I don't care about the money. I can make more money. I can afford to lose that money." He sighed heavily. "Maybe I should just pay it and not be a principled bastard for once. I won't pay the wanderers, but I'd pay an Elder Alpha to go the hell away and leave me alone. I think I could live with that."

"The world needs more principled bastards."

My phone hummed.

I pulled away from him and sniffled. I leaned over and fished it off the table. It was my brother's number. Jerron. What did he want? Not anyone I wanted to talk to. I almost ignored the call, then remembered how I regretted not pumping him for information on Sterling. No doubt Jerron knew what our father was up to. I wiped my face.

My father wouldn't talk to Sterling, and he wouldn't talk to me, but maybe he had sent Jerron as an intermediary. Jerron had been there; Jerron probably knew what the master plan was. Even if Jerron had just called to gloat, perhaps I could get him to start bragging and running his mouth.

"What, Jerron?"

"Beta Daniel just talked to Sterling."

Time to play stupid. "What? Why?"

Jerron's surly but triumphant tone was a strange and ugly combination that put me on my guard. Additional surprises were not welcome. "Ask Sterling about that. I just have a little brotherly advice."

Yeah, because Jerron had always been the protective big brother. Trying to keep my tone respectful and not sullen, "I'm listening."

"You probably don't know this, but Sterling didn't pay your bride-price."

"He didn't? You're joking. That can't be true!" I bit my lip and uttered a fierce, silent prayer. Jerron was surely up to no good, but I still held out hope that Dad had put Jerron up to being the middleman. Perhaps Beta Daniel was making a power bid. Perhaps Jerron and Daniel were in league with each other!

"Yeah, well, anyway, I thought I'd let you know Sterling's been told to settle up, and he's balking."

Perhaps because the price is blood and honor, you donkey! "Are you sure? Why is Daniel doing it? Dad should do it. He's my father and the Alpha. Daniel shouldn't be anywhere near this."

Jerron laughed, "Because the SilverPaw Alpha wants to talk to your mate? No way, Winter. Just try to keep Sterling from doing something stupid."

"Cut the too-good-for-names prestige shit, Jerron. We all know it's Dad we're talking about."

Jerron chuckled again, low and cruel. "Just reminding you of where you stand, Luna-of-Nothing."

I grabbed the edge of the bed and *squeezed* so I didn't scream at Jerron that he could go *fuck* himself, the little smarmy bastard. But I needed to keep him talking, and that meant humoring him. "I can't help if I don't know why Sterling balked. Why did Sterling refuse?"

"Sterling said it was too much to pay."

"Jerron, let's not play twenty questions. How much did Dad ask for? What's too much? Why didn't Sterling pay it back at the house anyway? Why am I just now hearing about this?"

"The price is obvious. The traditional ten percent." He savored the words and ignored my other questions.

"Dad wouldn't ask for that!"

"That's the price."

"Stop trying to stir up shit just because you want a fancy truck, Jerron!" I hated him so much I couldn't even lie to myself about it anymore. I *hated* him. It was a sin. A terrible sin, a bad omen, bad luck, but it was true!

"Sterling even made accusations about an ambush. What a rude thing to say about an honorable Elder pack." Jerron's dark voice made my skin crawl. The smug, malevolent satisfaction crept up from the phone and slid around me like miasma. This was not the shallow, selfish man-boy I knew.

Jerron had never truly frightened me before, and he had never startled me with being cunning. He had always been too lazy to be clever.

"Best set your mate right before he gets into trouble he can't purchase his way out of."

I managed to choke out that I would attempt to reason with Sterling.

I ended the call and dropped the phone on the floor.

"Did he threaten you?" Sterling asked.

"Not directly." I rubbed my hands over my wet face. I was still crying and hadn't realized it. I tucked my hands between my knees while the shaking passed. "Jerron has always been more like a mongrel to me. Junkyard dog. That wasn't a junkyard dog."

"He pulled the titles-not-names with you as well."

"Yes."

"That is a very bad sign."

I hugged myself. Titles-not-names drove home to a wolf how inferior they were, how below regard that they weren't even allowed to speak the name of the other wolf, and that the conversation being held was so distasteful that the only reason it was happening at all were reasons of strict protocol and absolute need. My family was no longer my family. I had been effectively disowned and disavowed.

I sobbed once. I wanted my mother. I had never needed her so badly. She would never have let this happen without explanation.

She was gone in a place I could not reach. I silently implored Gaia to keep me sane until morning. In the morning I'd wrap my head around all this. Just then I wanted my mother, even if there was nothing she could have told me. I wanted to lay my head on her shoulder, feel her fur under my chin, and her tail wrapped around me.

But there were just memories, a man I barely knew, and Gaia's presence buried under fathoms of concrete, glass, and steel.

Sterling and I called it a night and went to bed. Nothing like a few mental punches straight to the brain to make you want to clock out. We laid on our sides facing each other in the twilight. I think he wanted to say something, but he didn't know what, and I didn't know what I could possibly want to hear. We only stared at each other until sleep pulled us to the earth.

~*~ Winter's Dream ~*~

Although I could not see the walls, nor end, nor beginning, I perceived that I was in a dark, shadowy corridor. It was not a perfect darkness. It was the caliginous blackness after all lanterns had been snuffed out and the light had just now fled. The darkness felt soft and charcoal-gray against me. After only a few moments of confusion I did what seemed the logical course of action: I started walking. I knew which direction would take me to the end of the hallway, and that was where I needed to go.

I walked in silence for some time, but I wasn't concerned. The end of the hallway neared.

Just as I was about to reach the end, a shaft of moonlight burst from the not-present ceiling and illuminated a naked man. He stood with his back toward me, legs slightly spread. His arms were at his sides but his forearms raised, causing every muscle and sinew of his body to draw taut. Every dip and rise in carved relief under the moon's unforgiving eye. His short hair was silver and angled into a sharp point at the nape of his neck, then continued in a silvery-blue line down his spine right to the cleft of his flawless buttocks. He held an item in each of his upraised hands, as if he were a set of scales trying to divine the weight of each balanced against the other, and the strength of his body to bear them.

I crossed in front of him and was not surprised to see Sterling's face. He did not acknowledge me. His eyes focused on some distant point beyond my left shoulder. A small whimpering sound yanked my eyes to the item he held in his left palm: the brown wolf puppy I had seen before. Only this time the little one was so very young its eyes were still shut and its navel stump still present and damp. It squirmed and made little tender noises.

In his other hand he clutched a delicate silver chain, either unaware of or immune to its burning on his skin. At the end dangled a blue crystal spear, or a carved vial of blue liquid—perhaps it was both. I tried to move closer but found I couldn't. My feet couldn't go farther forward. But I could take a step back. Then I saw why: under Sterling's feet a shallow pool of water had shimmered into place.

The blue necklace danced in my vision. I wanted to reach out and grasp it and examine it more closely. What was it? I sensed its power and allure. Its secrets. Each time that I resolved to look at the necklace, the whimpering of the puppy in Sterling's other hand drew my attention, and the pendant swung just out of reach.

"Where the other two puppies? Where are the other puppies, Sterling?"

He may as well have been made of stone. His eyes did not even blink. The moonlight shone off his irises in a perfect, illuminated ring.

"Where are the puppies?" I shouted at him. "Sterling, the puppies! There are two other pups! Where are the pups? "

My shout made the blue pendant dance wildly in his grip, like an empty playground swing jangling on its chains.

The darkness seemed to expand and grow larger. My awareness of a non-specific boundary in the murky darkness increased. Just beyond where the ragged edges of moonlight did not touch. Beyond that rim of my perception were there eyes watching us? Waiting?

Shades drifted just beyond my awareness.

The silver puppies. Were they in those shadows, being held by clawed hands while hidden eyes watched me? I believed and disbelieved at the same time. I could not perceive the shadows, yet I knew they were there—was it a dreamer's paranoia, a fear of this non-specific darkness?

Now the blue-silver hair extended from the nape of Sterling's neck forward across his muscled shoulders in three claw-like slashes. But his face remained serene and human. The hand clutching the soft exposed body of the newborn didn't seem to cause the puppy any distress. It snuggled into his palm seeking a teat that was not there.

A terrible cracking sound, and six crevices snaked forward from the edges of the murky darkness to the pool of water at Sterling's feet. I jumped aside. The cracks clawed into the pool like spokes of a wheel. Water did not drain out, but a dark fluid flowed in. It was dark, thick, and when the moonlight glanced off its surface it had a silvery-blue film.

The scent of blood long dead hit me.

With the paralysis of a dreamer I was forced to watch as the brackish blood mingled with the water at Sterling's feet. It began to churn in protest, thrash like a living thing. It thickened, made terrible sucking and popping noises until the brew transmuted into liquid silver through some horrific alchemy.

"The puppy! The puppy!" I shrieked. The silver liquid's heaving tried to consume the blue necklace and globules burst upwards and smacked the back of Sterling's hand. It would hit the puppy soon! "Don't let it hit the puppy! Sterling! The puppy! It will burn the puppy! STERLING! STERLING!"

And I was also aware, the entire time, of eyes watching us from the shadowy umbra, watching the ordeal carved by the moon's circumference.

ALL THE TRADITION

Nothing made much more sense in the morning, but my emotions were distant, leaving my brain more clear.

On the surface it was a non-problem with a straightforward resolution. Pay the price, walk away, lick wounds.

Sterling wasn't at breakfast. Cye told me that he was already in his office and bristling with purpose. Jun and Burian passed some comments about someone on the other side of the world getting new orifices ripped open.

Cye had made French toast again. I indulged.

"You want some toast with that syrup?" Burian commented.

I jabbed a piece of bacon in his direction. "If I don't drown the toast it might get away."

Jun gave Burian two thumbs up. He approved of a woman having a hearty appetite.

Sterling emerged from the hallway as I finished my second piece of toast. He hadn't shaved, his shirt's buttons were mismatched, and he looked rougher than I felt. He ran a hand through his hair as he sat down. "Winter."

"Hmm? Oh, hold still." When everything else was messed up, I could easily fix that lopsided button job.

"Winter, I—" he tried to squirm away from me as I unbuttoned his shirt.

"Should we leave?" Cye asked sweetly.

I shot Cye a dirty look. He giggled. Sterling sighed and looked at the ceiling. "Winter."

"Oh stop. This buttoning job will drive me nuts." I also wanted to see if those three lines slashed over each shoulder onto his chest had appeared. I knew they hadn't, but I needed to reassure myself that Sterling's body was as I remembered it from the day before, not the dream.

Yes, still carved marble perfection. I ran my palm over his shoulder, then caught myself as the table snickered.

"I have need of a wolf lawyer," Sterling said to me.

"What a coincidence. I happen to be such an expert." I tugged at the second to last button.

He pushed my hand away. "What form does the payment have to take? I get to decide, right?"

I swirled my last bite of toast in my syrup and enjoyed it before I got on with the unpleasantness of my bride-price. "Yes. He names the price, you decide how to pay. Wouldn't be fair if he wanted five cows but you only had a flock of sheep."

"Are we talking about a bride price?" Burian asked.

Sterling nodded.

Cye's lips formed into a perfect 'o' as Burian and Jun exchanged glances.

"It's like a set of scales," I ignored the others and spoke to Sterling. "He puts the sum of his demand on one side, you fill your side with whatever balances the plates.:"

Sterling tapped his fingers on the table.

"Eat something." I pointed my fork at his empty plate.

"I'm—"

"Cye, shove some food in front of him."

Sterling frowned at nothing in particular, his attention inward at the problem. He ate about half of what Cye brought to him and then asked, "Winter, I don't see any way to maneuver around this."

I held my coffee cup to my lips and inhaled the scent. My emotions crowded at the door that I had sealed them behind. "I don't even know what *this* is, much less how to get around it. Or through it."

Money grab? Jerron engaged in a double-cross? My father being a scumbag? My father so desperate he was willing to sacrifice every shred of his honor?

"Are you saying you don't want to pay? That's not even an option, is it?" Sterling cocked his head to the side.

"The price always has to be paid. Maybe this isn't about *greed*, but it is about the money," I said with care. Suggesting an Alpha be benevolent toward an aggressor was thin ice. But this also reminded me of an ethical question posed to pups: if you were starving, was it better to try to steal a kill, or die of hunger?

I hated that damn question. My truthful answer of "it depends" was not allowed. It was steal or die, and that was ridiculous. In protest, I had always chosen the cocky and very "wrong" answer of *steal*. The appropriate answer was *die of hunger*.

The *point* of the question was to demonstrate to pups that, even in their dying moments, a wolf had to place the good of the pack before their own life. A wolf who stole the kill obviously won, but the chances of a starvation-weakened wolf winning were so slim it would not be responsible to make the attempt. The failure would diminish them, and diminish the aggregate prestige of their pack.

In my opinion it was a stupid question, and at least needed a follow-up question to point out the difference between hubris and prestige. And it wasn't like our history wasn't chock-full of stories about wolves who chose the "wrong" answer and became heroes for it, or the "right" answer and died idiots, or just made up their own answers.

If this business about my bride-price was that the SilverPaw were metaphorically starving, then this was my father trying to steal Sterling's kill. My father figured he had enough strength to succeed, and escape unscathed.

Sterling tossed down his fork. "Fine. There are ways to hand over this much money that won't put it in the hands of the tax man. If this is about need, tell me. I don't especially want anyone, human or wolf, to know about this, and I'm sure he doesn't either. We would both have reasons to be discrete, and he'll keep more of it in his own pocket if he works with me instead of making demands."

This time I asked plainly, "You'd share your kill?"

Sterling ground his teeth together, then answered, " I would for the sake of the packs."

I had been gone about a week, so my father might have had time to realize just how bad the finances were. I wasn't optimistic, but since my father had already chosen the "wrong" answer, perhaps I could argue some ancient history and convince him we could conjure an alternate answer. The cards were all in his favor, so not likely, but there was still a *chance*. "I'll try calling him. He should be in his office by now, and Jerron gone to work."

We retreated into the privacy of Sterling's office for the call.

"You're not here," I warned Sterling.

"I won't make a sound."

"This won't work if he suspects you're about."

"Not a peep," he vowed.

We sat on the little couch as I placed the call. On the third ring my brother picked up.

Shit. Jerron should be at work! He left at six a.m. to make it to the metal shop. Jerron never was late or skipped out on work. He liked the money too much. Jerron was greedy, but he was no slacker. One of his better qualities. "Jerron, let me talk to Dad."

"There's nothing to talk about."

"Drop the keeper of the gate shit, Jerron!"

Cold silence, then, "You shouldn't have called."

Dammit. He *never* missed work, and I was never going to get past him now. Dad didn't pick up the phone if he didn't have to, and usually he didn't even then. Dealing with Jerron was unavoidable. Stern and argumentative hadn't worked the night before. The syrupy tactic from the gala might.

I softened my voice and tried to sound just a little bit like

I was pleading with my big, strong, noble older brother who surely wouldn't want to see his little sister wounded so grievously. "I've spoken with Sterling. This is crazy. We don't need to do things this way."

"Butt out of the males' business."

"It is my business. It's my pack and my family at odds, and it doesn't need to be like this. Dad doesn't have to risk sounding like a hypocrite. If it's about the money—"

"The SilverPaw Alpha. Not 'Dad'." Jerron corrected.

"We all know who I'm—"

"The SilverPaw Alpha. Not 'Dad'." Jerron's blood-curdling snarl raked my skin.

I couldn't do the sweet little sister routine anymore. "If we just give you the money, you're going to lose half of it on taxes, not that *you'd* know that because you males never did the taxes. Mom and I did. If you need money, there's a better way. But you have to let me talk to Dad!"

"The price is the price. He set the price. It will be paid, Winter."

The sick triumph in his voice abruptly nauseated me. I choked down a gag. "That's the SnowFang Luna to you! You want to play formal games with me, dog? Use *my* title, you unranked pup!"

He hissed into the phone. Oh, it *hurt* him. "Then, *Luna*, remember this is between males. Stay out of it, and tell that cockless mate of yours, the SnowFang *Alpha*, to keep a male's business to himself."

Him saying *SnowFang Alpha* hurt him *so* much, the words itched on his tongue like fire ant bites. The rank Jerron wanted *so* badly for himself. *Alpha*.

"I know this was an ambush, and none of you SilverPaw even have the balls to admit it! You *used* me, you Gaia-damned dishonorable piece of—"

Click.

"Temper, temper," Sterling said, face stern but tone

laughing.

Call ended. Not even two minutes. One minute, thirty-seven seconds.

Used. A pawn. A cheap, worthless pawn. Just like the Alphas of old had used their daughters!

Sterling put his hand on my thigh. He took my phone away before I threw it against the wall.

I shook my head, dazed. "Stonewalled."

"Your brother is a mongrel."

Jerron skipping work confirmed it for me. There was no reason he'd miss a day's pay unless he was confident, and here he was playing Alpha's Messenger for our father.

I had done everything my pack and family had ever expected. I had tried so damned hard, I had been trusted down in the Archives, trusted with the sensitive secrets of strangers, and this was how it ended! Like *this*.

And why? Sterling's fatal, grievous flaws were a mystery. His father was clearly a wolf of wealth. Not prestige, but wealth. Maybe it was Sterling's father who was the problem?

Sterling asked, "So. About not paying them. Any options?"

"No. It's part of the named requirements of what defines proper Alpha behavior. You can't refuse."

This was no time to cry and mourn. I needed to assume *all* the SilverPaw leadership was involved, and that on some level, this had been a setup. They wouldn't even use proper names! We were *that* lowly to them. We needed to proceed as though the worst could happen. I pulled at my lips with my fingernails, cataloging every tiny detail from the past ten days.

I'll record the pairing myself.

What if he *hadn't*? Then Sterling and I were technically an unmated pair, and nobody knew how, or when, he had arrived, so the SilverPaw could close ranks and say I had run away with him. If my father wouldn't acknowledge our bond, then it might as well not exist at all. Our pups would suffer the bastard stigma. He might even refuse to allow them to be recorded. If we didn't give him what he wanted, he wouldn't need to kill us. He could just strangle us.

Or he could blackmail us, year after year. Keep paying, year after year, or be ruined.

I knew how terrible one wolf could be to another, and how Alphas could justify their behavior, or simply felt no need to justify it. My father could be *one* of them.

My pulse quickened in my throat. "We have to protect ourselves. To make sure they don't think we're an all-you-can-eat buffet."

Sterling cocked a brow at me. "How do you suggest we do that? We don't have anything to protect ourselves with."

Oh, but we *did*. Other packs might be helpless, but *we* weren't.

"Tradition," I sneered. "They want to play that card? I can do that too. I think my father forgot who he was dealing with! All the tradition they can handle, every single shred!"

My father wasn't the only Chronicler. He was *the* Chronicler, but there were numerous other adjunct Chroniclers who handled regional work. There was one down in Virginia, at the Elder Pack AmberHowl. She herself wasn't a member of the Elder Council, and *did* answer to my father as a Chronicler, but through the shield of her own Alpha.

I'd ask her to become the traditional neutral agent. The SilverPaw would file a formal request for payment, but wouldn't need to specify what the amount was. Once the agent had the formal request, we'd agree to pay, then pay the SilverPaw, and they'd send another letter telling the AmberHowl the matter was concluded.

If the record of our being a legitimate pair didn't exist, my father would have to create one to submit with the request. Two birds, one stone.

Our pairing, and the payment of the price, would all be on the public record, and we'd be protected from future interference. Well, hopefully.

"Sounds risky," Sterling said, "I doubt your father will appreciate another pack knowing about his antics."

"Mentioning the price isn't required. I'm afraid if we do, we'll spook the AmberHowl. We can pay it, right?"

Sterling shrugged. "I've already started to figure out how to do it."

"That part I don't think we can or should negotiate. The formal request can just say we've already agreed on it. I just want to make sure SilverPaw leaves us alone."

"Why are you so concerned?" Sterling asked.

"He told me he'd record our pairing himself."

"I'll bet he didn't."

"I don't want to lock jaws, I just want a witness, and to tighten the screws so that they know not to bother us again. That we're wolves, not chickens, and this isn't their henhouse."

Sterling nodded, "And how are you going to explain it so you tempt the Chronicler to help us, without spooking them?"

"Just the truth. That my father didn't name my price, and trusted you on your honor that it would be paid when requested. He's requested via proxy and invoked tradition, so we are responding in kind to show proper respect."

"Tell me she'll be smart enough to read between those lines."

"No doubt. And she probably won't ask questions she doesn't want answers to."

Sterling shook his head and his lips curved into a crescent smile. "Your father will get what he wants, but I will get some of his prestige in the process, in front of another Elder pack."

Sterling was right. This was going to cost SnowFang a great deal of money, and we wouldn't get a rousing victory from it, but we wouldn't come away empty-handed for our trouble. My father would be compelled to admit he had entrusted me to Sterling, and taken Sterling on his honor. No harm to my father, but Sterling would get a considerable boost.

I smiled, feeling sly. "More than a little. I'm sure he's not looking to do us any favors."

Sterling's fingers laced more tightly with mine. "Winter, he's still your father. I want to protect SnowFang, but we don't have to do it with your father's hide. We can just pay and if there's any doubt, the bank records will speak volumes. There is always that option."

"That might work in the human justice system, but this would be an Elder Council matter. We can't take our chance. My first duty is to protect the SnowFang and its future."

I unlaced one of my hands from his and shoved my index finger into his chest. "I will deal with the Chroniclers. You will figure out how to make this low-hanging fruit full of worms. Make whatever he thinks he's going to get as painful and inconvenient as possible."

His hazel eyes gleamed. "Did you think I'd just wire him cash? This is *my* area of expertise."

"Will it be a shipment of uterus paintings?" I moved closer to him.

"As tempting as that may be, beautiful wolf, I have something far worse in mind."

I ran my fingers over Sterling's unshaven jaw. "Good."

His other hand slid over my hip. My skin shivered in delight, and I murmured a soft sound when he tugged me across the couch and pulled me against him.

Our lips met, softly, lightly. That blissful warmth flowed over my skin, through my mind and bathed all the bad thoughts in warmth. My lips parted for him, my skin begged that hand on my hip to slide under my shirt, along my bare skin.

But it was the wrong time, and for the wrong reasons.

I gently pushed apart from him. "No."

"Yes," he pulled me back to him. His hand held my jaw. I could not escape the dizzying hunger. Not until one of his calloused hands moved along the bare skin of my side—

My entire body felt like it sparkled into existence for the first time.

Somehow I found the resolve to push him away again, even though his hand remained against my bare skin, unapologetic and heavy. "No. Not now. Not because we're angry."

For the briefest of moments—not even a heartbeat—I didn't think he'd comply. But he removed his hands. He was annoyed. I floundered a bit— I needed to get away from him, because I really didn't trust myself to not say to hell with it all and do exactly what my skin pleaded with me to do.

I'd regret it. I knew that.

"I will contact the AmberHowl." Being back to business didn't really cool the fever in my blood. "We shouldn't delay. Any delay will seem like avoidance."

His gaze drifted up and down my body. I wished he'd reach out with those hands and grasp me and pull me back down. My panties were uncomfortably moist.

"I'll start planning our gift," he said.

I nodded, turned on my heel and headed toward the door.

I felt his eyes on my ass. His gaze burned into me, the full force of his attention. He just grinned at me. "What?" he said, so devilishly innocent I nearly melted. "You told me I could look."

"Just keep enough blood in the brain that can count higher than one," I advised him. His grin flashed white teeth at me.

"Two. That other brain can count to two," he informed

me with a smirk. "Go change your panties, Winter."

Could he smell that, or was he just guessing?!

"Do your job!" I managed a somewhat composed scowl before fleeing the scene.

THIS COULD BE SIMPLE

In general, I had worked hard to be a credit to my family. There was, however, one secret blemish on that record: I had made a copy of my father's address book.

There wasn't some online directory or werewolf phone book. You had to know which wolf or pack you wanted to contact and figure it out from there. Often this meant involving another wolf or pack that had the information, or maybe knew somebody who knew somebody. It was a matter of safety to our kind. That wasn't the kind of thing you could just put up on the internet and hope humans never found it. It wasn't the best arrangement, but nobody had thought of anything better.

My mother's death had been quick and sudden. Thirteen-year-old me had barely wrapped my head around "cancer" before she was gone. After her death, a reoccurring nightmare started. In the nightmare, I came home from school to an empty house. I ran to the phone to call for help only to realize I didn't know how to find anyone, and I was alone. The dream always ended with me looking at my fingers over the phone buttons, the dial tone in my ear, not knowing what buttons to push.

Most nights the dream had been so vivid I woke up gasping and drenched in sweat, and driven to prowl around the house until assured my father and brother were still there. The unrelenting nightmare had eventually chased me downstairs into the workroom, where I had carefully copied every single name and number in my father's large associate roster: other Alphas, Betas, the adjunct Chroniclers, other wolves of prestige and note, family members, other SilverPaw. Once every six months, until the day I had left, I had snuck into my father's desk to keep my notebook current.

Hardly a crime, but a violation of his trust. I had justified it to myself that all I wanted to do was *sleep*. Knowing the crucial information was squished between my mattresses had let me sleep again.

I had felt guilty, but never guilty enough to stop doing it. I did devise a little code to obfuscate titles and phone numbers. Not trusting my grasp of cryptography, I also used the frilliest, sparkliest notebooks I could find, and plastered stickers and colorful doodles all over it. If it ever was discovered, my hope was it would be discarded as a teenager's diary.

It had also been the first thing I had packed.

The phone number for the AmberHowl Chronicler, MaryAnne, was still good, and she answered after a few rings. In as pleasant and casual a tone as I could manage, I explained the situation, although I did refer to my father as the "SilverPaw Alpha" to drive home that this was not a casual situation, and my request for her involvement wasn't nearly as silly as it seemed.

The bait worked. "Is the price in debate?"

"No. The price has been agreed upon. Once he files a formal request with you, we'll do our part." It grated to say that, but there was no legal room to wriggle on the amount.

"I'm confused. You're already with your mate? You've *left* SilverPaw?"

"I have, and am now the SnowFang Luna. The SilverPaw Alpha saw no reason to delay, and knew Sterling would honor the price when it was named." Might not be any wiggle room on the amount, but my father was going to have to sweeten the deal with some prestige for Sterling.

MaryAnne didn't believe a word of it, and she didn't want to get involved. I didn't blame her, anyone paying attention would smell how bad this stank. But on the surface it was nice and clean, without any reason for her to refuse. It fell square into her regular duties. Paperwork. Nothing but paperwork.

She reluctantly accepted and promised to be in touch.

Well. My job was done. Time to pass the baton to Sterling.

I went into the kitchen. Burian stood at the counter eating a sandwich. Cye said, "You look perturbed."

"Just sorting out this bride-price business."

"Shouldn't that have gotten paid before you got here?" Burian asked. "I'm no expert on the Law, but you generally pay for something before you take it home."

"You aren't wrong. But it wasn't, and now it's complicated."

"How complicated?"

"Complicated." I didn't trust Burian, and he was about as sympathetic as a cactus. I gave Cye a pathetic look. "What's for lunch? I don't feel like fighting with you over the kitchen."

He practically glowed. "I'll make you something!"

My phone rang just as I finished my food. MaryAnne shouldn't have been calling back that fast.

Her voice had some sharp, annoyed edges. "I spoke with Beta Daniel. He refuses to file a request. The SilverPaw are furious I'm involved."

The hell?

It took a moment to digest. Anger wasn't a surprise. If my father was determined to steal the kill, then refusing to let MaryAnne get involved made sense... except that pushing MaryAnne onto a Beta for a bride-price request was bizarre. Betas *never* dealt with bride-prices. It was always either the father or the Alpha. Even another male relative couldn't do it. If the Alpha wasn't available, it just had to wait.

If my father's hope was to keep this as discrete and hushed up as possible, this was not the way to do it. MaryAnne's Alpha would hear about it.

MaryAnne expected some kind of explanation, and I needed to choose my next move. My brain scrambled to re-order the chess pieces, but the board was a senseless mess. Jerron and Daniel being in league together made the most sense, except for the nagging detail of my father having been the one to give the ultimatum to Sterling.

I opted to keep up the sham of confused ignorance and formality. "I'm sorry, Chronicler. They said they wanted to be very traditional."

"What about this seems traditional to you?" she asked sarcastically.

"I'm just telling you what I've been told," I insisted, hoping she'd sniff out the dead body in the bushes without me having to explain it. There was a big difference between a Chronicler deciding to be the bad guy middleman, and asking them to champion something.

I fiddled with my chips during the silence. Gaps had formed between the acrylic and my cuticle. I needed to get fills before my wedding. Perhaps an ice blue, since Sterling liked blue.

"What *exactly* were you told?"

"Nothing, personally. Sterling spoke with the Beta, I spoke with my brother. Both told us they expected this to be handled in the traditional fashion. Everything else you know. There's just not much to this." I feigned confused, wide-eyed innocence as best I could manage.

Another span of thick silence. My fingernails cracked the chips. MaryAnne was going to balk, and tell me I was on my own. I couldn't let her. Crap.

Reluctantly, I added the dangerous detail I had told Sterling wouldn't be necessary. "Even the price is traditional. Ten percent."

The Chronicler sucked in her breath through her teeth. "Is that the problem?"

The proverbial water was deep, and it was very cold.

"No, as I told you, the price is not in dispute. We just don't have a formal written request, or proxy to handle the transaction. This whole thing is traditional, per their request." I think I sounded strangled, because I sure felt like a choke-chain was on my throat. This was getting complicated and dangerous–fast.

MaryAnne snorted, "You speak like a Chronicler."

No comment on that.

Another little sigh of frustration. Still fighting to not be part of this. "About how much will the price be, Luna?"

I took a deep breath and plunged into the water.

Silence.

After a very, very long pause to digest the amount and its implications, she spoke, this time in a voice heavy with something I couldn't name but understood. "I see. Unfortunately, the SilverPaw have made it clear to me they won't file a formal request under any circumstances."

My entire body felt a hundred pounds heavier. I had shown her my hand *and* wasted ten minutes.

"But," she paused, then continued, slow and measured, "given the price and circumstances, it shouldn't be a shock to the SilverPaw that *you* would know how these things work and are... complying... with their... preferences. It is not *my* place to demand an Elder Alpha do anything. I will have to take this matter to my Alpha."

I gasped, then slapped my hand over my mouth. The blood raced from my face and pooled somewhere else. On one hand, it was an offer for her to champion us. On the other, it involved asking the AmberHowl Alpha to growl at the SilverPaw.

If Elder Demetrius refused, our little show of resistance would meet a swift end, and SnowFang probably would too.

If Demetrius *did* help, even privately and discreetly, we'd be beholden to AmberHowl for some unknown, future favor. And the SilverPaw would be even angrier.

This had gone from sort of simple to a complete train wreck within two hours.

Sterling was going to have a kitten. A whole litter of kittens. All at once.

"Thank you, Chronicler," I said in as sweet a tone as I could choke out. "We'll pay the price immediately, but we're very confused about the SilverPaw's intentions."

"Obviously," she said sarcastically.

I ended the call.

Something about all of this was gruesomely wrong. It was too grabby. Too rash. Even if I factored in my father's arrogance, plus a little extra, it still came up short. He would never risk his status before the Elder Council. Quietly fleecing powerless wolves, perhaps, but risking his own neck and SilverPaw's reputation before another Elder? Never.

This reeked of Jerron, but Jerron didn't have this kind of influence over anyone. Unless my father intended to make Jerron the SilverPaw Alpha by letting him bring in a big kill and negotiating a high bride-price, but only Alphas and fathers could negotiate bride-prices. Well, it wouldn't have been the first time in the recent past my father had stopped playing by the rules and tried to keep it out of public view.

"I don't think we'll end up worse off than we already are," I told Sterling over evening coffee. He had spent the remainder of his day in his office working on his side of things. I had made Jun work out with me, then had a very long shower and forced myself to study.

We stood by the huge windows overlooking the city. I had coffee, he had a double whiskey. Cye and Jun were in awe that I had just called up the AmberHowl. Even Burian was impressed. Sterling hadn't asked how I had done it. Not yet, anyway.

Sterling took a long drink of his whiskey.

I added, "Which is to say we're screwed either way."

"Your father's reaction is not expected nor welcome."

"Don't you mean the SilverPaw Alpha?" I asked bitterly.

"I've met people who are so used to getting their own way that they sort of lose their minds when cornered. It makes them very unpredictable."

There was another consideration, "We don't know what the politics between SilverPaw and AmberHowl are. My father did support the AmberHowl elevation to Elder status. My father might know he's got AmberHowl in his pocket."

"Hmm." Sterling grunted agreement. "Possible. Or the AmberHowl Alpha may be furious your father tried to pull strings. I know I'd be angry. Your father is either being very stupid or very clever. Still," he cocked his head toward me, "this doesn't make sense to me, Winter. This is just off."

"It's probably my brother. My father wants him to be Alpha after him, but Jerron's not exactly doing himself any favors. Let Jerron bring home a big prize to prove his worth. With Daniel as the witness."

"You were never considered for Luna?"

I shook my head. "Elder Packs almost never choose a Luna."

"Foolish."

We stewed in mutual silence for a few minutes. Then I asked, "How do you intend to pay for me, Sterling?"

Sterling smiled at me.

My blood ignited with the hunt. I wanted to run under the moon with Sterling, the scent of prey in our snouts and our fangs ready to sink into flesh and bone. Sterling had to be as glorious a wolf as he was a physical specimen of a man. He couldn't be anything less.

"I'm putting together a lovely little portfolio of assets," he informed me in a low, devious tone that tap-danced the length of my spine. "Stocks and an ownership stake I have in a small little company. It's not worth much, but it will be very inconvenient for your father to own, because the company is profitable and pays dividends."

"The gift that keeps on giving! You are generous." I wanted to just grab the front of his shirt in both hands and kiss him, then rip it off him and run my hands all over his chiseled torso.

"I thought of giving him art, or gold," Sterling sipped his whiskey. "But he could just shove those things in his basement. Stocks and a company stake come with legal obligations. He's going to have to hire people to manage it for him. He'll pay taxes on the value today, and then when he goes to liquidate, get mauled again."

That apple would be full of poison, razor blades and worms like the worst of Halloween treats.

"If he's clever and hires smart people to advise him, it's a glorious nest egg for the SilverPaw and I wish them well. If he's just trying to rob the piggy bank..." a shrug. Then a smug little smile. "He's growled at the wrong wolf."

"Can he end up in real trouble for this? With humans? How nasty is this apple?"

"Federal prison flavored."

My eyes widened.

Sterling noticed. "Second thoughts? I could give him gold bars to put in the basement. This is a lot of money, Winter. Enough that the authorities are going to pay attention. If your dad, ahem, the SilverPaw Alpha, pulls this holier-than-thou crap he could end up in a lot of human trouble."

It required thought. We could just pay off the SilverPaw, and not endanger them. The money could really help the pack in their struggles, and there were a lot of wolves in SilverPaw who had absolutely no say in this.

Jun watched from the couch, face solemn.

It didn't change the facts of what had happened. My father had probably anticipated resistance from Sterling, and my horror, but he had no reason to think we could have fought back. My part in this had already been anticipated.

Except I wasn't blindly obedient little wolf he thought I was.

Even if the Elder Council found out, they'd never openly chastise him. The majority of wolves would never know. Oh, he'd lose prestige and face, but only in private. There'd be no public reckoning. Not when it was just one incident that he could probably find a way to spin and justify. Everyone would keep right on thinking he was trustworthy and noble. And I'd be left wondering if he'd do this to *me*, his own daughter, then what else had he done?

I wanted to be able to sleep at night.

"If he wants to play with fire, let him burn." I flung the words with contempt. "Just make sure you and I are well clear of the flames!"

"Whew," Burian said not quite under his breath. "Damn."

"I told you, man," Jun shook his head, eyes wide. "Don't fuck with the Boss Lady."

Burian raised his beer bottle to Jun. They clinked.

Pack first. Family second.

A CAGED WOLF

Throwing together the details of my bride-gift occupied Sterling's every moment. It had to be completed before we married in a few days. He came to bed long after I was asleep, and usually was on the phone with someone in some far-flung time zone before I even woke up.

Jun and Burian both attended school. Jun had personal training clients, and Burian tutored. Cye always had class, was busy around the apartment, or running errands—something. He was like a hummingbird who flitted from place to place.

The lack of any available escorts meant confinement. It could not be helped.

Desperate to get out and all alone on Friday afternoon—having been cooped up for two days, and my brain was mush from watching catch-up lectures for class—I decided to prowl around the building. I had errantly assumed it was an apartment building like a hundred others I had seen.

Silly me.

There was an indoor pool, a library, reading rooms, a vast room for parties and entertainment, a sound-proofed music room with grand piano, a small theater for private screenings, and a "meditation wing," which involved a yoga studio on one side, a completely sound-proofed room with a single futon mattress (for "stillness" the door plaque said), and a large room with a rock garden and indoor koi pond.

The rock garden was laid out in two squares with a carefully constructed koi pond merging the two halves. A path led from one end of the squares to the next so you could walk through the groomed sand, and over a small bridge to stand directly over the kois' abode.

I stood on the bridge and looked down at the black-bottomed koi pond in wonder. The big, fat fish ambled lazily throughout their lily-pad kingdom. It was not a trivial little slot of water, but a meandering creek about three feet wide and probably that deep, sprinkled with lily pads, koi and a few turtles. Great effort had gone into making it appear as natural as possible, and I sensed the fondness that the caretaker tended this place with.

In front of the garden was dark-paneled wood flooring with a few scattered cushions and mats. The ceiling there was normal height, but above the garden the ceiling extended two floors, with horizontal planters all along the walls to the glass ceiling. Real sunlight shone down onto the garden, and the air was blissfully clean and clear. I could *breathe*.

"Do you have names, fishes?" I asked them. Koi could live a very long time. Maybe some of these fat koi had been given names by their caretakers. They were in an array of colors, not just the orange and white. Some were brilliant gold, some were the same seductive silvery blue of the moon, some were black and white.

My phone buzzed in my pocket. My little pocket harbinger.

Sterling >> Where are you!

He had left before breakfast in a hurry and had said he wouldn't be back before six. Whatever he wanted couldn't be good.

Me >> Zen garden.

Sterling >> omw.

Five minutes later the door opened and Sterling stepped in. He hadn't even taken off his long gray coat or black gloves. He brought with him a storm on his shoulders that disrupted the patient calm of the garden.

"Why are you back so soon?" I asked.

"Got sent home for the day." He tugged off his gloves. His handsome face bent into a scowl. "I have to wait for other people to do their jobs."

"So you got told you were underfoot and to go play outside," I translated.

He shoved his gloves into his pocket like he intended to put his fist through the lining. "More like play in traffic. Have you heard from the AmberHowl?"

Sterling had two assistants to harangue. Last time I had checked, I was Winter, and hadn't magically transformed into Oscar or Andre. "No."

"Why not?"

I tapped nails on the bridge's wood. He shouldn't disrupt this place. "I don't know."

"Well, what does it mean?" He came right up to the edge of the garden. "Why not? Why haven't we heard from them?"

If this was how Sterling treated his staff, I hoped he paid them very well. "What crawled in your ear and started biting?"

"Winter, I've had a very stressful day, and no one seems able to get anything done."

A lot of ugly retorts passed through my brain. About how I was in an enchanted castle waiting out a storm, how Sterling's little pack couldn't ensure my safety or command enough respect anyone would care. How I wasn't staff. A lot of ugly things I wasn't proud of thinking at all.

"I don't know." I didn't hide my annoyance. One of the fishes flapped its tail and broke the surface with a splash. "It means the AmberHowl haven't told us 'no' outright. But that's all it means."

He growled and swore under his breath. I didn't recognize the language. He checked his phone, swore again at the world's general incompetence and lack of urgency, and the way his knuckles clenched around his phone I thought he might crush it. Instead, he pushed it back into his pocket with the same force he had visited upon his gloves.

The fishes splashed again. A yellow and a tricolor were

having a little fishy-tiff right under me.

"We're upsetting the fish," I told him. "Let's go."

"Upsetting fish? Winter, they barely have brains."

I descended from the bridge, stepped across the path through the sand and came alongside my stormy mate. His anger swirled around him like the clouds of a storm, and he was the seething center of convection. "You're upsetting their little pea-brains."

"They're fish. And they're not the only thing I've encountered today with pea-brains and more power than they should have. When will we hear from the AmberHowl?"

"No idea."

He made another little noise of disgust.

That was enough of his Mr. Bigshot behavior. He could come in angry and frustrated and raging at the world, but I wasn't his chew toy. "Sterling, I'm not your goddamn secretary, and the AmberHowl aren't some humans you're doing business with. So back off. I've done everything I can do."

Sterling's jaw visibly clenched. I heard his teeth grind together. He stared at the stone garden with a gaze so hot and angry it could have turned sand to glass.

With very delicate care, I took one step back from him.

He snapped his head back around. Noting the slightly longer distance between us, he said, "Will we hear from them at all?" He sounded peculiar, sort of ugly and despairing, all at the same time.

"Yes." At least I could give him that bit of assurance. "Wolves do call back. Until then, we wait."

"In limbo." His anger returned to a bubbling simmer.

"It beats being in hell."

"Well, there is that. And if they don't, we're on our own? There is no one else? No other Chronicler?"

"It would be in very poor taste to go Chronicler

shopping."

"So this is a one-shot deal. We make it happen, or we don't."

"We cannot *make* it happen. It's on the AmberHowl."

He became unnaturally still. Like he had been caged up for so long he had forgotten how to move, and simply stood rooted and broiling within.

The bond was an illusion; yes, we had been chosen for each other, fused together. It could mislead me into thinking I knew him when I didn't. Sterling had a hot temper that I found appealing, but I also wasn't completely convinced it wouldn't turn violent. Many people had bad tempers, and their tempers were harmless. They'd never do anything but scream and shout and maybe punch a hole in a wall.

Sterling's anger burned hot and intense, and there was an edge to it I respected. I just didn't know yet if his anger only boiled, or if it exploded.

My pragmatic brain started stepping through scenarios again, but as usual, I didn't have many answers. These were questions I had never considered. What would I do if he lashed out at me? Fight back? What did other she-wolves do when trapped with an abusive mate? Did they go to warform to defend themselves? Did it escalate into a bloody battle? Females could shift faster than males, so if I went warform, could I hurt Sterling before he really hurt me? Did they go wolf and run or cower somewhere? Did they remain human and take it? How far did it escalate?

What would I do when we had children?

After a couple of almost intolerable moments he looked back at me. He still seemed to vibrate with anger, but his voice was more familiar now. "Have you seen the roof?"

"Roof? I don't normally go prowling on roofs. I am not a cat."

"Are you afraid of heights?"

"No."

"Come on, then. I'll show you."

The roof was not the actual true roof, but was a mezzanine level several stories below. It was like a terrace garden: in the large center area were garden beds and grass, which were all now dead and brown and crispy-frozen, some corner areas for sitting amongst green, but all around the center landscaping was a stone track. Perfect for running.

The wind cut across the roof in gusts, the air was damp and bitterly cold. It burned my cheeks and made my eyes water. I huddled into my thin cardigan against the brutal elements. Sterling and I were the only souls up there.

"It's damp and brown now," Sterling told me. "But it's beautiful in warm weather."

Nobody had told me I could forgo the treadmill and run on top of a building. And that there was a lovely little stone patio in the center of everything where I could sit eye level with the rest of the skyline, watch clouds roll in, and surf the internet from a steel and glass perch.

Sterling shrugged off his long wool coat and held it for me. "Here."

I hesitated. His anger seemed to have cooled a little bit, but he still seethed. "I'm fine."

"You're freezing."

He lifted the jacket over my shoulders. His scent briefly engulfed me before the wind carried it away. Anger, frustration, and two other things I had never smelled on him before: fear and anxiety.

Sterling was a worrier. If he had told me he had worried himself gray, I'd have believed it. How strange. It gave a different color to the anger.

We walked to the dying grass. It had been two weeks since I had walked on grass, and I relished the crunch of frozen blades under my shoes. A luxury apartment complex with a koi pond and a rooftop running track and a huge indoor pool were hard to argue with as far as prisons went.

Sterling kept searching the skyline for something.

If ever there was a wolf who desperately needed to run and bark and howl, it was him, right then. I thought of asking him when the last time he had shifted was, or if he had ever been afflicted with City Sickness, but I didn't feel like I could pry just then. It was one thing to never feel the need to shift from one form to another. Some of us really did spend our lives in one form. Most of us felt the need to shift at least occasionally, and it was unhealthy to suppress the need over and over again.

"Is there a problem with the gift?" I ventured.

"Just that it's not ready yet. Nothing is ready yet. I—"

His phone rang. I fished around in his myriad of pockets and handed it to him. He seemed hopeful for a moment, then his face darkened. The wind blew his scent toward me: more anxiety, but of a different flavor. Nervous anxiety. He swore again and put the phone to his ear. Whoever it was didn't get the ass-chewing I expected.

"Ronald," he said, sounding more tired than genial. A long pause. "I haven't—no, yes. Yes. No. Ronald, I—yes, yes, I'm flattered but—no." He rubbed his head like it hurt. "I'll call you back. Yes, I will call you back. Ten minutes, I just got here."

He hung up, went to put the phone in his pocket, realized he wasn't wearing his coat, looked at me.

"Problem?" Sterling now seemed like a wolf who had just been dunked in water and hauled out.

"That's Ronald. You don't know him. Yet. But I'm in the middle of a very large business deal with him. We've done some deals before in the past. He's in town and wants to do dinner. I've put him off the past couple of nights, but he's being pushy. Wants to talk shop."

"And you're not interested?"

"No. The issue is he insists you come. He found out we're getting married and wants to take us out. Tonight. And he's not taking 'no' for an answer. It's not smart to decline this sort of thing. It's code for 'fuck you.' I've been putting him off all day with the excuse of I needed to talk to you. I was hoping he'd get distracted by some other obligation but that's not happening."

"Hmm." Secretly I was desperate to get out, Sterling was too. This explained the caged wolf, at least in part. We couldn't take Jun or Burian with us on this sort of outing. Good allies were also rare, and those relationships needed to be nurtured.

"This is a big part of my work," Sterling told me. "It's going to keep coming up. Let's do drinks, come to my ski lodge for the weekend, meet me in Bali, I'll be in London next Tuesday with So And So, you should come and I'll introduce you. I can only turn down so many invitations before I stop getting them."

If I hadn't had that notebook we'd have been severely screwed, since we had no relationships to fall back upon. Even within a pack bonds required nurturing and care. "I understand."

"Well, you do. But they don't." His face constricted in a prolonged wince while he rubbed between his eyes. By now he had to be freezing cold. The wind tore at his tie and suit coat. His shirt was a bright pink, of all colors, which was the brightest spot on that roof just then.

"We could go," I ventured.

"Winter. There are wanderers watching this building every moment. I'm not sure if going out at night is—"

"Well, we could. Are we going to go somewhere like the diamond district where the wanderers won't go?"

"Yes," he stopped rubbing his head. "You're game?"

"The way I look at it this is our job." The world wasn't going to stop spinning. Sterling's money and our cunning were the only two things we had going for us right then. "If we can slip away without the wanderers knowing, we shouldn't have a problem, right?"

"Great idea." Sterling suddenly brightened like a bolt of lightning had shot out of the sky straight into his backside. He seized my hand and hauled me after him back into the building. "Come on."

SNEAKING AROUND

"What are you going on about?" I tried to ask him, but he was already on his phone. I waited impatiently while he called Ronald.

"Can you be ready by six-thirty?" he asked me after he had already told Ronald we'd be there at seven.

"Yes." Did I have a choice? No. And I felt like I had missed the Obvious Bus—what the hell idea had I had? Because I didn't recall making a suggestion. The pack was going to protest bitterly about this.

On that last point I wasn't wrong. Burian got home before Jun, came wandering down the hallway thinking we were up to mischief of the naked sort, but realized fairly quickly that while we were in states of undress, it was to go out. Not stay in.

He stood in the doorway and glared at Sterling. "The fuck, Sterling?"

"Business dinner," Sterling told him.

I watched from the bathroom mirror. I could only see Sterling's back, but I had a clear view of a very grouchy Burian.

"Screw your business dinner."

"Can't."

"Are you dense or something?"

"We're going to sneak out of the building. They're always waiting at the front door. There's a way to get out through the garage. It's walled off from the outside for just this reason."

"So we're sneaking out?" This was the great idea Sterling credited me with? My brother had refined sneaking around to a high art, but I was a relative novice.

"We're sneaking out," he confirmed.

"That's your plan. Damn dangerous. And lousy," Burian told Sterling.

"So you'll come downstairs with us and make sure we're not ambushed in the garage."

I pulled my lower eyelid down and slid the pencil across the inside. I hated doing that. Made me so squeamish having the pointy end of a pencil by the globe of my eyeball. It also gave me something to do while Burian and Sterling argued.

"Tinted windows exist for a reason. Town cars come and go all the time out of this building. They've already seen me come in for the evening, Burian."

Clever point. This wasn't a joke, and it was dangerous, but that was the appeal. The same way that crawling into the neighbor's illegal rickety crop-dusting planes had appealed to me. Some temptations I couldn't resist even when I knew I should. Like gas station nachos: so delicious, and so terribly bad for you.

"I'm sure they've got someone covering the back of the building." Burian scowled.

"Maybe. Can't put this off, Burian."

Burian and Sterling argued for a few more minutes. In the end, Burian grudgingly agreed to go downstairs with us, and only if we texted him and Jun so they could meet us when we returned. He wasn't willing to bet against wanderers waiting inside the parking garage.

The matter settled, Burian left us in peace.

I hoped I had done a decent enough job with my attire. My nails needed fills badly. I had chosen a dark maroon dress that hugged my body—hopefully not too much. Mint had helped pick it out, so I was sure it was fine for some venue. Hopefully this was that venue, and this Ronald was not too versed in the finer points of a woman's attire.

"You look lovely," Sterling told me.

"Oh, thank you." His compliment caught me off guard. I looked around for my shoes. I thought I had pulled them out of the closet and now they seemed to have walked away.

"I have something for you." He didn't move from where he was standing.

"You do?" What could he possibly have for me on such short notice?

He went to the dark gray pants he had been wearing previously. He had just tossed them on the bed with the rest of his suit. The room was a bit of a mess in our haste to change. He reached into the pocket and fished out a black velvet box.

"Oh." I realized what it was. I suddenly felt a lump forming in my throat. Which was silly, because I already knew what it was. He opened the box and removed the ring. It glittered between his thumb and forefinger, more beautiful than I had thought it would be.

He picked up my left hand and slid the ring into its place. The metal felt cold. I stared at the shining gems. The blue diamonds reminded me of the necklace from my dream.

He admired my hand. "It suits you, Winter."

My name on his lips made me shiver from the nape of my neck to the point of my tailbone.

And I kissed him.

I slid my arms around his strong shoulders and the shiver spread to my whole body when his hands moved over my waist and hips to hold me close against him. Slow, deep, passionate.

"We need to go," he said in a husky voice that reminded me of old silk and raw velvet. It was like a caress unto itself. His scent was pine and musk and man, thick with a desire that made my blood shake in every vein and capillary.

I didn't unlace my fingers from behind his neck, I enjoyed the corded, muscled strength of his shoulders too much. He was so strong and solid.

His eyes took on a devilish glint. "Business awaits," he all but purred. One hand clasped the small of my back just a few inches too low, while he raised the other hand. With deliberate care, his eyes never leaving mine, he touched his index finger to the hollow of my throat, and pulled downward over my chest. Painful jolts of pleasure snapped through my breasts and arms.

His finger continued its feather-light progression downward until he hooked the maroon fabric, the tip of his finger resting between my lace-confined breasts. He held me pinned by just that finger, and I silently begged for more than just that, I wanted to feel his rough hands over my bare skin, ripping away fabric and lace until I was completely naked. His erection pressed against my hip, rigid and unmistakable, his lust consuming me, and my panties impossibly moist.

Gaia, I wanted him. Right then. Inside me, his fingers pressing into my flesh, taking what belonged only to him, what had only ever belonged to him. What had made him the standard by which I had unknowingly measured every other male, and found them lacking.

The kiss was so hot, so deep, his finger rubbing my nipple, sending shocks through my whole being that made me whimper, his manhood engorged and painful even to him, lewdly thrust against his slacks with just one objective. I wanted to run my hands over him, stroke him, explore his body with my hands and tongue, taste him as he tasted me, hear his rough breathing as he panted my name just before he couldn't hold back anymore.

He would let me do all those things. He would want me to. I wanted to.

He leaned close to me, his whisper ragged. "We have work to do, my Luna," he kissed me once, briefly, and it seared both of us with hungry desire we did not have time for.

I found my voice, breathless, aware of every inch of my flesh in a most peculiar way. "I'll step out if you need a few minutes."

Smug and amused, he informed me, "I only look like I am made of ice, Winter."

His hand slipped a little lower, and he tugged me hard against him. I resisted the urge to reach up, kiss him again. I knew if I did, it would be long and slow, and there'd be no going out that night.

Barely composed myself, "Do I seem surprised? I just asked if you needed a few moments without distraction."

His smile did not widen but did intensify, illuminating his entire face with a feral amusement that made my blood churn. "Go see if Burian is ready."

"So you do need a few moments. Perhaps if you removed your finger," I looked down at my cleavage.

"But you're enjoying it so much," he replied.

I brushed his hand away, he cupped my breast instead. I said, "Say it, Sterling. Tell me you're in no state to walk out of here."

"You just want me to confess to how hard I am? I like this game." The flash of light off his teeth made me click my own.

"Oh, I know," I breathed. He was like an iron rod. I wanted to wrap my lips around him, taste him, feel his fingertips digging into my skin and scalp as I tore control from an Alpha. What would his rigid manhood feel like between my lips? My mind conjured a thousand virgin fantasies, any one of which he could have destroyed or confirmed with a single demand. He felt so large, too large to fit easily within me, and that only made it so much worse, knowing the raw, feral lust that would bring us together, no matter what.

"You are entirely too distracting. Begone, wench." He released me and stepped backwards.

Wench! Lust transmuted into uncontrollable giggles. I plunked myself down on the edge of our bed, and looked anywhere but him, because he was laughing too. My brain grasped for something logical and not funny to cling to so I could float above the giggles.

My shoes! Where were my shoes?! I giggled so hard I snorted, which only made me laugh even harder.

Shoes. Shoes. I needed shoes. My shoes were on the other side of the bed. I slithered my way over there, trying not to cry, snort, or give myself the hiccups. I managed to get one shoe on, then the next.

"Do *you* need a few minutes now?" he asked.

"No, no." I stood up and tried to suppress the laughter bubbling through my voice. Sort of like trying to keep the cap on a shaken bottle of soda. "No, perfectly fine."

He looked down at himself. "Situation under control. Let's go."

"Sterling!" I shoved my hands over my mouth to hold in a squeal of shock or laughter. Not sure. "Did you really just do that?!"

His smile just oozed smugness and he gestured for me to precede him out the door. "What else should I have done?" he asked in an oh-so-reasonable tone of voice. "Or would you have preferred to check for yourself? You can look, Winter. In fact, don't limit yourself to looking."

I couldn't stop giggling.

"Could you focus?" Burian crabbed at me in the elevator as I tried not to snicker to myself about Sterling, who pretended he had no idea what I was on about. "There could be an ambush waiting in the garage."

"I'm fine. I'm fine." I was not fine. I teetered on the edge of another giggle fit.

"She's fine," Sterling told Burian. "Natural reaction."

"Natural reaction to what?" Burian asked.

To what! Oh Gaia! To what! I wheezed on giggles. Sterling opened his mouth to answer, paused, then changed course, "You know, forget I just said that."

"No, go ahead, tell him. Tell him what I'm laughing at!" I squeaked out. I slumped against Burian for support. I certainly couldn't breathe. I couldn't even laugh. It was not possible for my body to laugh that hard, so I just made noises like a suffocating cat.

"Focus, Winter. Focus," Sterling said instead.

Burian huffed. He shoved me upright again. "Get a grip, Luna."

Sterling checked his watch and tried to be dignified.

I fanned myself, and was somewhat composed as the elevator door opened. Burian stepped out first and looked around. Then we passed through two glass doors to the bitterly cold garage. A black town car with heavily tinted windows waited for us. Burian impatiently hustled us into the car and gave the driver the hairy eyeball.

"Burian is not happy," I told Sterling from the relative safety of my seat. I didn't care about Burian being unhappy, but it should at least be acknowledged. I also wanted to think about something other than how tempting Sterling was.

My mind kept conjuring very vivid fantasies.

He reached over to me and took my beringed hand, lifted it to his lips and kissed it lightly. His tongue darted for a brief sweep between my fingers. I suppressed a gasp. "Focus, Sterling, focus."

"I am. On you."

"No," I pulled my hand from his grasp. "My lipstick wouldn't suit you."

"We'll discuss this later."

"Perhaps."

Which was probably just the wrong answer to give to Sterling. Because Sterling loved the hunt.

WHOOPS, TOO MUCH WINE

Ronald was a black man in his fifties, his hair a precise iron-and-salt low fade. He had the physique of a disciplined man who also spent most of his time at a desk, and the face of a man who smiled a great deal for any number of reasons. He could afford to be benevolent because he was so well acquainted with being ruthless.

Ronald chided Sterling for not mentioning he was getting married. He had found out through a mutual business acquaintance, and was annoyed at the lack of a phone call. "And none of us knew you were dating anyone seriously."

"I wasn't aware I needed to keep the world up to date on my comings and goings."

"You're a strange duck, Mortcombe."

"Then everything is going according to plan."

Ronald laughed. He had a big laugh.

Just listening to Ronald and Sterling talk I saw more of the careful dance I had seen at the art gala party: asking enough questions to be genial, but not asking questions that might have had potentially awkward answers.

There was a ritual to it, just as if they had been wolves. There was the greeting, some vague pleasantries that established there were no hostile intentions, then some more personal questions to re-establish that their affiliation was more than business, but nothing deep that might convey a personal allegiance. Trusted business partners, but Ronald would never call us seeking a personal favor.

Confident that I understood the nature of their relationship, I was able to enjoy my wine. Which I should not have been drinking, but it had been poured for me. Nobody asked and nobody would appreciate being told I wasn't twenty-one.

"So, Winter," Ronald asked me as he refreshed my wine with the new bottle that had just been brought, "What do you do?"

"Still a student." Partially a lie, but close enough to the truth. I counted on him not asking too many probing questions.

"Oh? Where are you going to school?"

An excellent way to start my evening: tossed right into the deep end. "I'm a transfer. But still working on transferring somewhere."

"Ahhh. What are you studying?"

"Math and statistics." That was not a lie.

This surprised him. I was always surprised by men who seemed shocked when a woman said she was studying in a technical or scientific field. Out of the corner of my eye I saw Sterling give Ronald a look that conveyed my feelings. Ronald was from my father's generation. Perhaps in his world it was shocking.

"I'm in love with logic," I elaborated. I sure as hell didn't understand wolves or people anymore.

"Is that how you met Sterling?"

"No, matchmaker," Sterling supplied.

I almost snorted wine through my nose. Well, you could call it that! Ronald noticed, but Sterling kept an absolutely straight face. I patted my lips with a napkin and did my best to not look like I had just swallowed a fish. Sterling kept talking, "You should try it. For your... fifth wife? Maybe you need an outside objective opinion."

"I have a weakness for a certain type of lady who invariably breaks my heart and takes all my money. And fourth," he held up four fingers. "Fourth wife. I'm an eternal optimist."

"Right. Optimist. And you're optimistic I'm going to take three points on the deal. I don't need Winter to tell me that math is bad."

"I could get my calculator to tell you." Not that I had any idea how much a "point" was or how to do that math.

Sterling smiled at me. I caught a whiff of genuine amusement from him. Whew. I hadn't made an idiot of myself. Good thing Ronald wasn't a wolf. He'd be able to tell how nervous I was on the inside. But the wine was helping—when I wasn't snorting it through my nose, of course. Needed to be careful. I eyed my half-full glass. Time to slow down.

"I didn't realize I'd be outnumbered at this dinner." Ronald grinned.

Sterling's tone took on a bite of annoyance. "You thought I'd marry a stupid woman?"

Ronald didn't miss a step. "I thought she was an art aficionado."

I almost blurted out something to the effect of "there's a difference?" but caught myself just in time. Instead, I said something almost as bad. "I just adapt quickly and blend in with the herd."

That was the wine talking.

Ronald's grin didn't falter but something changed about it. Damn, I had shown my fangs and devious side. Up until then he had dismissed me as being of no real consequence. Not to say that he thought I was mindless arm-candy, but that I wouldn't be any kind of factor in his plans.

Now he figured that I was more involved in this deal than I was. That I would advise Sterling, and even worse, Ronald might try to involve me in the conversations where my ignorance would be fully exposed. I didn't doubt that I could learn everything I needed to know about Sterling's empire, but right then, at that table, I had overplayed my hand.

Annnnnd insulting everyone at the art gala and calling them a herd and pretty much stating I had faked the whole thing was not wise. I silently vowed to never speak of art while drinking ever again.

Sterling didn't seem rattled, just highly entertained. Maybe I had said what he had always wanted to, and I was in some sort of position to say it when he wasn't.

Ronald, for his part, wasn't intimidated by the perceived shift in intellectual power at the table. An otherwise bland, friendly-but-not business dinner had become intriguing.

I focused on smiling like I knew what the hell I was about and gave my water glass a little more attention.

The menu read like a foreign language, and no Cye to translate. That meant playing food roulette. There was a dish involving octopus, squid, some things I didn't recognize and squid ink. It was the ink part that sold me. Ronald ordered the steak—I thought that was an overly safe choice—and Sterling had something involving liver and a stuffed quail. When his dish arrived it looked gross but smelled intriguing, and I half-wished I had gotten whatever mysterious food medley from hell he had selected.

My seafood dish was excellent. The octopus suckers stuck to my tongue. It tasted so fresh I suspected everything on the plate had very recently been alive.

All during this Sterling and Ronald discussed the deal that had brought us here. It involved purchasing a large tract of land in Canada that had been fairly well mutilated by gold mining, then come up dry for crude speculators. The plan was to reclaim the land and then sub-license it back as either a wind farm or solar farm, while doubling as a natural preserve.

Ronald had gotten back some geological studies that suggested there may be veins of gold located in a corner that had not been mined previously, and Sterling was dead set against more mining. There was also a lot of conversation about the Canadian government, and upcoming bills to underwrite wind farm verses solar. In short, things that mere mortals would not have cared about, but people with millions of dollars paid close attention to. It made my ears bleed and my brain do pirouettes in my skull.

"We're not buying it to set up a mining operation, Ronald." Sterling balked once again at even discussing mining.

"I know, I know, but it wouldn't take us but six months," Ronald said. "And we can start work restoring the rest of the tract on the opposite side. By the time we work our way over to the prospecting side we'll be done."

Sterling just glared over the table. "You know I've never been interested in mining."

Ronald sighed. "You have your blind spots, Mortcombe."

This deal was very much not done yet, and this mining business could be a big point of contention. Ronald had brought the geological reports with him. Sterling refused to look. He brushed them away with his hand, "No. Not interested. Continuing the mining operations was never part of the original conversation."

"I'd like to see them." I had been sitting like a patient lump for all of dinner. I figured I could read some geological survey summaries that had been prepared for non-geologist investors. Ronald handed them over while he and Sterling continued to talk. Their words were pleasant but their tones steel-edged.

The graphs and technical details made no sense, but there was a summary in the front couple of pages. No actual gold had been found, but they had found concentrations of quartz and magnetite. Those indicated potential gold deposits. But there was also nickel, which indicated possible platinum, or even diamond veins.

Ronald's thinking made sense: the area he wanted to mine was at a far corner of the land, not all of it. Possible big pay day without harming the overall mission. At worst delay it a few years, but with considerable additional risks and costs. Sterling could possibly contract out his claim and let another group of speculators take their chances.

The waiter brought us our coffee and desserts. For me there was a bowl of vanilla ice cream blended with strawberries and mint. Ronald and Sterling continued their friendly sparring session. Two alpha males grumbling and pacing in front of each other, not growling but with body language that communicated they didn't want a fight but weren't going to back down either.

Ronald excused himself to use the restroom.

Sterling turned his gaze to me. "You haven't said much."

"I think I said enough earlier."

"It was a little off-color. As in wine-colored."

I wrapped a stray piece of hair around my finger. "Sorry about that."

"You put him on the defensive. Now he's gnawing at my ankles."

"He was always going to do that. He wants to mine the land, and you've dug in for reasons that sum up to 'I don't wanna.'"

"I was counting on those surveys showing nothing. I wasn't prepared to argue against it. Of course he ambushes me with the information at dinner. And you're right. I don't want to. I don't care what those surveys show."

I cocked my head to the side, realizing part of Sterling's resistance. "This is the high dollar table. It's a little too rich for your blood."

"Ronald is from the next rung up." He didn't appreciate being the smaller wolf.

Ahhh, that made sense. If he backed out, it had to be for reasons that weren't weakness. Sterling had the respect of an alpha stronger than he was and recognized him as a potential ally. That meant a very great deal. "I see we're not so different."

"I often wonder do the wolves get it from the humans, or

the humans from the wolves," Sterling mused. He pondered this a moment, then his gaze turned into something that warmed my insides. "You do look lovely, Winter."

"Hmm-mmm." Sterling and his sudden changes of subjects! "Flatterer."

"Will it get me everything?"

It had me flustered inside but was a lot more fun than thinking about him getting in over his head. We were in up to our necks in wolf drama. The last thing I wanted was our human life falling apart. "I'm not sure. You can try."

"I intend to," he informed me.

I tapped the survey report on the table. He needed to focus on something else for a few more minutes. "Just tell him you'll think about it. And go home and think about how you'll get out of it. He's a bigger wolf than you. He's going to see through your 'I don't wanna' pretty quick. Give him a few inches just to get some breathing room, before he walks away and takes this somewhere else."

Sterling let out a long, angry breath. "Fine. Fine. But you," he pointed at me, "Watch the wine. Your tongue is going to get us both into trouble at this rate."

"Deal."

"And I want a reward for putting my tail between my legs."

"If you're going to be vulgar," I sensed where he was going with that, "you'll regret it."

He grinned at me.

"I suggest you go back to flattery."

Ronald saved us from our wine-induced flirting, but the old wolf knew exactly what we were doing. "Convince him to at least read it yet, Winter?"

Damn. He was sharp. Had his trip to the bathroom been deliberate and well-timed? "I have," I told him sweetly. Let Ronald think I was on his side in this. And that I even understood what his side was. We couldn't afford for the only thing going for us to turn pear-shaped.

"I'll look at it. There better be something really special in there, Ronald," Sterling said.

"Call me next week," Ronald said easily.

Sterling stood up and offered me his hand. Dinner was over. I thought we were beating a bit of a hasty retreat, and maybe we were. But Sterling's not-very-subtle-at-all look at my cleavage told me the hunt from earlier had never left his mind.

THE NOT SO INNOCENT VIRGIN

Sterling had his hands on me, and his body against mine, even before the door to the car was closed.

"Sterling," I thought I'd dissolve into a little puddle. "Sterling, Jun and Burian will—"

He ignored me. His left hand pushed along my thigh and shoved my dress up over my hip. His palm swept over my rump and his fingers met just bare skin. "Naughty."

"Thongs don't leave panty lines!"

"They don't leave much to my imagination either." His fingers curled into my flesh and he pulled me hard against him.

"Sterling," I managed to push him away just enough so I could talk to him. "Jun and Burian. We have to text them. They'll be waiting. Remember? *Remember?*" I was the not-so-sober one, but apparently my compromised sobriety was worth more than Sterling's brain at that moment.

"I remember." His lips placed little caresses along my neck, under my jaw, right over my exposed jugular. It would have been so easy to just give in.

His hands pulled me rough against him, his breath a roar. "We should have a little fun, Winter."

Oh, I wanted to! But, with supreme effort, I pushed him back again. "Jun. Burian."

"Forget them," he growled, his mind on exactly one thing and one thing only: getting his body inside mine as fast as possible.

He yanked my dress down over my breasts, lifted the flesh to his lips and I gasped, then moaned.

"Come here, Winter," his voice was a command, bidding me to straddle his engorged, hungry body. He didn't wait for me to obey, instead he seized me and pulled me across his thighs.

My dress high on my own legs, his hands seeming to be everywhere, and I gasped, looking down at him, startled and thrilled at how rough he was. He tugged me forward, his erection pushing flush against me, teasing my sex through the combined fabric of my wet panties and his pants. He admired me, fingers of one hand digging into my hips, and the other hand teasing my breast.

No, we couldn't just forget the others, or what was at stake, even though it was hard to remember anything. "Jun. Burian."

His gaze smoldered. With one hand still on my rump holding me against him so I did not escape, he fished his phone out of his pocket. As he tapped out a text, the heat chilled enough that I felt the leather of the seat under my knees, and wondered how many other couples had done *exactly* what we were about to do on that very seat.

Moment over.

I tried to squirm out of his grip. He held tighter. "Content?" He tossed his phone aside. It bounced off the seat onto the floor somewhere.

"You shouldn't dismiss them. Or are you too distracted?"

He was *very* distracted, if that's what we cared to call it.

I squirmed off his lap, he humored me. I meaningfully looked down at his hand on my pale flesh. Then back at him.

"I'm enjoying that," he stated. "And you taste, sweet Luna, of desire."

"I'm certain you are, but we aren't going to be couple five-hundred-and-something to christen this backseat."

He sighed dramatically, feigning being more annoyed than he was. Sterling enjoyed it when his prey fought back a little bit. Or a lot. He may have sighed, but it couldn't hide the glimmer in his eyes, or the way he practically clicked his teeth. I pushed his wrist. He didn't let go. I gave him what he wanted and shoved harder.

Only for Sterling would I be willing prey and play that game.

I slid backwards to my own seat and shimmied and squirmed to right my skirt. He watched, then tried to recapture me. I swatted his hand away, and pressed myself against my side of the car. "Didn't we just talk about this, Sterling?" I wasn't completely sure he wouldn't get what he wanted in the end. That made the game that much more fun.

"I'm not sure," Sterling informed me. "I do know you smell better than dessert, and I fully intend on having a taste."

The little pragmatic virgin within me squealed a horrible, "*Oh Gaia, no!*" while the far more vocal hussy made some non-specific squeal of shocked delight. I think the look on my face must have been absolutely priceless.

"Do I play too rough?" He cocked his head slightly to the side as if this thought bewildered him.

He certainly didn't, and if he had half a snout he'd smell that I was anything but intimidated. I was only backed off by the matter of how many other couples might have entertained themselves on that very backseat. I tried to figure out how to tell him that without throwing a wet blanket on the whole evening.

Sterling jumped ahead with a question I hadn't expected, and one he clearly hadn't expected to ask. "Winter, are you a virgin?" He drew out the last word to almost three syllables, like he had never even considered this as a possibility.

"What?" Of course I was a virgin. My father would have beaten me with a 2x4 if I had even a handprint on me!

His face shifted to a lopsided half-smile of bewilderment, surprise, and discomfort.

"Ah... yes?" This was awkward and uncomfortable. I pulled at the hem of my skirt and tried not to squirm.

"No." He didn't believe me.

"Absolutely! Not a fingerprint on me except yours." I

gave a dignified sniff.

He rewarded my haughty declaration by looking at me like I had just started glub-glub'ing like a fish.

"This is a problem?" Confusion reigned right then. I had assumed he would assume that I was a virgin, because I came from such a traditional upbringing.

"No. " His expression was one of total, complete, non-comprehension.

"You thought I slept around?" I asked him.

"Women who like sex aren't sluts, Winter," he said with sudden annoyance, like it was a stereotype he tired of. "Just... not what I was expecting. You're... ah... um... ah... feisty."

Feisty? What, he had expected me to be some delicate, cowering little virgin, all squeals and "oh no, don't, that's dirty" and "oh, I'm not sure about this?" I was no little squishy pink human! And here he acted like I had done something wrong, or deceived him in some way. Maybe he had expected his mate to come with some training. I scowled at him. "You're five poorly chosen words away from sleeping on the couch tonight."

"Well, I'm glad I asked." Sterling chose his five words with some care.

"Does it make a difference?"

"It makes a difference to me."

"Why should it do that?!" This didn't merit a conversation at all. I thought most males wanted virgins anyway. Or at least didn't care one way or the other! Of course I'd end up with the one male who didn't want a virgin, for whatever weird reason made sense in his brain. "So what? It's a problem with a simple solution, assuming I don't bite you somewhere you'll remember forever first!"

He almost said something. Then switched to a different logic tree and reverted to his smoldering behavior of five minutes earlier. "Well, I'd have never suggested some fun here if I had known. The backseat of a car is so... cliché. So high school."

I laughed. "That's not what bothered me!"

He looked at the ceiling. "Is there anything else I should know?"

"I still don't see why you *need* to know it." I rolled my eyes.

"We'll make it a moot point shortly."

His phone dinged. He reached into his pocket, didn't find it. Patted his other pockets. "I just had it, didn't I?"

"You threw it somewhere in your eagerness to put that hand on me," I reminded him.

"Ahhh. Yes. I have my priorities."

"Clearly." I nudged him with my toe again. He flashed me a grin that made my insides squish.

He felt around on the floor and retrieved it. He was most certainly not putting that hand on me now. Covered in grit and road salt and Gaia-knew-what. Nope. He was just going to have to wait until we got back to the flat.

"Burian and Jun," he reported. "Our chaperones."

"Don't tell them that. It will give them delusions of grandeur."

"Jun has already threatened me within an inch of my life."

"Jun threatened you?"

"He told me if I dared to presume certain things from you, and he found out about it, he'd turn me into butter and smear me on his toast."

"You let him threaten you?"

"I don't object to the pack holding me to a high standard of behavior." He dusted off his phone and put it in its usual pocket.

"Really." Interesting idea. My own father despised anyone questioning him. Given recent events I was less inclined to think favorably of this.

"My father taught me a leader has to expect as much of

himself as he expects of his team."

I liked the sound of that. Very noble. Reasonable. Strong. He had opened the door, time to finally find out about Sterling's father. "Your father is an Alpha?"

Sterling frowned. "Well, not exactly. I'm adopted."

"So your adoptive father is an Alpha."

"No," Sterling said, "he's human."

ONE NIGHT, TWO DESSERTS

If I had been completely sober his revelation would have startled me. But I wasn't sober, he wasn't the first human-reared wolf I had ever met, and I had already been steeled for a revelation of a considerable order of magnitude. In fact, if his "dubious past" was he was simply human-adopted, that was so much better than some of the other bodies that could have been buried in the backyard.

Being raised by humans wasn't unheard of, and it wasn't against the Law. It happened a great deal more than most wolves liked to think, despite how it was frowned upon, and the stigmas that came with it.

Sterling watched me with wary uncertainty. "I thought you knew."

"My father didn't tell me anything about you except your name, remember? I'm not even sure he knows. Does he know?"

"I can't imagine he doesn't," Sterling said with caution.

Well, come to think of it, my father might not know about the *adoptive* human father. He had glossed over Sterling's male line entirely, but now it all made sense. Sterling's biological father had never been in the picture, which *probably* made Sterling the result of an unmated pair. Depending on when Sterling's adoptive father had come into his life, my father might not know about him.

It might be an important point, it might not.

"Does your father know you aren't human?" I had met three human-reared wolves when I had been a child. All three had different stories. None of the stories had happy endings.

"Yes."

"So is your mother your biological mother?"

"Yes. She married a human."

Important distinction: she *married* a human, not a human mate. I filed that away as well, still relieved everything was so simple. Stigmas be damned, I was beyond caring. It could have been so much worse. I changed the subject from his pedigree to my now having acquired a human extended family. "They're not coming to the wedding?"

Sterling actually smiled a tiny bit. "They're off glacier-watching in the far north. They'll be back in about a month."

His mother was likely a lone wolf who lived as a human, and probably had for a very long time. Maybe most of Sterling's life. If his mother had gone human, her son having a mate might not be popular with her. His father might not accept Gaia's will as a reason for his wealthy son to marry some random woman from Montana. "Because they don't approve of us?"

"My father doesn't really understand this whole 'mates business,' as he calls it. My mother is pleased. She won't cut her vacation short, but you'll have to meet her to understand. Are you going to put up a fuss and demand they're there? Because that would not go over well at all."

Even before the bride-price fiasco I wouldn't have expected my family to show up, but my family was all wolves. Sterling's family was partially human, and humans put a lot of value on marriages. I had expected they'd want to come right back to celebrate. But that wasn't a fight I was willing to have.

Instead, I smiled and nudged him with my foot. "No. I hope you have only told them good things about me."

"I haven't had a chance to tell them much. Unless it's on fire or dying, they have strict rules about being bothered on vacation. We are neither on fire nor dying—"

"Well, you did say just a few minutes ago how I would kill you."

"And if you happen to be the death of me, their numbers are in your phone, remember?"

If there was any evidence of how little time I had spent scrolling through the numbers, it was the fact that "Dad" and "Mom" hadn't leapt out at me.

Sterling's eyes trailed up and down my bare thighs.

I put my heeled foot on the inside of his knee. "Tsk tsk. And what were you just saying about needing to be gentle with your little virgin mate?"

He looked down at my foot. I pushed a little onto the heel so it dug oh-so-slightly into his skin. He rewarded me with a feral grin that showed his white teeth. "I do not have to have gentle thoughts."

"Oh, I know your thoughts are not gentle." I pushed a little deeper. I wasn't going to encourage gentle thoughts either. Gentle thoughts sounded so boring.

He grasped my ankle and lifted it away from his leg. "Good." He very gently bent my knee and guided my foot back to the floor, "We are almost there. We'll pick this up when we get to our room."

I shivered with anticipation.

Sterling stayed on his side of the car, rubbing his chin with one hand, and getting his mind right for the brief transfer between the car and the apartment building.

I straightened my skirt. There would be about two minutes where we were vulnerable, and if we had the stink of lust in our snouts we'd be prime targets. I tried to distract myself with how badly I needed to get my nails done. Another day and the gaps would be unsightly. Yes. Terribly unsightly. I'd have to get them done before Tuesday.

So I could rake them down Sterling's back.

Jun and Burian provided a much needed—but unwelcome—wet blanket. They stood in coats, hands shoved in pockets, and faces dark. They were in a foul, surly mood. Jun especially. He and Burian hustled Sterling and I into the building like it was an abduction.

"You're late." Jun turned on us once we were safely in the

apartment.

"We were starting to get worried," Burian agreed. Cye slunk out from the back and gave us a fearsome stink-eye. Even Cye was mad!

We *were* late. We had said we'd be back by ten, and it was now almost eleven, but that was barely an hour. They acted like we had stumbled in just before dawn. Tough crowd.

"We're back now," Sterling's calm, paternal voice would have made me want to bite something, but nobody else lunged at him.

"Good," Cye declared in tone too cheerful for my liking, "Now we can have dessert! I'll pop it in the oven, and it will be ready in just a few minutes!" He clapped his hands and darted into the kitchen. I noticed he was wearing his *DTF: Down To Fondant* apron.

Dessert? They had waited for us to have dessert? Ten o'clock was normally dessert and television, but that was a ritual that required Sterling and I to be present? So this grouchiness was due to their collective blood sugar being low, and Cye holding the kitchen hostage?

"But we've alrea—" I started to say, but Cye had disappeared. "I'd like a shower, Cye!"

"Oh no," he caroled back. "No time! Everyone just sit down!"

Burian muttered something about finally, and about damn time, gave a final 'humph' and drifted toward the sofas. Jun followed him, but not before giving Sterling and I the most sugar-sweet, ever-most-innocent look I had ever seen. He would have made any high school mean girl proud with that expression.

"Sterling," I whispered out of the side of my mouth.

"Winter," he whispered back.

"I think we just got cockblocked."

MUSCLE

A phone call jarred us awake at three. I was used to ignoring multiple buzzes throughout the night, but his phone never actually rang before five-thirty.

I rolled over and didn't bother to lift my head off the pillow. Sterling mumbled something, extended one arm and felt along his nightstand for the phone. "What, Oscar?"

He put his face back down into his pillow while he listened.

Then he raised his head again. "Fine, fine. Yes, yes. That's fine. Five. Yes."

Sterling threw his phone onto the floor and plunged his face back into his pillow. I thought he had gone back to sleep until he mumbled, "I have to go to Seattle."

"Today?"

He groaned and rolled onto his back. "I'll be back tomorrow morning."

"What's in Seattle?"

"The company involved in your bride-price. I have to go deal with this myself."

"Right now?"

"Plane leaves at five." He cricked one strong shoulder, then the next. "That will get me there in just enough time for the meeting at ten. Which will last until about two, then drinks and dinner, because they're all upset about why I'm suddenly dumping my stake, and want to leave me with a good taste in my mouth."

"What did you tell them?" I admired the curves and lines of the muscles in his back.

"I told them the truth," Sterling half-laughed. "That I'm going to give it to my future father-in- law. That's why I'm getting wined and dined. I'd take you with me, but you'd be bored and it's not safe."

Sterling's-I-have-to-get-on-a-plane routine seemed well practiced. I dragged myself out of bed to see him off.

"Call me if you hear from the AmberHowl," Sterling fished around on the floor for his phone.

"I will." I wondered how many phones he destroyed in a year. I treated mine like a jewel, and not just because it was in a glittering case. I wrapped my robe tighter and followed him down the silent hallway to the dimly lit foyer.

He shrugged on his long wool coat and gloves. "Stay safe. I'll be back as soon as I get this dealt with."

I felt a very peculiar pang as I closed the door after him.

He was part of me. The soul that Gaia had chosen, and there was something to that, even if so far it had been just drama and headaches.

I managed to crack a nail sometime after breakfast. What was worse than an acrylic just peeling off? Cracking into a sharp, dangerous claw. No more putting off fills, even if it meant inconveniencing Jun.

I risked texting Mint, because I couldn't get married like this, and I wasn't sure I could get an appointment between now and Tuesday without his help. His boss had told him to help me as a favor to Sterling, and part of Mint's job was being gracious and helpful and never letting the client know what a colossal pain in the ass they were. But if I was going to risk dragging my packmate to a manicure, I was going to make sure I got it right. In the grand scheme of things I'd rather burn a bridge with Mint than piss off people I lived with.

Winter >> Cracked an acrylic. Getting married Tuesday. Help?

I didn't hear an acknowledgment within ten minutes, so hauled my laptop out to the dining room table. Pushed my luck too far. Time to figure out how to get my own appointment.

Mint >> Three this afternoon?

On a Sunday? How the hell had Mint made that happen? Wait. He was Mint. This was New York City. Time to not question his good nature or extensive contact list and give Jun the bad news about his Sunday afternoon.

"Jun," I knocked on the door of his and Cye's room, and shoved my head inside. "Holy hell."

The room was a disaster. It was a trainwreck of clothes, magazines, laundry. There was also a suspicious amount of tissues in the little trashcan between the beds. No one had a cold as far as I knew. I only saw bits of the underlying floor through the layer of debris.

Drawing attention to the absolute disaster was Cye's painfully neat bed. It was like a little oasis of order, but it was worse than the entire room. It was so neatly made, so completely free of rumples and wrinkles that it seemed unreal. Military precision in the corners. The three pillows arranged just so. It sparkled and radiated an unholy neatness.

I don't think Jun's bed had ever been made. I hoped the sheets had at least been washed at some time in the past six months.

The room had the faint odor of male and dirty laundry, but not squalor. Jerron's room had been a filthy cesspit that assaulted the nose from beyond the door. Now that I had had a few seconds to take it all in, I saw most of what covered the floor was just laundry and magazines. Tons of magazines. Years worth of magazines. The tide of magazines originated from a massive pile in one corner, and spread outwards from there.

A number of the magazines looked very rumpled and well-loved. At least several were girly magazines. One might have been a lingerie catalog. One featured an extremely buff guy in a bandolier and a studded jock strap.

Jun stood in front of the closet. I marveled at the carefully arranged wall of items. That had to have been Cye's work. In each of Jun's huge hands he held a tee shirt. He had on a hideous pair of sweatpants, and his entire upper body except for his arms had been waxed bare. His eyes darted around the room like a trapped animal. Seeing no escape, he managed a terrified, shaky grin. "Um... hi."

He extended one leg with the grace of a ballet dancer and used it to push a girly magazine featuring an exceptionally curvaceous lady behind him.

"What the hell is that? Your and Cye's collective library?" I side-stepped into the room and eyed the magazines. It appeared to be a generous mix of years worth of muscle magazines, fitness magazines, titty mags, innumerable cooking magazines, and someone in the flat had a certain affection for huge guys in leather. The huge guys came in two apparent varieties: waxed and oiled, or those who had never encountered a razor in their life. Nothing wrong with variety but what, no middle ground? My choices were fully waxed or jungle overgrowth?

What I didn't spy: food wrappers, dirty dishes, or decomposing bodies. Rats in a flat like this? I would have died of mortification explaining that to the management. "I see nobody here has a degree in library science. So. Anyway. Are you free this afternoon around three? For a couple of hours?"

Jun would have given me anything to get me out of that room and forget I ever saw any of it. "Um... yeah! I can be. Where are we going?"

"Nails." I held up my afflicted hand.

Jun made a keening sound that I think was some attempt at laughter but choked before it got out of his throat.

"That's not an answer."

"Sure." He nodded vigorously. "Um... yeah. No problem."

Jun couldn't look me in the eye for about an hour, and I overheard him whispering not-so-quietly to Cye that I knew about their magazine collection. Apparently in their world "hiding" magazines involved me wondrously never noticing a floor carpeted with them.

Jun demanded Burian come along to make sure nothing happened. I didn't want Burian to come with, and Burian didn't want to go with. Jun brow-beat Burian into consent. I pretended not to notice.

Mint arrived at two-thirty, dressed in a flawless green herringbone suit, dashing brown shoes, and a pale purple top. He had a little purple pocket square tucked neatly into his breast pocket. "Mint," I felt as though I had just been saved from walking the plank. "Thank you so much. I'm sorry if I imposed."

"If I never wanted to talk to you again I wouldn't have given you my number."

"I know why you gave me your number." It wasn't for the type of superficial trouble I currently was in. I intended to pay close attention so I could manage this myself next time.

His smile didn't waver. He looked behind my shoulder to Jun and Burian. "Bringing company?"

"We're the muscle," Jun told him. Burian grunted.

Mint's face clouded in a delicate scowl, then he said, "Try not to get underfoot. I'm in charge."

Jun said, "We're just guard dogs. It's your show."

Mint's scowled increased a degree just so they knew he meant it, but then he smiled at me. "Come on, Winter. Let's get you ready for the big day."

THE UNFORESEEN PERILS OF A MANICURE

Mint was used to working with bodyguards, and instantly spotted that Jun and Burian were rank amateurs.

The salon was busy even on a Sunday, and was used to high-profile clients coming in with entourages. They assumed Jun and Burian were bodyguards, and seated them in comfortable chairs around a little table within line of sight, and tended to them with drinks and snacks.

Wanderers had been waiting outside our building when we left, and tailed us most of the way. They had wisely slid into the distance when they saw our destination.

Their persistence was more than a little unnerving. I needed to keep Mint uninvolved. Unfortunately Mint took my nerves to be from something closer to home.

"You work on Sunday?" I asked Tony as he clutched handfuls of my hair.

"For this hair? Any Sunday." Tony grinned at me in the mirror.

Mint stood at my shoulder and looked at my reflection. "Might as well get your hair washed and tended to why you're here. Tony, go find somewhere else to be for five minutes. Be discrete."

Tony nodded. He patted my shoulder. "I'll go get the basin set up and we'll get started!"

Mint and I were out of earshot of Jun and Burian. "Who are the goons, Winter?"

"It's not what it looks like, Mint."

"Winter," he clucked his tongue at me.

"Mint, I swear, it's not what it looks like!"

"Winter, listen." He pulled a handful of my hair as he spoke to make it look like we were discussing what to do with it. Jun and Burian paid no attention at all. "If you're in trouble I—"

"I'm not in trouble. I'm really not."

Mint gave me a steel-eyed stare. He did not believe me. I didn't want him to worry but I couldn't think of anything to tell him that wouldn't be more damning or sound like a lie. The truth wasn't an option, not that he'd believe it. I pled with his reflection to just drop it.

He sighed and nodded. Mint had watched a lot of bad situations unfold. When someone punched their partner bloody or ripped out pieces of hair, Mint was the one they called to get them cleaned up. And every single one of them refused his offer to help. They felt trapped in their situation, just like Mint now feared I was trapped.

Mint never stopped trying. Even if all anyone let him do was help them hide the evidence.

"I'm not in trouble, Mint." The truth was I was in trouble, and Mint could spot a lie like that from ten thousand miles away. I just wasn't in the trouble he thought. I felt terrible, but I didn't know what I could do to make him feel better. I didn't want him to help me because he was worried for my safety or felt sorry for me. He had other charges who did need his help.

A few times I glanced over at Jun and Burian. Jun read a magazine while Burian kept his nose tucked into his laptop. Mint supervised everything, and I tried to tell him again how appreciative I was and he hadn't had to go through all the difficulty. He assured me I could text him anytime for any sort of help.

"Mint, I know you did this because your boss told you to because he was doing Sterling a favor." I couldn't take it anymore. "And I don't want pity."

"I gave you my number so you could use it," Mint stated.

Mint wasn't a wolf, but I knew when someone didn't like their loyalty questioned. For whatever reason Mint had inserted himself into my life. He didn't need to, and he had done it for the wrong reasons, but I did feel better knowing that I wouldn't be totally alone. My thanks felt pitiful and inadequate.

Mint respected my quiet while he supervised my nails. As the artist carefully streaked the white tips so they looked like icicles running down the powder-blue nail I noticed Jun get up. This wasn't a casual wandering about to get a different magazine or stretch. Burian peered over his laptop towards the top of the stairs, his whole posture on alert. Just then I heard raised voices down below, and then a commotion.

The salon occupied three stories: the first story was the lobby, the second and third were the actual salon. Posh clientele were certainly not expected to wait for their appointments in front of windows to be gawked at like so many puppies in a pet store. There were two security guards in addition to the two front desk staff.

Shouts and things crashing.

A scruffy-looking man with wild hair and a huge beard and a dirty lambskin coat bounded up the stairs. The stench of urine and three-day old oil hit me, and under that, the musk of a wolf. A wanderer! Right here! I surged to my feet, Mint shoved me down. The artist clutched my fingers in a death-grip.

Burian jumped up, a few of the other clients screamed. The man, waving his arms wildly and howling, plunged towards me.

Jun burst forward and down, tackled the guy and flattened him. Jun slithered over him like a snake despite his huge size, pinned the wanderer's hips and delivered a stone-fisted punch right to the face. My nail artist flinched at the pulpy sound.

Holy...

The two security guards launched over the final step, grabbed Jun and hauled him off the now-bloodied wanderer.

The wanderer flipped onto his belly, shot up onto his feet and bolted into the room. The two salon security guards did their best to hold Jun down while the wanderer threw his head back and howled.

It was the howl of a male to summon females to him.

That was my cue to go in the opposite direction.

"Let me go!" I tried to yank my hand away from the artist, but his grip was clamped down and bolted shut with terror. Mint grabbed both my shoulders and held me in place, snarling at me to stay still.

They didn't understand. I had to get away! Away!

Another patron's security guard came out of nowhere, seized the wanderer's arm and deftly kicked the guy's knees out from under him.

He dropped like a sack.

Silence.

The two staff guards muttered about crazies and hauled the wanderer to his feet. As they turned him around his eyes zeroed in on me. He looked right at me, giving me a huge, toothless smile, and barked at me.

A courting bark. He followed it by licking his lips.

"We got this, buddy," one of the staff guards told Jun. "This guy is crazy. He's always hanging around this block."

Sweat poured in thin rivulets down my spine. He had... spoken to me... that way. One of his hive-mates speaking to me in human language about what he would do to me was bad enough, hearing it in howls and barks no human would appreciate was even worse. Human vulgarity I could ignore. It was thrown around so casually and frequently it carried little meaning.

Wolves never spoke that way unless they meant it, and were willing to die for it.

And it had been a scene. He had caused a scene. And my packmates had caused a scene. A huge, huge, huge scene.

Quickly, I looked up at Mint, but Mint's attention was

on Jun. He jerked his head down and looked at me. "Goon."

"What—happens now?" I stammered. My mind pushed aside the courting bark and began to turn through how bad this might be. Jun had decked the guy and basically assaulted him. The private security guard had so neatly and quietly taken the guy down. I didn't like to think about what would have happened without him.

"This kind of thing happens," Mint said, but he wasn't happy. He was thoroughly angry under that posh exterior. "Crazies and crazed fans storm in here. They'll throw the guy back out onto the street. Through a back door."

Mint's tone spoke volumes. The police could get involved. The nail artist took a little break until we both weren't shaking, and then resumed the work on my nails. Mint left my side to speak for some time with the manager. From their body language she was angry, and Mint was trying to reason the anger away.

I assumed a submissive, embarrassed posture. Not even here a month and already my pack had been in an altercation involving humans. And, of course, I had embarrassed Mint.

Mint eventually came back and resumed his supervision of my nails. Did I apologize for Jun? Jun had known what a huge threat this guy was, what he had said, and Jun didn't deserve to be fed to the humans. Surely in my phone was the number of at least one attorney, right? At the same time, I owed Mint, and he wouldn't appreciate being embarrassed by my goons, or me siding with them.

"Very nice," Mint said to the artist. "Excuse us for a few minutes."

The artist nodded and left.

"So," Mint said to me.

"So," I mumbled.

"I've smoothed things over. I explained your goons are your friends and the big one has an overprotective big brother complex and just reacted. Suppression is already being taken care of, so you have nothing to worry about. However, your goons are not welcome here. I told the manager it was only for today and she'll never see them again. You, however, are welcome back."

Suppression? I had no idea what that entailed but it sounded like a solution. "I'm so sorry, Mint."

"I know you didn't get any choice in having them with you, Winter."

"Mint, it's not like that."

"Winter, don't lie. The big one told me. Remember? Nobody but low-rent goons says they're the muscle. They're the sort of goons who cause incidents that can't be suppressed so neatly. Tell Sterling he needs to pay for some proper guard dogs or else he's going to have more attention than he wants. Kick these meat shields back to bouncing at third-rate clubs. If you can't tell Sterling, I'll complain to my employer, who'll tell him."

What else could I say to him? Defeated, I said, "Thank you, Mint. I... I'll deal with Sterling."

"You're welcome, Winter."

"I am so sorry, Mint."

"I know. No hard feelings. You can keep my number." He smiled at me.

Jun didn't seem the least bit contrite. He had no idea how much trouble he had caused, and how much more trouble had narrowly been avoided. Mint had saved SnowFang face without them even knowing it, and just by luck the salon would take care of the rest.

"Where's Burian?" I asked him as we left. Jun had Burian's laptop satchel over his shoulder, and Burian's coat.

"Went for a walk to get some air," Jun said.

Jun was a piss-poor liar. Mint gave me a look that said "see?" as we stepped into the dark, cold night. On the breeze I smelled oil and wolf. A wanderer was close, but no Burian. I glared at Jun. He tried to look innocent and stupid.

Blast. I couldn't just wait around for Burian. "Let's go, he'll have to find his own way home."

Powerless, helpless and worthless were words to describe my feelings.

I told Mint he didn't need to see me to my flat, and he just smiled. Jun hustled me inside with enough force that the doormen gave me a questioning look but said nothing.

"Back off," I hissed at him. Jun ignored me.

We headed across the main foyer and heard someone calling a name. I walked on a few strides before I realized the name they were calling was *my* name.

Or at least what my name would be in less than two days.

"Mrs. Mortcombe!" footsteps scampered towards me across the marble lobby. "Mrs. Mortcombe!"

I turned towards the voice. It belonged to a man in his thirties, wearing a suit, and he waved at me so I knew to wait. What now? Was it Burian? Sterling? The police? Rats in the walls?

He had an overly warm smile on his face. "We have a number of deliveries for you!"

"What kind of deliveries?" I didn't bother to correct him on my name.

"Fruit baskets, flowers, that sort of thing. Should we send them up?"

Wanderers had the cash to send poison-laced gift baskets? A memory of Ronald popped into my head. No, these had to be wedding gifts from Sterling's business associates. "Ohhhh. Yes, bring them on up. But any new ones hold down here. I don't like people wandering around my foyer."

Wanderers might not be able to afford a basket of hand-picked, perfectly-matched strawberries but they could stand in for delivery folks.

Cye sang happily in the kitchen and the flat smelled of something delicious.

Jun went to the foyer to wait for the baskets, which he

carefully inspected before bringing into the apartment, and Cye practically wet himself with glee at some of what was sent. Beautiful baskets of perfectly matched fruit, candies and sweets, a box of cigars I'm sure were illegal in the U.S., truffles, caviar, teas, spices, fruits, meats, incense, perfumes, wines, liquors, beers, all with notes congratulating Sterling and I on our nuptials.

Lots of booze and fruit. Beer for days. This must have been how the bar had ended up so well stocked.

I gathered up all the little cards and carefully noted which gift came with which card for thank-you notes while Cye informed me how rare and exquisite a particular type of fish egg was.

"Sterling only told his assistants," I told Cye, card between my fingers. "If this isn't proof that people gossip, and how fast it travels, I don't know what is."

Cye clutched the little tin of caviar in his hands and gazed at it lovingly. "Who cares! Oh my gosh. And this!" He set the caviar tin down and picked up a bottle of wine. "This! Do you know what this is?"

"No, and since when did you become a sommelier?"

He grinned. "A good chef always knows what's in the wine cellar! All this we'll have to put downstairs."

The building had a private wine cellar, and we had two cabinets. One was full, the other half-full. The everyday wine occasionally served with dinner Cye kept on the counter, the good stuff stayed in the cabinets. "We're going to need to start drinking it. We're running out of room down there."

"I'll have to make special dinners for that." He admired the bottle. "Especially this treasure."

"Am I really having the conversation?" I asked myself more than him.

Werewolves were no strangers to gifts, nor were Sterling's associates. Gifts were a constant thing. Like wolf packs, much of Sterling's business revolved around relationships and maintaining them. This required gifts and ritualistic social bonding in various forms, but always absolutely superficial and with the intent to one-up everyone else with cost and sophistication. After all, what did you get someone who had everything, and where did you take someone when they've been everywhere?

"Where's Burian?" Cye realized Burian was missing.

"I have no idea." My exasperation returned. "He wandered off while my nails were drying."

"Aww. Don't feel bad."

Oh, I didn't feel bad. I was miffed. Just wandering off when he was technically on some kind of pack task was not acceptable.

Jun slunk around the kitchen looking at all the goodies. His eyes fell on a tin of cookies and several different exotic beers. It all belonged to me (and Sterling) and he wouldn't presume to help himself to my food. I outranked him, and I was a female. Either of those two things put my food off limits. The two together meant he dare not even ask.

He had acted like a wolf, not a human, and that had nearly gotten us in a bad spot. He knew better, and if he didn't, he was about to learn. At the same time, I felt terrible for punishing him when he hadn't meant to cause problems and had put my safety first, and like Mint had said, he wasn't a trained bodyguard. I turned the food problem over to Cye. "Cye, you're in charge of all of whatever this is."

"Really?!" Cye squealed. He hugged a tin of truffles to his chest. "This is awesome!"

There was thousands of dollars of gourmet items on my kitchen counter. I didn't know the proper way to use any of it, and some of it I didn't even know what it was. Cye knew what all of it was and clearly how to best use it. Let him deal with it.

Jun tried to sneak the tin of cookies.

Cye swatted at him. "I'm organizing it! You wait!"

"While you're waiting." I took one of the chocolates for myself and leveled a dour look at Jun. "Where is Burian? You've got his coat and his laptop. Don't you dare tell me that means he went wolf."

Jun gave me the answer I feared. "He wanted to track the wanderer."

THE LUNA WILL BE OBEYED

I tilted my head back and let out a slow breath through my nose. Burian had gone out the back door (maybe), undressed, tossed his clothes somewhere, and shifted. In broad daylight. "Does he have a phone collar?"

Phone collars were just what they sounded like: collars with a waterproof pouch to carry a phone while in wolf form.

"Yep."

Despite this, calling Burian would be useless. His phone was almost certainly on mute. If it wasn't, he wouldn't just shift to answer. At least I hoped he wouldn't be that foolish. But he had also thought going wolf form on a Sunday evening in New York City to track a random wanderer was a good idea, so I didn't have a lot of faith in Burian's judgment just then.

Jun gave me a blank stare.

"You don't see anything stupid about this?" I said. "Nothing at all?"

"No." Jun lacked any comprehension of why this would be a bad thing.

I put the heel of my hand to my head. As if being in wolf form on the streets of a major city wasn't stupid enough, he had gone alone! Who knew where that wanderer would lead him. "And what experience does Burian have tracking anything in wolf form?"

Maybe there was some off chance Burian was a super-skilled city hunter. Maybe this wasn't as bad as it sounded. Maybe I should just shut up and not completely lose my mind until Burian returned.

"Um, not sure." Jun admitted. "I guess he's okay. I'm sure it's fine. He's just tracking."

Nobody ever "just tracked" something. That's how more than one ignorant tourist had gotten themselves attacked by a bear or rutting moose. The wanderer could be leading Burian right back to his hive... and into a mess we couldn't get him out of.

"Jun," I asked, "do you have any experience tracking?"

Jun scratched his shaggy head. "I mean, my brothers and I used to play hide and seek and all, but we lived in the city so we got yelled at for being in wolf form."

Jun and Cye were so ignorant they had no idea how ignorant they really were. I had never met wolves like this before. I checked my phone. Accounting for the time difference Sterling was probably at dinner right about now. This was something an Alpha would (should) know the answer to.

Winter >> How skilled and experienced a tracker is Burian?

This required chocolate and some of that gourmet coffee made from hand-crushed beans or something. It actually required liquor, but I needed to stay sober. I wasn't used to being the only wolf in the room who understood this sort of thing, I had never even been the expert. My daydreams about being The World's Greatest Hunter had been exactly that.

Sterling >> Why?

Winter >> Reasons

I scowled at my phone. I did not have time to explain this shit to Sterling. I just needed facts as best he knew them. He was too far away to be of any other use.

Sterling >> Good snout. Not experienced. Not skilled. City boy gone hunting some.

So much for lingering hopes. I racked my brain to remember what I had seen my father do to wolves who had made this sort of mistake, but the only thing I could remember was him growling at a lower-ranking wolf to deal with it. This sort of entry-level stupidity was never his concern.

Did I go out after him? Did we wait? If he returned unscathed, I'd have to do something then too. This simply couldn't be permitted. If he was captured, what on earth would I do then? Leave him to die, or send us all to our deaths trying to save him? Bring humans into it, at the possible risk of exposing our kind or ending up in a terrible legal mess of questions I couldn't answer?

Sterling >> Why?

Winter >> It's a long story and you're far away. I'll deal with it.

If we had to go out after Burian that had T-R-A-P all over it. Better to wait. The wanderers *probably* wouldn't bother him if he didn't blunder right into a hive.

Dinner was a subdued round of greasy but scathingly good New York pizza, and Cye had made us cookies for dessert. They were both still nonplussed at my anger and worry. Cye dared to venture that it was all right if Burian wandered. My glare sent him diving for the pillows.

In the middle of Jun's favorite historical drama his phone buzzed. He tried to be sneaky checking his text.

"Um," he said to my glare. "I'll be, um, right back."

"Burian?" I asked.

"Ah, yeah. He's... "

"He needs some clothes, perhaps?"

"Um... yeah."

"Of course he does. Cye, go with Jun."

"Me?" Cye squealed.

"You."

"Um... Cye's kinda..." Jun said lamely.

"Useless in a fight?" Cye confessed.

Not a surprise confession. Cye moved like bumbling distracted middle schooler. "I know. But if Jun and Burian have to look out for you, they won't be tempted to do something stupid, like wander off in search of more adventure."

Half an hour later they returned. Burian reeked of sewers and garbage. My disciplinary plan had gotten as far as not lashing out in immediate anger.

"It's fine, Winter. Nothing happened. Nobody saw me. I'm back, see?" Burian told me before I even spoke.

"It is not fine!" So much for no immediate anger. The first thing he did was dismiss my annoyance and concern, not apologize, not explain himself. He opted to disrespect and belittle me. He had gone wolf to hunt in a human-filled area without permission or obvious need and thought it was a good idea?

"I'm back. It's fine. No harm, no foul." He raised his hands and turned around. "See? All in one piece."

I had had enough of him and Jun just reacting instead of thinking about how their actions might cause problems for the pack. This carelessness had to stop. They had to start thinking like wolves, not like humans who knew a couple of nifty party tricks. This was survival, and they damn well were going to treat it with the appropriate respect.

His disrespect galled me, but I made one final effort to control my rage. I *was* the Luna. I had an obligation to teach, not just knock heads together. Explaining his errors might go farther than just scolding. "You aren't a trained tracker, Burian. According to your Alpha, you've been hunting a few times. You went wolf, in a city, to chase unknown, poorly understood prey. You could have been lured into a trap. You could have caused an escalation. You risked this *entire* pack without my consent!"

Burian's brows dropped to an annoyed slant. "You're overreacting. Lay off, Winter. Nothing happened. I don't need your permission to go for a walk around town."

Overreacting.

When a female got mad at a male she was *overreacting.* There was never a legitimate reason we'd be mad at a male. It was always we *overreacted* and they'd get huffy at us and talk about biology and female problems. Never admit they were at fault. No, we always *overreacted*.

His defiance was unacceptable. Without Sterling here to enforce discipline, I had to assume both roles. Was it the right thing to do? It seemed like the only option left. This couldn't just pass and me put my tail between my legs, and let him think that yes, I agreed I was, in fact, overreacting. Who knew what Burian would do for his next trick. Time for some consequences.

The feral shiver moved over my flesh, the hairs on my neck rose upwards. "There are only two words I want to hear come out of your mouth, Burian. And those are 'yes, Luna.'"

He looked down his nose at me like I was a hysterical little girl. "You're going to try to pull rank on me? Oh, real funny, Winter. Get off your little pedestal and relax, will you?"

Red mist erupted from my blood. The shiver roared over my flesh and fur bloomed from my skin. Smells came to me, sounds, my body felt liquid for just a moment until it reformed, and I dropped gracefully to four paws.

Males always said shifting was uncomfortable for them. I always felt a quiver of exquisite pleasure, like cool wind on wet skin. I tested my weight on my paws and made a mental note to try to avoid scratching the wood floor.

Jun jumped back and Cye squealed.

I bared my teeth and growled. Hopefully Burian understood *that*. He clearly thought being a Luna was just a word tacked in front of my name. Maybe to him.

Not to me.

I would stand before Gaia when my life was done and answer for how I had nurtured my pack, ensured their survival and named my contributions to the future. Confessing to Her that I had failed because I had been too weak, shy, tentative, or merciful to deal with mongrels like

Burian was not how things would end for me. He was about to get a lesson in just how seriously I took my pack's future, and just how violently I would deal with any who threatened it.

Burian held his ground. He reeked of confusion and indecision. And some disgust too—he thought he was too good for this. That this was stupid. That I was an overreacting little bitch.

I growled louder and advanced a step. If he didn't shift promptly I resolved to maul his soft human form. Distasteful, but needful.

Perhaps he'd make things interesting and go war-form. I almost half-wished he would. My bloodlust simmered, the rage building, fueled by my emotions from the past two weeks.

Careful, little wolf.

Burian reluctantly transformed. He was a skinny wolf in shades of mottled brown and tan. He could have passed for a street dog. I was not large for a wolf, but I was larger than him, and outweighed him by a good amount. He didn't immediately lower his tail between his hind legs and slick his ears. He just sort of held a confused and disrespectful posture while he tried to decide what to do. He cocked his head to the side. *"This is stupid. Get over yourself, Winter!"*

Not even a worthy challenge! I snarled my fury. This was not worth his blood, my fangs or even a ruined manicure. I would have howled my rage and frustration if I had been outside under the moon. Instead, I barked, *"Let me make it very clear to you, wolf!"*

He didn't even understand. He was a stupid little boy who needed a whooping, but he was going to get a man's injuries. By Gaia's Blood, if I couldn't make him understand, I'd teach him to obey!

I lunged at him. We tumbled onto the hardwood floor. Burian scrambled, still confused by what was happening. I snapped at his foreleg, grabbed it in my teeth and bit down—hard. Blood flowed over my tongue and tendons parted under my teeth, I felt the resistance of bone. *"Do you understand now?!"*

He yowled in pain, yanked it back and his amber eyes flashed before mine. Oh, so it finally dawned on him I meant business! His teeth snapped by my ear and he rolled. Blood from his wounded foreleg splattered my white coat and hit my snout.

My war-form stirred. The rage and power, all the past years of powerlessness and anger deep within my gut clawing to get out and rip into this little dog-wolf. I could kill him. He had challenged me. He had endangered the entire pack. I snarled from deep within my throat and a black, angry fury seeped into my blood.

All Burian wanted to do was escape. He didn't want to beat me, he just wanted to get away from me. He squirmed and yelped and scrambled, flailing like an idiot. Coward! Coward, weakling, dog! I bit down on one of his ears and yanked. He shrieked. Blood bloomed on my tongue, hot and coppery. He flailed and his snout went everywhere as he tried to grab at my ears, my throat, my forelegs, or find my throat through my ruff.

His cowardice and weakness goaded my darkest urges. My war-form scratched to be free and stabbed under my skin. There was no place for such a coward in my pack! The only thing worse than a coward was an idiot coward!

And speaking of cowards, why the hell was Cye screaming?

A Luna must teach first, punish second.

Burian flailed. His snout bonking into me was more uncomfortable than his fangs harmlessly raking my ruff. It reminded me of wrestling with my little cousins, who still had their soft puppy fur and milk-teeth.

My rage dissolved into annoyance. This fight wasn't even

worth my time. Burian wasn't worth killing or even seriously harming. I wrestled him to the ground. He was all just flailing legs and snout anyway. This needed to end. I plunged forward and clamped my jaw over his exposed throat.

He froze as the pressure on his windpipe increased. He struggled a few more token seconds. Disbelief. Complete shock and confusion. But he didn't submit.

Anger brewing, I increased the pressure until the tips of my fangs broke his skin.

The dark part of me stirred again. Yes, part of me wanted to bite right into his windpipe. Break him. My instincts howled he was still a threat and must be removed. *Tonight. Now.*

The dark, feral part of every werewolf. The place where human cruelty and lupine predatory instincts met.

How dare this wolf challenge me. How dare he question me. How dare he think he knew better...

He whimpered. He actually whimpered.

The dark squeezed a snarl from my throat. I growled and increased the pressure just enough that I tasted the first trickles of blood. My rage demanded I punish him, my heart said he had been punished enough, my brain whispered I had already gone too far.

He whimpered again. Louder this time.

Unsatisfying.

I spat out his throat and let him roll over to his chest. I slicked my ears back and curled my lips over my teeth. His scent dominated my nose. All fear and intimidation, and under that the confusion and anger. He still had no idea how clueless he really was. Stupidity and ignorance were worthless reasons to fight.

Even simple greed was a better reason.

He bled from the wounds on his neck, shoulder, foreleg, and ear. Although he was smeared with blood and it puddled on the floor, his wounds weren't serious. He'd stop bleeding on his own, and heal in a few days without stitches. Unfortunately there was more blood on the hardwood floors than I had intended. And some scratches. But my manicure seemed to have survived. The acrylics, with their glitter and rhinestones, were damned uncomfortable in the delicate membranes that housed the upper part of my claws. What adhesive did that salon use, anyway? This was the second time I had shifted with acrylics and I hadn't lost a nail yet.

Burian crept past me, tail between his legs, heading towards his room. The threat of his death past, he was now mortified and angry. He could just go be angry and nurse his bruised ego away from me. I growled at him, *"Do you need another lesson in how unimpressive you are? Get out of my sight!"*

He hurried down the hallway.

Jun flattened himself against the wall and looked away from me. Cye—well, Cye was curled up on the couch sobbing. That was another problem for later. For now everything was settled. I gathered up my clothing in my mouth and trotted down the hallway to change and shower.

Afterwards, I poured myself a drink. All my rage had been exhausted. It was a stupid fight to have had, and it wouldn't be the last. Burian still didn't get it. That meant each time he ran afoul of my priorities, we were going to fight.

He fought like a mongrel dog. Maybe in a street brawl that was something, but it wasn't anything against a trained warrior. I wasn't even very skilled, just somewhat better than average. I had only managed to be slightly-better-than-average because I had been so offended at being dubbed "average" that I had dedicated myself to clawing beyond it. Burian wasn't even good sparring partner material.

I didn't want to think about how useless he was in war-form. For all I knew none of these wolves had experience in actual combat. How much time had they even spent in that form? It was not an easy form to hold, it wasn't easy to control. There was a reason why human legends of werewolves always told of a war-form beast in a mad rage destroying everything in sight.

They had only ever seen us at our worst.

Cye had started cleaning up the blood while I had been in the shower, and now he just compulsively wept and scrubbed the floor over and over again.

Wearily, I picked up my phone. Three texts from Sterling wanting to know what had happened.

Winter >> I had to teach Burian a serious lesson.

Sterling >> In what?

Winter >> The Fourth Law.

Sterling >> Are you hurt?

Winter >> No. He was no match for me.

Sterling >> I'll be home in the morning.

I tilted my head back against the couch.

Sterling hadn't asked if Burian had survived.

INTERNAL BLEEDING

Sterling >> Where are you?
Winter >> Roof
Sterling >> 2 minutes

It was quarter after six in the morning. Sterling hadn't been expected back before ten or eleven. I paced a little circle in the frigid air while I waited for him. So much for finishing my run. Running in circles around an empty rooftop had a certain irony to it anyway.

When I heard the door creak open and saw Sterling step into the pre-dawn gloom my blood quivered in my veins at the sight of him. Just as I was about to put my arms around him, I froze.

"What happened?" he had a scratch and a mouse on his cheekbone. It was a fresh bruise, slightly raised and still reddish. It hadn't had a chance to gain a halo. The scratch had barely crusted over. Need I even ask! Wanderers!

"Trouble, of course," he said with wry, resigned arrogance. His hands grabbed my arms and pulled me the rest of the distance to him. "I handled it. What happened here with Burian?"

He looked worn, and his voice had a weary, torn edge. I ignored his question and surveyed him again. "Did you sleep, Sterling?"

"No. I left Seattle right after dinner. I needed to be here." He stepped back and critically eyed me from sneakers to earband. "You seem to be in one piece. You *are* in one piece, correct?"

"I'm fine. Not a mark on me. Burian, on the other hand, is bloodied up."

Sterling's lips curled in a bare frown. "Burian's mouthy, but he doesn't usually require a beating. What happened?"

"The short version or the longer version? Because there are two parts to this story, but only one part involves Burian."

"Short version for now."

"We were out." I skipped ahead to the part where Burian ran afoul of my anger. "There was a wanderer, there was a scene. My attention was elsewhere and he slipped away, went wolf and tracked the wanderer. When I laid into him for it he told me to not pull rank and to stop overreacting."

A few hours sleep, a night to relax and then a few miles running in circles up here hadn't done much to dissolve my anger. The entire previous day had been one big giant mess. Burian, unexpectedly, had become the cake-topper.

Sterling's fingers tightened on my triceps, and the scent of his anger mixed with the dawn gloom. "Unacceptable."

"My actions or Burian's? Because if you say—"

"Burian's."

"If he had apologized I'd have accepted it, but he gave me a lot of lip about how I was wrong. Sterling, you didn't tell me these wolves are so ignorant they don't even know they're worse than puppies. And by the way, Burian can't fight worth a damn in wolf form. I don't know how to deal with wolves that are this... incompetent... in their fur."

Sterling just shook his head and said nothing. There weren't really any human words for this.

"What happened to you anyway?" I just couldn't stop staring at the cloudy bruise on his face. I reached up to touch the welt. Someone had hit him square, not even a glancing blow.

He jerked his head away. "I'm fine. Two wolves. I had to fly commercial to get back here. I don't know how they knew I'd be at the airport, but they were. Ambushed me as I waited for a cab. They look worse than I do."

My body produced a jolt of adrenaline that only made me feel how weary I was. "Wanderers?"

"I'm not sure. Maybe they weren't our wanderers. Airports tend to have a lot of vagrants. Security chases them off but they always come back. Might not be noteworthy. Although if they were random wanderers, you think they'd be smart enough to not pick on an Alpha, eh?"

"How did they know you'd be there?" Sterling didn't want to talk about it, but I did. My Alpha coming back with a bruise and scratch from a street brawl frightened me. After the previous evening, I didn't know what I'd do if I was the most competent warrior in the pack. I needed Sterling to be at least as good as I was.

I had not really contemplated the legitimate possibility that he wasn't. It had drifted through my mind but I had swatted the thought away like a fly. Now it was right in front of my face and might require actual attention.

"Don't know. Not fully sure they were wanderers either."

"I can only handle so many problems." My voice cracked. It was too much. Down there in that apartment I'd be the strong Luna I had to be, because that was just pure damn survival, but up here in what now passed for my forest, I was afraid. My life had sprung so many leaks I couldn't bail fast enough. I needed an ally, and Sterling was my only (and hopefully, best) option. I couldn't do this alone and I didn't know what I'd do if he wasn't able to carry his half of things. Probably go insane.

Insanity was an increasingly plausible option.

He pulled me close against him. I wanted to believe in his strength, but I wasn't convinced he could use it. "I have no idea what those two had hoped to gain from me. I am no one to the wolves. But it's not the first time. Won't be the last."

"I know, and that's what worries me."

"It might have been random. Not like that doesn't happen in this city. Why two young punk males would think jumping an adult Alpha male would be a good idea I don't know. But that's probably why they're jumping adult males for kicks, and why I'm flying first class."

I refused to be amused. "You didn't escape unscathed!"

He met my anger with annoyance. "Winter, I've had six hours of sleep in three days. Cut your mate a little bit of slack. One of them got one good shot in the beginning. It didn't even stagger me. It just looks ugly. Sorry to inform you, but skin this pale shows every bruise in all its glory."

"Given what I've seen of the rest of SnowFang?" I grumbled but was panicked under that. "I have the right to be skeptical."

"Are you asking for a demonstration of my prowess?"

"Maybe," I muttered. At least his arrogance surfaced, like a male wolf raising his hackles and tail in offended pride. I tried to pull my arms away but he didn't let me go. I shot him a dirty look but didn't try to fight more. I hadn't had my first cup of coffee and hadn't slept.

Cye had cried and scrubbed the floor until the wee hours of the morning. Jun hadn't been able to get him to stop, and by three a.m. I had had enough, gone out there, grabbed Cye by the arm, dragged him into his room and flung him into his bed. I might have been too harsh with him. I didn't know. What was I supposed to do with a sobbing werewolf compulsively scrubbing imaginary blood from a floor? It wasn't healthy. Maybe physically yanking him from the scene had been the right thing to do. Maybe it had been the exact wrong thing.

"Winter, I'm fine. It was just a scuffle, it didn't last long." He conjured smug arrogance. "They lost their taste for me quickly."

Sterling's prowess could wait. Burian's actions had gotten him to the top spot of the What Will Kill SnowFang Fastest list, which was impressive given what we were up against. "I don't think I managed to teach Burian anything."

Sterling's breath coiled in the growing light. "Burian is

used to being smarter than everyone in the room, if you haven't noticed. Nothing makes Burian bristle like someone pulling rank."

"Are you making excuses for his behavior?"

"Of course not."

So far Sterling's version of dealing with his packmates hadn't been grabbing them by their scruffs. Sterling's father's lessons in how to be a leader might not be the right lessons for this problem. "Sterling, I had him by his throat, bleeding, and when I released him he was just pissed off. Not a bit sorry or contrite. I was the bitch who flattened him. You aren't going to change how his brain is wired. Or Jun. Or Cye. And what the hell is Cye's story anyway? He just screamed the whole damn time."

"Cye is... Cye. Go easy on him." Sterling shook his head like it was too long a story for just then. "There isn't a mark on you?"

"No." I'd feel a lot better about things if Burian had managed to scratch me. Even a little.

Sterling pulled me hard against him and kissed me.

His lips were warm in the bitter cold, and I wanted him. I wanted to let myself feel the comfort of my other half just then. For a moment I indulged. Then I had to push him away. "No. You deal with Burian. No rewards until then. You also have a bunch of thank-you notes to write. I guess you haven't seen the kitchen."

I had to dilute all the werewolf drama with some mundane human problem that had a simple solution. I needed the win.

He tried to recapture me. I shoved with more force. The only thing I wanted from him right then was assurance and comfort, and what would reassure me and comfort me wasn't physical.

Convinced he wasn't going to get what he wanted, he said, "I came up here from the street so I haven't seen anything. I guess you mean wedding gifts?"

"Yes. Including a bottle of vodka I'm told would cost me fifty thousand large on the street and a type of caviar that made Cye wet himself. I've collected the cards and put them on your desk."

"Call Oscar and tell him to pick them up. He writes all my thank-you notes."

"Sterling! That's—"

"How it is, Winter."

"Tacky," I said with delicate distaste. Granted, I hated writing thank-you notes, and I also hated getting them (what a waste of paper), but if they had to be sent and received, shouldn't they be from the appropriate hands?

"It's business, Winter, not personal. I don't send any gifts either. Andre does that. He just hands me lists of people I know and I mark them with a star system based on how nice a gift they should get. He chooses the gifts, then sends me a list so I can know for small talk."

"There are no words for how screwed up your version of the human world is, Sterling."

He grinned at me. It was a humorless expression. "As screwed up as the world of wolves you've pulled me into, oh noble SilverPaw maiden?"

He had a point.

Burian looked a lot worse that morning. Bruises and injuries usually did get uglier after a night to swell and crust over. Most humans thought werewolves could regenerate in all forms, but the heal-on-the-spot regeneration was a war-form attribute, born out of rage, and uncontrollable. Regeneration almost always meant we were dying. In human and wolf forms we only healed a little faster. Recovered a little faster from blood loss or illness, didn't need stitches as often, bones knit a little faster.

And cancer spread with a virulent force that made almost any diagnosis terminal.

In human form the injuries I had visited on Burian translated to a black eye (I had some vague recollection of smashing his head into the floor when I took him down), a severely split lip (no idea how he had gotten that), a wrapped gash above his elbow, bite wounds on his neck and a bitched-up ear. Ear injuries to wolf form weren't serious—just the ear flap, usually. But in human form cartilage and structures got involved.

He should have stayed in wolf until his ear had healed up. A basic understanding of wolf and human comparable anatomy was a good thing to have. There were some injuries you didn't want to shift from. The ear was one of them.

Another thing to make sure they knew.

They were already at the breakfast table eating when we came in. I headed for coffee, Sterling just stood and looked at Burian. Burian looked at Sterling, then down at his breakfast and muttered something neither of us heard. I didn't need to hear the words. His surly tone summed it up. As if his posture didn't communicate enough defiance already.

Burian hadn't learned a damn thing. This fight was far from over.

"Well," Sterling said in his most icy, scalding tone. It sent Cye huddling into his chair and stopped Jun in mid fork-shovel. "She understated the severity of the lesson you required."

In my opinion, Burian had gotten off pretty easy. I had seen wolves get so bloodied they had crawled away for similar offenses.

"You and I are going to talk later. What you did is the kind of thing no pack can permit."

Burian raised his head.

"Don't say a word," Sterling growled at him. "Don't say one word, Burian. The Fourth Law states the Luna will be obeyed. The Fifth Law requires her to teach you. If you refuse to learn, expect punishment."

That was Sterling's obligation as Alpha: enforce discipline and order. The Luna instructed on what those expectations were.

"And if I don't agree with her lessons?" Burian dared to ask.

I growled. Had Burian not just been ordered to stay silent? My gaze darted to Sterling to see what he would do about this blatant defiance.

Sterling just laughed. "What makes you qualified to argue with her? My father's hunting dogs are the ones who took you on your first hunt. You really think that makes you equal to your Luna's experience?"

Hunting dogs? What the hell. Had Burian learned to retrieve ducks or something?

Burian's eyes burned with the same defiance as the previous night. Cye made some whimpering noises and curled into as tiny a ball as possible on his chair. I didn't see how this pack could survive. Jun went blank in confrontations, Cye turned into a screaming mess and when Burian didn't get his way, he became a menace.

This wasn't Sterling's fault. It was impossible to know what kind of wolf a wolf was until the first time they were in a fight, or the first time things got ugly for the pack. SnowFang had been a bachelor pack, and that had kept things simple. Just like whole herds of stallions, or bachelor prides of lions that could live together for season after season. But the instant a female came into play, things changed.

SnowFang was on its way to becoming a mature pack, one that would move toward a future, and with it came a pack's problems... and in our case, problems bigger than ourselves. Problems that would make even bigger, stronger packs pale.

No wonder my little pack struggled.

My phone buzzed on the counter.

It was exactly 7:01, and it was MaryAnne, the

AmberHowl Chronicler.

My Monday was off to a great start.

Still hadn't had that first cup of coffee.

THE SPACE BETWEEN DARK PLACES

Somewhat steeled for whatever she was about to say (only because I had been beaten into the proverbial emotional pulp), I picked up my phone. "Good morning, MaryAnne."

Sterling's attention focused entirely on me, and a silence fell over the table.

This was now the most urgent matter facing SnowFang that morning. Burian and his drama could wait five minutes.

Despite her pleasant words, I heard an edge in MaryAnne's voice. Sort of like the words had a distantly unpleasant taste. "Good morning, Winter."

My pulse throbbed in my neck. This was the call we had been waiting for. Fear, anger, battle-lust jolted through my system. My body was too exhausted to keep pushing all these emotions through it.

Just five more minutes. Just five more minutes.

"The AmberHowl Alpha has demanded that the SilverPaw Alpha file a formal request if they want your bride price paid," she said. "Are you prepared to pay the bride-price right away?"

Alpha Demetrius had made a formal demand of the SilverPaw?

I wheezed, "Yes, yes, we are. Everything is arranged."

"Then I will be in contact when we have the formal request. I will forward a copy to you, and then we can make arrangements." The more she spoke the more the metallic tone in her voice emerged.

My father must have put up a hell of a fight. I cringed. A token struggle out of pride was to be expected, but this had escalated and now there were bad feelings between two Elder packs.

My stomach somersaulted. I gulped down a gag.

"Thank you, MaryAnne." My voice betrayed me and got a little rough around the edges.

This was too hard. All of this was too hard. It was just too much.

"Goodbye, Winter. I will be in touch."

I turned around. My knees quivered. After the events of the previous day, I couldn't show weakness. The AmberHowl were going to help us, but it wasn't a victory. Not really. The price would be so high. The few words I had wanted had turned into a great deal more. This was as bad as it could be.

The little SnowFang, a pack almost below recognition, playing the politics of Elders.

Sterling came over to me. He took in my tears. "What's gone wrong?"

"Nothing. The AmberHowl Alpha has forced my father to file the request."

"This is good news."

It *was* good news, but with the added stakes of the AmberHowl placing themselves between SilverPaw and us.

The triumph drained me. SilverPaw hadn't been prepared for us to fight back, thought we couldn't, that we wouldn't dare. My father and those like him had gotten away with this kind of thing for centuries because everyone in a position to resist lost their nerve. If he had done this to *me*, what else had he done?

Sterling moved to stand next to me but faced the men at the table. "The AmberHowl have compelled Alpha Rodero to file a formal bride-price request. This is a huge victory for us. But in practical terms, the SilverPaw aren't going to forgive us, and the AmberHowl aren't going to be happy to hear from us ever again. There's no doubt this will get around the rest of the high-standing packs. We have to be very careful."

"You mean more than we are?" Burian asked darkly.

Sterling growled at him, and meant it.

I picked up my cup of coffee. "I need a shower, Sterling. Excuse me."

"Good idea." He had shaved at some airport between here and Seattle, but hadn't showered since I had seen him the previous day. Under his coat he did have the faint scent of exhausted, unwashed male.

"You shower first," I told him as I sat on the edge of the bed. I hadn't gotten too sweaty jogging in the frigid cold, and I needed to sit a moment anyway.

He dropped his satchels on the floor by the closet. "Am I that offensive?"

"You are a bit whiffy." Body odor hardly offended me. If I had been in wolf form it would have told me where he had been, who had been around him. All I could smell in human form was how exhausted he actually was, and that his human skin would benefit from soap. Human form sweated. Wolf form did not. "I imagine your skin feels like it's covered in scum. I hate that feeling."

"Hm. Wonder if I offended everyone in first class. Or if that was just because I refused to sleep and kept a reading light on."

"Oh, woe is you. Having to fly commercial." Of course, here I was savoring a cup of some extravagant ultra-gourmet shade-grown hand-picked organic something-or-other coffee. It is easier to confront problems in the morning when armed with excellent coffee.

He shrugged off his button-down with a sigh. He threw the shirt onto the floor with his usual disregard, then paused to fish his phone out of his pants pocket. I crossed one leg over the other and leaned forward on my knee. Sterling's physique was a pleasant distraction that sent a little pitter-pat throughout my entire being.

He scrolled through various screens. Then I sighed as he

held it to his ear. Did this wolf never stop? Of course he didn't. He was Sterling, and I probably wouldn't have liked him as much if he wasn't driven. Although I wanted my shower, and the longer he took getting done with his, the longer I had to wait.

"Hector," he told the person on the other end of the call. "Are we ready?" He began to pace a tight little circle. Then, just as quickly as he had started, he stopped. "Good. Good. Thanks."

He tossed his phone aside. It landed on his crumpled shirt.

"Who's Hector?" What was it with Sterling and just throwing things? It was like he had never grown out of that phase as a toddler.

"My lead attorney. I have a few I work with depending on what I'm doing, but when I say 'my lawyer' I usually mean Hector. You'll meet him soon."

"And the gift is ready? Completely. Wrap it up with a bow and slap a name tag on it?"

"Shiny wrapping paper and all. I'm a little proud of myself for pulling this off." Sterling gave me that smug but tired smile.

"I am impressed." I had no idea how large a mountain he had had to move to do this, but I figured it was large and I should be suitably impressed. He practically preened under the praise.

He paused, and said, "We have to do this, Winter."

"I know."

"You have your doubts about if this is a smart thing to do or not."

"Don't you? We are sticking our snouts in an ant mound."

"It would be easy to give him the money. But doing the right thing usually isn't the easy thing, and going by that logic, I shouldn't just cut him the check." He frowned at nothing in particular. "We're in very deep now. Not that we weren't before. But if the AmberHowl actually had to tussle with him for us... usually on a chessboard you don't protect the pawns."

"Usually. But there are times it's a good idea."

He smiled at me. "What are the odds your father will have lost his taste for our flesh after this?"

With dark humor, I replied, "About zero."

"Ah hell." He shrugged his strong shoulders and unbuckled his belt. That got thrown onto the floor like everything else. Then he stepped out of his slacks and those ended up in a heap, followed by his boxers.

He was a glorious specimen of a man. I admired him with simmering smugness. My stress and concern got shoved aside as my thoughts turned to my mate. Allll mine. All of it. I had anticipated the lower half of him would be as glorious as the top part and he did not disa—

Wait.

I jerked like an electrical shock had been jabbed right into my bum. I had already seen him naked: in my dream.

Sterling's waking, physical form was exactly what it had been in the dream. I stared at him, my eyes searching him for a clue, a difference, something. Of course the slash marks over his shoulders weren't present, but in my dream that had not been part of him in a physical sense.

The memory of him standing, clutching the puppy and the necklace shoved itself into my brain, and I overlaid the image of him now with that memory and it matched perfectly.

I searched my memories—had I seen him before, completely naked? No. Not even a glimpse. I was sure of it. This was the first time. My eyes searched every part of him for something that wasn't what it had been in the dream. But he matched. It all matched. Every line, every curve, every angle, every arc, the knitted scar across the flat of his torso. A scar caused by silver, the burned, frayed edges were unmistakable.

"What?" His edged tone cut me out of my stunned thoughts. My eyes flew to him. He stared at me, cold and angry. "My body offends you?"

"No. Sterling, I—"

"You looked horrified," he snapped. "I can't undress in front of you? Or are you just gawking in maidenly horror?"

"You're not the first man I've seen naked," I retorted. I had seen many males completely naked. It came with being a werewolf. It was *this* man. This man's body I already knew and had seen in exquisite detail, but not in the waking world. I had *felt* his body against mine, but I had not *seen* it.

"So why are you staring?" His tone could have wilted a field of grass. He turned to face me fully, as if daring me to answer or judge him.

A little corner of my mind continued to admire him anyway.

I could have risen to his anger, but I softened my tone. We were tired, exhausted, drained. "Sterling, a few nights ago I had a dream. You know all female wolves have a little gift, right? From the Moon?"

"Yes."

"I have... a little more than most," I confessed. "Nobody knew but my mother. It's not worth telling anyone. It's not much. But you were in the dream, and you were completely naked and in human form. That's not unusual. I've just never seen you before. Not in this world. But your body is exactly like the dream. It's... it's exactly like my vision. With the silver scar and all."

Dreams were when our minds and gifts entwined to devour problems, and perhaps the Moon would whisper some insights into them. They were like unconscious prayers or pleas for help. *Visions* were when the Moon needed us to see something. To know. She deliberately spoke to us with great intent.

Visions had while scrying and deliberately invoking the Moon's Gift weren't all that rare if a she-wolf had enough of the gift. Sleeping visions were very rare. I had never had such a vision. My mother had said that the Moon always left a clue so that we'd know later it had been a true vision and not a dream.

Sterling was my clue.

His eyes narrowed. "What happened in this vision?"

"I'll have to tell you later." I was far too tired to have this conversation. "But you misunderstood. I was actually thinking how you're all mine. And then I realized I had seen you before. I'm sorry if I gave you the wrong idea."

His anger disappeared with suspicious swiftness. "I was wondering. You smelled very appreciative but your face was horrified. Anyway. Shower. I won't be long."

The view of his chiseled backside was quite nice. Except it was just like my dream. That was another splash of cold water. The puppy was an obvious symbol, even if I couldn't piece together exactly what they were supposed to represent. But that blue necklace—I wasn't aware of any symbolic value in a necklace. Any necklace. Or vials, or that shade of blue. The rest of the vision made no obvious sense. Everything I had seen could have multiple meanings. Except for the necklace that had no meaning at all.

I finished my coffee while he showered, then caved and picked up his clothes and phone.

I put the phone on his table just as he came out of the shower wrapped in a towel.

"I'm going to pass out for a few hours," he told me. "Then I'll deal with Burian."

"I'm going to shower and join you. I didn't get much sleep." My brain felt exhausted. Like it was just going to turn to goo and slide out of my skull.

He was still awake when I slipped under the sheets next

to him. He lay on his belly, head turned towards me on his pillow, and completely naked. His hazel eyes flickered over me. He dared me to say something.

I took the bait. "You normally sleep naked?" I was just in a chemise. Panties had proven to be too much effort. Nothing would have happened just then. Stick a fork in us, we were both done.

"Yes."

"Well, don't stand on ceremony for me." The bed was much better with him in it. I sighed contently, flipped onto my belly and turned my head to face him. This was nice.

"I didn't want to spook you." He smiled from his pillow.

"Spooking is not what I would have done."

"Oh? What would you have done?"

"Admire my prize."

We exchanged exhausted smiles. Gaia, it was sort of a wretched, laughable feeling. We just laid there like two overdone steaks.

He asked, "So. What was the first half of this long story? I'd rather hear it now and sleep it off."

I gave him the brief, point-by-point of the first half of the story. I also added Mint, and Mint's assumptions.

"I will never put a hand on you in anger." Sterling probably would have sounded more irate if he wasn't on the verge of surrendering to his exhaustion. Six hours of a sleep over three days would put down the mightiest alpha.

"I never told him anything like that. Or suggested you did."

"No, I'm sure you didn't. I guess I'm more troubled by Jun's actions. Mint is right about bodyguards. And... gah... Burian." He closed his eyes and sighed. He reached one hand across the sheets to me. His fingers gathered up a bit of the silk at my hip. He closed his eyes.

I expected him to say something else—but he didn't. He had fallen asleep.

THE LAMPREY

We only managed to sleep an hour. Then Sterling dragged Burian into his office for a talking-to. Jun walled himself into his room. I fully expected the meeting between Sterling and Burian to last five minutes before Burian stormed out. In anticipation, I examined the patch of floor Cye had scrubbed into oblivion.

"Damn," I rubbed the spot with my socked toe. Scratches from the tussle, then Cye's incessant scrubbing had trashed the varnish.

Cye had been in the kitchen since breakfast, medicating his anxieties by reorganizing the pots. At least that's what I hoped all the racket was about.

I worried about him.

My phone buzzed.

Sterling >> bedroom will call you don't speak mute

So now he and I were playing cloak and dagger in our own den. Unsavory. Maybe it was one of those dirty little secrets of leadership.

I made myself comfortable in the center of our bed just as my phone rang. I answered it, hit the mute button, and was drawn into a conversation between Burian and Sterling.

Burian's voice had that exasperated, impatient tone that made me gnash my teeth. "She overreacted. It's that simple. Nothing happened."

She being me, of course.

Sterling replied, "It doesn't matter nothing bad happened, Burian. You invited trouble. It's like my dad teaching us to never point a gun at anyone. Not because we intend to shoot, but because of what *might* happen. You just don't invite that sort of trouble."

"Me sniffing after a wanderer isn't a loaded gun."

"No, it's worse."

"Sterling." It was easy to imagine Burian clutching the bridge of his nose with his fingers. "I had just spent four hours trapped in some crappy salon while she got her bloody nails done. You bet I was done! Add a wanderer to that mess and you think that's how I want to spend my life?"

"Winter is a prisoner here. Jun had the good sense to ask for your help one damn time, Burian."

"And I did it with a smile on face. She never suspected how pissed I was. Sue me for trying to do something about the bigger problem!"

Sterling barked a caustic laugh. "Like a dog chasing a car. What the hell were you going to do if you had caught it? Did you even give a thought to what it'd do to this pack? It's a wanderer hive, Burian!"

Burian seethed in front of Sterling, full of rage and frustration with no outlet. "Big bad wolf now, eh? Dealing with Winter's snotty attitude is bad enough. Take your balls out of her purse and wake up, Sterling. You've let her get into your head!"

"Protecting this pack is my job. The job you wanted me to do. This whole pack was your idea. You're the one who pressed me to be the Alpha!"

That spun my understanding of everything right around.

It made no sense until Burian's next statement: "Yeah, because you're the one with the fucking money."

As a wealthy Alpha Sterling would have been expected to provide for his packmates. No Alpha capable of providing basic food and shelter could refuse a packmate in good standing. If Burian had been Alpha, Sterling would only have been required to pay a modest tribute. There was a very intricate formula to calculate the maximum any Alpha could demand from any given packmate.

The formula had existed for centuries. It was not a new thing, and all Alphas got a copy of it when the pack was formed, and once again every time a new Alpha came to power. Using packmates like cows was a crime. I had studied the formula and its history since I had been in middle school. It was fascinating and nauseating to see how life was valued, and each change had its justifications documented, and it often had seemed to me that everyone that had written those decisions seemed to share the same vague disgust for its necessity.

Burian had manipulated Sterling just like my father had.

But Burian wasn't a predator. He was a parasite.

"Ah." Sterling's voice was cold steel, but there was a wound there too, under the armor. That knife had gone deep into him, right between his ribs, and tore at tender tissues. "I see. When I ran a bachelor pack it was fine. But now that it's ugly and uncomfortable and inconvenient and not fun, you have second thoughts. Don't be a little boy, Burian. This is how packs are. You just wanted to play house."

No, Burian had latched on like a lamprey.

Betrayed in your own den.

That was worse than being sold by your own father.

"Play house? Winter got in my face. I walked in and she's in my face with the lecture before I was even out of my boots. I wasn't going to put up with that! She could have said thank you, asked what I had gone to do, what I had learned, but no. Not Princess Winter! I didn't ask Her Majesty's permission so I got my nose smacked. Tut, tut, Burian, we don't permit independent thinking in this pack!"

Sterling snorted. "You didn't accomplish anything. She knew that before you came home. Is this that you can't deal with a woman who can handle some things better than you, including her liquor?"

I couldn't handle my liquor at all.

A chair scraped on the floor and fell backwards.

"Forget this shit!" Burian's anger made his voice go up half an octave. Sterling had hit a nerve. "She's *your* mate and *your* problem. Stop spreading it around to all of us! You can shove this pack up your ass!"

Sterling's rancid tone burned through the phone as he crept towards the kill. The underlying viciousness pressed against my bones. The predator smelled blood and fear, and his victory very, very close. "So this is how it's going to play out. Things get tough and you're done. You're just going to quit. Like your dad quit."

Frantic footsteps, heavy breathing, scuffles as Burian started for the door, stopped, spun around, advanced on Sterling. Burian's voice sounded much closer, and shook with barely controlled rage. "Don't bring my parents into this. Cheap shot, Sterling. Cheap damn shot. This is nothing like that!"

"No, it's exactly like that. You're just too gutless to admit it."

"I don't have to stand here and listen to this, Sterling. I know where the door is!"

"You're just like your father," Sterling ground the salt in deep, slow and with dark relish. "This pack was your idea. Now it's become more than you can handle so you want out. Your father knocked up your mother, realized he was in too deep and left. When the fun was over, when the work started, that's when your dad left. Your mom crawled into a bottle. You can shout all you want, Burian, and you can stick your head so far in the sand you can talk to Gaia Herself, but it won't change anything. Your father was a coward. Your mother was a coward. And you are a coward."

Burian's heavy breathing was ragged and punctuated with the start of syllables that never became words. Then, finally, in an ugly, hideous tone, he said, "As you say, Alpha."las

The rest of the afternoon was the surreal, uneasy silence that felt like a blanket of eggshells. A sort of silence filled with thoughts and feelings but nobody dared break it with words.

Burian holed up in his room. Jun tried briefly to coax him out. This only resulted in Burian yanking the door open, telling Jun to get lost, then slamming the door over and over until the wood around the doorjamb splintered.

Of all the things Burian had broken that day, a door was the least of them and the easiest to repair.

After that Jun got a beer and despondently watched strong man competitions.

Cye asked me if Burian would eat dinner with us.

Not permitting a wolf to share in a pack's food supplies was one of the most serious punishments that could be given. That could range from denying a wolf treats, like dessert or liquor, to refusing to share meals but still allowing the wolf to eat alone, or it could be all food.

The ritual of sharing food with the pack was so deeply ingrained in us that food related punishments could break even the most defiant wolf. The longest I had ever seen anyone hold out was four days of eating alone. They hadn't crawled back to my father because of hunger.

Burian was once again my problem. Sterling had enforced discipline and expectations. Managing the disobedient, intractable wolf and educating him on proper behavior was my job. If he revolted again, back to the Alpha for punishment. Back and forth, back and forth.

I didn't know if Burian would appreciate food punishment for what it was. Was it learned or an instinct? On paper excluding Burian from shared meals seemed appropriate, and my heart demanded I punish him for what he had done to Sterling. It also would have just given Burian a rope to pull against, another perceived injustice to nurse, and if he didn't recognize it as the severe punishment it was, it would just undermine our authority.

Continuing to feed him would be seen as pity, and would gall him all the same.

When dinner came about Cye set out a plate for Burian

and I sent Jun to go get him. It took a little coaxing but eventually Burian came to the table. He said absolutely nothing to anyone and kept his eyes on his plate. Sterling didn't even have to pretend to ignore him—my mate was exhausted and just done with the day.

Jun filled the silence with chatter about dudes pulling loaded passenger buses with their teeth.

Burian took his dessert back to his room.

Sterling dug around in the liquor cabinets and pulled out a bottle of vodka. *The* bottle of vodka, as it were. He looked at me. "Join me?"

I wasn't in the mood to drown my sorrows in liquor but drinking alone was the worst sort of drinking.

Sterling got two shot glasses and poured us each a shot. Jun watched from the bar counter, and Cye worked feverishly over something that looked like an elaborate cake batter. Sterling leaned back against the counter, downed his shot and looked at the ceiling.

"Cheers," I told him before gulping down a shot that I figured was worth about five thousand dollars.

So these were the joys of being a small-pack Luna. Standing in a kitchen with your mate, only other two packmates, and doing shots of expensive vodka on the night before your wedding while wondering what your father was going to do next and contemplating if you were going to even make it to your wedding in one piece because your fifth and angry packmate might burn everyone to death during the night.

At least I could say my life was not boring. Small comfort.

Sterling scratched his evening scruff and poured himself another shot. "So. Burian."

"Is a lamprey." Burian had risked SnowFang the day before, but what he had done to Sterling that afternoon had drawn blood. Disgusting. Burian had no place in SnowFang as far as I was concerned. Alphas had to take a certain amount of abuse, but being a conniving little parasite in the guise of friendship had no place in my pack.

Sterling shook his head once, although it wasn't clear if it was disagreement or dismay. "I'm not giving up on him, Winter."

Wolves could be loyal to a fault. I frowned.

Sterling repeated, "I won't. Not yet."

It had been Sterling's friendship, and if he wanted to forgive Burian, he had known Burian far longer than I had known either of them. I limited myself to a doubtful look.

Sterling gestured with one hand. "Burian's a genius, Winter. A legitimate genius. His parents were a couple of lone wolves who had been lone wolves for a long time. The sort who drift in and out of groups, maybe packs that wax and wane. They weren't mates. Just two wolves who were together."

Sterling downed a shot of vodka and poured himself another one. "His mom was a functional drunk for I think most of his life. I never met his dad. From what I've heard his dad was sort of hapless. All talk and no spine who just found himself with a female and a baby. When they realized how smart Burian was they believed he'd somehow make them rich. Burian scorns his intellect, and most anything else he thinks people expect of him.

"Burian never told me anything specific, but I think the constant screaming matches got a little physical from time to time. She got drunker, and one day his dad just left. No forwarding address, no number, nothing. Burian never saw him again. His mom hit the bottle harder and blamed Burian for all of it. Two years ago she polished off her stash and passed out in the bathtub. Burian got home and there she was."

He offered me the bottle. I shook my head.

Sterling's tone was grim and resigned. "I can't really say it messed him up more than he was already messed up. Burian had probably already done the math."

"Did you know him then?" I asked, "Or did you hear this afterwards?"

"I met him at school six years ago just before his father left. We hit it off. My parents kind of took him in. As much as anyone could take Burian in. Our lives took different paths but we stayed friends."

To my unspoken question, Sterling elaborated, "I graduated high school early, finished college in five semesters. I wanted out the system, and onto my own life as fast as I could get there. Burian goes down to the dean and drops out every semester. Usually he re-enrolls in a week. He's so brilliant they just put up with it and give him back his scholarships. Until last night I never really believed it would extend to this. This was his idea, Winter. He wanted SnowFang."

I didn't have the heart to remind Sterling that Burian had explained his reasons: money, money, and, oh, money.

Sterling's strong shoulders bent under the burden. He poured himself another shot. Damn, he had good alcohol tolerance. I had just had two and already felt them. Sterling didn't even flinch.

"Burian's repeating history. Things get tough, he hangs on a while, then starts to fall apart and tries to escape. You came at him, laid into him and I'll bet all he heard was his mother riding his ass. Then you flattened him, which he deserved. But in his mind, you're just another bitch telling him what to do. Head for the door. I didn't think it'd happen, but I can't say it surprises me."

Burian had his demons. Did we abandon him to his demons, or did he like his demons and have tea with them? If he was struggling, we couldn't just leave him.

But I also couldn't let him destroy everyone around him.

Sterling expected me to say something. I settled for a

response somewhere in the middle. "It can only go on so long, Sterling."

Pack first, family second, allies third, friends fourth.

HOPELESSLY HILARIOUSLY ROMANTIC

"This is a formal event?" I asked Sterling with a smile. His suit was absolutely impeccable—even for him. An exquisite silvery blue that threw all his pale colors into brilliant relief, and for once, he had on a pale shirt. A pastel ice-blue. And a tie. I liked how severe and austere he looked.

"I believe it is," he informed me as his hands slid over my hips. I had chosen a sky blue dress embroidered with fanciful gold birds. It came just above my knee, and being somewhat vintage-inspired, probably didn't show enough of my cleavage for Sterling's tastes. I caught his eyes darting over my neckline. A night of solid sleep—assisted by a bottle of vodka—had done a good deal for both of us.

Burian had also not torched us in our sleep. That made today automatically better than the previous two days. So far.

"You look lovely," Sterling told me.

"Thank you."

"You do know that dress is going to be ripped off you in short order."

"No, no ripping. Slow and exquisite." The thought of his hands stroking me through the soft fabric, exposing skin inch by inch to his lips, making me quiver and plead in anticipation caused me to quiver in reality.

A knock on the door. Cye peeked his head around. "Um, Sterling? There are some ah… guys here."

Sterling lifted his hand off my hip to check his watch. "They're early. Tell them to wait outside, Cye."

"Sterling." I raised an eyebrow at him.

"I don't want to get into this today. We'll talk about it later. But I didn't want to put our safety on the others today. They should be able to enjoy it with us."

Hadn't answered my question. "Keep talking."

"They're bodyguards."

"Human bodyguards?"

"Human."

Oh yes, we'd be talking about this later. But our wedding was very important to Sterling. The discussion of human bodyguards could afford to wait a day or two. "How do you know these bodyguards? Are they good?"

"They're from the agency who does my parents' details." He gave me that little smile that bespoke a confession. "I texted my father and got some help from him to pull this off on such short notice."

"You broke the dead and burning rule?"

"No, that's a call. I texted. Mom was in the sauna."

"Sneaky, daring wolf," I teased.

He winked at me.

Jun owned a button-down. That fit. Tucked into clean jeans. Marvel of marvels. Cye was in slacks and a button-down in a bright shade of green. He clapped his hands as we entered the foyer and grabbed Jun's huge bicep. "They look so perfect together!"

Jun sniffled and brushed at a tear, then went to pound on Burian's door. "We're leaaaaaaaviiinnnng, Buriannnnnnnnn!"

"That would wake the dead." I tapped one ear.

"Then it might wake Burian," Sterling said.

Jun came back into the foyer, and behind him was a dressed, shaven, and groomed Burian. I hadn't expected him to get up, much less to be joining us. Burian gave Sterling and I a look that said we should just stay quiet. The day had earned a halt in the hostilities, and if nobody said anything about the obvious, we would all fake it for a few hours.

Fine by me.

Two men wearing dark suits waited in the exterior foyer. They were both average height, early forties, clean shaven, and dark hair with varying amounts of gray. The only thing that betrayed either of them as bodyguards was the way they moved.

Just as we got on the elevator one murmured into his phone they were on their way down.

Outside the building two dark gray SUVs waited. Sterling and I were directed to one, while our other three packmates to the other. The two guards split between the vehicles and joined the drivers in the passenger seats.

I spotted familiar scrubby faces in their usual spots. The breeze, however, blew their scent downwind.

The bodyguard in the passenger seat murmured to the driver about three more across the street, and one on each corner.

I brushed my finger over the fading bruise under Sterling's eye. The scratch had healed to almost invisible rough edges, but the bruise was still there and a little green around the margins, with a little knot of blood under his skin. "Are we safe with them?"

"Far safer than we were."

"But no promises."

"No promises."

That was more believable than some blanket assurance.

My fingers moved down his shaven cheek, feeling the texture of his skin. This was the soul Gaia had made for me. This strange wolf, in his flawed, frightening world. Looking back at the world I had come from, with the advantage of distance, my life at SilverPaw had only been what it was because of my ignorance. The world of the elite wolves must have seemed frighteningly foreign, harsh, insular, and perhaps even noxious to wolves like Sterling.

We made it to City Hall with no difficulty, and the wanderers trailing us drifted away. They did not want to be anywhere near City Hall. "Does this offend your sense of romance?" I asked Sterling as we waited in line to get through security. Our security guards had already made arrangements; but we still had to go through metal detectors.

Sterling *was* a romantic at heart.

"I'm sure it suits your pragmatism." He did not smile, but his face seemed to. "I still have to pay for the ceremony."

"Get a receipt," I quipped, and winked at him.

"Man. Twenty five bucks. Big spender." Jun grabbed Sterling and shook him once. "Dude. Man. I know you saved for months."

"Smashed his piggy bank, he did!" Cye chimed in. "I saw him counting his nickles."

"He almost had to bum a quarter from me. But he found that in the couch."

I handed my purse over to a City Hall security guard and shook my head. She chuckled. "Boys."

"They were all up late drinking," I told her.

"You were drinking with us, dear," Sterling reminded me.

Yes, we had finished off that bottle of vodka. I can't say that I found fifty thousand dollar vodka to be that much of an improvement over a fifty dollar bottle. It hadn't even had the decency to leave me even mildly hung over. For that price there should have been some lingering reminder of having drunk away a respectable annual salary.

And Sterling? Sterling hadn't even been slightly drunk. His liver was a creature of legend. Even by werewolf standards.

The judge was a man in his fifties or so, white hair with a bald crown, heavyset, and had a slow Texas drawl. He greeted us with a huge grin and meaty handshake. There was an intricate wooden cross hanging on the wall by his desk. Intermixed with his various diplomas and commendations were some cross-stitched Psalms and scripture quotes from the Christian Bible.

"I love having a wedding to do first thing in the morning!" he told us as he clapped hands once. "Starts my day right. So you're Winter, and you must be the very lucky groom, Sterling."

"Yes," Sterling answered.

The judge seemed so... jubilant.

"Don't ever let him forget how lucky he is." The judge told me in a not-so-quite confidential whisper. He clapped his huge hands together again. "So how long have you two been together?"

Was this a quiz? Could he refuse to do the ceremony if we gave the wrong answer? I had thought we'd just march in, maybe do a few my-name-is's, you say this, he says that, bam. Done. I looked sideways at Sterling. He had made these plans, so he should know the answers.

No, he seemed as deer-in-the-headlights as I was.

"Our families introduced us some time ago," Sterling recovered first, and conjured an answer.

I smiled and nodded. It wasn't exactly a lie.

"We're so happy they're finally getting married!" Cye chirped from my shoulder. Jun nodded vigorously.

Nods all around, like dashboard dolls.

Just marry us, please.

He clasped his right wrist with his left hand. He had a massive gold ring on his ring finger. He beamed at us. "My wife and I have been married for a blessed thirty years, and it hasn't always been easy. That's the thing about marriage. So many young couples come in here, and they have all the love in the world, but love is work, and they're just not prepared for the commitment. Are you two prepared for the commitment you're about to make to each other?"

Sterling didn't hesitate. "Yes."

I was more nonplussed. People went to the courthouse because they didn't want speeches and ceremony. "Yes."

The judge went on for a while about how any relationship was work, even one formed upon a solid foundation of real love. Bewildered as I was, his voice was still so hypnotic it was impossible to escape the sound of him, even if it was difficult to take in his words through the nervous hum in my brain. After everything else that had gone wrong, I expected a wanderer to burst into the chambers at any moment to protest, or for the judge to decide he wouldn't marry us, or some other abrupt, random calamity occur.

He finished his speech, then grinned. "Time to get started! Unless there are protests? Hmm? Boys? Protests?"

"Nope," Jun said.

"Marry 'em!" Cye insisted.

I don't remember the words I spoke. I remember that the words echoed the promises I had already made in my heart, and that perhaps Gaia had already made for me. It felt good to affirm them, and to hear them spoken to me.

Jun actually cried when we kissed. "It's so sweet," he howled. Tears streamed down his face. The clerk passed him a tissue.

The judge beamed and radiated paternal warmth that made me miss my father—or the man I had once believed my father to be. This judge that didn't know me from the next couple he'd marry, and we'd probably never see him again, but I felt he, in a genuine way, wanted Sterling and I to be happy. Our happiness would make him happy, and that he had done something very important that morning taking extra time to offer us counsel.

Burian face-palmed at Jun's sniffles. "By Gaia, man. It's a wedding, not a funeral."

"It's sweet," Jun insisted. "It's just so sweet. She looks so pretty and Sterling is happy and this guy is just so nice and it's sweet!"

"Dude," Cye muttered as Jun broke down into bawls.

There was a round of photos—half of which involved Jun or Cye clowning around— then the judge signed our marriage certificate with a flourish. "My lucky pen." He waved the old fountain pen at us with a big grin.

He wished us well, still beaming from ear to ear, and as we left, his clerk and another clerk tossed a little bit of rice at us before our security detail swooped in to escort me to change my name. Changing my name was less emotional than expected. Just hand over the Montana license without a thought. Took ten minutes. Sort of like it had taken all of ten minutes for my life to transform when I had met Sterling.

Back at the flat, I told Sterling. "I don't even know what just happened. I think somewhere in there you and I got married, but I can't be sure."

Sterling held up the marriage license. "Mission accomplished. It did, in fact, happen."

"The judge was nice," Cye said.

"He was downright wholesome," Jun said. "When I think of the word wholesome, I'll picture that guy."

On second thought, it had been much better than some perfunctory oath-exchange. There had been good advice, good intentions, and genuine laughter. No crappy bouquet toss or garter-with-teeth or wretched first dance to some horrible song or the flower girl throwing up in the champagne fountain. I felt like twirling about.

But I'd settle for taking my stockings off. Because the lace on my thigh-highs itched.

"Wait, wait," Cye urged us before Sterling and I could go to change. "Let me get a picture of you two with your cake!"

Cye darted into the kitchen and, honestly, I have no idea how he hid this cake from us, probably behind a wall of food in his carefully arranged fridge. Cunning Cye. He pampered me with prepared food so that I'd stay out of his kitchen and leave him to his evil schemes!

The cake was the same shade of blue as my ring's diamonds, three round tiers and drenched in exquisite white icing work, and delicate spun-sugar roses with blue touched petals.

"Wow," Jun said eloquently.

It was not a large cake—just meant for the five of us. Cye beamed at us and said, "Ta-da!" He whipped his phone out of his pocket and waved it. "Picture time!"

Cye and Jun indulged in snapping some shots, then compared notes while Sterling and I admired the hours Cye must have spent sneakily crafting sugar roses and piping icing lace.

Then we had to eat the cake.

It was a nutty, rich cardamom-laced carrot cake and the blue frosting was the most decadent cream cheese and sugar thing I think any of us had ever tasted. Cye paired it with liquor-laced coffee, and we stood around eating it and drowning in sugar.

Even Burian came around for cake. He didn't say much, but he wasn't bad company. Perhaps there was hope.

We ate the whole cake. And Jun ate one of the roses. Petal by sugar petal.

I had never dreamed of a wedding.

But my wedding day had been perfect.

LAST MINUTE LEGAL MATTERS

Of course the evening had to be interrupted by Sterling's lawyer calling. It served as a stark (and unwelcome) reminder that the SilverPaw were the biggest threat to SnowFang just then. It didn't mater what happened with the wanderers or Burian if this bride-price business went south. The AmberHowl couldn't force the SilverPaw to do anything. They could only lean and threaten, but if the SilverPaw dug in, the options were the Elder Council or well... nothing.

That would leave SnowFang very much on its own. My father's vengeance would be terrible, and he'd carve SilverPaw's "good name" out of our hides. If he was feeling generous he'd accept the payment, dissolve SnowFang, and disgrace all of us, striking us from the records and sending us to live in exile. More likely he'd demand the payment, dissolve SnowFang anyway, and brand all of us rogues. Rogue status would put a bounty on each of our heads. Perhaps he'd let *me* live in exile, just to see if I'd choose to die at Sterling's side or live as a warning to everyone who tried to defy the Elders.

It had been such a nice day, and here I was sipping coffee and staring out the window while contemplating all the ways my father could make my life a monument to stupid choices made by willful daughters.

Sterling emerged from the back, head still tucked into his phone, but his general direction pointed towards our bedroom. I followed him.

"Problems?" I asked, closing the door behind me as he sat down on the edge of the bed.

He frowned at his phone. "No, just some last minute thoughts from Hector. Hector is already not happy that I married you on what he calls a lark, and without a pre-nup.

You should hear him screaming. You probably will one day."

The world needed to go away for a few hours. I went over to the bed and knelt behind him, pressing into his strong back as I peered over his shoulder. "But are there problems with the gift?"

"Hmm. Last minute squabbling coming through. They're on Pacific time." Sterling skimmed through a series of texts.

I drew one of my nails down the side of his neck, pressing into the flesh enough to pull up a few curls of skin. Sterling shifted slightly.

He looked over his shoulder. "The wanderers are held at bay for the time being. I can pull this gift together. But it's the SilverPaw not yet caving to the AmberHowl that makes me nervous."

I sighed. We needed to stop talking about all this. I pushed my fingernail into the point of one shoulder, and pulled it, hard, over his skin to the other. "They have to. There's no reason for them not to, besides not wanting an official record. That's not a reason."

"It's a reason. Just not one the AmberHowl should accept."

"They won't accept it."

"You genuinely believe the Council is honorable?"

"I'd like to think the AmberHowl are doing it for honor, but they probably want something too. Not that I can fathom what they'd want from *us*. They *did* became Elder Council a few years ago. Possibly they don't like seeing it tarnished. Maybe it really is just the chance to growl at another Elder Pack. Prestige games still exist with the Elders."

He considered this.

I had humored him long enough. Conversation time was over. I reached around him and put my hand over his phone. "Enough, Sterling. Throw it away."

He grinned at me, but didn't give up the phone. "Oh? Why?"

"There is still work for us to do. I am not an expert on human law, but I seem to have some recollection that we are not actually married until we consummate the relationship." I pulled my fingernails down his neck again, harder this time, creating red lines in his flesh. His body shifted slightly, but the scent of lust was unmistakable. "We have enough legal problems, wouldn't you say?"

"We have quite a few. But you have my attention. Somewhat. Tell me." He pulled my other hand to his lips, examining the blue nails. "Did you get these just to rake down my back?"

"Blue is your favorite color."

He tossed his phone away. "So. Blue dress, blue nails... blue panties?"

"Maybe."

He slid his hand under my skirt, along my thigh to the top of the my stockings. His fingers explored the ribbons interwoven with the lace tops. "Blue ribbons."

"Hmm." I smiled mischievously. "Keep going."

The air on my thighs and the heat of his gaze drew a gasp from me. My panties (what there was of them) were indeed blue.

"Do you have a favorite color?" his lips brushed mine.

"Naked."

His fingertips slid around the inside of my thigh. He kissed my neck slowly, lips lingering and teasing, the hand between my thighs a light, lingering touch as well. It was torment. My dress was too tight, my breasts suddenly too heavy and confined, the panties an unneeded obstacle. My skin flushed another notch, and a hot coal of heat coalesced deep within me.

"Take this off." He pulled at my dress.

He released me and I slid off the bed. I turned to face

him, and he watched with a heavy gaze, unapologetic, and even that was a caress. He didn't want a show... he just wanted to be in control.

Fine. I'd play along for a bit. Might be interesting. And I could get my dress off. I tugged the zipper down, freeing my breasts from their confines, and sighed in relief.

He stared, taking it all in. I went to untie the ribbons holding my panties on my hips, and he said, hoarsely, "No."

"Oooohh, *really*." I tried not to laugh. Sterling had a thing for fancy panties, did he?

He reached out, grasped me by my rump and tugged me to him. He kissed my belly, moving lower and lower in a slow chain. I quivered as he kissed the blue silk covering my mound. The sensation of warm lips through the sandy soft silk made me squirm, uncertain. He held me in place.

Lower still, and his tongue, damp and warm through the silk, found where my slit began. I gripped his shoulders. My skin was too hot, and there was a throbbing emptiness within the deepest part of me. I closed my eyes and grit my teeth, fighting to stay upright as he slowly teased me, just teasing, nothing more. Flicks of moist silk grazed my jewel, tendrils of hot excitement snapped through me, dissolving my will and senses.

He moved back, and pulled me astride his thighs. I kissed him hungrily, tongue meeting his. I gasped as his hands pressed me down, rubbing our bodies together through a few thin layers of increasingly abused fabric. Then one hand pinched a nipple, sending shocks through my shoulder and chest that matched the tender heat between my legs.

"Wait a moment—" I said.

He ignored me and bent to take my nipple in his mouth, then moved to my other breast.

I grabbed two handfuls of his shirt and shoved him back. "What is this?"

"My shirt. Obviously." He humored me for about two

seconds, then bent to kiss between my breasts. He lifted me higher on him. Our bodies shifted together and my damp panties abraded my body, punishing me with jolts of pleasure.

"That's not fair." I think I sounded a little breathless. I *felt* breathless. Somehow the silk around my hips strangled my throat. I shifted again, trying to find some way to be astride him that didn't make the fever-pitch humming between my thighs find a new height. The shifting just made it worse and I gripped his shoulders as a pleased shudder went down my spine.

"Are we negotiating?" His body was taut, but his voice composed.

I was losing this battle of wills, because every shift of my body on his sent waves of heat through my brain that made me want one thing. His breath was just as hot on my skin, his hands tight in their grip, but he had the benefit of experience. "It's unfair that you are clothed, and I am not."

He pulled back slightly, cupping my rump, and he took in the sight of my damp panties astride him. His breath caught, and his fingers tightened to a vise, digging into my skin. He shifted me against him, and I almost melted, willing to do whatever he wanted so long as it involved at least one key part of his body unclothed within the next thirty seconds.

He corrected my statement, voice torn, "You are delectably adorned. Not naked."

Oh, so that was it, hmm? Sterling liked his prey in autumn plumage. I liked my prey naked. I used a fingernail to pop off one of his shirt buttons, and made it a point to slide my body against his.

He rewarded my efforts with a growl as he nipped my neck. "Behave yourself, Winter. You're testing my control."

"Oh, is *that* what I'm doing? Little virgin me just doesn't know these things." I shoved him flat onto his back. I put both hands on his chest and crouched down over him, keeping my weight over his erection. "Sterling, are you trying to be *gentle*?"

Stubborn wolf still thinking his little virgin mate needed to be handled *gently*. I wanted what was rightfully mine, and there was nothing gentle about the empty, hot hunger within me. Nothing gentle would feed it. Nothing gentle at all.

I growled at him.

He wasn't the least bit threatened, and just smirked. He pulled at the ribbons on my hip. "The thought had occurred to me to be gallant and not just throw you down and take what is *mine*."

Mine. The way he hissed the word made me moisten further, and my spine arched.

Oh, he could have done that. He most certainly could have done that. My skin surged with the hot flush not unlike a coming shift. I said breathlessly, "You'll bore me to death before you ever scare me."

Something about his grin made me even more wet, and the empty heat more intense and unbearable. He snapped the ribbons and flung my panties away. He shoved me off him.

I rolled into the blankets and kicked him in the thigh. He smacked my foot away. "Naughty little she-wolf," he growled at me. "You might regret what you've demanded."

"I doubt that," I retorted.

He pulled off his shirt, tossed it aside, and then the pants. Gaia, he was glorious. I stared, absorbing what was mine. Chiseled, his body's handful of scars flawing the otherwise uncomforting perfection. His rigid length was beyond impressive... perhaps even a little intimidating.

Good. I liked intimidating.

"You're staring," his voice felt like piano wire against my skin: taunt, threatening, thrilling.

"Damn right I'm staring, and if you insist on being gentle

with me, that's *all* I'll do."

"I think someone needs to learn some manners, especially about what she will and won't do."

I liked this game, but I also didn't think it was much of a game, which made it all the more entertaining. How far did I dare push him? Him throwing me down and taking what was his didn't sound like a punishment I wouldn't enjoy... but there was no guarantee that would be the actual punishment. I enjoyed the quiver of doubt, and twinge of wary anticipation.

Sterling came back to the bed, the scent of musk and power and authority on his shoulders. I curled around him, fascinated by the scent that demanded I *obey*. I ran my hand over the flat of his abdomen. He was so much stronger and denser than I was. There was nothing soft or gentle about him. The silver-burn scar met my fingertips, and I wondered briefly what had caused it.

"Keep going," he commanded, biting my ear a little too hard.

His shaft was thick in my palm, but the skin so very soft, and felt stretched tight over the swollen girth. The thick vein along the underside, then the littler veins. He pulled at my cheek with one hand, "Harder," he bid me, hazel gaze smoldering, and closed his hand over mine and pushed downward on the shaft. "Or do you think you'll hurt me?"

"Won't I?"

"No," The idea that little me could hurt *him* amused him to no end.

I gripped him, stroking upward, then downward, fingers curling around the base and pressing upwards, marveling at just how rough I could be. His breathing grew ragged, his kiss hotter and heavier, and the shaft slickened as he came closer.

Revenge was so sweet. So very, very sweet.

Alphas, so easily tamed.

"Enough," he growled. He shoved me onto my back, and I protested, but he ignored me.

Perhaps not so easily tamed after all.

He ran his hand over the inside of my thigh in a sweeping stroke. I squirmed. It tickled! His hand closed over my mound, which did *not* tickle in the least, stroking my slick lips, and he breathed, ragged, by my ear, "Your turn, and you seem more than ready." He bent and inhaled the scent off my neck. "But you will have to learn a little patience."

Patience! I growled at him. "Are you going to spank me next?"

His response was a sharp, stinging swat to my rump. "If you want."

I rubbed my stinging ass. He hadn't held back either. It was going to leave a mark.

He pushed me back into the blankets, feral smirk on his lips, daring me to misbehave again. He kissed me lightly, his fingers sliding over my sex, amusement and power and control on his scent.

His fingers explored my moist slit while he watched me, studying every reaction as he sampled each delicate place, leaving me suspended between pleasure and annoyance. So the male's drive to know their mate extended to sex? Unfair advantage that was! One finger dipped just inside me, just a bit, just enough for the hunger to clamp its jaws down, and for me to moan.

"I hate you." I panted as he tormented me, exploring just inside me, gently. This was not going to do anything! I could do this to myself! I squirmed on his hand uncontrollably, even though I didn't want to, but he seemed to know exactly where to touch, or not touch, and to keep me poised just on the edge

"Good." His finger slid deeper, which was better *and* worse, because it was *more*, but it wasn't enough. It was just teasing of a different order. The heel of his palm rubbed my jewel, bringing me closer and closer. Oh, Gaia, finally he was going to—

Abruptly, he pulled his hand away from me.

"You beast!" I gasped pathetically. "I only did that to you because you told me to!"

"Poor little wolf. Does she not even know what she wants?" He ran the thumb that had just been touching me over my lips so I could taste myself. Oh, I knew what I wanted, and I bit down *hard*, growling a challenge at him.

He snatched his hand away, grabbed my face, kissed me, tongue shoving past my lips. He moved over me, his other hand grabbed my hips and yanked me under him.

If I could have told him *yes* I would have, but I could barely think straight. His hand moved between us, guiding his body against mine. I froze momentarily, not sure what to do, if anything, torn for a second between icy uncertainty and raving lust. He pressed into me, and it hurt as he sank deep, but I didn't care. The ice melted, and I arched up to meet him and cried out.

Sterling pulled back, and I grabbed at him, fearing I had spooked him. But he filled me again, and I dissolved under him, the exquisite shiver of a shift flitting over my skin as every shred of me sparkled into life.

"You are perfect," he told me, ragged and torn, his groan against my neck. His teeth raked my skin, then his jaws closed over my shoulder, clamping down hard enough the dull pain balanced the sharp pleasure.

"Flatterer." I managed to gasp out around a tangled moan. My fingernails dug into the skin of his back as I clung to him, coming closer and closer. The burning built higher with each stroke, each movement, his raw desire burning into me. I was so ready for him, so eager. I clawed at him as he thrust deep again, and again, and again.

The pleasure tripled to an unbearable intensity that finally shattered in brilliant explosion.

Afterwards we lay panting and sweaty on the crumpled sheets.

He moved behind me, fingertips caressing the small of my back. He kissed my neck very gently. "Now that the legalities are over, beautiful wolf."

"Hmm?" I rolled over to face him, warm and content. I trailed my fingertips over his chest, still marveling at how strong and dense he felt, even just laying next to me. My shoulder throbbed. I touched it, and found the indents of his teeth. He had really chomped me. I smiled to myself.

I would have to return the favor.

"It is time to turn more attention to the finer details your pleasure," he leaned closer, "and mine."

RISING WATERS

My phone rang far too early the next morning. Sterling had muted his, but I had forgotten to silence mine. I debated not answering. Then I remembered how few people had that number, and anyone trying to ring me was probably someone I needed to talk to.

I oozed toward the nightstand. Felt around until I grabbed a phone. Realized I was on Sterling's side of the bed, and it was his phone. Threw it on the floor with a curse. Felt Sterling behind me. His arm slid over me. "Here," he murmured in my ear. He dropped my phone before my breasts.

It was the AmberHowl. I picked up the phone and tried to prop myself up a little more. If I got more vertical I might feel more awake. "Good morning, MaryAnne."

I hoped I did not sound as furry-headed as I felt. I rubbed my face with my other hand.

"Good morning, Winter."

Sterling kissed my shoulder. I tried to shake him away. His hand moved over my naked hip and made me quiver and almost gasp—that tickled! I elbowed him and got him right in the solar plexus. MaryAnne and I exchanged some trivial pleasantries. She told me the formal request for my bride-price had been received.

Well, that was enough to wake me up like some cold water. It was welcome news, but hearing about it still sent adrenaline through my system. Back to reality.

Sterling's hand continued over my thigh, and he brushed his lips against the back of my neck—apparently unaware of, or completely ignoring, my sudden focus on something other than him. I elbowed him again but it didn't make any difference.

MaryAnne didn't let me go so quickly. There was one last small detail: the AmberHowl wanted to know how we intended to pay my bride-price. I merely acknowledged the request and bid her farewell.

Sterling flipped me over onto my back. My phone fell out of my hand onto the mattress. "Good morning." He bent and kissed my shoulder, working his way towards my neck.

"Do not fondle me while I'm trying to talk to an Elder pack." I couldn't believe I even had to tell him this.

"I was not fondling you. I was caressing you. There is a difference. Now fondling you—"

"Will have to wait." I pushed on his shoulders. As much as I enjoyed his soft touch, he and I had something important to do that probably required clothing. Now that I was actually awake, I was also aware that part of my body felt like it had been on the losing side of a barfight. So much for the "it hurts a bit" line given to you in eighth grade health class.

"Why?" He refused to budge and instead kissed under my jaw, "It can all wait half an hour."

"We have a little homework assignment from the AmberHowl. And I feel like I've been in a bar fight." I pushed him off me and winced as I sat up. Dang. Bar fight. Right in the ladybits.

He frowned at me. "You should have said something last night, Winter. If I was too—"

I liked him better when he was aggressively pawing at me, and not when he was worried he had done something wrong. "I'm fine. Now, I'm going to shower. Alone."

He captured my wrist and tugged gently. "You don't have to put on an act for me, Winter. Not in bed, and not afterward. Don't ever do that."

"I'm fine, Sterling. Although my stockings." I nudged one of the fallen stockings with my toe and changed the subject. "I do not believe this one survived."

His eyes were inexorably drawn to the abused white

stocking on the floor. "Pity. I suppose you will just have to find more. "

"Mmm-mmm." I moved toward the shower.

A hot soak made everything feel better. Sterling let me have about ten minutes before he placed himself outside the shower door and asked the obvious question, "What is this homework for the AmberHowl?"

"They want to know what the gift is."

"Why? I thought we got to choose and it didn't matter."

I splashed water on my face and whined. "Can't I have a cup of coffee first?"

He yanked open the shower door. "No."

The AmberHowl wanted to verify for themselves the payment was of sufficient value and not 'overly burdensome.' Given the contentious nature of the proceedings it wasn't unreasonable. They were right in the thick of things.

I explained this to Sterling, who immediately bristled. "You told me I got to choose."

"You do. My father could still get to the table and refuse payment. It's happened before when Alphas just want to be dicks to each other. So the mediator gets to say if the payment violates the excessively burdensome rule. Like if you paid my father in pennies."

"We agreed this would be a poisoned apple. The AmberHowl will spot this for what it is. All this time putting it together and now you tell me it has to go through a final vetting?"

"Poisoned apples and booby-trapped gifts aren't prohibited. The exact language of the Law is 'overly burdensome for the value of the gift.' Don't worry, Sterling. If the AmberHowl wanted to make nice with my father, they'd have told us they weren't getting involved at all. This is just so they are fully prepared."

"You're sure," he said suspiciously.

I was *almost* certain, assuming the AmberHowl had honorable intentions, which might be an overly large assumption. "Trust me. I know how this goes. I'll write the formal response, but you'll need to fill in what the gift is."

Sterling could smell even the tiniest bluff from a thousand yards. "Do they need a copy of the contracts and documents?"

"Won't hurt to include it." The AmberHowl was a younger pack—just a few generations—and had come to prominence through skillful maneuvering, politics, and investments. They had achieved a voice on the Elder Council three years earlier. My father had supported it because the pack was so savvy, although he had encouraged the AmberHowl to also focus on more "traditional" pursuits and not completely immerse themselves in humanity. Quite a few doctors, lawyers, dentists, investment types, teachers, even some placed in human government.

I had never been introduced to the Alpha, Demetrius, but I had seen him at the Greater Meetings and always thought he had the bearing of a good Alpha. A smart, strong wolf, with a lovely and wise Luna. A good leader if he had wrestled his pack to Elder status so quickly. The first time I had seen him he had had his head cocked to the side as Luna Marcella murmured something in his ear, and I had been enthralled by their graceful, gracious authority.

I had even pondered what it would have been like to have mated into AmberHowl.

Including the contract might also give us a chance to demonstrate Sterling's considerable resourcefulness and quiet cunning to an Elder pack that valued such things. I permitted myself a little smile. An appropriately worded traditional response packaged with a modern day Trojan horse? I didn't see how it could possibly work against us.

I was going to go for every possible glimmer of hope and advantage we had. Maybe the AmberHowl had started this way.

Every big pack grew from something.

SnowFang wasn't going for a spot on the Elder Council —no pack made that in a single generation. I did intend to survive, and if we could possibly wrestle some prestige from this, so much the better. SnowFang's success and survival would be the best revenge.

Sterling closed the shower door but not before I saw his face had a dark expression on it. If this fell out from under us it was on me. I pursed my lips. I'd have to take my chances that not everything my father had let me learn had been a lie.

By the early afternoon we had the packet ready and in a courier's hands. The AmberHowl would have it in the morning. In characteristic Sterling fashion he told me we had a meeting at three. He mentioned this to me at five after two, while we sat in his office having just handed the packet off to the courier.

"A little warning would have been nice," I said.

"An hour isn't enough?" he asked blankly.

Something told me it was pointless to try to have this argument with Sterling. He was always a man on a mission. Always on the scent of something, and I could either keep up or be dragged along or stand there and fight with him. I chose to just shrug and go along with it this time. "What is it about?"

"Bodyguards."

Now I put my heels in. "Whoa. Back up there, Sterling. We haven't even talked about bodyguards at all. Now there's a meeting about it?"

"We can talk about it now, before the meeting."

I hadn't agreed to anything and he had already set up a meeting with some human to discuss the matter as if I had already agreed to it? I scowled at him.

"Do you want to be a prisoner in your own home?"

"I'm not your staff. You don't get to make a bunch of

assumptions, even if they seem logical to you," I retorted. "I'm your mate, and now your wife. It's called respect. Involving humans in our lives is a very big deal. Yes, I hate being a prisoner here. I'm also not sure I'd hate what comes with human bodyguards less."

"Fair enough." He didn't sound convinced.

I weighed having this fight with him, then decided I had enough conflict the past couple of days. Sterling's intentions were good. I shifted on the chair. I could not quite recall this particular chair being quite so unforgiving.

"Are you really in one piece?"

"Those scratches on your back aren't because I was trying to stop you." I winked at him. "I'm not sitting here worrying that those scratch marks were a little too much. You haven't said anything. Are you all right, Sterling? Was I too rough with you?"

He burst out laughing. His arrogance simultaneously made me melt onto the floor in a quivering puddle, and want to roll my eyes in the most dramatic fashion possible. "Hardly."

"I didn't think so." I clicked my nails together. "Hardly, hmm? I'll remember you said that."

He grinned at me. Although he was in human form, my mind saw glimmering pearl canines, feral and brilliant.

"Anyway. Back to me being annoyed at you." I waved my hand and smiled at how his eyes followed the blue tips with undisguised interest. He had enjoyed them the night before. "And you trying to convince me not to have a headache tonight."

"You fight dirty."

"Do I?"

"So. Bodyguards. Although," he cocked his head slightly and leaned forward, "I'm wondering if you have on pretty stockings again under that dress."

"I do not. Focus, Sterling. Bodyguards." I was without

any stockings at all. I hated them. They were sort of scratchy and caught on things. The only ones I could live with were the thigh-highs, but even those were uncomfortable after a time. They had been a special treat for Sterling the day before.

"Burian had one thing right."

Ah, Burian. Just the cold shower we needed.

"He's not a bodyguard. Nor is Jun. And Mint was right too. What happened at the salon could have been very bad for a number of reasons. Lucky for us, the other security detail suppressed everything. I got all this from my friend. Mint's employer."

And mentioning the salon incident was the ice bath that finished off any heat in my blood.

"It all got overshadowed by Burian's little Sunday jaunt, but it's every bit as serious for other reasons. This is too much for them. They're not trained for it. Not fair to you or to them."

"Or to you?" I pointed at his still bruised cheek. "We are talking about you too, I hope, Alpha."

"Yes, yes," Sterling grumbled.

"And we're talking humans. Not wolves."

"Yes, humans."

My gut reaction was absolutely not, but I already hid behind humans. Behind drivers, behind doormen, holed up in their buildings. I had no interest in adding more wolves to the pack just then. It was too much responsibility. I could barely manage the ones I had. But we clearly needed some kind of pest deterrent. After the previous day, the ease and polish and competency of professional bodyguards had left an impression.

He half-grinned at me. "When I was growing up, I had bodyguards. My mother had them. I was glad to get rid of them, because part of their job was to keep me out of trouble. Incident suppression. Handlers."

"Did they... know? About you? Your mother?"

"If they did, or do, I don't know. I don't believe so. They weren't there for wolf threats."

"So what did your pack think of this?"

Sterling shook his head. "My mother left pack life behind when I was seven. Now she lives as a human."

That must have meant his mother took MoonDark, an herbal concoction that suppressed our ability to shift. It had been developed as a restraint in lieu of silver-lined shackles, but it also was used as a treatment for werewolves who force-shifted, or werewolves who wanted to or needed to live as humans. Using it to "go human" by choice was a contentious topic. I personally was a little uncomfortable with it. We were a dying breed, and werewolves "going human" seemed like death by a thousand cuts.

At the same time, unhappy werewolves who didn't want to be werewolves weren't going to help our species either. Having met some, it was difficult to argue against their unhappiness.

Sterling took my silence for agreement. "So."

I took a breath and let it out through my mouth. "I see the logic, but what happens when we go places they can't follow?"

"That I don't know. How often is that going to happen? We have no place on the Elder Council. Hell, you and I wouldn't even be allowed at the Greater Meetings."

"True." I scratched my cheek with a manicured nail. "Maybe if such a time came, we'd have other options. I'd like to hope so."

"Winter, I travel a great deal. I want you to come with me. I don't want you locked up here. Our issues are either human, or we simply need a deterrent. Protection specialists know how to plug the holes. Deal with threats in discrete fashion before it even happens. Clean up messes. Suppress incidents. It's what they do. It's all they do."

"Would we tell them?"

"I'd rather not."

Sterling had mentioned his family in passing, but hadn't gone into too much detail, and some omissions, like his biological father, seemed deliberate instead of casual-things-he-never-thought-about. He spoke about his father more readily than his mother. Probably a risky subject, even though there was very little he could have revealed to me at this point that would have changed my opinion of him. One day we'd have to talk about it, but for right now, confining myself to immediate concerns seemed best. "Your mother lives as a human. But she saw you got a wolf education. You *clearly* have one."

I feared my mother-in-law and I would not have a good relationship if she had gone human, and I was determined to not lose that part of myself.

Sterling, after a moment of hesitation, said, "My mother has her reasons. But she didn't make them *my* reasons, and let me make my own choices. My wolf education is nothing like yours, but she did the best she could. I'm not a city wolf by birth."

I fidgeted. "Sterling, I'm not human. I don't want to be human."

Sterling didn't flinch. "Can you be practical?"

The lure of freedom was undeniable. I'd no longer be a puppy that needed minding. I was also a danger to anyone around me. If an innocent human got hurt because of me, I'd be riddled with guilt. A paid human bodyguard was an improvement, but I didn't know how I felt not being completely honest about what they might face.

Still, the odds of them encountering a war-form werewolf in this city were pretty slim. "Is it the agency from yesterday?"

"Yes."

"Who is the meeting with?"

"The owner."

"If I don't feel comfortable with him, I'm not going along with this."

"Fair enough."

"And we cut them loose if we start getting into wolf trouble. I'm not going to bring ignorant humans into a wolf fight."

"Agreed."

I let out the breath I had been holding. "I still don't feel good about this, Sterling. It's dangerous."

"We're playing the hand we were dealt, Winter. I don't have wolf resources. I have human resources."

"I worry about becoming too human. There's a difference between choosing to go human and losing your fur."

"I've lived with that fear for years, Winter."

SILENCE

At three, we went downstairs to one of the meeting rooms to meet John Case. He was a tall, lithe man, bald and with a face that reminded me of my freshman year science teacher, and the demeanor of a steel blade. He wore an impeccable dark suit with a pale blue shirt and dark tie. Everything about him told me no nonsense and understated severity. Case was the owner and CEO of a personal protection agency that dealt in the highest level VIPs. Not just the ultra rich, not just celebrities, but government officials and royalty when required.

He recognized Sterling as they shook hands.

Quickly, and wordlessly, he backed me off many of my concerns. I reflected, instead, that werewolf packs often had human allies. Even, on very rare occasions, human members. John Case was a man who could have stood with those human. A man I could trust.

Perhaps not with my greatest secrets, but he at least invited me to consider it.

"My wife," Sterling introduced me. "Winter."

"A pleasure." Case shook my hand. I appreciated his grip. Strong, but not domineering. I had never met anyone who so instantly coerced trust.

We spoke for a while as he picked over every detail of our lives. Hobbies, work, obligations, were we night owls or early birds, smoke, drink, any sort of weapons or combat training, if we wanted male or female guards, medical conditions. In return, I asked Case about some of the more extreme situations his teams encountered.

In the name of discretion he edited out a great deal, but his teams would have found a couple of war-form wanderers a typical day's work. He recruited his teams from the highest level of the human military and intelligence agencies.

Werewolves had a healthy respect for human warriors. Our war-form exceeded them for strength, speed, pain tolerance, regeneration. It was a hard form to hold, and with it came a feral rage that clouded the mind. Cool-headed, well-armed humans were legitimate threats. We couldn't out-regenerate a bullet into our brains or ripping through an aorta. One expert shot in the right place would end any wolf, silver tips not required.

I'd have felt better had I been able to be completely transparent with them, but I comforted myself that what I would ask of them was probably less risky than other assignments. We weren't going into contested territories disputed by five armed factions in bad terrain a hundred miles from anywhere with no local law enforcement present. I wasn't a celebrity that would cause traffic accidents and mob crushes if I went for a jog.

Case told us it would take about two weeks to put a permanent detail in place, but that until then his agency would supply a temporary detail for me during the day, and any necessary coverage for Sterling.

Sterling didn't say much on the elevator back to the flat.

"Do you think he knows?" I had the oddest feeling he *did* know.

"I don't know. How long will it take for the AmberHowl to get back to us?"

"No idea." It might take a day. It might take a month. I dreaded the prospect of it taking months. I changed the subject back to the bodyguards. "So you've had this sort of detail before, right? Following you?"

"Mine were handlers," he told me with a mischievous glint in his eye. "They knew where I was allowed to go, who I could be with, when I needed to be home. They knew all the tricks. Especially when pretty women were about."

He flung the door to the flat open. "After you, dear."

"You are too kind."

He swatted my rump as I passed by him. Hard enough that it stung. "Fresh!"

"So I'm only allowed to swat you when you're naked?" He was suddenly right behind me against me, his body pressed along mine. One of his hands slid over my stinging flesh, the other held my arm. "Not that I mind such a requirement. Clothing is easily removed."

My skin flushed so hot it would dissolve into a million delicate particles. He drew the back of his fingers along my bare arm, igniting every nerve, painful prickles raising my skin towards his. "Sterling—"

He murmured, "The AmberHowl interrupted my plans for this morning."

"Sterling," I whispered in apology—and disappointment—, "I don't think my—I'm still sore. The barfight, remember?"

"I haven't forgotten. I will just have to show you my gentle side." He drew his fingertips along my throat, just a feather-light touch, but his teeth pressed into the soft flesh where my shoulder met my neck.

The combination of a feather-touch with the dull, threatening press of his teeth was almost more than I could stand. How could such a thing even exist? His fingertips moved in delicate patters over my dress, just barely pressing into my skin.

Gentleness was such exquisite torment.

"Very, very, gentle," he whispered.

I whimpered.

"Move along," he nudged me towards the hallway.

* * * * *

We did not hear from the AmberHowl the next day. Or the next. Or the next. We had bodyguard interviews to distract us, and Sterling his usual work, and I had the absolute novelty of being able to move about New York on a whim. I could go anywhere, do anything. It wasn't just being able to go, I also had unlimited means to do so.

I also had to go alone. Sometimes Sterling met me for lunch, but usually I found myself with just two bodyguards for company. It was hard for anything to have too much of a shine when there was no one with me to share it. Two days exploring the Natural History Museum and as I sat underneath the big blue whale having a cup of coffee, watching everyone else, very alone. There was no one to exchange texts with, no one to meet after this, or the next day.

Freedom lost its appeal and I threw myself into my math homework, apparently with such fervor that Jun and Cye both worried I was obsessed.

Sterling and I went out to dinner a few times, but each day that passed without word from the AmberHowl he got more and more twitchy. By the next Monday he was almost crawling the walls. I stretched a smile across my face and continued to assure him it would be fine.

Secretly, deep inside, I panicked a little more each day.

Sterling knew I was lying to both of us. He could smell the fear and anxiety on my skin, just like I could smell his doubt and growing frustration.

"You can't make them call," I finally said on the eighth day. Sterling had spent most of the night pacing, and trying to figure out something he could do to nudge things along. "They'll call when they're good and ready."

"You are the one who assured me this would not go to hell, Winter," he snapped. "I took you at your word."

It was his tone that stung, and it laid right into my increasing guilt and worry that I hadn't had as good a grasp of the game as I had thought. "It won't go to hell."

"It is not such an easy thing to just pull that much cash out of the air," Sterling growled. "I'd need a few weeks to do it. And now I'm thinking I need to do it just in case! Gaia forbid that one stock in the portfolio tanks. Rumor has it the company is for sale and has a watery balance sheet. I need to get rid of it. Quickly. I cannot keep waiting around for the AmberHowl! If I had known this could take weeks, I'd have done things differently."

I had seen these mediations a few times at home, and it always seemed to happen quickly. Speaking with care so as not to cause another burst of anger, I said, "It usually doesn't. There's no reason for the mediator to drag things out. It's probably just that it was a complicated gift and they want to make sure they know what they're backing. It's Elder on Elder, Sterling."

"Unless the mediator is negotiating with your father for a cut," Sterling said sourly.

"They wouldn't do that!"

Sterling gave me a scathing look, as if I had said something supremely stupid. "You *also* told me your father wasn't going to try to fleece me. Don't be naive, Winter. This is two Elder Alphas against me. After everything, it didn't at least cross your mind?"

"Well, yes, but... but, that's suggesting the entire Elder Council is corrupt!"

"Maybe it is." Sterling circled around me. His gaze sliced thin layers off my skin, his anger burned into me. I held completely still, afraid of what might happen if I even twitched. "Maybe the AmberHowl have some debts to pay off after making it to Elder status in three generations."

"No," I whispered. I wouldn't believe it. I couldn't believe that we had been lured into a trap like that.

"You are so naive."

I swallowed. The tears burned my eyelids. I willed myself not to cry. I would *not* cry.

Sterling's tone took on an edge of mocking contempt, as if I were a wretched simpleton. I had faked my way this far, but now it was over. "Do you *really* think your father would have let you be his assistant and create his own adversary? I'm starting to think you were raised to be naive and idealistic, cleverly disguised as educated and pragmatic. Plenty of knowledge, but no *truth*."

Panic curled claws into my bones like fine silver wires, burning and relentless. Sterling paced around me, re-assessing my value. There was nothing to counter his accusations. Since this had all started I had been playing as if I knew the rules, but everywhere the rules had been bent or broken. Sterling might be right: my father had *always* had more pieces on his side of the board, and I had been the piece he knew best how the manipulate.

But the AmberHowl were a wealthy pack. Why risk their public face for a piece of my bride-price? Yes, it was a good piece of money, but nothing they didn't already have. That was just wild speculation, so I didn't dare say it. Sterling was done with my speculation. The ball of anxiety pressed up into my lungs, the silver wires jerked my body. A tear managed to escape.

Sterling stopped and faced me. His voice would haunt my nightmares, a tone I never wanted to hear again. It crawled down into the bond between us, silver seeping into my blood. "This is the gambit. And we'll play it until the bitter end, Winter."

He left.

If I let the tears fall it released some of the pressure in my chest, but the burning in my blood and the wire in my bones did not ease.

Unwanted.

Perhaps not, but a failure all the same.

That night he chose to sleep in wolf form at the foot of our bed. In the darkness I could not see his form, save that he was pale-coated and large.

He had left our bed, but not our room. I shifted, and crept up to him, tail tucked and legs bent so my belly was lowered, offering an apology and trying to snuggle up with him.

He growled at me. I keened a whimper. Surely he didn't mean it! He could growl just to make his point, but he wasn't really going to banish me from his side over this!

He snarled and snapped his jaws shut. His teeth made a cracking sound that hit the walls.

I fled to the top of the bed and buried myself in the pillows.

In my dreams, I was alone in the dark hallway, wandering up and down the endless corridor, trying to find Sterling and the puppies.

THE EDGE OF FAILURE

Shifting two nights earlier had popped off three acrylics, and now I had a museum-hosted charity gala event to attend. Another day at the spa, this time with silent, stony human bodyguards and a watchful Mint tending to me. Avoidable mistakes being avoided.

Through no intentional act, I had mostly failed as a Luna. I had given my Alpha bad advice that had directly led to a political nightmare. One that could have been easily avoided if I had not overestimated myself.

Silence from the AmberHowl continued.

Sterling had only slept alone that one night, but now he didn't blame me for my ignorance. His anger at me had been replaced with a sort of shitty, privileged pity for my ignorance. He blamed *himself* for trusting me and deciding to play against two Elder Alphas.

"I should know better. I am not wealthy because I play a bad hand," he had told me. "I should have known to just write the damn check."

Being forgiven as incompetent was worse than being blamed for being just plain wrong.

"I can't believe the Elders are a corrupt old boys' club," I had mustered.

"Believe it," he had replied, but given me a look of pity for how surely I had been outfoxed by my own father, and played perfectly into his plans.

I didn't want Sterling's forgiveness, and I didn't want his pity! I wanted to fight with him. Not just have him back away and forgive me as an uneducated feral. I wanted his anger. I wanted him to be mad at me. I wanted to be *worthy* of his anger. I wanted to be worthy of being responsible for this!

Another gala, this time in a museum. I just sat on my side of the car, hands folded in my lap and the new necklace he had given me an anchor around my neck. I hated the silence between us but I didn't know what I could say to him.

He was impossible to deal with when he was pulling at his chains, snarling at everything. He had promised he'd never put a hand on me in anger, but his anger seethed and churned. The physics of a pressure vessel were frightening. Finally, he turned to me and said, "Winter, don't be this way."

"What way?" I kept my eyes forward. I didn't want to talk to him. I had to keep things together for this party.

"This way. You've been frost and ice to me for three days."

"You're the one who growled at me, Sterling." Being growled at and banished from my mate's presence had cut right into my bones. I preferred to think he didn't know, or didn't appreciate how deep a wound it had left. Let him think I was angry. Burian had betrayed their friendship, and Burian had still been allowed to eat with the pack. I had, at worst, made a stupid and naive mistake, for which Sterling had banished me from his presence. It had only been for a night, but it still didn't fit the crime.

Being forgiven because I was the village idiot didn't make it better. It made it worse.

"I was angry."

"You made that very clear." This wasn't about that anymore. If he thought I was holding an angry grudge about *that*, he was wrong.

He sighed. "You are impossible, Winter. Your damned pride."

"*My* pride? What about *you*? What if they haven't called because they haven't gotten around to it. Maybe we're not *special* enough to screw. We're not important enough to be anyone's priority."

Sterling huffed. "If I had thought a delay was possible, I'd have done a different gift. Something not so toxic. I'll use my claws if I have to, I'm not afraid to get roughed up, but I'm not going to walk out in front of a firing squad!"

Back to this again. He had told me it wasn't my fault, but he sure acted like I was to blame. He needed to make up his damn mind. I blinked my eyes. Crying with this much makeup on was out of the question.

It was an old conversation by now. I was just a naive country bumpkin. Now I was off to some lovely museum gala for some function Sterling couldn't remember the purpose of. Just that we needed to go and be seen so Sterling could schmooze and succeed some more at human games. This time it was *his* business, not his father's, but he couldn't even be bothered to remember why we needed to go.

Just like in the beginning, where he hadn't cared where I was or who I was with, so long as I showed up to be at his side at the appointed time.

Oh, and the sex. Not that he had so much as looked at me in seven days. For that I was grateful, because being good enough to fuck but too stupid to be responsible wasn't a turn on.

"Winter."

Apparently he wanted some kind of response. I summoned the energy. "What do you want me to say? Do you want me to pretend you're not angry? Pretend that you didn't make me sleep alone when you let Burian keep eating with us? It's either my fault, or it's not, just decide already!"

"Winter, I am sorry about that. I was just angry."

"And I was the available target. I'm the source of the anger. Just admit it!" It was better than pity for my stupidity. Tell me I was competent enough to be held responsible!

"No. I overestimated you. I overestimated myself. I underestimated your father. And when I think over it, I'm the one who's played these games more often than you. I should have spotted the potential trap and planned around it."

"We've had this conversation." My voice tightened to cracking. His matter of fact honesty was the worst kind. It gripped your ribs and you knew it was true. Sterling had been the one to admire my knowledge, and now he tossed it aside. All that seemed to be left of me was the Winter in the backseat of a driven car dripping in diamonds and plastered with makeup, expected to play nice with the humans and not cock that up. "It doesn't matter if they ever call. You've said your part."

"So what I said was unforgivable?"

"It was unforgettable."

"I don't like you so far away from me."

I didn't like it either, but I didn't know how to cross the distance between us. We somehow needed to. We wouldn't survive long like this. I sucked in a breath. "I gave you the best advice I had to give. I've seen this before. I can't accept the AmberHowl are that dirty. Not until I don't have a choice. We haven't lost yet."

He ran a hand over his face. I envied his lack of makeup. "You and I are from two different worlds, Winter. You're from the world that believes. I'm from the world that's seen how the Elders treat the weak."

"I won't apologize for still having some faith. You must still have some too." Us being together at all was proof of that.

"Maybe we shouldn't."

"You and I are mates. There's that."

"There's that."

There was something beyond us that would demand accountability when we died. I wasn't about to indulge self-righteous spiel about dying martyrs and fighting for what was right, because I believed such things to be nonsense best confined to fairytales, but in the darkness, I clutched my faith like a candle. Not much to see by but better than complete darkness. I simply couldn't believe my faith was futile or silly.

Just difficult.

The party was at least interesting. The museum had set out a custom showing of priceless works spanning a thousand years and eighteen countries, and of course it was beautifully catered and people fluttered and preened at each other. Conversation was slightly less meaningless than the art gallery. I confined myself to soda water with a little lime, and admired all the artwork, drifting with the crowd of tag-a-long spouses that weren't there to do business, just be present.

I was congratulated multiple times on my recent nuptials. Each congratulations was like a punch to my chest, but I smiled and said my part. And when I was asked where we had met, I told the same lie Sterling had told to the judge. "Oh, our families introduced us."

Sterling disappeared. I could have found him, but I didn't see any point to why I should. My job was to be the perfect little human wife, and smile prettily, and say meaningless things. I could do that properly. Or at least I hoped so. The nature of the exhibit, and my past appearance at the art show, let me sit on the benches in front of each painting and seemingly contemplate it. People just murmured that I was appreciating the art.

Because I was an art aficionado, according to the society pages.

That I managed to lie so well and pretend to be something with such ease made me sick. I was just a cracked clay pot that was about to be thrown away. I had served my father's purpose and had no further use.

Even Sterling re-evaluated my worth, like he contemplated balance sheets and projection reports weighing how much anything was worth to him.

Just used and forgotten, discarded, disposable, the worthless space between stars.

The AmberHowl had to call eventually. Then I would know better how bad things were. Eventually this would all be over. Until then I just had to not lie down. Storms only lasted eons on the outer planets. Even Gaia's rage had limits. Her Wheel would turn in time and this would all move with it.

My little purse vibrated on my wrist. What now? Had Jun burned down the apartment? I tugged the beaded handles off my wrist, snapped it open and fished out my phone.

Eventually was right then.

"Excuse me," I murmured to the people around me. I hurried out of the room and tried to retreat to a quiet part of the museum floor, but the party was sort of a far-flung affair and it was hard to get out of earshot of everyone. Adrenaline made my hands shake. "Hello, MaryAnne."

"Good evening, Winter." A pause. "What's that noise?"

"I'm at a charity gala." I couldn't believe I told her that. "But we can talk."

"We received the packet," Her voice was completely neutral, and superficially pleasant. "Alpha Demetrius finds your gift is appropriate and of sufficient value."

I collapsed backwards onto the wall. My knees shook so hard they bumped into each other. My throat closed over and I had to fight to choke out, "That is welcome news. What is the next step?"

Who was this person talking to her? Because it sure didn't sound or feel like me.

"Alpha Demetrius would like to conclude this matter here, on the AmberHowl estate," MaryAnne said.

Good thing she couldn't see my face. And good thing I was already supported by a wall. Normally packs chose neutral ground for this sort of thing, and sent proxies. We had planned to send Hector. But summoning all the players straight to the heart of AmberHowl! A shimmer moved over my skin and I grabbed it, fought it, nearly panicked that I had felt a shift begin. Instead, I heard myself say, "That is fine with SnowFang."

Who was this person talking to MaryAnne? It sounded like me, but I was down somewhere deep inside myself screaming.

"Alpha Demetrius anticipated that. The SilverPaw have also agreed. It will be this Saturday, at ten AM."

Two days? Focus. I had to get through this. "That is fine. I will need the address."

Address? Address! Crap! I looked around. The bar. I scurried over to the bar, not really caring who saw me rushing about, and snapped a napkin from the corner of the table. The bartenders looked at me with polite inquiry but that was all. Now. A pen. "Hold on," I told MaryAnne. "Just a moment."

I looked around, didn't see anything, then remembered that in the lobby was a low table that had the guest book and a large bowl for checks. I thought I recalled seeing some pens as we had come in. I picked up the hem of my dress in my other hand and less-than-gracefully clicked my way down the marble steps to the lobby.

Don't break an ankle, don't break an ankle...

The low table was indeed there, and I spied two orphaned pens lying on the dark blue tablecloth.

"Ready?" she asked me for the third time.

"I am now." I clutched my prizes. She told me the address of the AmberHowl estate, and then gave me the AmberHowl Beta's phone number and email. He would coordinate picking us up at the airport. We would not be expected to make our own way to the AmberHowl estate, or be unescorted. That was the first normal thing in this entire debacle.

I leaned both hands on the table and panted. I needed to get a hold of myself. I swallowed, straightened and, fearful of losing the napkin, carefully tapped the information into my phone.

So much for *eventually*. There hadn't been any release or conclusion. Just another carrot waved in front of my face. Sterling was going to crawl up the walls.

My guts informed me I was going to throw up.

More to the point, my guts wanted to throw up, and I was just getting enough warning so I could find a quiet corner. How polite of my insides.

There was no one in the bathroom, and since I hadn't eaten anything but some toast that morning, it was just the agony of dry heaves.

I slumped against the cold tile wall, sitting on the floor of the handicapped stall, and rested my forehead in my hand. I shook all over. The hot sweats passed to cold shivers, and left me empty.

I was just twenty years old and barely knew how to run my own life. I knew nothing about leading a pack. Especially not a pack of wolves who didn't know how to be wolves, and one of whom I couldn't trust. And another who screamed at the least little bit of blood. I didn't know how to be a Luna, a wife, or a mother. I didn't know how to live in this world of ungodly wealth and privilege, or survive in a concrete jungle. And now I was in so impossibly deep with Elder Alphas that I didn't know up from down anymore.

But twenty or not, I couldn't just sit here on a museum's bathroom floor.

I wanted to splash some water on my face, but I hadn't managed to ruin my makeup, so I resisted the urge. Instead, I just stood in front of the mirror and inspected myself. I couldn't go back to the party looking like I had just been told the beatings would continue until my morale improved.

What was I going to tell Sterling? His gift had been accepted, but we had to go in person to deliver it. My father would be there. Probably with Second Beta Arnold, perhaps even Daniel, a few enforcers, probably Jeffers the pack lawyer and who knew who else.

I hadn't had time to think about ever seeing my father again. I wasn't prepared to see him. I didn't want to see him.

My guts informed me they wanted to do another round of dry heaves. I tried to convince them otherwise. My phone buzzed on my wrist. I tried to swallow, pulled my phone out to distract myself and saw it was Sterling demanding to know where I was.

That did make me heave.

The door to the bathroom opened. I was lucky I had had it to myself so long. I tried to muster enough of a damn to get up off the floor, but it wasn't going to happen. Not just then. Screw it. Who cared.

"Winter."

I leaned my head back against the blissfully cool wall. "What are you doing in here, Sterling?"

"Looking for you."

"Go away, Sterling. You'll scandalize the next woman to come in here."

"I'm not leaving you in here! Are you on the *floor?* My wife on a bathroom floor at *this* party?"

"Oh, believe me. I'm well aware of my situation." His anger and annoyance poured through the raw bond between us. Gaia, why did it have to be so strong? I couldn't handle the press of his emotions against my own. What the hell would happen when I told him we had to go to the AmberHowl and deliver this gift personally? Score another one for Winter not guessing right.

"Winter, you can't hide out here."

Just when I thought the last round had gotten all the wretched feelings out of me... well. Sterling standing there wasn't helping. Dry heaves were the worst. My body fished around inside me for whatever offended me so it could get rid of it, but it didn't seem to know it wouldn't find that in my intestines.

"Go away, Sterling," I rasped.

I heard metal rattling. Sterling deftly picked the bathroom door with a credit card, and invaded my questionable sanctuary. "You should have told me you were sick."

"Go away," I snarled. He did not get to stand over me and glare at me while I threw up.

"Come on." He pulled me by my elbow. "We'll leave."

"I'll be fine. I'm not sick."

"You can't throw up on these people, Winter. As much as some of them deserve it."

That would probably be funny later. I tried to shake off his grip. "I won't."

"We're leaving."

"I'm not sick," I insisted, even though I still felt a little unsteady and clammy.

"Do you know how I found you? I felt it. I knew you were in trouble. So. We're leaving," he snapped. "I'm not playing, Winter. This isn't for conversation. We're leaving. You are not well."

"They called," I blurted out.

His fingers tightened on my arm. "*They* did."

I nodded.

"Bad news." His finger continued to tighten.

"I don't even know anymore." I laughed, completely undone. "I don't even know, Sterling. Don't ask me. Like fuck I know."

"We can't talk about this here."

No shit. Really? His fingers tightened to a vise. "You're hurting me."

He immediately loosened his grip.

"I can make it through the rest of the party." Now that I wasn't the only one holding the news inside me, my insides settled down.

"No."

"What, is my mascara smudged?"

"No. But you're not up to this," he said with rough concern.

"I am," I insisted. "I'm not sick. This is all just too much."

"Exactly."

Sterling dragged me out of the bathroom and escorted me downstairs. The bitter night air felt wonderful on my clammy skin. I breathed a sigh of relief. He handed me off to our bodyguards with a murmur I wasn't well, and then went back inside to say a few strategic goodbyes.

"Ma'am." One of the guards handed me a red striped mint.

They were always prepared. For anything.

Sterling didn't take long. "All done."

"What excuse did you give?"

"That we had something come up and have to go deal with it," Sterling said. "Made an excuse about time zones. You scooting around scribbling frantically made nobody question it. Everyone there knows about things that won't wait. How are you feeling?"

"I'm fine." I was grateful for the mint. I leaned my head into my hand and watched the people on the sidewalk as our car pulled away. I could sense Sterling's watchful, concerned silence. "What time is it?"

"Nine-thirty."

"Call Hector." I spoke carefully, just in case the words started me gagging again. "Tell him he's going to Virginia on Saturday morning."

"Why—"

I held up a hand and shook my head. My throat started to close over. I gagged once.

Sterling did as I asked. Hector apparently had had plans for Saturday, and Sterling had to bully him into changing them to suit our needs.

Cye and Jun immediately suspected something had brought us home too early. I kicked off my shoes in the foyer and headed straight for the bedroom. I desperately wanted to brush my teeth, then I needed to sit down on the bed, lean forward on my knees, and put my face in my hands.

"Can you talk yet?" Sterling asked.

"Not if you're going to loom over me like that."

He sat down next to me.

"Ten AM. Saturday." I dug in my purse and shoved the napkin at him.

"Who's the name?"

"Their Beta. He'll coordinate getting us from the airport to the estate."

He nodded. "Lucky for us we don't have our formal security detail yet. We can leave them behind here without causing trouble for ourselves."

"I suppose." I hadn't thought of that. "But we're bringing Hector."

"I'll tell the Beta."

"Sterling," I rubbed my face, smearing my makeup. "I know my opinion might not be worth much, but they're bringing us to them for this in person, to their *heart*. Usually this would be done somewhere else, a little more... ah... visible. Just in case."

Sterling turned the napkin over in his hand.

"Believe what you want about me, but this is unusual."

"No," he said quietly. "I know getting an invite to their estate to settle a dispute is unusual."

"Yes," I echoed.

Sterling looked at the napkin. "Your father put up a hell of a fight about all this."

I nodded.

Sterling twisted the napkin. "The AmberHowl saw the poisoned apple and have spent the past week deciding how to play it. This is a statement. I'm not sure what the statement is, or who it's for, but that's the play."

"If the AmberHowl are strong-arming the SilverPaw, it's going to create bad feelings between the packs."

"That's what worries me. I would never piss on someone's leg unless there was a big payoff for me. So what's the AmberHowl's payoff?"

"Honor? Doing the right thing?" I asked dryly.

He frowned. "I'll allow for *maybe*. Because my father is the kind of man who would stick his snout into this. But predators generally don't vary much between species. I'm wondering if we'll get out of it alive."

"The AmberHowl wouldn't lure us there to kill us. They're the neutral party. Even if they aren't, that's how they're playing it. It's not like a couple hundred years ago where they'd kill us and take our property by conquest. They intend for us to get in and out alive. The AmberHowl have their fingers in human pies, they won't want to be the last people to see us alive when we don't come home."

"Could be maybe it's just the chance to stand over the SilverPaw." He didn't like that option either.

"Don't count on it. When the SilverPaw come back at us, don't think the AmberHowl are going to help us."

Sterling sighed. "Make a statement, get in and out, no muss, no fuss. You and I get bloodied up."

"I already feel bloodied up," I muttered.

"So do I."

We sat in heavy silence for a long time. Sterling eventually pulled out his phone and transferred the information from the napkin. I took that shower and got off my ruined makeup.

Still just guessing.

Guesswork had gotten me this far but now this was so far beyond my abilities and knowledge I didn't even know what game I was playing anymore. The sheer magnitude of it all hit me. This was not just a minor embarrassment that would be noted in the annuals of our history, and perhaps Alpha Demetrius and my father would eye each other but never speak of it.

This was not private. This was the whole of AmberHowl would know this happened.

Which meant eventually, everyone on the Elder Council would know. And all the major packs and powers would as well.

But I didn't foresee any formal or public decree vindicating SnowFang and punishing SilverPaw (which would mean SilverPaw could not feud with us), I just foresaw this being embarrassing, and AmberHowl using it to their own advantage (somehow), while SnowFang—too small and worthless to be anyone's concern—suffered SilverPaw's rage for the dishonor.

"How are you feeling?" Sterling's voice asked from outside the shower.

"Battered."

He opened the shower door and stepped inside.

"Who invited you?" I mustered some humor.

"You are taking too long."

He leaned against the opposite wall and sighed under the water. He closed his eyes. "We didn't even realize when we drifted into uncharted waters."

"No," I said softly, "we didn't."

Another long pause with just the hiss of water. I didn't want Sterling's forgiveness, nor his pity, nor an apology. He hadn't been completely wrong, and I hadn't been completely right. This had stopped being about my bride-price a long time ago. We just hadn't realized it until the AmberHowl had deigned to inform us of the obvious.

"Do you figure there's any dessert left?" he broke the thick silence.

I breathed some laughter. "Knowing Cye? Probably."

"Good. Because I'm going to find it. And eat it. And perhaps share it with you. But perhaps not."

"Oh, you will share it with me. Or there will be a fight. Right there on the kitchen floor."

"Then I am most certainly not sharing it with you." He smirked at me through the water.

My insides still felt raw, and my veins ragged and exhausted, and my blood like exhausted sludge. I was so tired, and I had to muster the energy for one last fight. But if Sterling and I could admit that everything had always just been our collective best guess, I could live (and perhaps die) with that.

But first, he needed a lesson in sharing his hunting spoils.

UNCHARTED WATERS

Sterling coordinated our arrival with the AmberHowl Beta, Henri. The specifics of that conversation only confirmed to Sterling there was a much larger play. He and I sat in the living room, eying each other, and trying to figure out what the next day would bring. It was comical pretending we weren't flailing around like a kid drowning in the deep end of a pool.

"The AmberHowl are a wealthy pack. I can't remember how they made their money. Do you think you could make some discrete inquiries to see if the Alpha's name pops up in any human concerns? Let's assume he's done that for you. Maybe you'll bump into each other."

"It's worth a try." Sterling didn't sound too optimistic. "There are a lot of places to look. Unless he's a big player, or a splashy one, he won't be easy to find on short notice."

"And a gift." I had found some little foam stress balls and rolled one around in each of my hands. Sterling watched me pace from his place on the couch. Now I was the one pacing. "It's traditional to bring some kind of gift in a situation like this. Since we're being oh -so-traditional."

Sterling shook his head. "I wouldn't have the first clue what to bring, Winter."

"Hah. Neither do I!" I tossed the two balls between my palms. "I don't even know exactly what sort of situation it is. It's nicely painted as being traditional, but we all know that's a lie."

"Do we have to bring a gift? Might be better if we don't."

"We don't have to. But it would be in our favor if we did." I had seen many gifts given to my father and the SilverPaw over the years. There was a very delicate etiquette surrounding gift giving. It could not be too trivial, and offer insult. It could not be too grandiose and be seen as a bribe or ostentatious or above the perceived station of the gifting pack. It ideally would be something that represented the strength or character of the gifting pack, and something that the recipient's entire pack could enjoy and benefit from.

As an added complication, we had to be careful not to offer something that would offend the SilverPaw as well.

My instincts told me a gift would be highly appropriate. But now I wasn't sure where my instincts stopped and my luck had begun, and I didn't want to tap out my supply of luck.

"We could give them almost anything." I clutched the balls in my fingers and squeezed. "And I can't think of a damn thing."

"This is why I have Oscar and Andre handle this sort of thing. Don't risk it unless you're sure, Winter. What's this Alpha's human birth name?"

"Demetrius Logan. His Luna's name is Marcella."

Sterling tucked into his phone while I tried to figure out what—if any—gift to give. I paced around the apartment looking for inspiration. I needed something idiot proof, but that would represent SnowFang without offending anyone, or being above our prestige.

I wandered into the kitchen. Cye cut vegetables at the counter.

I squatted down in front of the liquor cabinets and yanked open the doors to contemplate the vast array of gifts that had been sent for our wedding. So many consumables. I pulled out a tin of some weird-looking taffy in a strange flavor: lilac. Who ate lilac candies? I put it back into place. That would probably be there for another ten years.

We didn't need to bring a gift. Nobody would expect a little pack like SnowFang to bring a gift.

Which was exactly why I wanted to.

But it was that attitude that had gotten me into a fight

with Sterling. We were playing a game way over our heads, and perhaps it was time to fold and wait for the next hand. I grimaced and resigned myself to being the humble little Luna. It was just hard to accept there wasn't something in the whole of Gaia's creation that couldn't be the perfect gift and I could not somehow obtain it.

My trainers in SilverPaw had always said females didn't know when to back down. They had said that with admiration and frustration: rile up a female enough that she felt the need to fight, and she'd die before she quit. They had always believed it was because we could carry life in our bellies, and risked our own to bring it forth. When a female decided she had to fight, she fought with all the conviction Gaia had fused into her core.

At the time I had wondered why my teachers had acted like this tremendous ferocity was so dangerous. Now I had an inkling. It was given to us so we'd fight to bring forth our children, it was given to us so we'd fight to the death to protect them, that we would never flinch even when faced with our own demise and suffering. Turned to any other purpose it was too powerful. Too dangerous. It was like the rage that consumed us in war-form.

We had to learn to control that rage. Did females have to learn to be more selective in their battles?

I wished my mother was around so I could ask her.

Cye gave me a carrot from his pile. "Looks like you could use this."

I spun around on Cye. Cye jumped back with a squeal, yanking up the knife he was holding as he shielded himself from me.

Getting stabbed by a panicked Cye sounded like a bad idea. I backed away from the shiny blade.

He realized what he was doing, squealed again, and dropped the knife. It clattered onto the kitchen floor. He raised his palms in front of his face. "I'm sorry! I'm sorry, I didn't mean to!"

I ignored it. He looked about ready to faint. "Cye! I need your help!"

He lowered his hands. "You do?" He peeked at me through his fingers. "For what?"

"Our gift!"

"Um, okay."

"Cye. We need to take a gift to the AmberHowl tomorrow."

"I know." He squeaked, ashen with terror. "Am I the gift?"

"Are you the gift? No, of course not." I had no idea what Cye meant by that. I carried on, "No, but I need you to make the gift. I want to take them food. Dessert."

Cye dropped his hands and his skin brightened. "And you want me to make them tasty treats?! Me?" He clapped his hands together and illuminated like a mercury vapor lamp.

"What do you think would be best?"

SnowFang might be small, but we had Cye's spectacular abilities, and anyone who ever came to SnowFang as a guest would dine upon his food. It would be a humble gift masterfully executed.

Which made it so very SnowFang.

Cye pushed a finger into his cheek. He stared at the ceiling as he ticked off the considerations. "Let's see. It has to be ready to go by tomorrow and it has to transport well, and be easy to transport."

"And most would have to like it. Nothing like those lilac candies under there. For simple tastes." Because sometimes Cye got a little crazy with flavors, and while I'd eat just about anything I didn't have to cook myself, I didn't want the AmberHowl scrunching up their faces at some of Cye's lemon, thyme, and rose-oil infused sugar cookies.

Cye yanked his tablet off the counter and pawed through

his collection of recipes. "I'll think of some things and get back to you."

I accepted this as my dismissal and left Cye to his plotting.

One victory. I'd take it.

Then I had something less entertaining to do while Sterling tried to dig up something on the Logan family.

Burian still had his door closed. Ever since the fight he had remained holed up in his room, refusing to do more than eat with us. Sterling had not pressed the issue, and neither had I. There were other problems besides Burian and his little self-entitled snit.

Since Sterling and Burian did not currently have a personal relationship, that made me the intermediary between the Alpha and those not in the Alpha's favor. Burian had been disciplined, in a fashion, which bounced him back to my care for teaching so he wouldn't screw up again (that was the theory, at least). That meant I had this unpleasant task, especially when I was the last person Burian wanted to see. I had been the spark, even if the tinder pile had been there for a good long time.

I rapped on his door, waited one breath, and then opened the door.

Burian was at his desk.

We eyed each other for a moment. He looked back at his computer screens and mumbled some sort of acknowledgment.

I stepped into the room but left the door open. "We're going to AmberHowl tomorrow to settle this matter with the SilverPaw."

He mumbled another acknowledgment. Sullen. Still sulking, like a child.

"We want you to come." I ignored the attitude. "Cye and Jun will come. But this is an Elder pack, Burian. Two Elder packs, and we're right in the middle of what could be a nasty fight. We are coming back with the SilverPaw as our enemies. The best we can hope for is making a good impression on the AmberHowl that will back the SilverPaw off us. I have to know I can trust you. If you won't play along, then say so and you can stay here."

"Is that a trick question?"

"No. It's your choice."

A normal wolf's instinct would be to go with the pack. I no longer assumed Burian had normal instincts.

"You been to meetings like this?"

"I have been to meetings where my father mediated disputes between two packs. Never a meeting with Elder packs involved."

"So you're going to extrapolate based on that experience and you might be wrong about all of it."

Burian didn't get to talk to me like Sterling had. "Yes, but you pissing on someone's leg *will* make it a scene."

Amusement tugged at his lips and I saw a little feral glint in his eye. "You don't like me much."

No chance in hell of him baiting me into a confrontation. I was just here to tell him what was expected and leave. He had given me every reason to despise him for what he had said to Sterling, but I caught myself before I revealed that. To me it was obvious I'd know, but perhaps no so obvious to Burian. If he didn't know, or didn't suspect, he could stay ignorant.

Instead, I told him, "You've made it very clear you look out for number one first, and if this pack's interests conflicts with that, you side with yourself. No one trusts selfish wolves who put themselves before the pack. Going to AmberHowl tomorrow is about the pack. If you can't or won't play by the rules, then you shouldn't be there."

Burian visibly weighed his decision before answering. "I'll go."

I feared he'd go to cause us headaches, just to prove he

couldn't be made to obey.

Still, Burian had been Sterling's best friend for years. Somewhere in there, there had to be something worthy of redemption.

* * * * *

At quarter to five the next morning we arrived at the airport. Patrick appeared at the jet stairs, his face washed pale by the plane's lights. Another car was already there waiting for us. The world was still purple and dark, asleep and cold.

Sterling's gloved hand held mine. "It's time."

Another figure emerged from the waiting car. A man of about my height, stocky in build, and also wrapped in a long, pale gray wool coat. He had a well-worn russet leather messenger bag over his shoulder, which looked like it might have been about his age. He appeared to be late thirties, maybe early forties, dark hair speckled with gray, and a square, dusky face deeply creviced with an equal balance of smile and frown lines.

He and I sized each other up quite frankly. I wondered what he made of me, and everything Sterling had had him do the past few weeks. I didn't blame his skepticism and I sensed another struggle waiting for us.

Sterling indicated the plane's stairs. It was too cold and noisy to speak outside. As we passed Patrick, Sterling asked him to help Cye secure the trays of food.

This plane was a little different on the inside from the previous one. There were regular seats, as well as the more informal furniture. There was a small round table, two chairs, and along the cabin a built-in couch. Sterling took my coat, then shrugged off his, then took Hector's. He disappeared to hang the coats up, and it gave Hector and I another chance to eye each other.

I sat down on the couch and tucked one ankle behind the other. Hector took the chair opposite me and unbuttoned his suit jacket. His suit was, as I would have expected, completely impeccable. Dark blue with pale blue pinstripes, white shirt, elegant tie, modest gold cuff links. When he placed one ankle over the opposite knee I saw his shoes were a standard-issue brown leather, save for a thin stripe of alligator skin along the edge.

Sterling returned and sat down next to me. "Morning, Hector. Winter, this is Hector. Hector, Winter. But I can see you two have already sized each other up."

I looked sideways at Sterling and gave him a little smile. "Hector and I are on the same side."

"Woweeee, in style, man, in style." Jun flung himself down in a seat and ground his considerable rump into it. "Oh yeah. I could so get used to this."

"Is it too early to drink?" Burian asked no one in particular.

"I bet it's open bar, man."

Hector swung his head back around to Sterling. "This looks like a regular dog and pony show."

No ponies, but he was half right.

Sterling shrugged.

"Why are you bringing the roommates?" Hector smelled a rat. No, Hector smelled a whole damn deer-sized corpse. That had been dead for a few weeks. In a low-lying marsh. In high summer.

Burian was a loose cannon, Jun might blurt out something inappropriate, and Hector might learn our secrets. Ah, this day was off to a promising start. When Patrick appeared to ask me what I wanted to drink I asked for mint tea. I was *wide* awake and didn't need any caffeine sending my nerves over the edge.

"And you brought cookies." Hector prodded Sterling's silence. "Who the hell brings cookies to a closing?"

"I do."

"Is this deal so fucked you're sweetening it with cookies?"

"Something like that."

"Oh yeah. A real kindergarten deal. Will we have naptime too? Juice and little cartons of milk? Sit in a circle and sing songs? Then have Show and Tell? Here, kids, this is what a 'retirement fund' looks like?"

"He gets a little grumpy when forced onto a plane before dawn," Sterling informed me.

"Sterling, it's about damn time you told me what this deal is. You're bringing cookies and the peanut gallery to a Saturday morning closing."

I dipped my teaball up and down. Jun and Cye were too busy pressing all the various buttons that could be pressed, and Burian had pulled a blanket over his head. Hector gave them all another look, then turned back to Sterling. "You need to tell me what I'm doing, Sterling. I don't do bad business."

Maybe Burian had it right about wondering if it was too early to drink. The last thing we needed was Sterling's lawyer thinking we were mobbed up or had fingers in some other toxic pie. Sterling shook his head. "There is nothing illegal going on, Hector. Directly, indirectly or otherwise. This is a bride-price payment."

"A what?" Hector held out his coffee cup towards Patrick for a refill.

"A bride price." Sterling flicked a finger at Hector's bag.

Hector asked me. "For *you*?"

"It's a long story."

Hector held up his hands. "Wait. Wait. Sterling bought you? The fuck, Sterling. You bought a bride? A guy like you does not need to buy his bride. No offense, Winter."

"None taken." I half-lied.

Patrick set the coffee cup down in front of Hector and melted away again, but not before his eyes fluttered over me. The same look Mint had given me. Another man who thought I was some kind of damsel in distress.

Unfazed, Sterling said, "That wouldn't be a long story. That would be a very short story. This is a little more traditional, and things between her father and I got ugly."

I marveled at how Sterling just hid the truth in plain sight. It just came out of his mouth so easily. He made this sound like it was all so perfectly reasonable.

Hector was familiar with Sterling's smooth talking. "Complete load of shit, Sterling. What the hell am I involved in? Nobody does that kind of crap anymore."

"That's where you're wrong."

"I don't do cloak and dagger, Sterling. I'm a shark, not a snake."

"This is all completely above board. It sounds strange to you, but this is how some people still do things."

Hector scoffed at this. I couldn't fathom what might have been going through his head right then, and Sterling wasn't going to throw him off the scent. Calling on a lawyer's trust? That almost defied the fundamental laws of nature.

"Just go along with this, Hector. I promise you aren't involved in anything unethical. In our community, there's an old tradition that the father gets ten percent of the groom's wealth. That tradition has been largely abandoned as burdensome, and Winter's father is one of the people who's spoken out against it. Suddenly I come along and that's what he wants."

"Plucked like a nice fat hen," I muttered.

"So that's why you didn't just cut him a check," Hector said suspiciously.

"Exactly."

"And it's gotten dirty and heated."

"Winter's father is a man of some influence. He thought I would be easy to quietly fleece. He wasn't expecting us to fight back, and now another heavyweight has gotten involved as the mediator."

"And I have your word this is completely above board.

No drugs, no gangs, no mafia, no organized crime, nothing smarmy."

Sterling snorted a laugh. "No. More like the Amish. Committing crimes draws attention and violates our principles. It results in being outcast. We keep to ourselves and follow our traditions and that's that."

I nodded my agreement to this and said, "The Logans have done us seemingly a big favor, but I'm sure there's a price. Not from my father, but from the Logans. This is all very dirty and unpleasant, and them getting involved is going to make it something to talk about for a while."

"In our community," Sterling told Hector, "I am a no one. No prestige, no status. No one at all. Nobody does someone like me a favor, or gets involved in this kind of messy business unless they've got something to gain. Winter and I just haven't figured out where their profit is because we have nothing of apparent value."

"Our community does not value material wealth the same way as the greater population," I clarified.

Hector slumped down in his seat. He rubbed his head, then folded his hands in his lap. "So it's basically the shit I do everyday. Everyone at the table wants something, nobody's saying what and nobody says why."

Sterling grinned. "Your area of expertise, Hector."

It was a two hour flight to the small airport in Virginia, and from there it would be another hour and a half to the AmberHowl compound. The day was clear and bright. The trees were already brown and the leaves had fallen, and despite the clarity of the day, when I put my hand on the window, it was frigid.

Sterling took my hand as the plane taxied down the runway.

I did not want to see my father. I was not ready to see my father. Or any of the SilverPaw.

The plane turned off the main runway, carried on a bit,

then came to a halt.

"Oh no," I breathed. Outside the plane were no less than five vehicles, and six men in suits of varying colors. But that wasn't what made my heart clog my throat or my stomach twist like a wet rag.

"They said they were picking us up, Winter," Sterling's said, although he sounded a little concerned.

Standing by one vehicle, and flanked by two men, was a tall, dark-skinned woman with raven hair, a strong physique and dressed in an exquisite dark purple skirt and pale blue top that rippled in the wind. I recognized her instantly. I had only ever seen her from a distance, but Luna Marcella of AmberHowl was impossible to forget. Her very presence burned itself into the mind.

"No. That's Lu—Marcella," I told Sterling in a low voice.

"Are you sure?" Sterling glanced out the window, then back at me. "It can't be."

"I'm sure." I could barely whisper.

An Elder Luna was here to greet us personally.

"Sterling," Hector's voice cut through to us.

There was no way to avoid the truth. Sterling had to answer. "That woman is sort of like a queen." He raised his voice, "Cye, Jun, Burian. The woman is Marcella. Their Boss Lady."

We couldn't say "Luna". Titles would not be used in front of Hector or Patrick. Jun's impromptu title for me translated to all of them.

"I shouldn't call her Boss Lady, should I?" Hector asked.

I shook my head.

"Gaia's tits, what the hell is the Boss Lady doing here?" Jun plastered his face up against the window.

"Fuck." Burian untangled himself from his blanket and smoothed his hair.

Cye whimpered from his seat. "Winnnntterrr, whyyy?"

Good question.

The plane taxied to a halt. In a few seconds the little metal tube would crack open and we'd all spill out, prepared or not.

"Now we find out if we're the pawn, or the rook," Sterling whispered.

Then I was going to play this like a rook, and no pawn. I got to my feet, smoothed my skirt and ran a hand through my hair. I straightened my rings, my necklace, shook myself, and tried to remember the protocol for two Lunas meeting on unequal and unhappy terms. Couldn't really remember. I had studied the Law, not the finer points of obscure protocols, so I fell back to the basic introductions. "Sterling, at my right shoulder, but I'll greet Marcella first. Everyone else, three steps behind me."

That was the best I could come up with. That's usually how exchanges like this went. Marcella would probably have forgiven me for not being up to snuff, but I didn't want to be excused as ignorant or young or inexperienced.

"So at what point should I start swimming?" Hector asked no one in particular.

"Oh, about ten minutes ago," I quipped. "Or did you not feel the tide carry you out from shore?"

Hector gave me the sort of helpless grin of a man resigned to whatever the day would bring. "And who are you in all this? Because you're not just the chattel."

"Winter is *our* Boss Lady," Jun said with pride that both warmed and terrified me.

DANCE, LITTLE WOLF, DANCE

My heels met tarmac. Cold air cut into my bare legs. Wind tore strands of my hair from its confines.

Sterling stayed close at my shoulder, his attention on everything, ready for anything.

I glanced around, noting where every wolf stood, and approached Luna Marcella. I kept my steps measured, not too quick, expecting any of the wolves around her to leap between us.

My pulse tapped a nervous rhythm in my neck.

"Marcella." I dropped her title for the greeting due to Hector being nearby. I tried to keep my tone neutral but respectful. I wasn't sure how I should address her. I was a Luna as well, and while our ranks were equal, our prestige was not.

"Winter." Her dark eyes flicked over my shoulder to Sterling.

I took the cue and gestured to my mate, "My husband, Sterling."

That sounded very strange to say.

"Marcella." Sterling inclined his head politely.

Marcella's gaze took him in, and I felt a twinge of pride for the subtle approval. I don't know if I met with her expectations or not, but Sterling had not disappointed at first glance. Her attention returned to me, then noted my three packmates, and Hector. She knew who they all were and they did not require an introduction.

One of her wolves stopped forward with an empty basket.

"Phones," she said.

"Why?" I didn't move to hand over mine.

"Security and discretion."

326 | Merry Ravenell

There was no reason to argue with her. There wasn't anyone we were going to call if the AmberHowl decided to sink their teeth into us. Sterling pulled his phone from his breast pocket and dropped it into the basket.

Burian just sighed, and he was also told to turn over his laptop. Hector was the least thrilled. He gave Sterling a burning look that promised we'd be having it out later. It was hard to blame him. To an outsider I'm sure this looked like some kind of cartel drug deal.

Hector's ignorance was also one of the few advantages we had. Letting the Lunas speak instead of the antagonized males would only go so far. We all needed Hector to be ignorant at least a few hours longer.

Satisfied that all devices had been confiscated, Luna Marcella told me, "You'll ride with me."

I did not want to be separated from Sterling or my pack, but I couldn't refuse. The only option would be to get back on the plane and leave. Assuming they let us leave. My moment of hesitation drew a look of cold expectation from Marcella.

Unwillingly, I turned to Sterling and nodded.

"Separating us was not part of the arrangement." Sterling kept the glare intended for Marcella on me.

"Just keep everyone in line. I'll see you at the house."

We had come too far now to blow everything picking a fight over procedure. If the AmberHowl wanted us dead, or to hold one of us captive, they didn't need to be sly about it. I squeezed Sterling's hand and felt the stiff circle of his wedding band.

In the backseat of her car, I tried not to fidget. Or seem too stiff. The Elder Luna crossed one leg over the other and tapped a message into her phone. She had natural nails, I noticed, painted in an elegant pink-tipped manicure that suited her. I envied she could grow her nails enough to have a natural manicure. I had on my society-required acrylics, still painted for the party a few nights earlier.

Marcella was in her late thirties or early forties. It was hard to tell. Maybe she was even older. She was the sort of woman who was not beautiful, exactly. Not beautiful in the way that lines and aging skin could affect. She had a beauty that pushed through her skin and into the world around her, and could not be challenged by something as trivial as age.

I had only ever met a few lower-prestige Lunas before, and only by accident. Even though I had been the daughter of an Alpha and Luna, it hadn't entitled me to introductions to highly ranked wolves. I had been a child, then an unmated juvenile female of no specific rank, then a female of questionable value. My family's prestige had allowed me to be present in certain company, but no more. Children who misunderstood where their family's prestige ended and their own began disappeared from the sight of adults until they learned their place.

Now I was a Luna. Sitting next to one of the highest prestige Lunas in our society. I didn't seriously think I was a match for Marcella's experience, but I intended to give a decent account of myself.

Behind us was a train of cars. Hopefully Hector wasn't about to leap out the window and run for the hills.

"The SilverPaw arrived earlier this morning," Marcella commented.

My stomach flip-flopped. I acknowledged this with a nod. It was all I could muster.

She gave me a very strange look, and she didn't even try to hide it. She waited for a reaction.

"That's good." I fumbled for something to say.

Marcella shifted in her seat enough to convey that it was intentional and should be noted. The scent of watchful consideration was echoed by her weighed tone. "Indeed."

Okay...

Marcella rested one wrist on her knee. "I'm told you

spent the past few years as Rodero's assistant."

I glanced sideways at the slight inflection of *assistant*. No doubt it had been mentioned in the Elder Council, at least informally. "Only as a scribe."

"So you were very familiar with his work," Marcella prodded, looking at me that strange way again.

"I knew my place." I shied away from answering directly. My father no longer deserved my loyalty, but the position of Chronicler still did. Perhaps Marcella was trying to tease out how I had been able to contact MaryAnne so easily.

"So you were never down in the archives."

"No." For the most part I had only ever seen what my father intended me to see, which was more than most but not nearly as much as a true apprentice. My answer was mostly not a lie.

"So it was just an excuse to get you in front of many males, hmm?" She raised her perfectly groomed brows at me.

Humiliation burst onto my cheeks, and that old tear-riddled fury in my chest. All the worst memories of the worst parties marched to the front of my awareness. The snickers, the looks, the whispers, the cruel comments, the dramatic mock sniffing. "He never said it so plainly, but it was obvious."

"He brushed it off to us as being a restless wolf, but we all figured he was trying to find your mate."

"I had no say in it. He is the Alpha."

Her tone softened a little, almost maternal now, "Of course you didn't. Did you ever go to any Elder packs?"

There would have been no reason for us to go to Elder packs. Marcella was after something. The answer to her question was simple, though. "No."

"But this is how you figured out how to contact MaryAnne."

"Is that what you're fishing for? You want to know how I could fight back?"

Marcella's lips curled. "Look at the fangs on you, she-pup. They're almost sharp."

I yanked my eyes down and to the side, and ducked my chin to acknowledge my mistake.

"Temper on a leash, Winter. The males are ready for a fight, and things are very tense. Don't provoke the situation further."

"Yes, Luna Marcella." Obedience might be difficult.

Silence for a few minutes. Then her gaze rested on my wedding rings. "You and Sterling are married."

"He wanted to formalize it for human society right away."

Even though Marcella didn't outwardly betray anything, this meant something to her. A few minutes later she casually picked up her phone and typed in a message.

She jumped around from obscure inquiry to inquiry, and never stayed on one topic too long. And what did I do? I stood like a confused doe trying to figure out what her plan was. Time to re-focus on saying as little as possible, and only answer the exact question asked. This wasn't little SnowFang. I wasn't a puppy tottering behind my father. I was a Luna, playing a Luna's game.

It was like playing chess for the first time. Knowing what all the pieces did and how they moved was almost meaningless. Chess was easy to learn, but a lifetime to master.

Luna Marcella had years on me, and she wasn't *just* an Elder Luna. She had *made* herself one. She had stood before the other Elders and commanded that esteem and respect for herself, her mate and her pack, and she had gotten it.

My mother had gone to Elder Council meetings, but I had rarely seen her as a Luna. My memories were just of my mother, and I hadn't been much more than a child when she had died. She hadn't raised me to be a Luna. I didn't know if I'd raise my daughters to be Lunas. I just wanted them to be good she-wolves, capable of being a credit to any pack or rank they found themselves.

But my father had been raising Jerron to be an Alpha, even though the position was not often hereditary.

The forest gave way to landscaped white fences and pastures. The caravan turned up a long driveway through an iron gate, climbing yet another hill along an avenue lined with ancient trees, and finally came to a huge brick house.

The heart of AmberHowl.

It was a mansion, actually. An old Virginia mansion, white columns and all, atop a hill and overlooking the hills and forests.

The cars curved around the cobblestone cul-de-sac before the front entrance. A man came to my door and opened it, and murmured, "Luna Winter."

"Come," Luna Marcella bid me before the other cars stopped. Clearly, she meant to keep me a few steps apart from Sterling. I followed her up the stairs and through the front door of the massive house.

I smelled Jerron's scent right away.

What business did my mangy brother have doing here! I smelled many other strange wolves, but no other scents I could easily identify by name in human form, except the shocking absence of my father's familiar scent.

I stopped at the doorway, hands on either side of the doorframe. "My father isn't here?"

Sterling and I had been summoned, but my father had sent a proxy?! He had sent my brother!? My fingernails curled into the wood. What game was this! My brother! My no-rank, jerk, arrogant sod brother?!

Marcella gave me that strange look of pity again. My own father hadn't dirtied himself coming to this, he had even snubbed an Elder pack to drive home how below him all this was.

"Luna Winter," a male wolf murmured over my shoulder. "Your coat."

"No titles, Jake." Marcella corrected.

"Yes, ma'am."

"They have brought a gift, Jake. See that it's properly handled," she bade him.

I hoped she didn't mean properly handled as in thrown promptly in the trash. That would not be a good start. Luna Marcella's sad, resigned expression remained. Sort of like *poor little rabbit, she doesn't know what she's in for.*

Oh, I had no illusions. Marcella need not worry I had hoped that my father and I would embrace, shed loving tears and be grateful it had all been one happy misunderstanding.

Another wolf in slacks and a polo shirt, and almost as large as Jun, emerged from the side hallway. He was in his early fifties, which made his physique all the more impressive. "They're in the conference room."

"Good. We can get started right away."

That was the one thing going according to my expectations. Get us in and out as fast as possible. I wouldn't want this sort of sordid family squabble in my territory either.

Sterling's storm rolled in behind me. I swallowed my tangible relief. He brushed his fingertips over the small of my back, and dipped his head low to catch the scent along my neck. Our three packmates lined up behind us, and Hector at Sterling's right. Cye was very close to my left shoulder. I hazarded a look over at him. He twiddled his thumbs nervously.

Luna Marcella just waited.

It went on long enough I wondered what we were being held for. Our phones were not given back to us. The basket containing them passed in front of us on its way to some secret location within the house.

Hector sighed.

Finally, Jake and another two wolves appeared with the trays containing our gift: three of Cye's most exquisite cookie flavors. One was chocolate chip, but the other two did not involve any chocolate at all. Some wolves could not tolerate it.

The trays were presented to Luna Marcella for her to inspect.

Perhaps I should not have trusted Cye.

Luna Marcella looked at each tray in turn. She tapped the chocolate chip cookie one. "And what are the other two?"

I murmured to Cye to answer her.

He crept around me, squirmed, looked anywhere but her and managed to say, "Ah. Um. Ah. Those are butterscotch chai, and the others are lime-and-apricot soda shortbread."

She picked up one of the lime-and-apricot ones and bit into it. Cye darted behind me, and peeked over my shoulder. Of course she chose the weirdest one of the lot.

She looked at the cookie, flicked her brows, and then popped the rest of it in her mouth.

"Told you!" Cye whispered to me in triumph.

"Liar, you were sweating!" Jun whispered to him.

"Shut up," Burian hissed to the both of them.

The trays of cookies were taken away. Marcella beckoned us to follow her.

SnowFang had at least one point in its favor.

Or we hadn't lost points.

The upstairs conference room was a large, wood-paneled room with an ancient dining table. The scope of the table reminded me of Sterling's desk, complete with imposing claw-and-ball feet. Between the wood paneling were recessed flat panels painted in hunt coat red. It struck me as a very odd choice for a conference room.

Sterling and I stopped dead, halfway between the door and the table.

Jerron smirked at me from the far side of the table, sitting as an Alpha with two Betas, Arnold and Daniel, flanking him. A few other SilverPaw males I didn't recognize waited in the shadows of the wall.

Marcella weighed me with that same, sad expression again, then, far too gently, said, "Rodero is dead, Winter."

THE SHAM SACRAFICE

"The fuck." Burian's whisper was the only thing I heard over the roaring in my ears.

Jerron wasn't old enough. He wasn't prestigious enough. Daniel and Arnold sat like stones flanking him, their faces unreadable, betraying nothing of how this madness had come to pass. An Elder Alpha with no prestige, no victories, no accolades, and no mate?

He had drunk the grocery money not a month earlier, for fuck's sake!

My father was dead?

My father *had* been dead.

He had to have died shortly after I had left. Or had been dying.

Sterling's hand pressed to the small of my back, steadying my spine as I gave Jerron the shocked, stunned, horrified reaction he had hoped for.

Alpha Demetrius rose from his seat at the head of the table. Like Sterling, he wore an impeccable suit, but no tie, for the occasion. He was a little shorter than I recalled, still completely bald and clean-shaven. His skin was dark obsidian, and when he spoke his gleaming white teeth flashed in fierce contrast, even when his tone was genial. There was nothing genial at all about the veiled threat he carried on his shoulders, or the chapped scabs and callouses on his hands. This was an Alpha who had guided his pack's march to Elder status, and ultimately, fought for their right to be heard as Elders.

My father had not *made* SilverPaw. He had continued an established tradition. Demetrius had wrestled prestige from the jaws of everyone, and convinced all the other Elders to accept his AmberHowl among them.

Luna Marcella took up a seat at the other end of the table, and the two of them exchanged a grim, unhappy, look.

My father was dead, but he had been very much alive when he had refused to name the price that had brought us here, so was Jerron just continuing work in the wake of Rodero's sudden and unforeseen demise?

If that was true, how had Jerron brought the rest of the SilverPaw leadership in on whatever scheme this was?

"Were you not informed of Rodero's death?" Alpha Demetrius asked me.

I couldn't make my throat work. Sterling answered for me. "No."

Nobody asked Jerron why I hadn't been told. Jerron's cruel triumph was the explanation.

"Jerron sits there by—claim," Demetrius gestured to my brother.

Sterling's contempt was tangible.

Oh, so Jerron *wasn't* the Alpha yet. He was Alpha-By-Claim. He had made a bid to be Alpha,, but the pack wanted him to prove he was worthy. He needed to bring back something of great value. A kill, a conquest, a victory, something, because the pack had not accepted his authority on its own merits. My bride-price, in all its toxic glory, had to be what would seal him as the Alpha of SilverPaw.

If only I had *known*, we wouldn't be there at all! Me having already left the pack would have allowed us to slip through a very tiny legal loophole. The debt had belonged to my father, it didn't pass to my brother. It *could* have passed to the new Alpha, except for the tiny detail that the price hadn't been named by the time I left SilverPaw. An unspecified debt was outstanding, but the new Alpha would be powerless to negotiate the actual price for a female that was no longer legally a member of his pack.

If I had known! If only I had known... Jerron could have choked on it! That debt could have existed in legal limbo, acknowledged to exist but nobody having any power to give it a value. Jerron's deception had tricked Sterling into all this!

Well played, you mutt. Well played. I'd believe it if you double-crossed our father in your little conspiracy and murdered him so it could all be yours. Gaia will have your soul for this!

Jerron wasn't going to get my tears to go along with the money. No, he had lured me here, but I was going to figure out how to make him regret it!

Hector introduced himself to Jeffers, the SilverPaw lawyer. Then Hector leaned over to me and whispered, "Can I eat him?"

"Raw," I murmured back.

Hector snorted a laugh.

Given a few moments to square up, Demetrius turned to Sterling and they exchanged a few pleasantries until a tray of cookies was brought in. Luna Marcella indicated the tray with her hand. "A gift from the Mortcombes, Demetrius."

"Ah." Demetrius helped himself to several of them.

The AmberHowl present enjoyed the cookies. The SilverPaw refused the offer to share.

Everything went according to protocol. All wonderfully normal and polite, except it wasn't.

Alpha Demetrius put a large stack of papers bound by a huge metal clamp onto the table. The pages were tagged with many little sticky flags in an assortment of colors, and had the look of having been gone through multiple times. "We have reviewed the bride-gift, and decided that it is acceptable."

My brother looked at the stack of papers with justifiable distrust.

Demetrius went on, "Jerron, you assert your predecessor wanted the traditional ten percent, and you intended to honor that request."

It didn't matter how true or not that detail was. My father had been scheming something when he had thrown me out with Sterling. His dead paws were dirty as he stood before Gaia.

The AmberHowl Alpha continued, "Within a day of receiving your official request, Sterling provided us with the details of the gift. There is no argument as to the debt being owed, and the price agreed upon. We are here to conclude the exchange."

Sterling rested his hands in his lap, fingers laced, and eyed my brother.

The Betas were wary, but my brother already gloated. Probably imagining all the things he was going to waste the money on, patting himself on the back for how cunning he had been to get this far. He hadn't realized what his Betas had already figured out: Sterling wasn't going to make this simple.

Perhaps this was what had taken so long. The AmberHowl shock that Jerron had somehow become an Elder Alpha, and trying to figure out how my father had died so quickly... and conveniently.

I focused on the matter at hand, which was shoving the poison down my brother's gullet and watching him choke on it.

"Hector," Luna Marcella said, "the official paperwork, please."

Hector fished into his russet bag and pulled out the clamped paperwork. Jerron blurted out, "What the hell is this?"

"It's this," Demetrius said like it was stupid, tapping his own marked up copy. "Same as what I have."

"But—" Jerron looked back and forth between the two stacks.

Marcella gave him a withering look.

Hector pushed the paperwork across the table, "Enjoy your prize, runt."

Jeffers adjusted his glasses. "I'll need a few days to review this."

"That is not what you are here for," Demetrius informed him. "*We* have already reviewed it and deemed it acceptable. It is a simple transfer of common stock and an equity stake in a company out of Seattle. Value at close of markets yesterday is just over the ten percent requested."

My brother snapped. "This is not acceptable."

"I have determined that it *is*." Demetrius raised a brow.

Jerron thought there'd just be a check waiting for him, and they'd walk away instantly rich, fat, happy and smug. Like they had won some sick lottery. It was amusing to watch Jerron squeak and flap like a baby bird.

He grabbed the bundle and flung it back across the table. "No! Unacceptable!"

"You named your price and I am prepared to pay it, Jerron," Sterling's tone dripped ice.

"It is overly burdensome."

Demetrius didn't budge. "Disagreed. You were aware of Sterling's wealth when you named your price. Any manner of payment would have had some level of burden. You are showing your considerable ignorance not recognizing this."

Hector shoved the packet back across the table. "Spread 'em wide and take it dry, big boy."

My brother's eyes moved from Sterling to Demetrius to me, and when they touched me they burned so hot it went right through my ribs.

Why are you doing this?

It wasn't just simple greed. It was something else, and I had been a naughty little pawn. I hadn't played by the rules, and Jerron wasn't smart enough to figure out what to do to make me obey. He was also cunning enough he realized he was in a corner. If it wasn't simple greed, what the hell was it? He was so *angry!*

Demetrius, quite calm, said, "This is the payment, Jerron. Accept or walk away. Unless you want to escalate this to the Council itself."

I heard the great beast from my dreams breathing, felt it chasing me and herding me down that hallway to where Sterling waited like scales made of flesh.

Why!

The words escaped me, "I just want to know why!"

"Stay out of this, Winter," Jerron told me.

My emotions threatened to break all my ribs. "This isn't just you, Jerron! This started with Dad. Why? *Why?* You're getting what you've always wanted, wealth and power, is that all this was? Tell me, dammit! You owe me that much!"

Jerron barked a short laugh. "Deserve? You don't deserve a damn thing, Winter."

Luna Marcella silenced Demetrius' next words with a glance.

"Do you know what Dad went through on account of you taking your sweet time to find your partner? Do you even know who Sterling is? You have no idea how humiliating it was for him! For me! Having to suffer my pathetic sister, and now your scab of a husband."

"My husband is not a scab." I snapped. "And if you're so upset, remember I had no say in how any of this happened. You know I begged Dad to stop, you know I saw how it was hurting the family. He *wouldn't* stop, and somehow it's *my* fault?"

"It'd have been *better* if you'd been Unwanted," Jerron mocked me, "than paired with *that*."

"Tell me the truth, and stop with the playground games! There's nothing wrong with Sterling! I have no idea how he got onto Dad's last resort list, but at this point, I think it's probably bullshit!"

He laughed at me. "You don't even have a clue, do you? All that time spent helping Dad, and you didn't even catch a whiff of it!"

He somehow succeeded in being gleeful and cold at the

same time, and he savored it, laughing at how he got to break the news to me. He glanced at Hector, visibly annoyed at having to mince words and spare me some of the pain.

Jerron leaned forward on his forearms. "Dad was desperate to save that maternal family. He *should* have just let it die. But he was young and stupid. He opened a Pandora's box and turned to science. It gave him permission to violate Gaia's will, even though he knew it couldn't be right. Now look what he let into the records. *That*. Nobody was ever supposed to know outside the Elders and Chroniclers, but then you had to go and get paired to it! That... half-breed."

Half-breed. He meant a hybrid, and science must have meant DNA testing There was talk in the Elder Council that Sterling was a *hybrid*? Sterling's biological father had been proven through DNA testing?

No wolf had ever been recorded that way, and as far as I knew, it had never been permitted at all. There was too much doubt about the science not holding up for werewolves. Our human-form DNA was supposedly identical to regular humans, but we clearly weren't human. One day science might reveal our secret, and the thought sent fear through all of us, and there were even proposed additions to the Law forbidding us to give DNA samples for any purpose, fearing the more data that was out there, the more likely we'd be discovered.

Hybrids could only partially shift, if they could shift at all, and almost without exceptions, had more serious problems, ranging from infertility to insanity. I had *seen* Sterling shift. I hadn't seen him clearly in the darkness, but he hadn't struggled, and he hadn't seemed to be unusual in any way. There had always been rumors of hybrids who could pass as purebreds, but those were just rumors, and there were plenty of confirmed, suffering hybrids as evidence to the contrary.

Jerron didn't wait for me to digest any of this before he

went on, "Dad told me sometimes he wondered what he had done. That's why the group application sat there. *Sterling*. Dad had hoped since Sterling had been adopted and his mother had... ahem... *left* us, that Sterling would just disappear. Dad decided the best way to keep things quiet was to simply approve the group and hope it went away again. Then he decided to risk introducing you to him. Like I told you back at the house, the only thing he has going for him is his money."

I filled in the blanks. "So to sweeten it up, you decided to make him useful."

"He's not useful. His *money* is useful. Do you get it now? You couldn't just stop at being *Unwanted*. No, you had to be such a failure She decided to pair you with an abomination."

My mate was not an abomination! My mate had a sense of decency and honor, who didn't treat the weak like they were his own personal henhouse. Hybrid or not, blank pedigree or not, it didn't matter! I growled, but restrained myself. I might make it sound like I knew something. All I knew was Sterling was a purebred.

Or believed he was.

I couldn't think about that just then.

It'd be easy to think this entire scheme was all Jerron, that he had murdered our father and seized control. But the AmberHowl wouldn't have been involved in that part, and the delay had probably been them making damn sure they weren't getting involved in a bloody coup. It had all started with my father, now Jerron picked up the damn flag and kept running.

I snarled. "And we still managed to drag your mangy ass here. You and Dad thought I'd be an easy mark. I'll give you your due for tricking us into being here at all, but I didn't spent four years following a Chronicler around and not learn how things work. The rest of the world won't know what you've done, but I will, and so will your peers. How our father abused his power, abused a man who couldn't fight him, thinking he'd get away with it, and then you carried the tune. You'll *never* be free of this stain, Jerron. *Never.* Even if you kill me, you'll *never* erase this from the Chronicles, or the memories of the Elder Council."

Jerron's lips curled back over his teeth. "And you'll always be some mongrel's bitch. Some fucking hybrid's wife."

He had said hybrid in front of Hector! Well, there might be a way to explain that away, but oh Gaia, Jerron was dense at times.

"Watch your language," Luna Marcella snapped, and her tone was so sharp Jerron jerked like someone had yanked his collar.

I laughed at Jerron's idiocy. "I know he isn't, not that I'd care if he was! He's the soul chosen for me."

Jerron snorted. "No surprise in Her choice, stupid bitch."

"I don't feel punished by Her. Stop trying to put the blame somewhere it doesn't belong! Whatever Dad's mistakes were, they were his, and not ours! He always said to never hold the younger generation responsible for the sins of those who came before!" My eyes were bright with tears, rage needled my skin, a growl, bubbling in my throat. It was only kept at bay by the profound sadness.

Sterling, his temper at an end, reached over, grabbed the much-abused clump of paperwork and shoved it back across the glossy table. "Eat your poisoned meat like a good little cur, Jerron. Or let's go play with the Council. This mongrel will go right for your throat."

Jerron jumped to his feet, grabbed the table's edge and his face mottled purple with fury.

Sterling goaded my brother. "I dismantle corrupt assholes like you before breakfast. You're an amateur pretending to be a man!"

Jerron roared and lunged across the table.

I scrambled out of the way. Almost fell over Hector, who didn't move fast at all and just blurted out, "Holy shit!" as Jerron and Sterling's bodies smashed together and chairs fell over onto the floor.

Jerron had more training than I did, and that might not bode well for Sterling. I spun around in terror and gasped as Jerron delivered a bare-knuckle punch to Sterling's jaw.

Hector grabbed me and hissed, "What the fuck! Nobody's stopping it!"

No, nobody would. Sterling was an Alpha, and another Alpha had attacked him. Only Sterling could answer the challenge.

Sterling pushed Jerron back against the table, ate another punch to the liver and snaked his arms around Jerron's neck and clinched his fingers behind Jerron's head, yanking Jerron's head to Sterling's shoulder. Jerron tried to pull back and worm his arms under Sterling's so he could burst free. With a snarl, my brother wriggled one arm between them and cracked Sterling in the jaw.

The men broke apart, Jerron lunged at him, they crashed into the wall, and Jerron dropped Sterling with a knee to the ribs. I almost cried out in shock and jumped up, Hector had the presence of mind to grab my wrist before I even budged. The blow only had Sterling startled a moment, he flung himself out of the way before Jerron's next knee smashed his head, and scrambled up as Jerron swung again.

"Pathetic hybrid." Jerron spat. "City half-breed!"

Jerron ate a punch that probably would have dropped anyone else, the cracking sound hit the walls it was so loud. Jerron tagged Sterling again and laughed.

Sterling snaked to the right, then sprang forward. He seized Jerron in the clinch again, and snapped one knee up. Jerron twisted, expecting a body strike, but Sterling stomped Jerron's foot with his heel. Jerron jerked off balance. Sterling snapped back, smashed Jerron square in the teeth, sending him reeling back against the table. Sterling's final punch to my brother's solar plexus dropped him to the ground.

My brother dropped forward with a sound of choking agony. He slid off the table and crumbled onto the floor, choking for air.

Sterling snarled, grabbed a handful of Jerron's hair and yanked his head back, knuckles white and--

"Enough," Luna Marcella demanded. "He's been beaten. Smashing his head into my table is not needed."

Sterling growled at Jerron, loosened his fingers one by one and stepped back. Bruises had already started to fill on his jaw, and his knuckles were bloody, and he was breathing hard.

"That was pathetic," I blurted out, astonished a young, would-be Elder Alpha could be bested so handily. My brother had been trained since he was a boy. It said something that Sterling had beaten him with only moderate difficulty.

"Agreed," Luna Marcella's dignified tone said.

Jerron staggered to his feet, not looking at Sterling, but did glance at Marcella. Despite the Elder Luna's dissatisfaction with his performance, the SilverPaw Betas didn't seem inclined to vacate their support.

Chasing the money.

Alpha Demetrius was not amused. "This is not a cock fight, Jerron. Remember that. You aren't some adolescent mongrel. Do not act like one, and do not fight like one."

Sterling straightened his jacket, ran a hand through his hair, and reclaimed his seat.

Demetrius' patience was at an end. "That is the deal, Jerron. The gift is acceptable. You take it, or you do not."

Jeffers leaned over and murmured to my brother. Jerron tried to shove him off, but Jeffers grabbed him and hissed at him. My brother had three choices: accept the gift, refuse the gift as being overly generous but then be forced to explain that to the impoverished SilverPaw, or pick a nasty fight with the AmberHowl by going to the Elder Council.

Going before the Elder Council would officially strew this carcass everywhere. It was the worst possible outcome I could fathom. The AmberHowl might be willing to privately growl, but the entire Elder Council chastise one of their own? Even if the AmberHowl championed us, it wouldn't matter. They were the youngest and newest Elder pack, and the SilverPaw were one of the oldest. The rest of the Council would be reluctant, and had historically *always* been reluctant to entertain charges brought against their peers.

Sterling whispered. "Thoughts?"

Hector twirled his pen on the table.

The patterns of light and the grain of the table's wood surface bent into the squares of a chessboard.

Time to find out if we are the rook, or the pawn.

Historically, pawns are the ones sacrificed.

My vision blurred, then refocused. On the table, now, were a black rook, a white queen, a white king, a white bishop, and the black bishop. The white king loomed, in a precarious yet powerful position. Something large breathed, heavy and slow, and a shadowy hand moved over the board. It reached first for the white bishop, released it, and the fingers closed over the white queen.

A nudge from Sterling.

I whipped around, grabbed his sleeve, and whispered. "He's going to sacrifice the queen instead of the bishop!"

"What are you talking about?!" he whispered back, gripping my fingers. "Your hands are like ice. Winter, what are—"

"Listen to me! He's going to do something stupid!"

"He's already doing something stupid."

"Stop him. Stop him before he plays the queen!"

Blabbering in whispers about sacrificing queens instead of bishops and demanding Sterling somehow magically make this not happen sounded completely sane, of course. I looked back at the table, but the vision of the chessboard was gone. The rest of the table watched us, waiting for us to sort out whatever we were whispering about, but Luna Marcella observed with a degree of knowing. Or suspicion.

Sterling thought fast, fished into his jacket pocket and retrieved his checkbook. He tossed it down onto the table.

My brother's eyes lit up.

Sterling reached for Hector's pen. "Since it seems like ten percent of my worth is beyond your ability to deal with, and I wouldn't want you to go back to your *impoverished* and *starving* family with your hands empty, I'll make you a cash offer. Assuming the mediators will permit a last minute substitution."

"Yes. Please end this quickly." Marcella just wanted to be rid of this entire matter.

Sterling named a cash price that was a shred of the paperwork-prize's value. Only a moron would take it. It was a basic intelligence test that had two results: "protozoa" and "multi-cellular organism."

Jerron didn't tell him to screw off. He demanded double, which was still a pittance compared to what he stood to gain.

I looked at him like he had three heads. Luna Marcella did not hide her disgust. She rolled her eyes and turned her body away from the table to face the windows.

Sterling wrote the check.

The stupidest thing was that if that was what had been requested from the start, it'd have been paid.

Jerron had settled for a tiny little fraction. He had also scrambled out of his own trap: no one would ever know what had happened in this room.

It robbed me of my brother suffering any public discomfort. The SilverPaw were also so desperate and broke, they'd probably take this as sufficient to prove my brother's right to rule.

All of this for nothing. And if I had known my father had *been* dead, we wouldn't have been here at all.

Hector grabbed the packet and shoved it into his russet bag. "Motherfuckers."

Demetrius summoned MaryAnne to alter the original request so that the last-minute substitution of a cash payment in lieu of ten percent was what my brother had willingly and "eagerly" accepted.

"*Very* eagerly," Luna Marcella instructed the Chronicler.

Just another entry in the history of the wolves, and only perhaps a curious historian one day would notice it.

Once it was all done, my brother stood up, and looked down at me. His face twisted into rancid disapproval. "You look like a painted whore. Bought and paid for."

I met his gaze, and simply answered, "I look like my mother."

CONCERNS FOR DAWN

Hector summed it all up perfectly: "Well, that was completely fucked up."

I was beyond crying. Or shaking. I was just numb.

A tray with four coffee cups arrived. Luna Marcella handed our three packmates off to one of her wolves. They left without complaint and Jun closed the door behind him.

"So now we discuss what I owe you." Sterling didn't stand on diplomacy with Demetrius just then. "Because I know you didn't get dirty out of the goodness of your heart, Demetrius, even if you wanted to see your newest peer in the flesh."

Demetrius used a little spoon to stir a cube of brown sugar into his coffee. "That was worth something."

"You can't tell me you're going to accept him as an Elder."

"You put him on the floor, Sterling, but he's still an Elder. Don't get confused."

Luna Marcella was going to have a lot to say about that.

Sterling ignored his coffee cup. "What do you want, Demetrius?"

"You have nothing of immediate interest to me, Sterling. Marcella and I were intrigued by the fight that you were willing to put up."

The AmberHowl still wanted something. He was just trying to sidle up to it.

Demetrius went on, "We have no interest in getting mixed up any further with you. But I would suggest that you tell your father that buying up all of New York draws a great deal of attention to himself."

"So he's been told, and he doesn't care."

"He should. And you should suggest to him to keep his

eyes off Virginia."

"Ahhh. I see. That's why we're *really* here. Nothing to do with Jerron. You want me to prevail on my father to not buy the Apharaia Spread."

I stirred cream into my coffee and listened carefully, my own aching wounds momentarily forgotten.

"It's a little close to my territory for my comfort. Your father isn't ignorant. Tell him to stay north in his own territory and stop looking at mine."

"My father isn't one of us. He doesn't hold territory."

Demetrius shook his head, lips curled. "Your father is abusing his privilege, and he knows it."

Sterling didn't flinch. "I don't expect my father to pay my debts for me. Negotiate with him yourself."

"I don't talk to the consorts of no-name loner females who have produced bastard offspring who may or may not be what she claims," Demetrius replied.

The slight annoyance in Demetrius' voice suggested Demetrius had already attempted to discreetly get rid of Sterling's father. Now he could use Sterling to get what he wanted. Sterling couldn't resist him. The matter of Sterling's pedigree meant we needed the AmberHowl at least *not* as our enemy.

Nobody seemed to do anything anymore because it was the right thing to do. Shouldn't it have been enough that one Elder held another Elder to some basic standard of behavior? The Law defining an Alpha's duty to his pack and station did include phrases like *decency* and *honor*.

"My father doesn't interfere with those that live on his land. That's the whole point. If he doesn't buy it, development companies will."

Demetrius snorted. "I don't care about *now*. When your father dies, *you* inherit the land. He's abusing his privilege. Flagrantly. The groups in the north are impoverished mongrels, and they're grateful to have him. The groups down here don't want or need him. You and your wife have proven you're at least worth talking to, so I'm talking. I forced Jerron's hand. Force your father's in return."

Luna Marcella took us back to the airport. Sterling and I were separated again. I wanted to be near him. So much for thinking this meeting would pull us from the currents back to recognizable shore.

Marcella said. "You knew Sterling has been accused of being a hybrid. It's a conversation you two have had. You weren't surprised at the suggestion."

A conversation had in a fashion. I evaded the question. "Jerron meant that Sterling was DNA tested to prove his parentage. Right?"

"You two *haven't* spoken about this." She was surprised.

"I don't think Sterling thought it was a rumor with teeth. My father didn't tell either of us anything about the other. Sterling told me his mother married a human who adopted him as his own, but that he never met his biological sire."

Marcella twisted towards me, one hand over the other. She had a beautiful diamond ring that had polished pieces of amber flanking the central diamond. "What your brother said is true, as far as the Elder Council knows it. Sterling is the last real representative of his maternal line, but is a bastard all the same. Your father allowed the use of DNA to prove Sterling's sire is who she claimed so at least he wouldn't have a blank pedigree. That wolf did state he had had a brief fling with her around the time Sterling could have been conceived, but has never acknowledged Sterling. The Council let it stand, but forbid further DNA testing, and heavily criticized your father."

"Is it science that worries us, or Gaia's will?" I asked.

"Both. But I can also speak as a biologist, and I have my concerns. There's nothing I've seen that conclusively shows it's flawed, but there's so much new research coming out that challenges what we think we know about DNA. We aren't at the point of certainty that werewolves are genetically similar enough to trust human science."

"But I thought that our human form DNA was approximately identical."

"If we were genetically identical to humans and wolves when in those forms, then hybrid offspring shouldn't exist. There's something deep in our DNA that causes hybridism. That same thing might introduce an unacceptable margin of error into even basic parentage tests."

The logic was so simple and obvious! Superficial DNA work showed we were human or wolf in those forms, we could receive blood transfusions from dogs or humans depending on form, we blood typed to those species. But there had to be something else, unless we wanted to believe it was something in our souls. "So you do believe Sterling is a hybrid."

"Personally? No. In my opinion the technology is perfectly adequate to prove paternity. It's the X chromosome that concerns me, but there's no dispute about who his mother is. The rumor about Sterling being a hybrid has persisted for years, but I don't know how it got started."

"So if popular *opinion* is that Sterling is a hybrid, he's a hybrid. Popular opinion said I was Unwanted, that made me Unwanted."

"Has he told you who his sire is?" Marcella prodded, her dark eyes full of expectations and searching for clues.

"No, and I do not care. I don't think Sterling knows. He doesn't care. He has a father." I did not want to talk about this anymore.

"These things don't lay quietly, Winter. They'll sleep for years and years until something gets them out of their grave."

"Why are you telling me this?" I refused to play any more games that day.

"In some form or fashion, what happened here today will not simply go away. You and I both know there is a storm coming."

The storm was already here. Wanderers in the city, a population crisis, hypocrisy. We were dying by inches, and instead of *demanding* Sterling's biological father admit his indiscretion instead of forcing his son to wear a shameful brand, the whole Council would let the rumors persist. Just like the AmberHowl only helped to get to Sterling's father, just like my brother got off with only a slap on the snout.

The AmberHowl had had a profitable day, and it was time to cut them off.

It was only two-thirty when we arrived at the airport. Our phones were returned to us. Sterling and I thanked Luna Marcella for her help, and on some level, we were grateful. It had all been recorded, and Jerron hadn't impressed anyone. That much at least would get around the Elder Council, and he'd suffer before his peers, if not before the rest of us. It was a large victory for such a little pack as ours.

"Well, that was a regular carnival," Hector announced. He told Patrick to bring him a shot glass and a bottle of something painful. "Fucking amateurs. What the hell, Sterling? That was insane."

"He knew the paper gift would eat him before he even got home," Sterling said. "He knew I had outsmarted him and didn't like the taste of it."

"You weren't kidding when you said your group doesn't view wealth like I do." Hector poured himself a shot. He downed it, then poured another one.

"We don't." Sterling's sighed.

As the world retreated under the plane's wings, I wondered if my mother and father had been a happy pair. She had the Gift. How could she have not known the monster my father was? She had always spoken of her past with him in a wistful, sad way. I thought it might have been fondness, now my older self wondered.

Jerron had always been his favorite.

Hector downed a third shot.

I moved closer to Sterling. He was all I had left. I didn't have a past anymore. Not one I wanted to claim.

"I've decided," Hector gestured grandly with his shot glass, "That I don't want to know. Don't want to know a damn thing about your weird-ass little society."

"You're not firing me as a client, are you?" Sterling asked.

"No. But I've got a husband and two kids and I have this gut feeling that whatever you tell me is going to keep me up at night. Maybe in a week, I'll ask. But right now? Nope." He downed his next shot. "Right now, I drink."

It was one less thing to worry about. Hector had a good nose for knowing who to trust. And as he'd say, when a skeleton in a closet had a perfectly reasonable explanation for staying there, it should stay there.

Much later that night, when Sterling and I were in our room, trying not to think too much about what had been said, I asked him, "Are you going to talk to your father?"

"I don't have much choice."

"Will your father listen to you?"

Sterling shook his head once. "I don't know, Winter. My father gave me my seed money. I've made all the rest. He doesn't believe in backing off or bailing out, and I'm damn sure he's not going to be happy about me attaching his name to a deal he wasn't part of."

"You wouldn't be happy if he did the same to you."

"I wouldn't. I also don't know how far into this deal he is. Might be too late."

"There was an unspoken threat there, Sterling. There were a couple of them." I didn't tell him about Marcella's comments in the car. That could wait until the next day. Or the next week. Or maybe never. Maybe I'd never say anything because there was no point rattling Sterling, or his parents, with worries that might not materialize.

But I did wonder what Marcella knew. Marcella hadn't been chatting to fill up the silence.

"Getting my father to understand that will be difficult." Sterling ran a hand through his hair and shifted his spine. I heard a crack. "And he'll ask what he taught me to ask. If he gives on this point, what will be the next thing they ask for? If I could promise him it would just be this one thing, but I can't."

The AmberHowl could nibble and nibble, and who else might nibble? I didn't know a thing about Sterling's father's politics, or even the man's name, but I knew that ceding territory was not a small thing. "Consider if Elder Demetrius brings to Council revoking your father's human privilege."

Wolves were tolerant of human allies, their activities and even human consorts like Sterling's father. But when they got too close to pack politics, that's when they ceased to be seen as humans.

Sterling put his phone on his nightstand and slid under the blankets. "Enough for today, Winter. Tomorrow. We fended off the SilverPaw, one thing done. Now Wanderers, AmberHowl, and my father."

I crawled up towards him and sighed contently as I settled next to him. "Our task list is not getting shorter."

"We did solve one mystery ,and get one thing resolved. The rest can wait."

His fingertips pulled along my skin, down my cheek, my throat, trailing lower and lower until he oh-so-gently caressed my breast.

"Don't tease. Not tonight," I breathed.

"Just think of it as a different sort of torment."

"Cruel, cruel man."

"You wouldn't want me gentle."

"No, I wouldn't." But I did wish he wouldn't have chosen that night to torment with me tender caresses that left my skin aching. I had never thought tenderness could be such exquisite torment.

He pressed me down into the blankets.

"One turn of the moon," I whispered to him, "is all it took."

"Blessed irony." He kissed my throat. "My moon-come-down-from-the-sky."

I drew my fingernails along his strong back, tracing red lines in his pale flesh like the marks in my dream.

The moon turned in my mind as She pulled at the tides, drawing us further and further out into the waves.

About the Author

Merry Ravenell lives in the San Francisco Bay Area with her husband, David, and two cats.

She enjoys coffee, running the occasional 10K (slowly), coloring books and cheesy movies.

www.merryravenell.com

Made in the USA
Lexington, KY
18 September 2017